RUSH OF
BLOOD

MARK
BILLINGHAM
RUSH OF
BLOOD

Atlantic Monthly Press
New York

First published in Great Britain in 2012 by Little, Brown

First published by Grove Atlantic, February 2017

Printed in the United States of America

ISBN 978-0-8021-2591-0
eISBN 978-0-8021-8985-1

Atlantic Monthly Press
an imprint of Grove Atlantic
154 West 14th Street
New York, NY 10011

Distributed by Publishers Group West

groveatlantic.com

17 18 19 20 10 9 8 7 6 5 4 3 2 1

For Mum and Dad

PROLOGUE

FLORIDA

It's all wrong.

The light winking on the blue mirror of the pool, the sun hats and the sweating beer bottles clutched in their fists. The drone of insects. The smell of warm skin slick with suntan lotion.

All of it.

It couldn't really be any more unsuitable, bearing in mind what's happening. One of them thinks there's a word for it, for that . . . clash, but he can't remember what the word is. The six of them just listen and shake their heads, trying their best not to let the woman see how awkward they're feeling—God, that would be terrible, all things considered—but it only makes the situation worse. Now, they're worried that they just look even more relaxed, even more insensitive. Like they don't give a shit about the missing girl.

It makes them all feel even guiltier.

I mean, clearly it's just a question of 'context' or whatever you call it, because for the previous thirteen days the picture could not have been more perfect. Wasn't that exactly what they'd paid their money for, and weren't they there to relax? But that was before the flashing lights on the roofs of cars were visible through the palm trees. Before there were cops and State Troopers running about and radios crackling.

On top of which, the woman herself seems pretty relaxed about it all.

'It's so crazy,' she says, and raises her hands in a 'stay where you are' gesture when one of them tries to get up from the sunbed. 'I feel stupid putting everyone to all this trouble.' She takes a step away and says, 'No, really,' when another asks if there's anything they can do. 'It's fine, honestly . . .'

Later on, talking in whispers, one of the men says, 'Why should we feel guilty? I mean, there was no shortage of people out looking for her, and it's not like we didn't offer to help, is it?'

His wife shrugs. 'There's not much we can do about the sunshine, is there?'

A couple of the others nod.

'Disparity,' one of them says. 'Is that the word?'

So, they eat their final meal together and try to enjoy the last night of their holiday. They talk about how the woman's daughter has probably just gone to the mall, if she hasn't turned up already, and keep talking in much the same way even though the police cars are still around the following morning. On a full flight back to Gatwick, they try and fail to sleep. Scratchy-eyed, they eat their foil-wrapped meals and watch movies, and several pick at the skin that is already peeling from chests and shoulders. They stay cheerful, more or less, but each of them is thinking about the woman by the pool and a smile that quivered and died. That kept on dying, a little bit quicker each time it was cranked into place.

Thinking about her insistence that everything would be fine, that everything was fine, and the words—spoken with something approaching irritation—when she glimpsed what she took to be sympathy.

'She's missing,' the woman says. 'That's all, just missing. So, don't even think it.' And her voice rises just a little and cracks, and just before she pushes her sunglasses back into place, there's something fierce and tight around her eyes.

'My daughter is not dead.'

PART ONE

ANGIE AND BARRY

From: Angela Finnegan angiebaz@demon.co.uk
Date: 16 May 17:31:01 BST
To: Susan Dunning susan.dunning1@gmail.com
Cc: Marina Green marinagreen1979@btinternet.com
Subject: Dinner!!!

Hi All!

You know how you meet people on holiday and say things like 'we really must stay in touch'? I bet you're regretting swapping those email addresses now. Ha ha!

Seriously though, it was an amazing holiday even if it did end a bit oddly, so I thought it would be great if we could all get together. So, me and Barry would love it if the four of you could come to dinner on Saturday, June 4th. I know it's a bit of a trek down here to deepest, darkest Crawley but I do a mean bread and butter pud and I promise to send out sherpas if you get lost!!

Talk to the boys and let me know ASAP, but I really hope you can all make it.

Lotsa love,
Angie xxx

PS. Been looking at the local papers on the internet and still no sign of that poor girl. Can't imagine what her mother must be going through. Horrible, just horrible.

PPS. Can't remember, but is anyone a veggie?

ONE

Angie moved slowly along the aisle, nudging the trolley with its squeaky wheel past white meat and along to red, picking up some bacon—which they needed anyway—before turning and heading back again. Still trying to decide between chicken and lamb. Chops or *coq au vin*.

She'd originally wanted to do something themed. A holiday-style menu to remind them all of their fortnight in the sun, with piña coladas to kick things off. Seafood had been the obvious choice, a chowder perhaps—if she could find the clams—and then some sort of fish for a main. She had even gone online and found a recipe for Key lime pie.

Barry had said it was a stupid idea, so she'd let it go.

She glanced down into the trolley, wondered if she should get some ice cream to go with the frozen pizzas she'd picked out for the kids. It was all quick and easy and it would be handy to get dinner for the pair of them done and dusted before her guests arrived. She knew that Laura and Luke would be happy enough with that arrangement; keen to stay out of everyone's way and not have to join in with boring grown-up conversations. One night in front of the computer couldn't hurt, assuming that any homework had already been done.

Barry was in charge of all that.

She picked up a large pack of chicken breasts. She saw that the meat was organic, clocked the price and quickly put it back again. Right idea though. Lamb was nice enough, but it could be a bit tricky, what with some people preferring it pinker than others, and Barry had always enjoyed her *coq au vin*. She reached for a cheaper pack . . .

'I just thought it would have been nice,' she had said. 'A bit different.'

'I don't see the point.'

'There's no *point*, it's just a bit of fun, that's all. Cooking something Floridian.'

'*What?*'

'Something that comes from Florida.'

'I know what the word means,' Barry said, eyes narrow. He crushed the empty beer can he was holding, opened the lid of the bin in the corner of the kitchen and tossed the can inside. 'I'm just trying to work out why the hell you're saying it. It's poncey.'

'Look, it doesn't matter.'

'The whole thing's poncey, you ask me.' He slammed the lid of the bin shut and walked across to the fridge. 'You'll make us look stupid.'

'Fine, I'll just do chicken or whatever.' Angie reached for the cloth that was draped over the edge of the sink. 'That OK, then?' Rubbing at a smear on the granite worktop, she watched as her husband stared into the fridge for almost half a minute, then closed the door again without taking anything out. There was a bit more hair gone at the back, she noticed, and the mottled roll of fat above his collar seemed that little bit thicker. Not that she was in any position to talk, of course. 'OK, then,' she said to herself.

'Yeah, fine, whatever.'

He walked behind her, put his hands on her shoulders and kissed the back of her head. She carried on rubbing at the granite, though the smear had already gone.

'Can't see why we're even bothering though, to be honest,' he said. He moved away and pulled out one of the seats at the breakfast bar. 'Haven't we got enough friends?'

'It's just a get-together, that's all. Sort of an add-on to the holiday kind of thing.'

'Why do we want to do that?' he asked. 'I mean, it all went a bit weird at the end.'

'Only at the end.'

'That girl and everything.'

'All the more reason. It's something we've got in common, isn't it?'

'So, because of that we have to go to all this trouble?'

'*You* don't have to do anything,' she said.

'You know what I mean.'

'You got on all right with Ed and Dave, didn't you?'

He shrugged. 'They were nice enough.'

'And the girls.'

Barry rolled his head slowly around on his neck. 'Ed's wife was all right, but that what's-her-face . . . Marina . . . got right on my nerves.'

'Really?'

'A bit full of herself, I reckon.'

Angie just nodded, happy to let him think he was being clever. She knew very well he was only pretending not to like Marina Green because he fancied the arse off her. Because he was a sucker for big tits and an over-the-top dye job. Angie had watched him ogling her on the sly, saucer-eyed behind his knock-off Oakleys, pretending he was still reading his paper as she climbed out of the pool in a bikini that anyone could see was too small for her.

'Well, *I* think she's nice,' Angie said.

'Up to you.'

'I think they're all nice, and providing you make an effort we'll have a nice evening.' She could hear raised voices in the lounge, an argument about what to watch on TV. She opened the kitchen door and shouted at her children to stop bickering. When she turned back into the kitchen, Barry was standing, rubbing the belly that strained against a maroon polo shirt.

'What about the diet?' he asked.

She considered the fact that he was almost certainly more concerned about *her* putting on a few pounds than *him*. She thought about the two cans of lager he'd got through in the half-hour since he'd come in from work and the empty crisp packets she was always digging out of his car. 'I'll do fruit for pudding,' she said. 'It's just one night.'

'It won't be though, will it?' He slid a hand beneath the shirt, began to scratch. 'We have them over here, then each of them invites us to their place, whatever.'

'What's wrong with that?'

'Like I told you, we've got enough friends.'

'Name them,' Angie said.

'Excuse me, could I just . . . ?'

Angie blinked and apologised to the man who was stretching to reach past her for something. She nudged the trolley with the squeaky wheel out of his way and wondered how long she had been standing there, staring blankly at the meat like a mad woman. She glanced down at the pack of chicken that was still in her hand.

The shiny pink flesh, pressed tight against the polythene wrap.

She dropped the meat into her trolley and moved quickly towards the till. Remembering that last meal the six of them had eaten, the blood-red sunset and all the police cars back at the resort. It would be strange, she thought, to see them all again, eight weeks and a world away from where they had met.

A holiday to remember, in spite of everything.

Finnegan *Bros*. That's what it said on the signs and on the sides of the vans and on that overpriced headed notepaper he never wanted in the first place.

Bros. Brothers. *Two* of them . . .

You wouldn't know that though, Barry thought. Not the way he was spoken to sometimes, and dismissed. The way he got given the runaround like he was just another employee.

Adrian was the younger brother, that's what made it even harder to stomach. Three years younger, but while Barry had been getting his hands dirty, Adrian was the one swanning about at college just long enough to get some poxy business management qualification. Now he seemed to think he was Alan Sugar or something and that some pointless bit of paper made his contribution to the firm more important than Barry's.

Well, it fucking *didn't*.

Barry slammed the heel of his hand against the steering wheel, pulled it left and put his foot down hard to take the Audi past some idiot doing forty miles an hour in the outside lane like a tit in a trance.

Forty-five minutes each way, just to take abuse from some moron who was still complaining that work on his loft extension had 'not been completed to a satisfactory standard'. A window that didn't shut properly, a radiator that leaked, shit like that. Forty-five minutes each way, on a Saturday afternoon, while his brother sat at home watching Sky Sports and playing with his kids.

His jammy bastard brother, who still got to *see* his sodding kids.

A Saturday, for crying out loud, when he'd been working his arse off all week . . . and to cap it all, the punter had *still* not been happy. Whined like an old woman, called him a cowboy, then, after all that, said he might just as well phone Adrian to get it sorted out.

Typical.

'Should have spoken to the organ-grinder in the first place.' That's what the cheeky bastard had said. Took a good deal of self-control on Barry's part to keep his fist from flying into the little turd's sweaty, red face . . . a job he'd *certainly* have completed to a satisfactory standard.

It was time to get things straight with his brother, Barry knew that. Time to have it out. It was a speech he had rehearsed often enough and the list of grievances just kept on getting longer.

'*Saturday, Ade? You're taking the piss, same as you always do . . .*'

Not that he hadn't been happy enough to get himself out of the house while Angie was busy cleaning the place from top to bottom, digging out the flash crockery, getting everything ready for dinner.

And he guessed that she was equally glad to see the back of him while she arranged the candles and polished the sodding cat.

'You should *say* something to him.' He could hear her saying it. *Had* heard her saying it, too many times. 'You need to tell him you're not putting up with it any more.'

Easy for her to say. Same crap he used to get from his ex.

Stand up to him, you're the eldest.

Be a man . . .

He leaned on the horn, up the arse of some other idiot who refused to move out of the way. He saw the bloke check his rear-view. Barry raised his arms and shouted, 'Come *on* . . .'

'Barry's the practical side of the firm and I'm the nous.' Adrian was fond of trotting that one out. A hand on Barry's shoulder, like as not, while Barry did his best to smile about it.

'He's the muscle and I'm the charm . . .'

He *was* though, that was the problem. Always had been. *Your little brother . . . birds from the trees . . . sand to the Arabs . . .* all that carry-on. Adrian was the one who found the customers and pitched them quotes at just the right level. Who kept them sweet when every job went over time and over budget. He was the one who kept the fresh contracts rolling in, which was what paid for the Audi and the child support and the holidays to effing Florida, which was why Angie needed to shut the hell up and stop needling him.

Which was why, for the time being at least, that speech would stay undelivered.

Barry pushed in the cigarette lighter then reached across to the passenger seat for his Benson & Hedges. A sigh became a belch as he flipped open the lid of the gold pack. The last thing he needed was this stupid dinner party.

What was it she'd wanted to cook? Something *Floridian*? Christ on a bike . . .

'Make an effort,' she'd said, more than once, and 'Behave yourself,' which he knew damn well meant 'try not to get pissed and show me up'. It was a shame, because having a few drinks and sneaking the

14

odd look down Marina Green's shirt were just about the only things he was actually looking forward to. Besides, Angie was a fine one to talk, the way she'd been putting it away lately. Truth was, she'd been off her face on wine and pricey cocktails almost every night on that holiday; talking too loud and laughing at Ed's stupid jokes, so all things considered it was a bit rich, her telling him to mind his Ps and Qs.

She needed to show a bit more respect, Barry thought.

He lit his cigarette and cracked the window an inch to let the smoke out.

Bad as his brother . . .

He'd tell more of his stupid jokes, Ed would, and Dave would laugh along and Susan would roll her eyes. They'd talk about how quickly their tans had faded and how polite and friendly everyone was in the shops over there, not like the surly bastards you got here.

Ed would drawl 'Have a nice day' in his crap American accent.

Then later on they'd talk about the missing girl, bound to.

Which Barry didn't much fancy.

TWO

'*Sarasota has all the great beaches anyone could ask for and a stunning array of wildlife . . . while the variety of museums, galleries, concerts, and other artistic activities on offer have led to the area being known as the Culture Coast.*' Angela Finnegan lays down the complementary tourist guide that was handed to her when she and her husband picked up their hire car. 'Sounds good, doesn't it, love? Be nice to see some wildlife.'

The man behind her grunts, not really listening.

She opens the small, photocopied 'brochure' she was given when checking in to their accommodation and continues to read out loud. '*Siesta Key is one of several barrier islands which separate Sarasota Bay from the Gulf of Mexico. At its centre, the bars, souvenir shops, and restaurants of Siesta Village are clustered around the beach road, and, ideally located at the heart of this vibrant community, the Pelican Palms Resort offers premium quality rentals to holidaymakers and snowbirds alike.*' She puts the brochure down and closes her eyes. 'Well, no complaints so far. I think it's lovely, don't you?'

Actually, *Resort* is probably overstating the case a little. It's a complex of fifteen units: one, two or three bedrooms, each with separate entrance, private patio and barbecue grill; a communal swimming pool and two

16

hot tubs. At $615 per week for a queen-bedded unit that sleeps two, it prides itself on being reasonably priced, especially considering that each cabin comes with a fully equipped—if modestly sized—kitchen and that the resort is a 'stone's throw from a dozen or more great places to eat and five minutes' walk from the award-winning beach'.

'Paradise on a budget'. Of course, you can never be sure just how genuine any of the comments left on these websites are, but that was how one satisfied customer of the Pelican Palms had described the place. On the second morning of their holiday—just after eleven and already 28 degrees and climbing—that's more or less what Angela Finnegan is saying to her husband.

'It's not as though we're going to be spending much time here anyway, is it?' she says.

'I suppose not,' he says.

'Not inside the cabin at any rate. I think it's pretty good value, for what it is.'

She is dangling her legs in the pool, while behind her, Barry is spreading towels across their sunbeds. His gut hangs over the waistband of his multi-coloured Vilebrequin shorts and his shoulders are already burned having overdone it on the previous day. Like her husband, Angie is thirty-six years old and second generation London-Irish. Unlike him, she is content to keep her belly out of sight beneath a diaphanous floral wrap and a navy-blue one-piece swimming costume.

'Which factor sun cream do you want?' Barry asks.

A woman walks up and, in an English accent, asks if the empty sunbed next to Barry's is going spare. Barry says he thinks so and when Angie turns round, the woman looks over and says, 'I think we were on the same flight out.'

When Angie sits down on the edge of her sunbed, the woman sits on the edge of the spare one. 'Where are you from?' Angie asks.

'We're from Forest Hill,' the woman says. 'South London.' She nods across to a man who waves back at her from one of the hot tubs. He is pale and wiry with fair hair that looks greasy but might just be damp and a wisp of beard. 'That's Dave and I'm Marina.' She smiles,

17

showing a lot of straight, square teeth, and when Angie and Barry introduce themselves she says, 'Nice to meet you.'

Marina Green is thirty-two. She is mixed race, pretty with straight black hair dyed red at the tips, and though her body is not perfect, she is happy enough to show off her best bits in the white and gold bikini she bought from Monsoon at the airport.

'What about you?' Marina asks.

'Sorry?' Angie says.

'Where are you from?'

'Crawley,' Angie says. 'About five miles from Gatwick.'

'That's handy,' Marina says.

Barry laughs. 'I knew there was a reason we were living there.'

'It's not so bad,' Angie says. 'The schools are pretty good.'

'Oh.' Marina looks around. 'I didn't see any kids.'

Angie grins and leans towards her then lowers her voice, mock-conspiratorial. 'We left them at home. We wanted a bit of peace and quiet.'

Marina smiles back. 'Actually, it's one of the reasons we chose this place,' she says. 'On the website it said there weren't usually too many screaming kids running around.'

'Same here,' Angie says.

'How many kids have you got?'

'Three between us,' Angie says. She casts a quick glance in Barry's direction. He is slathering sun cream on to his chest and does not appear to be paying a great deal of attention. 'Only my two live with us, though.'

Marina says, 'Right,' and raises her face up to the sun for a few seconds.

'I like that,' Angie says. She points to the small diamond stud in Marina's nose.

'Oh, thank you,' Marina says.

'Did it hurt?'

'I can't remember.' Marina places the tip of her finger to the diamond. 'Had it done when I was a teenager. I think I was just trying to annoy my mum.' She notices a man walking around the edge of the pool carrying two bottles of beer and nods towards him. '*They're* Brits as well,' she says. 'From north London.' The man kicks off his sandals and sets one of the bottles down next to a woman who appears to be asleep, face down on a sunbed.

'Oh, really?'

When the man turns round, Marina waves. The man raises his beer bottle in salute, has a drink then slips his sandals on again. They watch as he walks towards them.

'He's called Ed,' Marina says. 'And she's Sue, I think. They've already been here a week. Well, you can tell, can't you?'

Apart from being well tanned, Ed Dunning is tall and muscular, his head and chest thick with tight, black curls and a stomach which—while not quite a washboard—is about as flat as any forty-two-year-old could reasonably wish for. When he reaches them he smiles and pushes his sunglasses to the top of his head. Says, 'Nice day for it.'

'More Brits,' Marina says.

Ed shakes his head. 'We should have gone to Skegness,' he says. 'Can't get away from them.' Then he laughs at his joke and Marina and Angie join in. Marina makes the introductions and Ed steps across to shake Barry's hand and say, 'All right, mate.'

They talk for a few minutes about the resort and about Sarasota, and, with just a trace of a Midlands accent, Ed tells them that this is the third straight year he and Sue have visited. Angie says they must really love it here and he tells her that there's nowhere like it. He tells her he knows all the places she and Barry *really* need to see while they're here. The best bars and restaurants, the boat trips that won't rip them off and the secret beaches the tourists don't know about. He puts on an American accent and says he gets 'all the skinny from the locals'.

'So, where's good for dinner then?' Angie asks.

'You been to SKOB?'

Angie shakes her head.

'Siesta Key Oyster Bar,' Ed says. 'You've *got* to go there.' He turns and points. 'Just a few minutes' walk towards the beach. Fantastic food, great atmosphere. There's live music every night and you can sit outside.'

'Sounds good,' Angie says. She turns to Barry. 'What do you think?'

Suddenly there is shouting from the shallow end of the pool. A young girl, thirteen or fourteen, is splashing about and shouting to her mother. The woman is smoking at a table beneath a tall coconut palm. She is bottle-blonde, wearing denim shorts and an American Eagle T-shirt and does not look old enough to be the mother of a teenager. She puts a finger to her lips, but the girl just shouts louder, squealing with excitement as she slaps at the surface of the water. The girl is heavy and round-shouldered and when she is not shouting, her mouth opens and closes slowly.

The woman gets up from her chair and stubs out her cigarette. She sees the two men and two women watching from across the pool and holds up her hands. She mouths a 'Sorry' and walks towards the water saying, 'Be quiet, baby . . .'

Ed turns back to Angie and Marina. 'Listen, why don't we all eat there together?' he says.

Angie instinctively turns towards Barry. Marina looks across at Dave who is just climbing out of the hot tub.

'I know the bloke who runs the place,' Ed says. 'So I can definitely get us a decent table on the balcony. Quesadillas, crab cakes, jugs of frozen margaritas . . . what d'you reckon?'

'Don't you want to eat with your wife?' Marina asks, looking towards the woman who is now sitting up on her sunbed and swigging from the bottle of beer. The woman smiles and waves. She is slim and small-breasted. She is wearing a broad-brimmed sunhat and a black one-piece swimming costume.

Ed pulls a face. He says, 'She does what she's told,' in some kind of mock-cockney accent and laughs.

Once again, Marina and Angie join in the laughter, and Angie's cheeks flush just a little.

'You two have a think about it.' He looks from Angie to Barry and back, then turns to Marina. 'And you have a word with . . .'

'Dave,' Marina says, helping him out.

'Yeah, see what he fancies doing,' Ed says. 'It's not a big deal either way. Might be a laugh, that's all.' He turns then, wincing a little at yet more squeals from the other side of the pool, and they all watch as the woman wraps a towel around the young girl's shoulders and ushers her gently back into the shade.

From: Edward Dunning <Edduns@gmail.com>
Date: 16 May 22:14:17 BST
To: Angela Finnegan, Marina Green
Subject: Re: Dinner!!!

Ed here (Sue crap at answering email etc) and dinner sounds great. Hope M & D are up for it too. The Florida sunshine seems a long way away, doesn't it? Maybe the girls could wear their swimsuits just for old times' sake and I'm happy to rub in suntan lotion as always. It's a dirty job but someone's got to do it! I'll bring the margarita mix.

See y'all soon,
Ed x

Sent from my iPhone

THREE

Ed hissed a passionate 'Yes' to himself when his opponent's lame attempt at a drop-shot caught the top of the net. He clenched his fist as he turned away to fetch some balls from up against the fence. Now, he was serving at 40–15 to go 4–3 up in the deciding set.

He shoved a ball into the pocket of his shorts, began to bounce another.

He whispered, 'Come *on*.'

Ed didn't know the bloke he was playing terribly well. Simon something-or-other, bought and sold top-end cars. The important thing was that he was three places above Ed on the singles ladder, which meant that Ed was only a couple of games away from a *very* significant scalp. The bloke was friendly enough and it had been a good-natured match up to this point, but glancing across the net as he prepared to serve, Ed could see how badly Simon something-or-other wanted it.

Not enough though, Ed thought. Not as much as I do. Which is why I'm going to kick your arse.

He glanced across at Sue, who was sitting at one of the tables outside the clubhouse. She wasn't looking his way, which was a shame, because he felt an ace coming and he wanted her to see it.

25

His first serve was a foot long.

'Long,' the car dealer shouted.

Tosser.

The second serve was too high and far too slow and the bounce gave his opponent all the time in the world to get over the ball and put it away very easily. Ed glanced across to make sure that Sue hadn't seen it.

'Forty–thirty,' the car dealer said.

Ed trapped a ball between racket and shoe, flicked it up and walked over to the backhand court, muttering. 'I know the score . . .'

'Sorry?'

Ed shook his head and bounced the ball. This time, the first serve was right in the corner. He pushed off hard towards the net.

'Long,' the car dealer shouted.

'*What?*'

His opponent, who was already moving across for the next point, stopped and looked back at the mark the ball had left. He shrugged and raised his racket. 'OK, play two.'

Ed stared at him, watched the cheeky bastard move grudgingly back and get into position to receive the serve again. Shaking his head like he was the one being generous, when he was clearly just a cheat.

He netted the first serve, but his second was pretty good and Ed watched, delighted, as a mis-hit return came ballooning back, the fist already clenched by the time the ball had landed a good few feet beyond his baseline. The car dealer dropped his racket in exasperation. Ed looked towards the clubhouse again.

'Game,' he said, good and loud.

At the chairs, they both opened water bottles and watched the two women playing on the court behind theirs. Both were pushing fifty, but Ed thought that one of them looked quite dirty and had a backside that was still very tidy indeed in tight, grey tracksuit bottoms. Her name was Carol and she and Ed had exchanged near-the-knuckle comments at various club gatherings. This had become even more exciting since someone had told him that, even though she was married to some duffer in the seventh team, she was shagging the club captain.

'That's nice to look at,' the car dealer said.

Ed was pleased to see that his opponent, who was a couple of stone heavier than he should have been, had yet to recover his breath and was sweating heavily. 'Up for it as well,' he said. 'From what I hear.'

'Really?'

They stared as the woman bent to pick up a couple of stray balls then walked back to her baseline. When she served, Ed nodded to the car dealer, raising his eyebrows at the glimpse of surprisingly toned-looking stomach on display as she stretched towards the ball.

Ed took a swig from his water bottle.

'So, how's business?' the car dealer asked. 'You're something in the book trade, aren't you?'

Ed worked as a sales rep for Macdonald & Hughes, a medium-sized publisher of academic books and technical manuals. Two of his colleagues had been laid off in the previous three months. He tossed his water bottle back into his bag and said that yes, he worked in publishing and that business was pretty good actually.

'I can never find the time to read,' the car dealer said. 'Just a couple of thrillers on holiday, you know. Jeffrey Archer or Frederick Forsyth. That bloke who writes the Jack Ryan books, what's his name?'

Ed didn't know. He put his hands on his hips, rolled them around. 'I've just always loved books,' he said.

The fact was that Ed hated books. The boxes of the bloody things he had to hump to and from the boot of his car every day. That he had to transport the length and breadth of the sodding country, working a territory that got bigger each time another one of the sales team got the boot. He'd seen it coming, of course. The damage that the internet would do to the business he was in. Who the hell wanted dirty great encyclopaedias, dictionaries and technical manuals when they were all available for nothing on your computer? On your phone, for goodness' sake.

He was still flogging eight-track cassettes when everyone was listening to MP3s.

Thank God he'd always been one of those with a nose for which way the wind was blowing. He'd seen the way things were heading long before anyone else and even though he knew he would be the last one to get the push, he'd started sniffing around for something else good and early. Putting out feelers. Nobody had bitten as yet, but he was confident he'd be able to jump before he was pushed and was still waiting to hear back from one or two contacts. There were several new leads to chase up. He had a meeting that sounded promising early the next week.

'So, shall we get this finished?' The car dealer picked up his racket, bounced the head against the heel of his hand.

They walked back on to court.

Ed thought, *I'll* get this finished.

He walked to the baseline and beyond, until he was just a few feet away from where Carol was gathering balls on the other side of the high, cross-hatched fence. He glanced quickly across to where Sue was still sitting, then said, 'You winning, Carol?'

She turned and smiled. 'Just,' she said. 'What about you?'

Ed stepped closer and hooked his fingers through the fence. 'Well, I am at the moment, but if you keep on bending down like that I think I might lose my concentration.'

Behind him, the car dealer shouted, 'Four–three, then.'

Ed winked at Carol, then turned to see his opponent jumping up and down; ready to serve, man-boobs jiggling. Ed raised his racket to signal that he was ready, then bent his knees and tried to focus. He decided that, whatever else happened, he was going to call the next shot that was remotely close to the line 'out', and that not only was her arse in lovely nick but Carol had very decent tits as well.

Sue Dunning slowly turned the pages of the *Daily Express* she had found in the clubhouse. With one ear on the mindless chatter from two women a couple of tables away, she cast an uninterested eye across the pictures and the headlines, taking in little as she sat waiting like a good wife, and hoped that her husband was winning his match.

From where she was sitting, the body language of the two players suggested that things were looking good.

That was a relief . . .

She knew that an evening she was already dreading would be a damn sight harder if Ed lost. That the bad mood which inevitably followed when he came off worse at tennis, or poker . . . or *anything*, come to that, could last for hours. She could not bear the thought of what already promised to be a hellish drive to Crawley being made grimmer by his childish, sulky grunting, though the alternative— as he relived the highlights of his triumph—was only marginally preferable.

'I was striking the ball so *well*, Suze. Volleys, ground strokes, you name it. It's like I was really . . . *seeing* it, you know what I mean?'

He was certainly seeing that old slapper on the next court, Sue could tell that much. Not that she cared a great deal any more. It was funny really, and *so* predictable, and she would quite enjoy waiting for just the right opportunity to say something. Maybe she would have a quiet word with the woman's husband at the summer barbecue; let him know just what his wife had been up to at the quiz night the previous month, on her knees behind the clubhouse. She could always have a chat with the captain's wife, of course. Or she might just volunteer to help out with the drinks and spit in the old slag's punch.

There was all manner of fun to be had.

A woman on the nearby table laughed loudly at something her companion said. Sue looked over and smiled when she caught the woman's eye. 'Isn't this weather great?' she said.

'Fabulous,' the woman replied.

Sue looked back towards the tennis courts. Ed watched a ball drop near the line and called it out. On the court behind him, the woman in the grey tracksuit squealed as a lob lifted the ball a few inches over her outstretched racket.

'Fingers crossed for a good summer,' Sue said.

Twenty-five years together—since the sixth form, for heaven's sake—and married for twenty-two, Sue understood by now that Ed needed to do these things. He defined himself in terms of his pulling prowess and she wasn't so naive as to believe that in twenty-odd years he'd never done anything about it. She knew that he craved the occasional adventure and she was content to let him get on with it, because over the years she had come to believe that they actually made their marriage better. In fact, Sue wondered what life would be like for them both the day Ed woke up and stopped believing he was attractive to women. Actually, she was not giving him his due, because she knew that in most instances he *was* attractive to women. She knew that Angie fancied him for a start. Silly cow couldn't stop blushing and laughing at the silly jokes and voices. She wasn't sure about Marina, that one was a little harder to work out, but she would not have been surprised.

Ed certainly thought Marina was sexy. He and Sue had talked about it when they'd been on holiday of course, and several times since, once they'd received that bloody dinner invitation.

Not that she'd even known about that until it was too late.

It had been perfectly fine in Florida, fun and games for the best part of a fortnight, but Sue had certainly not harboured any desire to see any of them again. You *said* those things because it was impolite not to, because you were tight-arsed and British, for God's sake, but people never really meant it.

We should definitely stay in touch . . . same time next year . . . it really feels like we've become friends.

She and Ed had had a minor bust-up when she found out that he'd intercepted Angie's email. That he had actually replied to say they were going.

'These things are always a nightmare,' she had said.

'We've never done anything like this before.'

'There's a good reason for that.'

'Come on, the six of us got on all right, didn't we?'

'We don't want people . . . latching on.'

'Who's latching on? It's just dinner.'

'You're thrown together on a beach or around a pool or whatever, and you're best friends for a few days, but that's supposed to be it. It doesn't mean you want to do it again. It won't be the *same* if you try to do it again. It's like a one-night stand . . .'

That last comment had made Ed smile and he had made a grab for her, and the argument had run out of steam fairly quickly afterwards.

Not that Sue would have known, of course. What a one-night stand felt like, or two nights or three. In those twenty-five years together—'since we were passing soppy love notes in that playground in Birmingham, for heaven's sake'—the opportunity had never presented itself. Or if it had, she had not recognised it for what it was.

She closed the newspaper and asked herself if that was truly the case. Had she simply been afraid to transgress? Had she known deep down that while she was willing to tolerate Ed's flings and flirtations, he would never have been as understanding?

That in spite of everything, she was far stronger than he was.

She looked across and saw that the two men were walking towards the net. Ed got there first, jogged the last few yards, and stood with his hand outstretched.

Thank God . . .

She stood up as the players gathered their things and watched them walk towards the gate. Ed raised his racket and she waved back. She would need to wait around a little while yet, as etiquette dictated that he buy his opponent a drink and spend another half an hour gloating.

The women at the nearby table turned as the two men approached.

'Your husband?' one of them asked.

'I'm afraid so.'

'Which one is he?'

Sue smiled. *You mean, is it the fat, balding one? Or is it the tall good-looking one you wish you were sharing a bed with?*

'The one who won,' she said.

FOUR

Before anyone has so much as picked up a menu, Ed volunteers to order for them all. If anybody has a better idea, they keep it to themselves. They kick things off with pints of local Landshark lager for the men and a jug of frozen margaritas. Then a few minutes later, the waitress—who tells them her name is Traci, and scribbles it on the paper tablecloth in case they forget, dotting her 'i' with a heart—delivers an enormous platter of mixed appetisers. A dozen buffalo wings and a mountain of nachos covered in salsa and melted cheese; battered oysters, clam strips and popcorn shrimp.

'The portions are always so enormous,' Marina says.

'That's why it's best to wait,' Ed says. 'Just order your starters.'

Barry helps himself to a chicken wing and says, 'Well, you're the expert.'

They're seated at a large table on the balcony, near the bar. The bar itself is decorated with dollar bills—hundreds of them, each with a message scrawled on it in marker pen by satisfied customers: *Best margarita in town! Love Bob and Marsha*; *Thanx for the warm welcome and the awesome fish tacos xx*. It's no more than a degree or two cooler than it was at midday, and the few fans scattered about aren't helping much. In the far corner, a guitarist—white, with dreadlocks—sits on a stool, swapping banter with the customers closest to him and playing an inoffensive selection of songs rather well: Paul Simon, Bob Marley, the Beatles. It's loud, so they all need to lean in close to one another and raise their voices to make themselves heard.

'You ask me, the trick is to take it that bit easier before the holiday starts,' Ed says. He slaps his belly through a salmon-pink, short-sleeved shirt. 'Go on a diet for a week or two, then make sure you get some exercise while you're out here. Play a bit of golf or tennis or something.'

'I try and swim every day,' Sue says.

'Me too,' Dave says.

Ed leans towards him. 'You a swimmer then? See you in the pool.'

'I prefer the sea,' Dave says. 'But yeah . . .'

'You don't need to lose any weight,' Angie says to Sue. 'There's nothing of you.'

Sue is wearing a plain white halter-neck which accentuates her slender figure and shows off nicely tanned shoulders. Her long brown hair is held up with a clip. She tucks a loose strand behind her ear and smiles. 'I just like swimming,' she says.

They all clap politely as the guitarist finishes a song and announces that he's taking a short break. Marina insists she likes the music, but says it's good that they don't have to shout any more. Barry has finished his beer, so Ed signals to Traci as she passes and orders him another.

'Right.' Ed drums his palms on the edge of the table and looks from one face to another. 'Where did everyone meet? That's always a good way to kick things off.'

Angie looks at Barry, who is sitting at the other end of the table. 'No point in couples sitting together,' Ed had said when they'd been sorting out the seats.

'It's a good story,' Barry says.

'We met when I was having some work done on my house.' Angie reaches for the jug and tops up her glass. 'Ten years ago, was it?' She looks at Barry again and he shrugs, unsure. 'Barry was my builder.'

The others at the table make suitable noises of surprise and interest.

'She was looking for a quotation, so you gave her one.' Ed laughs at his innuendo and winks at Barry. 'Right?'

'We just started seeing a lot more of each other as the job went on,' Angie says. She stares into her drink, stirring it with a straw. 'We'd both been through bad break-ups, both had kids, what have you. We both needed shoulders to cry on, I think.' She looks up. 'So, anyway.'

'At the end of the day, *I* got a second wife . . .' Barry leaves it hanging and looks towards Angie, having set up a punchline that has obviously been trotted out many times.

Angie picks up her cue. 'And *I* got fifty per cent off my extension.'

Everyone laughs. Marina says, '*Fifty,* is that all?' then everyone laughs some more.

Dave and Marina are holding hands across the table. He signals to her and when she passes him her handbag he reaches inside and pulls out a blue inhaler. Ed watches him shaking it and says, 'You an asthmatic or something?'

Dave nods and takes a puff.

'That like a steroid?' Barry asks.

'Sort of . . .'

'They shrink your balls, don't they?' Ed says. 'You end up with bollocks like Maltesers.'

'Can't say I've noticed,' Marina says, and all the girls laugh.

'So, what about you?' Angie says to her. 'How long have you two been married?'

'We're not married,' Dave says, quickly. 'We are *planning* to, when we get ourselves a bit more organised.' He leans towards Marina and blows a kiss. 'Right, babe?'

Marina nods and smiles, then turns back to Angie. 'Boring really,' she says. 'We met at a party. God, when was that, Dave?'

'It was almost exactly two and a half years ago,' Dave says. He smiles at Marina, tugging at his scruffy goatee. 'October.'

'I'm impressed,' Angie says, pulling a face at Barry.

34

Sue leans across the table and pokes Ed's arm. 'Can you remember what month *we* met?'

'I know it was your lucky day,' Ed says.

'Well, I suppose it *was* a long time ago.'

'I think Sue and I have got you all beaten,' Ed says. He takes a mouthful of beer and smacks his lips. 'We've been together twenty-five years.'

'You're kidding,' Marina says.

'Married for twenty-two.'

'Bloody hell,' Barry says.

Ed sits back and folds his arms. 'Now, if that's not worthy of some kind of long-service medal, I don't know what is.'

Sue looks at Angie and shakes her head. Says, 'Cheeky sod.'

'You must have been kids,' Angie says.

'We were both in the sixth form.' Sue puffs out her cheeks. 'Long time ago.' She picks up a nacho, carefully bites it in half. 'He'd already gone out with most of my mates.'

'Only because she was playing hard to get,' Ed says.

'Where were you at school?' Marina asks.

'Birmingham,' Sue says, then pops the rest of the nacho into her mouth.

'Oh, I thought I could just make out the accent.'

Ed leans forward and raises his voice. 'Yow alroight, our kid?' Angie laughs and he leans across her for the last chicken wing. 'This grub's bostin' ay' it?'

'We moved to London twelve years ago,' Sue says. 'Ed got a job with a company down there.'

'What do you do, Ed?' Dave asks.

Ed licks sauce from his fingers. 'Publishing.'

'Sounds interesting.'

'I've just got one of those Kindle things,' Angie says. 'They're fantastic. Do you do those?'

Ed does not appear to hear the question above the chatter from adjacent tables and the clink of glasses. He nods back at Dave. 'So, what game are you in, then?'

'Computers,' Dave says. He snores and chuckles. 'Very dull.'

'Not dull at all.' Marina turns to Angie. 'Your kids play computer games?'

'Can't get them off the bloody things,' Angie says.

'I bet Dave helped design some of them.'

'Wow,' Angie says.

'What about you?' Ed nods across at Barry. 'Still in the building trade?'

'It's his own company,' Angie says. 'A family business, you know?'

'Do *you* work?' Sue asks her.

Angie shakes her head. 'Well, only if you count running around after two kids.' She laughs, reaching for the jug again, and pours what little is left of the margarita into her glass. 'I'm a kept woman.'

'Sounds good to me,' Sue says.

'Don't get any ideas,' Ed mutters, looking to Barry and Dave for a reaction.

'You?' Angie asks.

'I teach,' Sue says.

'Infants or juniors?'

'Well, it's a private school, so it's years four to eight. Nine- to thirteen-year-olds.'

'Sounds like hard work.'

'Sometimes.'

'Nice long holidays, though,' Angie says. 'Right?'

Sue just nods and turns to look at Marina. It takes a few seconds before Marina realises that she is being invited to say her piece.

'Oh . . . I'm sort of looking around a bit at the moment,' Marina says. 'I'm working part-time as a dental receptionist, but it's not exactly my life's ambition.'

'Marina writes and acts,' Dave says. 'That's what she *should* be doing.'

'Shut up,' Marina says. She pushes him playfully in the shoulder, but looks happy enough to talk about it. 'I take some acting classes, that's all, and I've written a few short stories, which nobody's ever seen.'

'I've seen them and they're great,' Dave says.

'You're biased though, because we have sex.'

Angie and Sue laugh and Angie points to Ed. 'Well, now you've met a publisher,' she says. 'You never know, you might end up being the next J.K. Rowling or whatever.'

'I don't think so,' Marina says.

'What kind of stuff do you write?' Ed leans towards her. 'Obviously, I can't make any promises, but I might be able to point you in the right direction. Get it in front of a few people . . .'

Traci arrives at the table and asks if everyone is enjoying themselves. Ed says that everything is great, as always. Traci says that's awesome and cheerily asks if she can clear some of the empties. When she moves away again, dirty plates and bowls stacked on one arm, a young girl is standing next to the table.

She is wearing shorts and training shoes and a glittery pink top that doesn't quite cover her belly. Her dark hair is tied back with a glittery pink scrunchie. She stares at them and tugs at her ear.

'Hi,' Marina says.

Angie says, 'Hello,' recognising the girl they had seen earlier, in the pool at the Pelican Palms.

'Everything all right?' Sue asks. She looks around and eventually sees the girl's mother down below them on the pavement. The woman is talking to a dark-haired man whose back is to the restaurant. He looks well built and Sue can just make out tattoos creeping beneath the sleeves of his T-shirt. The woman gesticulates lazily—an unlit cigarette between her fingers—while the other hand is casually laid first on the man's arm, then across on to his chest. Sue nudges Marina, cocks her head towards the street and quietly says, 'There . . .'

'Where you from?' the girl asks. Her voice is high-pitched and nasal.

'We're from England,' Angie says. 'What about you?'

'I'm from America,' the girl says, frowning. 'I'm not from England.'

'OK . . .'

The girl steps forward and holds on to the edge of the table. 'I saw England on the TV though.' She nods slowly, eyes down, and when she looks up again, her face breaks into a beaming smile. 'When the

37

prince and the princess got married in the church that had the trees growing inside and all the kings and queens from everywhere in the world came there to watch.' She looks towards the group, but as she speaks, her eyes are fixed on a spot six inches or so above the head of Dave, who is sitting at the furthest end of the table from her. 'That was my favourite show of all time, and we have it on the DVR, so I can watch it whenever I want.'

'That's good,' Marina says.

As Ed refolds his paper napkin and Barry slowly drains his beer glass, Sue looks past the girl and down towards the street. She watches as the girl's mother begins peering frantically up and down the street, and Sue opens her mouth to shout. At the same moment, the woman looks up, so Sue and Marina wave, and when the woman spots her daughter, she raises her hands in relief and shakes her head.

There is no longer any sign of the man she was talking to.

She jogs up the steps on to the balcony and walks quickly across to the table. She puts her hands on the girl's shoulders. Her daughter is several inches taller than she is.

'Hey, baby.' The woman's voice is low and smoky; a Southern accent. 'I told you to stay close to me, didn't I?' She nods towards Sue, who is closest to her. 'I hope she wasn't disturbing you.'

'Not at all,' Sue says.

'She gets over-excited, you know?'

'It's fine.'

'We don't get out of Georgia a whole lot, is the truth.' She smiles and rubs the tops of the girl's arms as though she might be cold. 'Anyway, thanks for being so nice about it, and have a great evening . . . and now we'll let you get back to your dinner, won't we, honey?'

'They're from England,' the girl says. 'Like in the show we like.'

'OK, then.' The woman grins, and reddens, then turns and leads the girl away from the table and down the steps.

Before anyone can say anything, Traci reappears to take orders for the main course. Ed recommends the fish tacos, which Dave is happy to go along with. Angie and Barry order burgers and sweet potato fries, while first Sue and then Marina declare that they want to skip the main course and leave room for pudding. Angie asks if anyone else is moving on to wine, so Ed chooses one and they order a couple of bottles. Barry wants another beer.

'I'll be right back,' Traci says.

'So.' Ed leans forward and lowers his voice a little. 'Anyone else think that girl was a bit . . .'

Dave grunts and nods.

'I don't know what the word is,' Angie says. 'What you're supposed to call it these days.'

'Retarded,' Barry says.

'I don't think you can say that,' Angie says.

'Don't look at me,' Ed says, shrugging. 'We called them a lot worse than that when I was at school.'

'I think that's what Americans *do* call it,' Barry says. 'I saw something on TV, somebody talking about "mental retardation".'

'It's another one of those stupid made-up words,' Ed says. 'Like relevancy or burglarisation.'

'Right,' Dave says. 'I hate that.'

'You've got to feel sorry for the mother though,' Angie says. 'Doesn't look like there's a husband around.'

'Looked like she was doing fine to me,' Sue says.

Nobody says much else until the drinks arrive. Ed tastes the wine, tells Traci it's fine and starts to fill the glasses. 'Say "when",' he tells Marina, then, when she does, he laughs and proceeds to ignore her.

'We're on holiday,' he says.

Angie slides her glass across and says, 'I'm not arguing.'

'So, who fancies going on somewhere afterwards?' Ed asks. 'There's a fantastic little bar a bit further up towards the beach.'

Dave looks at Marina and says, 'I'm up for it if you are.'

'I'm not sure,' Barry says.

'Why don't we just play it by ear?' Sue says.

'Suit yourself.' Ed nods towards the corner, where the guitarist is taking his seat again and tuning up his guitar. 'There's a proper band on. Dancing if you fancy it.' He bites down on his lower lip as he shows off a few moves in his seat. While Angie and Dave are laughing, Ed looks across at Sue and his eyes narrow. He says, 'Some people just don't know how to enjoy themselves.'

From: Marina Green [mailto:marinagreen1979@btinternet.com]
Sent: 18 May 20:36:42 BST
To: Angela Finnegan
Cc: Susan Dunning, Ed Dunning
Subject: Re: Dinner!!!

On May 16, at 17:31, Angela Finnegan <angiebaz@demon.co.uk>
wrote:

*<<So, me and Barry would love it if the four of you could come to
dinner on Saturday, June 4th>>*

Angie,

What a brilliant idea, and thanks so much for getting this organised.
Dave and I will be there with bells on. Not sure the bikinis are a very
good idea though (nice try, Ed!) Still trying to shift a few pounds after
all those fries and crab cakes. Might have to make an exception for
your bread and butter pud though. Sounds delicious.

Can't wait to see everyone.

See you soon and let me know what you want us to bring.

Love and snogs,
Marina XXX

FIVE

On Saturday mornings, Dave drove them across to Brixton. He would drop her off at the little theatre tucked away behind the town hall, then park the car. He would pick up fresh fruit and veg on Acre Lane, read the papers over coffee in a bar on Atlantic Road, then be back in time to pick her up when her class had finished. They would walk back to Brixton market together and mooch around for a bit if the weather was nice. Once in a while, they might buy cans of Red Stripe and takeaway jerk chicken from one of the market stalls, but more often than not they would have lunch in a little pizza place in one of the arches.

That was what they did on a Saturday morning. What they had done for the best part of a year, since Marina had started the course. Both of them liked the routine.

In the small dressing room they all shared, Marina took her time changing out of her tracksuit bottoms and trainers. She said goodbye to some of her classmates who were heading off for a drink together. They didn't ask her to join them because they knew she had other plans, same as always. She said she'd see them next week. As it happened, she was hoping to grab a few minutes alone with Philip, their acting teacher, before Dave came to collect her, so she was happy to let the others drift away.

She leaned in close to the mirror, wondering why nobody ever did anything about the fact that two of the light bulbs around it had gone. She teased out a handful of hair and held it to the light. It was definitely time to get the tips dyed again.

'You going to stick with red?'

Marina saw Trish, one of her fellow students, move up behind her and lean down so that she could share the mirror.

'Not sure.'

'The red looks great,' Trish said. 'But you could always try something else. Purple, maybe?'

'What about blonde?'

'That would look amazing,' Trish said. 'You know, with your colouring and everything. Really original.' She ran fingers through her own hair, then said that she needed to run. She kissed Marina on the cheek and left.

Marina continued staring at herself. She wasn't altogether sure about the idea and was even less convinced that Trish gave a stuff about whether her hair looked any good or not. They had done quite a few improvisations together in recent weeks and Marina was starting to think Trish was hogging things a bit on stage. That she was trying too hard to draw attention to herself, which was absolutely not what it was supposed to be about.

She had toyed with saying something to Philip, then thought better of it. She did not want to seem whiney or competitive and besides, he would have seen exactly what was going on.

Actually, blonde *might* be an interesting idea, she decided. Something different. She wondered if she could get an appointment for that afternoon, have it done in time for the big reunion dinner in the evening. She rooted in her bag for her mobile, flipped it open, then tossed it back in again. Even if the hairdresser could fit her in, a style and colour would cost the best part of a hundred pounds and that wasn't fair, not when she and Dave were supposed to be saving up.

Looking to get something better than two bedrooms in Forest Hill.

Dave would tell her to go ahead and get it done, she knew that. He would tell her that it didn't matter. He would say, 'Actresses are supposed to get noticed, aren't they, Maz?' He would squeeze her hand and say, 'Anything that makes you stand out is good, isn't it?'

In the mirror she saw herself smile, thinking about him. About *his* smile, and his voice; the faintest trace of a stammer when he was nervous or excited. Perhaps she would mention the hair thing casually, when they were walking to the market.

'It might be fun for tonight, that's all, but I know it's ridiculously expensive . . .'

See what he thought.

Thinking about the dinner, she realised that they hadn't yet talked about what they were going to wear. A lot would obviously depend on how much of an effort everybody else was going to make and there would be no way of knowing that until they all turned up. She guessed that Angie would dress up a bit. That she would badger Barry into doing the same. Ed wouldn't need much encouragement to wear something flash, while Sue was one of those people who put a lot of effort into looking like she'd made no effort whatsoever. It was a tricky one, all things considered, but she and Dave usually worked this sort of thing out between them.

Well, Dave asked and she told him.

Another smile, before she picked up her bag and turned off the light.

In the small auditorium, Philip was leaning against the stage talking to Trish, which annoyed Marina because hadn't Trish told her that she was leaving? She'd suggested as much, anyway, when clearly she had just been waiting for the right moment to get Philip on his own.

Trish raised a finger. Only be a minute. Marina smiled and raised her hands, like it didn't matter.

She walked across to the window and, once it was clear that she could not hear what Trish and Philip were talking about, she thought about the best way of putting things, when she got her turn. They were working towards an end-of-term show, something that Philip had been piecing together through their weekly improvisations. Now, it was only six weeks away. There probably weren't even going to be any 'leads', not as such, and it was only a couple of lunchtime performances for friends and family, but still you never knew who might be sitting out there and it couldn't hurt to give yourself the best chance to shine, could it?

'You should push yourself forward a bit more,' Dave had said. Was *always* saying. 'It's not being pushy, not when you know you're the best.'

I just wanted to make sure I was heading along the right lines. I just thought I'd ask if there was anything else you were looking for. Anything I'm doing wrong . . .

She turned when she recognised the rhythms of a conversation being wound up, and moved slowly towards the stage. She nodded to Trish as they passed one another. Philip was putting his notes into a satchel.

He looked up and shook his head. 'I'm so sorry, Marina, but now I'm *really* late.' He slung the satchel over his shoulder. 'Can this wait until next week?'

She nodded quickly and said, 'Yes, of course.'

'Sure?'

'Absolutely. It's not a big deal.'

'Great, bless you.' He moved past her then turned, walking backwards towards the doors. 'Listen, good stuff today, all right?'

'Really?' God, this was exactly what she needed to hear. 'Is there anything I can do to improve—?'

But Philip was already saying 'next week' and pushing out through the doors.

Marina stood there and listened to the squeak of his footsteps as he walked away, towards the front entrance of the theatre. After a few minutes she could hear voices in the foyer. There was some kind of dance and fitness group for the over-fifties that took over the space fifteen minutes after the acting class finished.

She looked at her watch.

She walked back to the dressing room, where the first of the middle-aged dancers had already begun to change. One of them asked her if she was all right.

She pulled a chair close to the mirror and took out her make-up.

By now, Dave would almost certainly be waiting for her outside, but she did not want him to see that she had been crying.

Dave Cullen kept trying, but he had begun to doubt that he would ever learn to enjoy espresso. It was way too strong for him and it was only two mouthfuls, for heaven's sake, but he persevered because he understood that those who drank it were far more sophisticated than those who didn't. More grown-up. His friend Kevin always ordered one after lunch at the Italian sandwich bar below their office, and Dave envied the casual way he slurped at it and moaned in pleasure. The slightly smug look on his face as he savoured the hit, just like he was a proper Italian or something. Maybe Kevin was only pretending to like it too, but if he was, he made a damn good job of it.

'This is *nice*,' Kevin would say. Something like that. '*Really* hitting the spot.'

Dave pushed the stupid little cup to one side, went back to the counter and ordered a latte with extra vanilla syrup. Over the months he had come to know the guy who was serving pretty well. His name was Devon, or it might have been Deron.

'Looks nice out there today.'

'It's great,' Dave said. It was certainly one of the warmest days of the year so far. Dave was wearing the cargo shorts he had last worn in Florida, a T-shirt with the name of a band he'd seen once on *Jools Holland*.

'What you got on this evening, anything exciting?'

'Just dinner with some friends,' Dave said. 'Well, not friends, people we met on holiday.' He put extra sugar in his coffee. 'Might be good fun, might be bloody awful.'

Devon or Deron laughed. 'You got to approach these things with the right attitude,' he said. 'All about the attitude.'

47

Dave carried his coffee across to his table and continued trawling through the Saturday *Guardian*.

If he were being honest, he felt much the same about the posh papers as he did about the coffee. He checked results in the sports pages and looked at the TV and film stuff, and he would read anything gadget- or computer-related—obviously—but he just glanced at what was in the rest of it. He skipped anything that looked like news or comment. Life was just too short to plough through it all. He might occasionally catch the evening news on TV, but mostly he picked up what was going on in the world from discarded copies of the *Standard* or *Metro* on the train. Enough to hold his own with Kevin, or anybody else if it came to it.

He had certainly been the smartest one of that Sarasota group. Or he'd appeared to be at any rate, which was as good as. Not that he'd needed to show off or anything, it had just been pretty obvious. He couldn't *stand* people who showed off.

Fitting in was always the most important thing.

He drew out the review section from the main body of the paper and slipped it into his shoulder bag. He always kept it for Marina. She liked to look through the book and theatre reviews, see if there was anything she might like to read or a play she fancied. If she did pick something out, he was usually happy enough to tag along, but it was very hit and miss. Stuff in the West End was stupidly expensive, so they tended to go for the fringe end of things, upstairs in pubs, and to be honest a lot of it was rubbish. Last thing they went to see was just some woman in a floaty nightdress droning on about being raped. I mean, he understood it was a serious subject and all that, but he'd still spent the last twenty minutes asleep, and Marina had had a real go at him in the pub afterwards.

He wasn't sure why she carried on going to these things. He knew very well that all she did was sit there wishing it was her. Thinking she could make a better job of it.

The truth was he didn't know whether Marina was any sort of a decent actress or not. He always said the right thing of course, but he'd never really seen her in anything, only when he was testing her on lines for her lessons or whatever. Same thing went for the writing, those short stories she'd given him to read.

He had no idea.

Problem was, he didn't read enough to compare it with anything, not enough 'stories' anyway, because he only really ever bothered with non-fiction. He picked up the odd graphic novel occasionally, but even then he would have been happier with a few less words. Again, not enough hours in the day. He'd still managed to join in when everyone had been talking about what they were reading on holiday, though he'd mostly thrown in the odd comment about downloading books off the internet, which Ed had not been very happy about for some reason. Mind you, Ed was the sort of bloke who disagreed with what you were saying just for the sake of it.

Ed was probably the one Dave was least looking forward to seeing.

It would be good to see Sue and Angie again, though.

They were nice.

Barry was a bit of a black hole, but harmless enough . . .

He spooned out the last of the froth from his mug and wondered what *they* all thought about *him*. He thought through the time they had spent together, ran through as many of the conversations as he could remember. He felt pretty sure that they would all think he was OK. Even Ed.

He'd certainly worked hard enough.

Dave checked his watch. It was time to head across to collect Marina. He picked up his bag and, on the way to the door, he placed his empty mug and cup back on the counter.

He said, 'Laters,' and Devon or Deron said, 'Yeah.'

SIX

While Dave stands in the shallow end and watches him, Ed is swimming lengths. He has done ten or more already, taking care to steer clear of the middle-aged woman who is moving rather more slowly than he is, and the young boy, eight or nine years old, who keeps throwing a nickel into the water before diving down to retrieve it.

Each time the boy comes up clutching the coin, a short, hirsute man on one of the sunbeds claps and shouts, 'Way to go, Timmy.'

Barry walks slowly along the edge of the pool. Though he is a better colour now, he wears a baggy, black T-shirt over his shorts and a straw trilby to protect the bald patch at the back of his head. He reaches into his bum-bag for his cigarettes. As he is about to light one, the woman sitting at the table beneath the coconut palm says, 'You want one of these?'

Barry turns round and says, 'Sorry?'

The woman is sitting across from her daughter, smoking and flicking through a magazine. The girl is frowning as she scribbles in a colouring book. The woman picks up a yellow packet of cigarettes from the table and holds them out. 'American Spirit,' she says. 'All natural. None of the crap, you know?'

'Yeah, I'll give it a go,' Barry says. 'Thanks.' He puts his own cigarettes away as he walks over, and takes one from the woman's packet. She leans forward to light it for him. She is wearing a bikini today, and her blonde hair is tucked away beneath a white baseball cap with an 'A' embroidered on the front.

She sees him looking at it. 'Atlanta Braves,' she says. 'You know anything about baseball?'

'Same as rounders,' Barry says. 'Just a bit more complicated.'

The woman shakes her head, not getting it. She lifts her sunglasses and puts a hand on her daughter's arm. 'Thanks again for the other night, by the way. For being so sweet about everything.'

'Not a problem,' Barry says. He takes another long drag and says, 'These aren't bad, as it happens.'

The girl looks up and blinks at him, then turns to her mother. 'When can I go swimming, Mom?' she asks.

'Soon, OK.'

'I want to go swimming now.'

The woman rolls her eyes at Barry. 'The pool's still a little busy right now,' she says. 'So you'll have to wait.'

'I want to go swimming.'

'She's hot,' the woman explains to Barry. 'But she can get a little noisy, well, you *know* . . . so I thought I'd wait until things got quieter.'

It's not clear if either Ed or Dave has heard what the woman or her daughter were saying, but Ed stops at the end of the next length and Dave moves to the end of the pool and climbs out. Dave walks back to his sunbed to pick up a towel before moving across to stand next to Barry. Ed just heaves himself out of the pool and walks, dripping, towards the table. He stops just short of it and shakes his head like a dog.

The girl watches him, her mouth opening and closing slowly. When he looks at her, she goes back to her colouring. Her mother picks up her cigarettes again, waves the pack at Dave, and then at Ed. 'You guys want one?'

'Not for me,' Dave says.

51

Ed hesitates for a second or two then says, 'I will.'

The woman shakes one out and hands it to him then leans forward with her lighter. Her smile suggests that she can see it is not something he does very often. Not something he does when his wife is around. As if to confirm her suspicions, Barry nods and says, 'Naughty . . .'

Ed shrugs. 'So? I'm on holiday . . . and these are the ones without any additives, right?'

The woman nods. 'Right.'

He pulls out one of the tatty wicker chairs around the table and drops into it. 'These fags are actually *good* for you. It's like one of your five-a-day!'

Behind them, the boy surfaces and holds the coin aloft. His father's enthusiasm shows no sign of abating.

'So, you guys on your own today then?' the woman says.

Ed nods towards Barry. 'His wife's at the mall.' He takes a drag and exhales through a grin. 'Giving the old credit card a hammering.'

'She wants to pick up a few bits and pieces for the kids,' Barry says. 'T-shirts and what have you.'

'Is that stuff cheaper here?' the woman asks.

'Yeah, loads cheaper.'

'And our two are at the beach,' Ed says, with a nod in Dave's direction.

'They'll be back in half an hour or so,' Dave says. Dry enough now, he drapes the towel around his shoulders and looks back at Ed. 'Are we all going out to get some lunch?'

'That's the plan,' Ed says.

The woman puts her cigarette out and reaches for a bottle of suntan lotion. She squeezes some into her palm and starts rubbing it on to her arms. 'So, you guys all work together, something like that?'

Dave says, 'No,' and the others shake their heads.

'He's a builder,' Ed says, pointing. '*He's* a computer nerd, and I'm a professional racing driver and part-time male model.'

Dave laughs.

'You're a full-time wanker,' Barry says.

52

'You're yanking my chain,' the woman says.

Ed says, 'Only a bit,' and tells her he's not really a racing driver.

The short, hairy man walks to the edge of the pool and tells his son that it's time to go get something to eat. The boy asks if he can dive down one more time and the man says, 'OK.' A few feet away, the middle-aged woman is climbing slowly up the steps out of the water.

'You do all know each other from home though, right?'

Barry shakes his head and Dave says, 'We met out here.'

'Wow.' The woman starts rubbing the lotion into her legs. 'So it's just Brits sticking together.'

'I suppose so,' Dave says.

The girl looks up from her colouring book.

'Ganging up on us, huh?'

'What about now?' the girl asks, pointing at the pool.

The woman looks across and sees that the boy is climbing out, that nobody else is swimming. 'Yeah, OK.' The girl puts down her pencil and stands up, excited. She is wearing a striped blue and white one-piece swimsuit that is stretched across her large breasts and the soft roll of fat around her belly. 'You got plenty of sun cream on?'

'Got cream,' the girl says.

Dave, Ed and Barry watch as the girl reaches into a plastic bag for a pair of goggles and pulls them over her face. Once her mother has adjusted them, the girl walks quickly away from the table, smacking her hands against her legs, fingers outstretched. As soon as she reaches the edge of the pool, she bends her legs and presses her palms together. She pushes her arms out in front of her, mouths something to herself, then fearlessly belly-flops into the water.

Dave sucks in a fast breath and Ed says, 'Ouch.'

The girl instantly begins flailing her arms in a frenzied attempt at front crawl, which sends water flying in all directions. She stops after half a dozen strokes and holds out her arms. She shouts, 'Mom, look!'

'What about you?' Dave asks. 'Did you come here with anybody?'

The woman stands up and waves at her daughter. She shakes her head and says, 'No, it's just me and her,' then she walks across until she is only a step or two away from the edge of the pool. Dave follows a few seconds later and, once they have stubbed out their cigarettes, Ed and Barry drift across to join them.

They stand there and watch the girl.

'She's great,' Dave says.

'Yeah,' the woman says. 'She is.'

The girl scoops up handfuls of water, throws them in the air, then squeals when the water comes back down on her head.

Barry laughs and points. 'Look at her face.'

'Happy as Larry,' Ed says.

SEVEN

It was just her smile, no more to it than that.

When people write about these things—in those paperbacks you see in racks at stations, the ones with the blank faces of the so-called monsters staring out from the front covers—it's never quite that straightforward, is it? Maybe they need to *make* it complicated, to justify the fact they've written a stupid book in the first place. Maybe they really believe such and such a terrible thing happened because X was locked in a cellar when he was a kid, or Y had to wear his mother's clothes or whatever it was. Or maybe they just don't want to admit that, in the end, it's usually something nice and simple.

The colour of a shirt, a smell, a smile . . .

Trigger, that's the word they use, isn't it? 'Psychologists believe the trigger in this case was blah, blah, blah.' It's not the word I would choose myself, but at least it gives you some idea how quickly these things happen.

We might as well stop going round the houses.

This thing.

Thinking back, I suppose it *was* virtually instantaneous. Just the time it took for that smile to appear . . . wet-lipped, wide and a little crooked, and for me to see it. Having said that, there must have been *something* different about the girl's smile that day, because it wasn't as if I hadn't seen it before. So, her smile was different, or I was different, I'm not sure it really matters which. Or perhaps, for all my going on about how simple it all was, there were other things going on which I couldn't possibly be aware of. The time of day, the weather, some song on the car radio, the combination of *all* those things, whatever. There's no way I can know any of that stuff, that's up to shrinks and scientists to figure out. I can only tell you what it felt like to me at the time.

I can only tell you about that smile.

What I *can't* say for certain is that I knew what was going to happen the moment she recognised me. Not all of it. I remember that my mind was all over the place and that I could feel myself starting to sweat, but I can't remember much of a plan. I just started to drive and before too long, just a few sets of traffic lights further on from where she got in, I was starting to put it all together. She was gabbling, asking questions ten to the dozen, and I suppose I must have been answering her, but all I was thinking about were the wheres and the hows of it all.

I needed good spots. I needed to figure out the timings.

It was strange, but once things came together in my head—when I decided where I was going to pull over and where I would be going later on—I actually found myself starting to calm down. I think I needed that, so that I could focus. So feelings wouldn't get in the way when it came to the crunch. The trigger or whatever you want to call it, that was *all* about feelings . . . but I was kind of detached from everything that came afterwards, and I think you'd have to be, wouldn't you?

The things I did in the car, the things I said and did later on.

Thinking about it—and obviously I've thought about it a *lot*—I've asked myself if what happened was . . . avoidable, and you know, there's every chance it might have been if she'd stopped smiling. It's all hypothetical, obviously, but worth mentioning. Maybe I could just have dropped her off somewhere or she could have wandered back to the resort, but the fact is she wouldn't stop.

She kept on pulling that trigger.

She smiled, swigging from that water bottle, telling me about her pets and her friends and all the people who lived near her house.

She smiled, asking me where we were going.

Why we were stopping.

Where her mom was.

She smiled . . . wet-lipped, wide and a little crooked, right up until the end.

EIGHT

Barry's visit to yet another dissatisfied customer had not left him in the best of moods, though he had hardly been dancing a jig when he'd left the house first thing that morning. With a big dinner in the evening to come, Angie had plumped for a light lunch and had watched as Barry worked his way stolidly through a cheese sandwich and a packet of crisps, looking like he was a hair's breadth away from topping himself.

A face 'like a smacked arse'. One of his favourite expressions.

Angie had kept smiling. She had passed the pickle when it was wanted and refilled her husband's glass with Diet Coke. She had known very well that his foul mood was down to the whole business with his brother, it usually was, but she also knew better than to say anything. Not right then, at any rate. It was all about choosing your moments when it came to that particular hot potato, and picking the wrong one was definitely something to be avoided. It was frightening how quickly Barry could go from being somewhat pissed off at his brother to being seriously pissed off with her.

'That temper of his can turn on a fucking *sixpence*. It's a bastard, I'm telling you, so you want to go a bit careful.' Something Barry's younger sister had told her once. Flushed and full of herself, after one Bacardi Breezer too many.

'You should put your feet up for a couple of hours,' Angie had said, wiping the surfaces. 'Go back to bed, even.' There had been a grunt of interest then, and he had not needed too much persuading before he disappeared into the living room, with lager can, chocolate bar and remote control all within easy reach. Angie knew that—crashed out in front of the TV all afternoon while she did all the work—Barry would not feel the smallest twinge of guilt, but the fact was that she would not want him to, because with dinner for six people to get organised, this was how she preferred it.

With the kitchen to herself, she turned on the radio, tuned it in to Radio 2.

As far as the food itself went, there wasn't a great deal to do. She got the veggies ready and into pans, chopped the slab of paté into six equal portions and hulled the strawberries. She would put the chicken on as late as possible, let it finish cooking while everyone was tucking into nibbles and dips.

What she really wanted to spend time on was the table.

She dug out the best plates and the posh knives and forks and wiped dust from the crystal glasses that her mum and dad had bought when she and her first husband had got married. She tried to remember the last time they had used any of it. Decided it had probably been the previous Christmas . . .

Eleven for lunch that day. Dry turkey, sprouts and snide remarks.

On top of Angie's parents, and Barry's father—who wasn't really all there any more, poor old sod—Adrian and his lot had sat around while Angie had waited on the bunch of them hand and foot. His idle wife and spoiled kids. It didn't help that *her* kids had been sullen and barely spoken to his, while Barry had been in a foul temper with just about everyone because his ex-wife had gone away for Christmas and taken his son with her. He'd finally managed to get a few minutes on the phone with Nick while everyone else was watching *Doctor Who*, but it had only made things worse.

Sitting there afterwards, red-faced and muttering 'bitch' in his paper hat.

In the end, Angie had decided that she was just going to get rat-arsed on Buck's Fizz. Let the miserable bastards sort themselves out . . .

Half an hour on from ironing the tablecloth, she laid the last serving spoon on the table, stood back and decided she'd made a nice job of it. She leaned down to straighten the decorative candleholder she'd picked up in TK Maxx the previous week. She would light the candles just before the guests arrived. Once she'd showered and changed. Now, she poured herself a large glass of Pinot Grigio and sat down at the central island to work out a seating plan. Boy, girl, boy, girl went without saying, with her and Barry at either end of the table. She *had* been toying with place cards, but had finally decided they would be that one step too far, like napkin rings or a cheeseboard.

She took a slug of wine. Partners opposite one another? Directly or on the diagonal?

From the radio, she recognised a song that she and Barry had heard almost every day in Florida. On whatever that station was the radio in the hire car had been tuned to. She closed her eyes, just for a few moments, and remembered the feel of salt drying on her skin.

The taste of daiquiris and ice cream and prawns as big as fish fingers.

The sound of the drummers on the beach nearby at Siesta Key and between the beats, just for a moment before it is drowned out by wind and rhythm, the wail of a woman shouting out her daughter's name.

She stood up when Barry came in. She slid the wine glass away and watched as he walked across and stared down at the dining table.

'Bloody hell,' he said.

'What?'

'It's a bit . . . over the top, isn't it?'

'I don't know why I bother,' Angie said. 'We'll just send out for pizza, shall we?'

'I'm just saying, all this.' Barry waved a hand towards the table. 'It's a lot of trouble to go to.'

'Not for you it's not.'

As Barry wheeled away to make for the fridge, Angie swore out loud, realising that she had completely forgotten the big surprise. Her finishing touch.

'What?' Barry asked, turning.

Angie eagerly opened one of the cupboards they had built in beneath the island and pulled out a plastic bag. She removed a rectangular package and ripped off the wrapping, then proudly handed one of the six items inside to Barry.

He stared at it.

'It's a tablemat,' Angie said. 'With a picture of all of us in Sarasota.'

'I can see what it *is*,' Barry said.

'I got them done at that Snappy Snaps place, when I had the photos put on to a disk.' She took the others out and laid them in a row on top of the island. 'They do placemats, mouse pads, all sorts . . . and I just thought it would be something unique, you know? Something special for tonight, and the best part is, afterwards, everybody can take one home as a souvenir.'

'Christ,' Barry said. 'Why don't you just go the whole hog and have T-shirts printed up?'

Angie picked up a placemat of her own and looked at it. She moved her hand to her mouth. 'Oh, God,' she said. 'You know who took this, don't you?'

They both stared at the same picture of the six of them.

'This was on our last morning,' she said. 'Remember?'

'Yeah, outside the main entrance.'

'It makes you feel a bit funny, doesn't it?'

Barry pointed. 'You can just see a bit of the sign.'

'Ed asked her, you remember? And we gave her our camera.' Angie laid the placemat back down next to the others and reached across for her wine glass. 'Her daughter was definitely with her, standing next to her, because I can remember she was holding that colouring book. I remember that one of the pictures was only half coloured in. Bloody hell, Barry, this can only be an hour or two before . . . bloody hell.'

'Nice souvenir,' Barry said.

He could hear the shower running upstairs as he walked across to the table and sat down to study the picture. He picked the placemat up carefully so as not to disturb any of his wife's meticulously arranged tableware. He leaned it up against a wine bottle and sat back.

Barry and Angela, Ed and Sue, Marina and Dave.

Not that anyone was necessarily standing next to their partner. He remembered them bundling somewhat awkwardly into a line, squeezing together as soon as the cameras had been handed over. Sue on one end standing next to Angie, Ed up close to Marina in the middle, then Barry and finally Dave at the other end.

Some more tanned than others, more at ease.

Barry didn't dwell overlong on his own appearance. He almost always thought he looked like a bag of shit in photographs. There were a couple of him and Nick he was reasonably fond of, but that may have been because they were the only pictures of his son he possessed. That he was *allowed* to possess. He looked predictably awful in this one though, in a shirt Angie had forced him into buying which was too big and way too flowery.

'He reckons it makes him look like a gay darts player,' Angie had said. She was a glass or two to the good, in one of the bars near the beach, a night or two after the six of them had got together. She leaned across to kiss him on the cheek. 'Don't you, darling?'

'It's not me, that's all.'

Ed, of course, had been unable to resist. Flapping his wrist around and lisping, 'One hundred and eighty!'

Fucking hilarious . . .

In the photograph, Ed was showing a few too many of those nice, straight teeth, whiter than white against his tan. Angie was smiling too, more or less, and Marina, while four-eyed Dave on the end had that slightly superior look you caught sometimes, when he thought nobody was looking. Maybe the picture was taken before he was quite ready, but he definitely had that expression, something close to a smirk; *you should think yourselves lucky I'm even talking to you idiots.* To be honest, whatever face he had, Dave Cullen was a funny-looking sod: skinny as a stick, with bad skin and a wispy beard like some student or whatever. Geeky, that's what Angie had said. Certainly not what you'd call an oil painting, though Marina didn't seem to have any complaints, so maybe he was hung like a donkey or something.

It was Angie who had said that as well, like *she* should be so lucky. Like Barry had nothing worth writing home about.

Looking at the six of them, in shorts and sandals, brightly coloured shirts and sunhats, he decided that Sue probably looked the most . . . natural. A half-smile sort of thing, as though she'd just turned around and found a camera pointed at her. She had her hair up, showing off her shoulders. In fact, all of her was looking pretty good and Barry tried not to compare her slender figure with Angie's, but it was hard with the pair of them standing side by side like that. Funny, but in terms of being sexy or whatever, it wasn't an in-your-face thing with Sue. Not like it was with Marina, who was a bit, you know, *obvious.* In actual fact, you wouldn't give Sue a second look nine times out of ten, but every so often you just got this feeling—at least Barry did, at any rate—that whatever she wanted people to think, she probably went like a train given half a chance.

There'd been plenty of talk about what Sue and Ed got up to. Dave and Marina too, come to think of it. As per bloody usual, Barry and Angie had talked about sex a damn sight more than they'd actually done it.

Down to him, no getting round that.

Angie had been good about it while they'd been away, he couldn't fault her on that score. Saying that it didn't matter, because she was happy enough just to read her book and that it was far too hot to be doing any of *that* anyway. Letting him off the hook.

It wasn't too hot in bloody Crawley though, was it?

He let his head drop, then lifted it again, trying and failing to ease a little of the tension in his back and shoulders. It wasn't difficult to work out what was going on, was it? There was no great mystery about why certain parts that *should* be working *weren't*, no need for cuddles or counselling. He had a cow of an ex-wife and a bossy twat of a brother and both of them wound him up to the point where he felt like something was going to snap.

End of story.

'You just need to relax,' Angie kept saying.

Oh . . . you *reckon?*

He did his best to keep calm and to pretend that *he* didn't think it mattered either. Truth was though, he knew it was only a matter of time before she started dropping hints about 'seeing' someone. Made some joke about buying tablets off the internet. The sad, simple, sodding truth was, the tension was everywhere except his cock, and the irony was that not being able to do the business in the bedroom was making him even angrier.

A vicious cycle, or circle, whatever the fuck it was.

He realised that the water had stopped running upstairs. He listened, heard Angie's footsteps as she walked from the bathroom to the bedroom. He should probably go up himself and change into a clean shirt or something.

Make an effort.

Barry took one last look at the photograph as he carefully laid the placemat back in position. Five people staring straight at the camera. And him.

He wouldn't say anything, but he couldn't help wondering if this was really the best photo that Angie could find. If there was not one when, at the crucial moment, he had at least been looking the same way as everyone else. His eyes where they should be, on the woman with the camera, and not fixed on something two feet to the left of her.

One of the pictures only half coloured in.

NINE

Detective Jeffrey Gardner awoke thinking about Patti Lee and Amber-Marie Wilson. He lay staring at the ceiling for a few minutes, until the urge to visit the bathroom proved too strong, then he tried to slip out of bed without waking his wife.

The clock said 05.17.

His wife asked him if everything was all right and he said 'shush' and told her to go back to sleep. When she threw back the covers, he told her there was no need for her to get up as well.

'I'm awake now anyway,' Michelle Gardner said.

He was still thinking about Patti Lee and Amber-Marie over breakfast, while his five-year-old daughter was busy decorating the kitchen floor with Froot Loops. While his wife cooked eggs and tried to talk to him about something they were supposed to be doing that coming weekend. She could see that he wasn't really listening and called him on it. He apologised, and when he told her what was on his mind, Michelle nodded, and said, 'I think that woman needs to go home.'

Gardner knew his wife was right. He'd heard the same thing every day for a couple of weeks now. Almost every one of his colleagues on the Crimes Against Persons Unit thought it was crazy that the girl's mother was still around, but there were few volunteers to have that awkward conversation and plenty of reasons people could think of not to bother.

'*It's not like she's hurting anybody, is it?*'

'*Her choice, right?*'

'*What's that place cost anyway, like fifty bucks a night . . .?*'

He thought about it on the way to drop his little girl off at school. Then, once he was alone in the car, he began to think specifically about what he might say; trying certain phrases out loud as he drove south through the city towards Sarasota Police Department Headquarters.

'You need to be at home, Patti. You need to be around the people that care about you.'

Gardner was not convinced that Patti Lee Wilson would respond to that kind of cheesy crap, to *any* kind of crap now he thought about it, but it was the best he could come up with. He talked it through with a couple of the other detectives during the morning. He asked what his sergeant thought, while he wrote up reports and fielded telephone calls. The place was busier than usual, the atmosphere in the building a little more serious. The Chief of Police had been knocking heads together the day before and the entire Criminal Investigations Department was still buzzing following the murder of two elderly French tourists the previous week.

'Now's a good time, Jeff,' the sergeant said. 'It's been six weeks, and with everything that's going on around here right now, the truth is nobody's paying that woman's case a whole lot of attention at the moment.'

'We're still treating it as a homicide though, right?'

'For sure,' the sergeant said. 'We're looking for a body now, no doubt about that.' He waved an arm towards the dozen or so detectives who were working flat out on the tourist murders. He lowered his voice. 'But we *got* bodies with this one, we got two of the damn things. There's nothing much we can do on the Wilson case until that little girl turns up.'

'I guess not,' Gardner said.

The sergeant—a well-built black man, same as Gardner, but a dozen years older—reached for his coffee cup and swirled what was left in it around, like it might help. 'And there's no point in that little girl's mother being here to see us do *nothing much*, is there? You know what I mean?'

'I know what you mean.'

As far as the Sarasota Police Department was concerned, it might well have been a good time for Patti Lee Wilson to go back to Atlanta. It certainly made a degree of sense in terms of workloads and the allocation of manpower, but this was not the reason Jeffrey Gardner had woken up thinking about the mother of the missing girl. He knew that going home would be the right thing for Patti Lee Wilson. How in God's name could sticking around in the place where she'd lost her daughter, waiting on the only news she was ever going to get, possibly be doing her any good?

Until that little girl turns up . . .

At lunchtime, Gardner sat in a delicatessen full of cops on Ringling Boulevard—a paper napkin tucked into his collar to keep food off his shirt and tie—and tried to come up with other things to say that might convince the poor woman to leave. Perhaps it would be better to take a more common-sense approach to this, he thought. Be practical about it. In the end, he decided he would just start talking and see how it went, so as soon as he'd finished his turkey-breast sub, he got in his car and went to pay Patti Lee Wilson a visit.

It had been on Good Friday, six weeks and one day earlier, that Amber-Marie Wilson had been reported missing from the Pelican Palms Resort on Siesta Key. That initial 911 call—Patti hysterical and struggling to breathe—had come in just after four o'clock in the afternoon, and by Easter Sunday, Gardner had known it by heart.

Every whisper and strangled sob.

'*She just wandered off . . . must have . . . and I've searched and looked everywhere and . . . she wouldn't go far, she would never do that.*'

'*Could you repeat that address?*'

'Jesus Christ, you have to get over here right now, OK?'

'You need to try and stay calm, ma'am.'

'Listen, you need to know that she has some problems, you know? She has some . . . mental difficulties. Oh God . . . she'd trust anyone. Do you understand what I'm saying? Anyone . . .'

He drove five and some miles east on Fruitville Road, then turned south just shy of I-75. He was soon moving through an area of town dominated by industrial parks and warehouses. He could hear the sand and grit striking the side of the car as he drove. He passed lumber yards, repair shops and plumber's merchants, then slowed as he approached a budget motel next door to a low-rent strip mall.

Where she had been living this past month and a half.

By sundown on that first night, the smart money was on Amber-Marie having been taken. Every shop and bar had been checked, every inch of beach and, as soon as the Marine Patrol had been brought in, as much of the water as could be usefully searched before the light had gone.

Siesta Village was hardly a hot spot as far as crime was concerned and apart from a couple that had been put up privately by security-conscious bar owners, there were precisely two surveillance cameras on the main stretch of Beach Road. Amber-Marie could be seen walking out of the Pelican Palms on the single camera at the resort's main entrance/exit, but there was no sign of her on any other camera anywhere in the village.

In whichever direction she had walked, Amber-Marie had simply wandered on to the street and disappeared within a few minutes of leaving the side of the pool at the Pelican Palms. Nobody questioned in those first few days had any useful information. Nobody remembered seeing her and, despite repeated appeals, not a single witness came forward to say that they had seen anything suspicious.

'She'd trust anyone.' Patti said that to Jeff Gardner the first time she saw him, and she kept right on saying it.

She was not going to argue with the smart money.

68

Gardner understood that those first, 'golden' twenty-four hours probably seemed an eternity to Patti, but for him and the other detectives brought in from the Crimes Against Persons Unit, they went by in a flash. They became forty-eight hours quickly enough too, and long before that first week was out, the case had slipped off the front page of the *Herald-Tribune*, and was no longer a lead item on the local TV news.

Careful to make sure that the girl's mother was nowhere within earshot, most detectives began to talk about Amber-Marie Wilson in the past tense.

A homicide case, in everything but name.

Not for Gardner though, not completely. How could he not have at least a shred of hope? How could he see the unconditional love on the face of his own little girl and write off Patti Lee Wilson's daughter? He could not bring himself to give up on her, whatever common sense told him. He had to keep faith, especially with a girl who was . . . damaged.

'Makes her special though,' Patti had told him that one night. Beer on her breath in a parking lot near the beach, shivering a little as the temperature fell. 'Amber-Marie doesn't see the same things other kids see, you understand? She doesn't see the bad things.'

Gardner had wrapped her jacket around her and put her into the back of a cab. He had thought, not until now.

He slowed and turned into the front lot of the Brigadoon Suites, parked up next to a faded orange Subaru with a battered front wing. Climbing out of the car, he glanced across at some of the brightly lit signs in the strip mall next door. Not for the first time, he thought how handy it was for any guests at the Brigadoon Suites who needed twenty-four-hour dog grooming or refurbished computer components.

He walked towards a two-storey block of rooms, a wooden stairway at each end.

Almost every inch of the place was the colour of an old ballet shoe, dusty pink or rose or whatever they called it on the side of the tin. Gardner had seen plenty of similar colour schemes at places like this.

Wall-to-wall purples, greens and gunmetal greys. The owners had clearly seen little need to splash out and had opted to save money on paint by bulk-buying colours that were—quite rightly—unpopular elsewhere.

He saw the door of the manager's office open and watched an old woman walk out. She looked at him, but he just raised a hand. He did not need telling the way.

Climbing the pink stairs, his hand on the flaking pink banister rail, he tried to get at least a few words clear in his mind. He did not want this to take all day. It was after lunch, and he wondered if she would have started drinking yet.

He walked to the door of Room 1224 and knocked. Stepped back and waited. Knocked again.

'You looking for the mother?' He turned to see the old woman from the manager's office. She had followed him and was already halfway up the stairs. 'The mother of that girl who disappeared?' The woman was leaning on the handrail, panting, a hand pressed to her narrow chest. 'Well, she's not here, so . . .'

Gardner said, 'Thanks,' and walked away from the door, swearing under his breath. Why had he wasted his time driving all the way out here, when he'd known all along where she would be?

TEN

'I'm happy to drive back, you know,' Marina said.

'It's fine.'

'I just thought you might want a drink.'

'*A* drink, singular, maybe,' Dave said. 'When have you ever seen me drunk, though? When have you ever known me to *want* to get drunk?'

'I was just saying, because you always drive, that's all.'

'I want to drive.'

'Fine then.'

'Why aren't we *moving* . . .?'

Having studied the map earlier that day, Dave had decided that they would probably be better off heading south towards the M23 via Crystal Palace and Croydon as opposed to the series of back roads that were an alternative during busier periods. He didn't think there would be too much traffic through south London early on a Saturday evening. Within ten minutes of leaving the house, they were held up, Dave tapping his fingers impatiently on the wheel. 'Should have gone with my first instinct,' he said. 'A23's *always* a nightmare . . .'

'It's fine,' Marina said. She looked at him, a half-smile. 'We've left plenty of time.'

They had left the house in Forest Hill at six-thirty, for a journey that should have taken no more than an hour. Dave had been waiting at the door in his jacket, the car keys in his hand, shaking his head as Marina hurried down the stairs, her make-up only half done. 'I just think it's rude to be late,' he said.

'We won't be late.' She flipped down the sun visor and checked her make-up in the small vanity mirror. 'We're not supposed to be there until eight. If we hadn't hit a bit of traffic, we'd have been early.'

'We don't want to be the last ones there, do we?'

'Don't we?'

'Well, you miss out on . . . conversation, whatever.'

'You think they'll talk about us if we're not there?'

Dave glanced over at her.

'Good,' she said, flipping the visor back into place.

The tapping of fingers on the wheel had now become the smacking of palms. 'See, where we are, as far as getting to the motorway is concerned, we're just that bit too far away.'

'One more reason to move,' Marina said.

Dave barked out a laugh. 'Doesn't matter how many reasons we've got if we can't afford it.'

She turned in her seat, adjusted the seatbelt. 'Is this about me going to the hairdresser's?'

'What?' He shot her a look, panicky. 'No . . .'

'I *said* it was just a thought.'

'I know—'

'I *told* you it would be ridiculously expensive, that I wasn't bothered one way or the other and you were the one who told me to go ahead and get it done.'

'Yes, and I was right, because it looks great,' he said. '*You* look great.'

'You sure?' She opened the visor again.

'Possibly a bit *too* great.' The traffic had begun to move and for the first time in ten minutes Dave managed to get the Fiat 500 into top gear. He grinned. 'Ed starts paying too much attention, I might have to smack him one.'

72

Marina laughed, closed the visor. 'Yeah, right.'

'Did you bring your stories, by the way?'

'No . . .'

'What?'

'I didn't think it was such a good idea.'

'Oh, for God's sake . . . I *told* you.'

'It just feels a bit pushy,' she said. 'Like I'm desperate, or something.'

'That's stupid.' Dave's eyes flicked to his wing-mirror. 'They're great stories and now we've met somebody who might be able to help.'

'Look, I'm sure we'll have to invite them round to us at some point, so why don't I just wait and do it then?' She leaned back and turned her head towards the passenger window. 'Then, you know . . . I can just nip upstairs and get them because we're at home, rather than looking like I've brought them specially.'

Dave said he supposed that would be all right, that he was only thinking of her, then leaned over to switch the radio on. They listened to the last few minutes of *Loose Ends*, then he retuned to a music station. He put his foot down on a clear stretch of dual carriageway between Thornton Heath and Croydon.

'Do you really not think I'd step up?' he asked. 'If Ed was out of order?'

Marina appeared not to have heard the question, and said, 'Why don't you ever get drunk?'

'Sorry?'

'I mean, everyone should get pissed once in a while.'

'Why?'

'It doesn't do any harm, does it?'

'So, everyone should lose control, once in a while? Everyone should do things they're ashamed of or embarrassed about, or that they can't even remember?'

Marina said nothing and shifted in her seat. They drove another mile or so without saying any more.

'I was at college with this bloke,' Dave said. 'He was a mate, I thought I knew him, but the first time he got really smashed I could see that he was somebody else entirely. He was ugly and aggressive. He was pathetic, you know?' He looked across at Marina and smiled. 'I just don't get it, I never have. This desire to be off your face, to lose it completely. I mean I'm not trying to stop anyone enjoying themselves, but you know . . .'

'What about on holiday?'

'What about it?'

'Weren't you a *bit* drunk on the last night?'

Dave shook his head, as though he had no idea what she was talking about.

'Come on . . . when we were in that flashy restaurant, the Bonefish or whatever it was. When we were all talking about that girl and what had happened. The business with the police.'

'I don't think so.'

'You seemed to be drinking a lot.'

'Maybe because it was the last night.'

'Well, there we go then.'

'I drank no more than anybody else,' he said. His voice was good and even and his hands were tight on the wheel. 'And I was certainly not drunk. Not even a bit.'

'All right, it doesn't matter.'

Dave turned the radio up and after a while he began singing along with a song that Marina did not recognise. During the instrumental he turned to her and smiled. He said, 'I don't know what you're trying to start an argument for anyway. We're supposed to be going out to have a nice time . . .'

ELEVEN

The manager of the Pelican Palms was a short, weasel-faced individual named Cornell Stamoran whom Gardner did not consider one of the nicer people that the Amber-Marie Wilson case had brought him into contact with. He had hair that was suspiciously dark for a man in his fifties and today he wore a checked golf sweater over a lemon-coloured polo shirt and khakis. At least one layer too many for the June temperature outside, but Gardner guessed that Cornell Stamoran would do his very best to avoid leaving his nice, air-conditioned office unless he absolutely had to.

Stamoran stretched an arm towards the window, the pool visible beyond, the shouts and splashes clearly audible above the drone of the air-con. 'She's been out there since ten o'clock this morning,' he said.

'I know.'

'She just sits there.'

'Right.'

'She doesn't *do* anything.'

'I understand your position,' Gardner said.

'You do?'

Gardner nodded, thinking: yes I do, because you've been calling us every other day for the last few weeks, whining like a little bitch and *telling* us your position. 'Of course,' he said.

'Good, because this can't go on.' Stamoran opened a large ledger on his desk and began turning the pages. He shook his head and clicked his tongue. 'We had quite a few cancellations right after the girl went missing. Families, you know?' He waited for a reaction, acknowledged Gardner's sympathetic look. 'Well, I'm sure you can appreciate that what happened wasn't exactly the best advertisement for the place, but myself and my staff are knuckling down and trying to turn it around. So, I guess what I'm saying is . . . the *last* thing we need right now is for her to be sitting out there like . . . what do you call it, like the spectre at the feast or something.' He glanced towards the window, began straightening things on his desk. 'Looking the way she does and spoiling other folks' vacations.'

'I'm here to talk to her,' Gardner said.

'I really wish you would.'

'Well then . . .'

When Gardner stood up, Stamoran did the same, then came quickly around his desk to shake the detective's hand. 'The last thing I want is for you to think I'm unsympathetic, by the way.'

'Of course not.'

'What happened to that poor woman is just beyond awful. I mean, you remember that me and the rest of the staff passed the hat, right?'

'I remember.'

'Fifteen hundred dollars, give or take. So, you know.'

'I'm sure she's grateful,' Gardner said, turning away. He heard Stamoran saying something about waiving all rental charges on Miss Wilson's vacation cabin as he opened the door and walked out towards the pool.

Despite the manager's concerns about how the place was doing, it certainly looked busy enough. There were half a dozen people in the water and maybe three times that number sunning themselves poolside.

Gardner could see many of them watching him over the tops of their newspapers and magazines as he walked towards the far corner of the deck. It was understandable. Not too many people favoured a grey suit in ninety-degree heat and he guessed that most of those who didn't have him pegged as a cop would think he was a salesman of some kind. Maybe someone who had stopped by for a dip on his way to church.

He was certainly tempted.

There were as many eyes on the woman he was walking towards; the one sitting at the table in the shade beneath the coconut palm. Some clearly knew exactly who she was, but Gardner could easily believe how even those to whom her identity was unknown would find something compelling about the figure at the table. Her stillness. Her total lack of interest in *them*. The way her dirty-white sneaker tapped against the tile, and her arm snaked slowly forward every few minutes to her plastic water bottle or cigarette pack. Just sitting in the corner, staring out across the pool towards the white-painted fence and the street beyond.

Patti was wearing denim shorts and a Budweiser T-shirt, the same Atlanta Braves baseball cap she usually had on. She was also wearing sunglasses, big ones, but Gardner saw her head shift just a fraction as he approached the table. He saw her shoulders tense. He shook his head, a small shake, just to let her know that she could relax, that he was not there to deliver news.

'Hey, Jeff.'

'Patti.' He took off his jacket and hung it on the back of the chair before he sat down. He loosened his tie. 'Nice to be in the shade.'

'You want some water?'

'Sure.'

She reached down to a coolbox beneath the table and took out a small plastic bottle. 'Got enough in there to last me the day,' she said, handing the water over. 'Plus a couple pieces of fruit, something for my lunch, whatever.'

Gardner opened the water, took a swig, then a deep breath. Said, 'What's all this for, Patti?'

'All what?'

There appeared to be no expression, but of course he could not be sure what was happening behind those big sunglasses. 'What good can it possibly do?'

'I don't have any choice.'

'Sure you do.'

She shook her head and reached across for her cigarettes. 'I can't leave her.' She took out a cigarette but the movement was fumbled. 'You think I should leave my daughter?'

'No. I'm just saying.' Gardner picked up her lighter and leaned across with it. 'Why does it have to be here?'

She sighed out smoke, looked out across the water. 'This was the last place I saw her,' she said.

'I know, but—'

'We came back from lunch and she wanted a swim, so I went back to get her swimming things from the cabin. She promised she'd wait for me right *here*.' Patti Lee touched the grimy glass table-top, then spread her arms out wide. 'I was five minutes. Five . . .'

'I understand,' Gardner said.

'Do you?'

'Really, I can see why this place would be . . . significant for you. But if she comes back . . .' He caught the tilt of her head on the word *if* and tried not to hesitate. Tried to pretend that he didn't mean it the way it sounded. 'You really think she's going to come back here? Amber-Marie's going to come waltzing in here like she just popped out to get a candy bar?'

'She went to get an Easter egg.'

Gardner nodded. He had heard it before. He had heard it *all* before.

'When we were on the way back from lunch, she saw this egg in one of the windows. Just stood there staring at it, you know? Enormous thing, all wrapped up, shiny and red. She said she wanted it and I told her I would think about it, I mean it was like fifty dollars or something stupid like that.'

'That's a lot of money.'

'Right, what the hell was I supposed to do?'

'Patti . . .'

'I think that's what she did.' She drew hard on her cigarette, leaning towards Gardner and nodding fast. 'No . . . I'm *sure* it is. I don't even know if she would have remembered the way, but the fact of it is, Amber-Marie walked out of here to go back to that shop, like they were just gonna give that stupid Easter egg to her if she told them she wanted it. She never quite understood that life wasn't like that, you know? That people wouldn't just hand stuff over if you asked them nicely.' She turned away and took off her sunglasses, just long enough to wipe a finger across each eye, for Gardner to see just how red and wet they were. 'You didn't come over for a chit-chat, did you, Jeff?'

'You need to get yourself home now,' Gardner said.

She looked at him for a few seconds, then stubbed out her cigarette. The ashtray needed emptying. 'Is this about the cost of the motel?'

'No.'

'You sure?'

'It's nothing to do with the money,' he said.

'Because, you know, flashy joint like that, I certainly don't want to be responsible for bankrupting the city.'

Gardner shook his head, loosened his tie a little more. The Police Department had been paying for the room over at the Brigadoon Suites since the day Amber-Marie had disappeared. It was far from being the most expensive place in town and if the powers-that-be were starting to grumble about the cost, he had certainly not heard anything. The city was not stumping up for any kind of day-to-day expenses though, at least not as far as he was aware, and he was curious.

'What are you living on?'

'I had some spending money left,' she said. 'Plus the cash that the manager here raised for me. He's been very kind, you know? Very supportive.'

'Right.'

''Sides which, I don't need much.'

'It's going to run out.'

'I know that, which is why I was thinking I might get a job.' She nodded towards the street. 'One of the restaurants or bars maybe. I've worked in plenty of bars.'

'It's no good,' Gardner said.

'What isn't?'

'You need to be at home, Patti.' He leaned towards her. He thought just for a moment about putting a hand on her arm, then decided not to. 'You need to be around the people that care about you.'

'Which people might they be, Jeff?'

Gardner knew that neither of Patti's parents was close to home, that there were no siblings. He knew that Amber-Marie's father had long since left the picture and could not even be sure that the man knew his daughter had gone missing. 'There must be someone,' he said.

'You would think.'

'You seeing anyone down here?' The manager at the Brigadoon Suites had told him a couple of weeks before that a man had been seen leaving Patti Lee Wilson's room on more than one occasion. Different men maybe, the manager could not be certain. Gardner had not been overly concerned. He could hardly begrudge the woman seeking a little comfort after what she had been through and clearly any man she had met since her daughter had disappeared could not reasonably be considered a suspect.

'Nobody worth talking about,' she said.

So, nobody who might be interested in taking her back to Atlanta and caring for her. Equally though, nobody worth staying in Sarasota for. 'It's time for you to go, Patti.'

She swallowed and shook her head, but now there was little vehemence in it. 'I can't leave her.'

'You won't be leaving her,' he said. 'Because she's in your heart.' She nodded, slowly. 'And while you're back at home where you should be, I want you to know that I'm here for Amber-Marie one hundred per cent, whatever happens.'

She looked at him. Whispered, 'You swear? Because I would need to know that.'

'I swear. Finding your daughter is my number one commitment, that's the plain truth, and any news, you will be the first to know. I can guarantee that.'

'That's good to know.'

'So, I want you to think about what I said, OK? I really want you to think about going home.'

This time she did not even bother taking the sunglasses off, just pushed a finger up behind each lens. 'Fifty dollars isn't so much,' she said, her voice catching. 'I should have just bought her that stupid egg, shouldn't I?'

TWELVE

Ed appeared in the bedroom doorway holding up two shirts.

'Which do you think?'

Sue was sitting at the dressing table in black bra and panties. She glanced in the mirror, then switched off the hairdryer and turned. 'Either's fine,' she said. 'They're both great.' She looked back to the mirror, watched as Ed tossed the shirts on to the bed. 'You'd better get a shift on.'

'We've got bags of time,' he said. 'An hour tops to get there, I reckon.' He sat down on the edge of the bed behind her and unbuttoned his shirt. He kicked his loafers off, lay back and unzipped his jeans.

Sue thought the journey would be more like an hour and a half, but said nothing. She switched the hairdryer back on.

'What do you think the house will be like?' Ed shouted.

She switched the hairdryer off again. 'What?'

'The house? Angie and Barry's.'

Sue thought about it. 'Blimey, I've got no idea. Modern . . . uncluttered. Very clean, I'm guessing. She struck me as a bit of a clean freak.'

'Big TV, definitely.'

'*We've* got a big TV,' Sue said.

'Yeah, but ridiculously big. You know how it works . . . the less taste the people have got, the bigger the screen. Fifty-inch plasma to watch *Deal or No Deal*. Surround sound speakers so they don't miss any of the dialogue on *EastEnders*.'

'Garden gnomes?'

'Every chance,' Ed said. 'And some of those little stone animals on the patio. Oh, and I bet you they've got one of those signs over the front door, with the name of the house made up from their own names.'

'Definitely,' Sue said. She rubbed moisturiser into her hands.

'Barrangela.'

'Angelarry.'

Ed laughed: dry and fast. 'Just like their ridiculous email address,' he said. 'Angiebaz, for God's sake . . .'

In the mirror, Sue watched as her husband stood up, wearing only his underpants, and took the step across to stand behind her chair. She saw the look on his face. She turned.

'Really?'

'Bags of time.'

He reached down for her arm and lifted her from the chair. She was breathing heavily as he eased the thin straps from her shoulders, ran his hands across them, then pushed her down on to her knees. As soon as she had removed his underpants, he moved his feet apart a little to steady himself. Took a handful of damp hair into his fist.

Said, 'Do it.'

They were no more than a few feet away from the window and, looking down, Ed could see a woman walking a dog on the far side of the road. He watched her as he pushed his hips forward, willing the dog-walker to glance up and see him, but she did not.

Sue looked up at him though, her eyes wide as she worked.

'I think their house will be full of cheap, ugly tat,' he said. 'Trinkets and tat.' His voice was quieter now, spitting out the words like they were hairs in his mouth. 'I bet there's crystal glasses from a petrol station and nasty white leather sofas. I bet we'll have Simply Red on the stereo and after-dinner mints. I bet there's built-in his-and-hers wardrobes and a bidet in their ensuite and I *guarantee* there are nice matching bedside tables, where he can stuff his wank-mags underneath his copies of the *Reader's Digest* and she can hide her Rabbit in among her knickers . . .'

Sue moaned in agreement, in approval.

He pulled away and told her to get up.

To get on the bed.

'I'll need another shower,' she said.

He shook his head. 'I like the smell of it on you. I like being able to smell *myself* on you . . .'

'Who am I?' She dropped on to the bed, turned over and crawled towards the wall. 'Who do you want me to be?'

Ed stood by the dressing table, touching himself. The woman with the dog had walked past. 'I don't know yet.'

'Marina?'

'Maybe later.'

'Maybe in the car on the way back.'

'Lie flat,' he said.

He got on to the bed and moved towards her. She swept the pillows on to the carpet, pressed her face into the mattress as he nudged her legs apart with his knees. He lay down on top of her—his full weight on her back and buttocks—and put his mouth close to her face.

'I was watching you today on the tennis court,' he said. 'You knew that though, didn't you, *Carol*, you knew I was watching? You were putting on a show . . .'

Sue whispered, 'Yes,' and closed her eyes.

THIRTEEN

When the pager she has been given begins to vibrate, Angie jumps up and says, 'Here we go.' There are red lights flashing on the top and as they walk towards the reservations desk, Ed takes it from her and says it looks like a Taser. He presses it against his neck, then pretends to convulse as though from an electric shock. Everyone laughs, so he repeats the gag as they are being shown their table, and the young waiter, who wants to do everything he can to ensure a decent tip, laughs too.

'That's awesome,' he says.

They have been waiting ten minutes in the bar of the Bonefish Grill, drinking beer and cocktails. Trying to make themselves heard over the noise. There is a good deal of chatter at the bar and from the booths on either side, as well as the commentary from dozens of TV sets mounted on the walls, which are showing baseball, basketball and football games.

'You know what they'd be showing if we were back at home?' Ed had asked when they'd arrived. 'Darts, snooker and rained-off cricket matches . . .'

'Snooker and what?' Barry had said. 'I can't hear.'

Ed shook his head like it didn't matter and Angie said she'd tell him later.

It's a large table, right in the centre of the busy room. There are several families with children eating, plenty of chit-chat, but it's still a lot quieter than it had been in the bar. The waiter takes their drinks orders—beer and white wine—then when he's gone, Ed raises the glass he's carried through from the bar. He asks the others to do the same.

'To a great holiday,' he says. 'And one that's been all the better for making new friends.'

Glasses are raised and clinked together. Marina says, 'To a great holiday,' at the same time as Angie says, 'New friends.' The others mutter one or the other. Barry says, 'Cheers.'

'Funny old day though,' Ed says.

'Horrible,' Angie says.

Sue leans forward and, one by one, the others do the same. 'So, what do we think?' she asks.

'She's wandered off,' Barry says. 'That's all.'

'Oh God, I hope you're right,' Angie says.

Dave nods. 'It's easy enough to get lost in a strange place, especially if you're a bit . . . you know.'

'Maybe she just went to the mall,' Marina says.

Ed shakes his head. 'Too far to walk.'

'Plus, I think they'd have found her by now,' Sue says. She looks at Marina, who recoils slightly, as though her suggestion has been dismissed as rather silly. 'It was probably one of the first places they looked though, so it's a good thought.'

'It's not what the police think.' Ed puts down his glass. 'That she's just wandered off, I mean. You can tell from their faces.'

'Tell what?' Dave asks. 'You can't tell anything.'

Ed looks at his watch. 'It's been what . . . four hours already? They'll have searched everywhere, talked to anyone who might have seen her. This long after someone goes missing, a child I mean, they know damn well someone's taken her.'

'I don't think that's true,' Marina says. She stops as the waiter comes back to the table. The drinks are laid down along with some bread and olive oil, and the waiter tells them that he'll be back in a few minutes to take their orders for appetisers. 'For a start, she's not an ordinary child, is she? She might not have a normal sense of time or distance or whatever.' Dave nods, next to her, and swigs from his beer bottle. 'She might just be walking round a supermarket, or sitting behind a rock on the beach somewhere, colouring in that book she's always got and thinking that her mum is coming to get her.'

'I hope you're right,' Angie says again.

'Well, yes, obviously.' Ed sits back and folds his arms and says that he just thinks it's important to be realistic about these things. That the *police* certainly will be. 'I'm not trying to be morbid, I promise,' he said. 'It's the last night of the bloody holiday, after all.'

'Bad things can happen anywhere,' Barry says, quietly. 'Even somewhere like this, where the sun's shining and everything seems like it's perfect, you know?' He's peeling the label from his beer bottle. 'Probably *more* bad things.'

There is nodding around the table. Angie puts a hand on Barry's arm.

'It was freaky though, wasn't it?' Marina says. 'Talking to the mother, earlier on I mean, by the pool. I felt terrible, her chasing around and panicking and the six of us just lying there, desperately trying to soak up a last bit of sun before we go home.'

Angie agrees, says she's been feeling guilty ever since.

'It's only natural,' Sue says. 'Especially if you've got kids.'

'Not our fault,' Ed says, shaking his head.

'No, but it was still weird, didn't you think?' Marina turns to him. 'Her face, like you could see she was going over and over all the terrible things that might have happened, and us just lying there . . . sunbathing.'

'Why should we feel guilty?' Ed asks. 'I mean, there was no shortage of people out looking for her, and it's not like we didn't offer to help, is it?'

Sue shrugs and looks at Marina. 'There's not much we can do about the sunshine, is there?'

'Disparity,' Dave says. 'Is that the word? You know, when what you're talking about doesn't match the surroundings? Like somebody talking about their child being missing when . . . you know, like earlier.'

'Never heard of it,' Barry says.

Angie says, 'Come on, Marina, you're the writer.'

The waiter appears at their table and asks if they're ready to order their appetisers. Nobody has really looked at a menu yet and so they hurry to take in what's on offer while the waiter, who still has an eye on that tip, smiles and tells them there's no rush.

'Take all the time you need,' he says.

They order spicy shrimp, corn chowder, calamari and spring rolls. Sue says she is not very hungry, that she got a little too much sun maybe and is happy to wait for her main course. Dave asks for another beer and Barry tells the waiter to make that two.

'So, what did everyone say to the police?' Marina asks.

Shortly after the three couples had encountered the mother of the missing girl late that afternoon, uniformed officers had begun asking questions of everyone at the Pelican Palms. By that time, only Marina and Dave had been left at the pool. The other two couples had gone back to their cabins. Barry had said he fancied a nap before dinner and Sue said that she wanted to spend some time online in the resort's small computer room, to which guests had access at the cost of ten dollars per half-hour.

'Just answered a few questions,' Angie says. 'That's all. Same as you did, probably. We had a policewoman come knocking on the door.'

'Bloody embarrassing that was as well.' Barry shakes his head. 'Ange shouted through that the police wanted a word, so I came to the door in my pants, didn't I? Never thought it would be a woman.'

'What did she want to know?' Dave asks.

Barry shrugs. 'All just routine, that's what she said. They're follow-ing up a report that a fourteen-year-old girl has gone missing, blah, blah, blah.'

'When was the last time we saw the girl?' Angie says. 'Had we seen anyone dodgy hanging around the resort?'

Ed nudges Barry, and says, 'Apart from Dave, obviously.'

Angie continues. 'Where were we when she went missing? Same questions they asked you, most likely.'

'You two were still at the beach, weren't you?' Marina says.

Angie nods. 'Trying to make the most of the last day.'

'Same here,' Ed says. He looks mock-daggers at his wife. 'Though for some unknown reason that involved the pair of us traipsing round the shopping mall.'

'There was stuff I needed to get,' Sue says.

Ed looks at Dave. 'What about you two?' He puts on a silly voice: a pantomime copper. 'Would you be so kind as to confirm your movements between the hours of one-thirty and two-thirty this afternoon?'

Dave laughs and takes another swig of beer.

'Still having our lunch,' Marina says. 'That place opposite the Oyster Bar, whatever it's called. We got back about three o'clock, met you lot by the pool around half past . . .'

'Right,' Ed says, nodding. 'Next thing, the woman starts screaming and ten minutes later there's cops all over the place.'

'She had plenty to scream about,' Angie says. 'You don't even want to think about it, do you?'

'So *don't* think about it.' Barry takes the last piece of bread and mops up what's left of the oil. 'Nothing we can do.'

Nobody says anything for a while. They pass a bottle of water around the table and cough and straighten cutlery. After a minute or so, Ed looks towards the kitchens and asks if anyone else thinks the food is taking a long time.

'We should make another toast,' Sue says, suddenly. 'We should drink to that girl.' She holds up her glass. 'To everything being all right and to her getting back safe and sound to her mummy.'

'Hear, hear,' Angie says.

They all raise their glasses and touch bottle to bottle, which is when they realise that not a single one of them knows the missing girl's name.

89

FOURTEEN

Let's not kid ourselves, everybody lies.

Sorry, I'm busy that night.

I was just looking at something on YouTube.

I love you too . . .

Twenty-five times a day on average, they reckon, and men twice as often as women, mind you I've never been convinced about *that*. Before that bloody strange Easter Friday in Sarasota, I don't know if I was more or less honest than anyone else, but I never had much of a problem saying whatever made life easier. For me or whoever I was talking to. Even so, I was seriously impressed with how easily it came to me when it needed to.

The degree of it, I mean.

It's funny, isn't it, how you can just throw that switch when you have to, and become whoever you need to be for however long and get the things done that need doing? The normal things. How you can talk or eat or whatever it is, without slipping up, not even for a second.

You don't look at your watch.

You don't sweat more than you should, or scream suddenly or glaze over.

You don't say, 'She's in the boot,' when you mean to say, 'Can you pass the salt?'

I'm joking, obviously . . . exaggerating to make the point, but hopefully you can see what I'm talking about. I can never get over it, that's all I'm saying.

The things we're capable of.

Like I said, all the time this was happening, the everyday stuff and the ordinary conversations about this and that, I was amazed at how well I could look after myself. It just kicked in immediately, to tell you the truth, because even while I was busy in that car—while that girl bucked and kicked and tried to slap my arms away—I'd known I wasn't going to drive straight to the nearest police station and tell them what had happened. I knew a hundred per cent that I was going to say and do whatever was needed to avoid getting caught. I'd started to think about exactly what those things might be.

I've never really bought into this idea that, deep down, some offenders want to get caught. Everyone wants to stay out of prison surely, it's a natural instinct, isn't it? It certainly felt natural to me. I felt—I *still* feel—that punishing me for what I'd done would be wrong. That seemed blindingly obvious, even then. I was positive that if I *was* ever caught, the powers-that-be would see sense pretty quickly. Once I'd explained, as soon as they'd been made to understand about . . . fairness, then any kind of punishment wouldn't really be an issue.

Don't get me wrong, I'm definitely not *planning* on being caught. I just don't think it would be the end of the world. That, worst-case scenario, I could talk my way out of it.

Ironically enough, just by telling the truth.

That smile, what it did, and why.

Meanwhile, let's not forget about all those lies being trotted out every day. Husband to wife, colleague to colleague, doctor to patient; snow-white, pitch-black or somewhere in between. A good many of these liars do what they do for very good reasons. Some of them have the best of intentions. Now, I'm certainly not claiming to be one of them and I know there's no way you can measure these things, but I do wonder if those twenty-five small lies every day would equal one big one.

My big one.

I heard a vicar or someone on the radio once, saying that being able to lie is what 'perverts' us. It's because we find it easy, so he said . . . that's what makes us all corrupt and spoils what might otherwise be perfect. That's rubbish, come on, you *know* it is.

Even then, before any of this happened, I never believed that.

Lying is what makes us human.

THE FIRST
DINNER

FIFTEEN

'Are we the first here?' Marina asked.

'It doesn't matter, so long as you're here. How was the journey?' Angie beckoned Marina and Dave in from the porch. She took the proffered wine and chocolates, said there was really no need, then pointed towards the kitchen and invited them to 'go through'.

'Somebody's got to be first,' Dave said.

While Marina and Dave stood hand in hand, making all the right noises about the kitchen, Angie deposited jackets and bags in the utility room and Barry took orders for drinks. Marina said that red wine was great if there was already some open and Dave asked Barry what *he* was having.

'I'm on the beer for now,' Barry said.

'Sounds good to me.'

'This is amazing,' Marina said when Angie reappeared. 'It's huge.'

The kitchen had been large enough already before being extended out towards the garden, an orangery-type glass roof now sitting above what was a conservatory-cum-dining area decorated in a Mediterranean style. Angie talked about the feeling of space, and told Marina where she had bought the dining table and the big terracotta pots. Barry pointed out where the RSJs had been fitted. Something jazzy and melodic was playing quietly, though the source of it was not immediately obvious. Angie saw Marina looking around, finally spotting the white speakers mounted high on the wall, and said, 'Jamie Cullum.'

'I'm surprised you've done such a lot to the place,' Dave said to Barry. All four were standing in the conservatory looking out into a large garden. It had been a bright, warm day, but now it was clouding over a little and the light was starting to go.

'It's what I do, isn't it?'

'Exactly,' Dave said. 'I'd've thought *because* you're a builder, it might have been the last thing you wanted to do. You know, like the cobbler's children always going barefoot.'

'Come again?' Barry said.

'Where are the kids?' Marina asked.

Angie nodded upwards. 'Laura and Luke are upstairs with a couple of mates and some pizzas. I should probably get them down to say hello,' she said. 'Prove they've got *some* manners.'

'Don't worry,' Marina said. 'Leave them to it.'

Dave turned to Barry. 'And you've got one of your own, right? A son, is it?'

'Nick,' Barry said. 'He's with his mum.'

Jamie Cullum sang uninterrupted for those long few seconds until the doorbell rang.

'There they are,' Angie said.

When Barry had followed Angie out of the kitchen, Marina raised an eyebrow at Dave.

He said, 'I can't bloody stand Jamie Cullum.'

Marina nodded out towards the front door and whispered, 'The kid's a bit of a sore point, I reckon.'

They listened to the noises of greeting, the exclamations and the kisses on the cheek, until, half a minute later, Angie came back into the kitchen carrying an enormous bunch of lilies.

'Look at these . . .'

Ed, Sue and then finally Barry appeared in the doorway and, once Dave and Marina had welcomed the newcomers—exchanging enthusiastic kisses and greetings of their own—more drinks were organised while Angie dug around in a cupboard to find a vase for her flowers.

'Your hair is amazing,' Sue said to Marina.

Angie moved across to join them. 'Yeah, I meant to say.'

Marina leaned towards the other two conspiratorially and said, 'It was stupidly expensive, to be honest. I'm not sure Dave's too thrilled.'

'Sod him,' Sue said.

The women laughed. 'Spot on,' Angie said. 'I mean it's him you're looking gorgeous for, isn't it?'

On the other side of the kitchen, the men were talking about the football season that had recently finished. Barry was an avid Arsenal fan, while Ed still followed Aston Villa, the team he had watched as a boy. On holiday, Dave had rashly confessed to being a Manchester United supporter and now the other two happily took up where they had left off in Sarasota, mocking his support for a team that, as a southerner, he had no natural affiliation for. Dave stood his ground, saying that he'd followed them for years, but when Ed asked him to name half a dozen members of the current team he fell three short.

'My mum knows more than that,' Ed said. 'And she's got Alzheimer's.'

Barry laughed and told Dave he was a lightweight.

'You should always knock ten per cent off the cost of a visit to the hairdresser's,' Angie said to Marina and Sue.

'Same with shoes and bags,' Sue said.

'We can hear you, you know?' Ed punched Dave in the shoulder and walked across to join the women.

'You making fun of my old man?' Marina said.

Ed grinned. 'Just winding him up. You know what he's like . . .'

'Yeah, *I* do,' Marina said. 'But you want to be careful.' She narrowed her eyes, theatrically. 'He can *turn*.' She smiled at her boyfriend over Ed's shoulder. 'Can't you, babe?'

'Definitely,' Dave said, a little red-faced, as he and Barry walked across.

'Barry's got a temper on him as well,' Angie said. She slid an arm around Barry's waist. 'He's like the Incredible Hulk sometimes, storming round the place.'

Marina leaned into Ed. 'What about you?'

Ed's face was a picture of innocence. 'Me?'

'No way, not Steady Eddie,' Sue said. 'Happy as a pig in shit, aren't you, my love?'

'Well, I *can* get a bit strict with you sometimes,' Ed said. 'When you've pissed me off.' He winked at the boys. 'But only because you like it . . .'

'Right,' Angie said. 'The chicken's taking care of itself, so—'

'Smells gorgeous,' Marina said.

Angie put down her wine glass. 'Who fancies a quick tour?'

'We should have given these to the police,' Angie said. She looked up at the others. 'God, do you think we still should?' She carefully lined up three photographs, tapped a bright-red fingernail against several of the figures in the background. The missing girl and her mother, then a number of anonymous men and women captured behind the main subject: sitting around the pool; walking in one direction or the other through the back of the shot; more than one of the strangers looking towards the photographer. 'He might be right here in one of these pictures,' she said. 'We might be looking at whoever took that girl . . .'

The offer of a 'tour' had not been taken up by everyone. Ed had hung back in the kitchen, along with Barry who pulled a face and opened them both another beer. Dave had hesitated, looking from the men to the women and back, before eventually deciding to trot along after Marina, Angie and Sue.

'How gay is that?' Ed had said, as Barry handed him his drink.

Fifteen minutes later, when everyone was gathered back in the kitchen, Angie had put plates in the oven, given her main course a final stir and told people to find a seat. Her 'special' placemats had caused every bit as much interest as Angie had hoped and served to remind Sue that she and Ed had brought photos of their own to share.

'We got three sets printed up,' she said. 'Ed was going to email them, but as we were getting together anyway . . .'

'I didn't think,' Angie had said. She wiped her hands and came over to the central island to take a look. 'I'll get two more sets of ours done as soon as I get five minutes.'

'It's a great idea,' Marina said.

They gathered around the island and began to look at the photos that Sue had handed out. The majority were of Sue or Ed themselves of course, a handful of them together taken by one of the other four and a few of the entire group. There were shots of them at the beach and in assorted bars and restaurants, shots against sunsets, some with pelicans or egrets silhouetted against the pink-orange sky behind, but many of the pictures had been taken around the pool at the Pelican Palms.

It was a group of these photographs that had captured Angie's attention.

'We should have given them to the police,' she said again. 'At least let them look at what was on our cameras.'

'They didn't ask,' Sue said.

'You're being ridiculous,' Barry said. He nodded down at the pictures. 'What are the chances that this bloke who took her, *if* anyone took her in the first place, is sitting there in his Speedos or whatever?'

Angie shook her head, adamant. 'The police did this thing, a few years back, on Brighton beach or Southend or somewhere. They were looking for someone who they knew had been spotted in the area, so they asked anyone who'd been on the beach on that particular day to send their snaps in.'

'I think I read about this,' Marina said.

'Right. And when they looked at all the photos, they identified about a dozen known paedophiles.'

'A dozen?' Dave said. 'On one beach?'

'Maybe a few less than that,' Angie said. 'I can't remember the exact number, but it was really shocking.'

Dave looked at Barry.

'No, she's right,' Sue said. 'I saw something about it too.'

Ed leaned down to take a closer look at the photographs. 'I still don't see why that means anything as far as these are concerned.'

'What if he'd been watching her?' Marina asked.

Sue nodded. 'If it was someone who was already there, he might just have seen her wander away and followed her.'

'It would have been far easier for someone to take her if he was someone she recognised,' Marina said. 'Someone she knew, even.'

They all stared at the photos for a few more seconds, until finally Ed dropped the set back on to the worktop and stood up. 'All well and good in theory, but the police questioned everyone who was there, didn't they? So they must have spoken to everyone in these pictures.'

'Not necessarily,' Sue said. She laid down the photograph she was holding. The others waited. 'I remember talking to one couple who weren't actually staying there at all and just paid a daily rate to use the pool. So there's no guarantee that everyone in these pictures was a resident or was around when the police were questioning people. Also, I'm pretty sure that some people just sneaked in whenever they felt like it and used the pool.'

'Definitely,' Marina said. 'There was nothing to stop anyone doing that and it wasn't as though anybody checked, was it?'

'There you are then,' Angie said.

Barry held his hands out. 'There you are, *what?*'

She waved a photograph. 'I'm just saying. What if he's on here?'

'So contact the police or whatever,' Barry said. 'Email them the sodding pictures if it's going to keep you awake at night.'

Ed was nodding his head in time to Jamie Cullum. A somewhat frantic version of 'It Ain't Necessarily So'. 'It's all far too late anyway,' he said, reaching for his glass. 'It's been a month or something now, hasn't it?'

'Month and a half,' Dave said.

'So, she's dead—'

'*She's* called Amber-Marie,' Angie said. 'I saw it when I was checking on the internet.'

Ed nodded. 'Right . . . so, *Amber-Marie's* dead, the police probably don't give a toss any more and whoever killed her is hardly likely to still be knocking about at the Pelican Palms eyeing up his next victim.'

Sue shook her head. 'God's sake, Ed.'

'I'm just being realistic.'

'We should eat,' Angie said. 'Before all my timing goes tits up.' She asked them all to go and sit down and, while she laid the paté out and Barry got more wine from the fridge, the four guests walked across to the dining table.

Standing at the table, Dave leaned towards Ed and muttered, 'A dozen paedophiles on the same beach? *On the same day?*'

Barry heard it, turned round and shook his head as if to say, 'Ignore her.'

'An ex-girlfriend of mine once accused me of being a paedophile,' Ed said.

Dave looked at him. 'What?'

'I told her that was a pretty big word for a ten-year-old.'

Dave laughed, one eye on Marina's reaction.

'Just sit anywhere,' Angie shouted.

Seeing that Barry had finished his main course ahead of anyone else, Angie said, 'Go and ask the kids to come down.'

'Do we have to?' Barry said.

'Probably the last thing they want to do,' Sue said. 'Come and talk to boring old farts like us.'

'They should at least come and say hello,' Angie said.

As the others continued to eat in silence, Barry went out into the hall and shouted up the stairs. After half a minute or so he shouted again, a real edge to his voice this time. He came back in and sat down, shaking his head, and they all listened to the thump of footsteps on the stairs, then watched as the two teenagers—a boy and a girl—trooped wearily in and waited at the end of the table.

'Say hello,' Angie said.

They did as they were told, though the boy somehow managed to make the word monosyllabic. He looked as though he'd rather be having teeth pulled, hands thrust deep into the pockets of his hooded top. The girl seemed marginally less uncomfortable, manufacturing something that might almost have been a smile as she shifted from one Ugg-booted foot to the other.

'What have you two been up to then?' Ed asked.

'Just watching TV,' the girl mumbled. 'Me and my friend.'

'Anything good?'

'Not really.'

'No need to ask Luke what he's been doing.' Angie rolled her eyes. 'He'll have been glued to that bloody Xbox. Honestly, he forgets to eat sometimes.'

The girl's smile broadened and she leaned into her brother's shoulder. The boy leaned back into hers, far harder.

'Hey,' Barry said.

'Dave works on computer games,' Angie said. 'Maybe he can give you a few tips later on.'

The boy brightened just a little. 'Did you work on *Call of Duty*?'

'I'm afraid not,' Dave said.

'*Halo*?'

'No . . .'

The boy went back to staring at his trainers, the conversation clearly going nowhere.

Ed looked at Dave and shook his head. 'And there we all were, thinking you were "down" with the kids.'

'Tell him some of the ones you have worked on,' Marina said. It wasn't clear if she was asking Dave to tell Ed or the boy.

Barry spoke up before Dave could say anything. 'You need to get off that bloody computer now anyway,' he said. 'Haven't you got homework?'

'He can do it tomorrow,' Angie said. 'Can't you?'

The boy mumbled a 'yeah' and took a step away from the table, his eyes pleading with his mother.

'OK, go on then,' Angie said. 'Don't let us keep you.'

102

The boy was out of sight in seconds, but the girl lingered. She nodded towards Marina and said, 'I love your hair.'

'Thanks,' Marina said.

'You might need to save up,' Dave said.

The girl touched a finger to the side of her nose. 'That's cool too. Do you always wear a stud?'

'A ring sometimes,' Marina said. 'You should get one.'

'I don't think so,' Angie said. She reached across for Marina's plate.

'Loads of the kids have got them now,' Marina said.

Angie said, 'Yes, well,' and told the girl she should probably go and get back to her friend upstairs.

When the girl had left the room, Ed said, 'Nice kids.'

'Bright,' Sue added.

Dave looked across at Barry. 'Do they all get on? Laura and Luke and your lad?'

'Nick doesn't see them,' Barry said. He stood up and took the empty plates from Angie, carried them out into the kitchen.

Angie leaned in to the table and whispered. 'It's all a bit tricky with Barry's ex.'

The others took the hint and voices were lowered.

'That's awful,' Marina said. 'You know, when kids are involved.'

'She's a total bitch,' Angie said. 'She uses that poor kid like some kind of bargaining tool or whatever. It really gets Barry down, to be honest.'

Marina shook her head. 'Awful,' she said again. 'I mean whatever happens between a couple, you never stop loving your kids, right?'

'Some people shouldn't be allowed to have them,' Dave said.

Sue said she'd go and give Barry a hand. Angie said that he'd be fine, but Sue stood up anyway. Ed grinned and told Sue to make sure it was just a hand she gave him.

'Right then,' Angie said. 'I hope everyone's left room for pudding . . .'

When Angie came out of the downstairs toilet, Sue was waiting to go in. They smiled at one another, then swapped places outside the door, laughing for no good reason.

'Listen, thanks for doing this,' Sue said. 'It's really nice to see everyone.'

'No, thanks for *coming*,' Angie said.

'Our place next time, all right?'

'Oh that would be great.' Angie stepped forward and hugged Sue, pulling her close while the cistern refilled noisily on the other side of the toilet door. When they had separated, Angie glanced towards the kitchen. 'I *think* everyone's having a good time.'

'Oh definitely. The food was amazing.'

'Ed certainly seems to be enjoying himself.'

'That's one way of putting it,' Sue said.

'I take it you'll be driving?'

Sue laughed. 'It's fine.' After a few moments of staring at feet, just as Angie was about to turn away, Sue put a hand on her arm. 'Listen, I know Barry was a bit sniffy and Ed was being a wanker about it, but you should send those photographs to the police if you really want to.'

'I don't know,' Angie said.

'What you were saying made perfect sense to me.'

'I've probably just read too many thrillers.'

'It's up to you,' Sue said. 'But it can't hurt, can it?' They looked at each other and Sue shrugged, then said, 'Right, well . . .' and pushed open the toilet door.

After she had popped upstairs to check on the kids, Angie walked back into the kitchen in time to hear Marina groaning in disbelief or perhaps exhaustion at something Ed had said. He was leaning back in his chair, looking pleased with himself, while Dave stared down at his plate and picked at what was left of his cheese and crackers. Barry was outside on the patio, smoking.

'Right, who wants coffee?' she asked.

Marina and Dave both said yes. Ed passed, but said he thought Sue would probably want one.

'I can do you one of those special little ones, if anyone fancies it,' Angie said. 'Expresso or whatever it is. Barry bought us this flashy machine.'

'That sounds great,' Sue said, walking back in.

'Me too,' Dave said.

'Right then.' Angie turned and half walked, half danced her way back out into the kitchen. An hour or so before, Jamie Cullum had given way to Michael Bublé and finally, Amy Winehouse.

A few minutes later, Angie carried the coffees across to the table on a tray, along with a carton of cream and a box of Swiss chocolates. As she handed out the cups, Barry began piling up dirty dishes, leaning across the table and asking people if they'd finished with their cutlery. Angie told him to sit down. She said that people had not yet finished eating, but Barry insisted that he was happy to make a start on getting things cleared away and continued ferrying plates and glasses out to the dishwasher.

'Don't knock it,' Sue said. 'I wish Ed was that bloody helpful.'

Ed pursed his lips, made kissy-kissy noises.

'So, we all going back again next year?' Marina asked.

'God, that reminds me,' Angie said. 'Did you hear about those tourists being shot?'

'In Sarasota?' Dave asked.

'When I was searching online to see if there was any news about the girl . . .'

'Amber-Marie,' Ed said. 'Her *name* is Amber-Marie . . . if you can believe that.'

Sue told him to be quiet, told Angie to carry on.

'There was all this stuff on there about this French couple that were murdered.' Angie took a mouthful of red wine. 'Shot in the head for a few dollars. Really nasty.'

Ed leaned towards Marina. 'Well, I think that answers your question,' he said. 'We should avoid the place like the plague, because it's clearly become the crime capital of Florida.'

'Bad things can happen anywhere,' Barry said, reaching across Angie for a plate.

'You came out with that little gem before,' Angie said, a little sharp.

Barry reached towards her wine glass. 'Maybe I should take that.'

105

'I'm still drinking it,' she said.

'I know.'

'Seriously though,' Marina said. She looked around the table. 'Do you think you would go back there again?'

'I would,' Angie said. 'Me and Barry loved it.'

'You'd go back to the Pelican Palms?'

'Well, maybe not there, you know . . . because of what happened.'

'I don't think we'd go back there, would we, Suze?' Ed said, looking at Sue. 'Not because of the girl or anything, I just think next time we'd want somewhere a bit more upmarket.'

There were a few seconds of silence before Barry said, 'You what?'

'With a better class of guest, you mean?' Marina asked. She wasn't quite as far gone as Ed, but the look on her face made it obvious that she was happy to take him on. 'Where there weren't people like us lowering the tone.'

'I didn't mean it like *that*,' Ed said, a little too loudly. 'I just *meant* that if we go again, we might treat ourselves to somewhere a bit more expensive. A hotel or whatever.'

'Somewhere where there weren't retarded kids running about making too much noise,' Barry said. 'Spoiling the view.' He picked up a plate, added it to the pile he was already carrying. 'That what you meant?'

'Now you're just being ridiculous,' Ed said.

'Come on,' Angie said.

Barry turned and walked back into the kitchen.

'I don't get it.' Ed shook his head and held out his arms. 'It just came out wrong, that's all, and now you're all looking at me like I've shagged your mum or something.'

Marina laughed and sat back. 'Sorry, I didn't mean to sound quite so aggressive.'

'Remind me not to get on the wrong side of you,' Angie said, laughing.

'I think we're all feeling a bit weird about everything,' Dave said. 'The holiday and all that, because of what happened to that girl.' He put his hand over Marina's and leaned across towards Ed. 'Everyone's just that bit more sensitive than they might normally be, that's all.'

106

'Why though?' Ed asked. 'There's worse things than that happening every day of the week. Serial killers and terrorists killing hundreds of people at a time. Jesus, you've only got to turn on the television.'

'Yes, but we were *there*.'

'We should think about making a move,' Sue said.

'It's early yet,' Angie said. 'Isn't anyone up for a brandy or something?'

'Brandy sounds nice,' Marina said.

Dave said he was fine and Sue said nothing. Ed said it would be bad manners to let Marina drink on her own. Angie called Barry in and asked him if they had any brandy in the cupboard. He shook his head, and said, 'There might be some Baileys.'

'Even better,' Marina said.

'It's not quite a piña colada,' Angie said. 'But it'll have to do.' She watched Barry go back into the kitchen, then said, 'I was thinking that it might just have been the best thing, that girl being . . . the way she was. It might actually have been a blessing.' She spoke slowly, taking care to avoid slurring her words, as though keen to elucidate something that she had been considering for some time. She looked across the table at Marina and Dave, then round to Sue and Ed. 'If you can't understand what someone's going to do, if you don't *know* what those horrible things are . . . then maybe you aren't afraid.'

SIXTEEN

Marina's head was back and her eyes were closed. She had kicked off her shoes and her bare feet were braced against the glove compartment.

'You asleep?'

'Nearly.' Her voice was thick with sleep and booze. 'Where are we?'

'Croydon,' Dave said. 'Probably best to keep your eyes closed.'

She laughed. 'That was fun, wasn't it?'

'It had its moments.' He glanced at the speedometer, eased his foot off the accelerator. Keen as he was to get home, there were a lot of speed cameras on the road. 'Last half an hour was . . . interesting.'

'She had tears in her eyes,' Marina said. 'Angie did, did you see that? When she was talking about the girl, about whether or not she would know what was happening to her. She was really emotional.'

'She was pissed,' Dave said. 'So was Ed.'

Marina lowered her feet to the floor. She rolled down the window an inch and leaned towards it to get some air. 'Terrible,' she muttered.

'What?'

'They should be ashamed of themselves, losing control like that.'

'This is exactly what I was talking about,' Dave said. 'People having a few too many and then saying stuff they don't mean.' He glanced across, smiled at her. 'It's the only time you're ever bitchy.'

'Is it, babe?'

He reached across and rubbed her leg, but she did not react. 'I did like it when you had a go at Ed, though. He can be such a knob . . .'

'Guess what?' she said, leaning her head back again. '*I* know more Manchester United players than you.'

Dave laughed, but not loudly. 'So what?'

'Lightweight,' she said.

He slowed as the car approached a speed camera, stayed at thirty across the lines on the road and then put his foot down. 'I mean, I'm bloody sure you *don't*, but still, so what?'

Marina closed her eyes again and slowly began naming footballers.

Most of the tableware had been cleared away and there were just a few napkins and unused items of cutlery scattered about on the table. Red wine rings and a couple of candles all but burned out. Angie wandered across to where Barry was busy at the sink. The dishwasher was already full up and running and now he was starting to wash the remaining pots and pans by hand.

Amy Winehouse was singing 'Back to Black' for the second time.

Angie held up one of her souvenir placemats. 'Look, somebody forgot to take theirs home with them.' She tossed it on to the worktop and sat down at the island. 'Now I'll have to post the bloody thing.'

'You don't have to do anything,' Barry said, his back to her.

'Course not, I can give it to them next time.' She sang along for a few bars, humming when she didn't know the words. 'Forgot it, or left it on purpose, what do you think? The placemat.'

Barry said nothing, choosing to ignore the question, or else not hearing it above the music and the dishwasher's hum and the clatter of pans beneath the suds.

'It was good tonight, wasn't it?' Angie asked. 'You think it was good?'

'Went well,' Barry said.

'*I* think it was good.' She hummed along with the song for a few seconds, then said, 'Sue told me to send those pictures to the police. She said she agreed with me about whoever took that girl being in the photos. That there was a chance, you know.' She picked at a few crisps that were left in a bowl on the central island. She laughed. 'She said Ed was being a wanker . . . and he *was* . . . all that "Amber-Marie" stuff, taking the piss.'

'He just wants to be the centre of attention.'

'Poor thing can't help what her name is, can she?' She emptied the last few crumbs into her palm and poured them into her mouth. 'It's funny that, isn't it?'

'What?'

'I still say "is" and not "was", like she's still alive.'

'We don't know she isn't,' Barry said.

Angie sang along with the chorus, then stood and walked across to the sink. She moved up behind Barry. 'Why don't we leave it until the morning?'

'Best to get it done,' he said.

She wrapped her arms around his chest and leaned into him. 'Come on, leave it and let's get up to bed.'

He pushed back just hard enough to make her step away and reached for a tea towel to wipe his hands.

'Don't be like that.' She stretched out an arm, but he walked past it. 'I only wanted to cuddle up, that's all.'

Barry picked up his cigarettes on the way out into the garden.

'Well, there was a disappointing lack of garden gnomes . . . as far as I could see, anyway.' Ed let out a small belch. 'Maybe they were hiding. There was no sign outside saying *Bazza 'n' Angie's Place* and I was wrong about Simply Red.' He raised a pointed finger with a theatrical flourish. 'But there *was* a fluffy toilet-roll cover in the shape of a poodle.'

'I think Angie's nice,' Sue said.

'I'm not arguing.'

'They both are.'

'I never said they weren't.'

'You're taking the piss.'

'Didn't seem to bother you earlier.'

They had made the journey from north London to Crawley in Ed's Volvo estate. There was a little more room than in the battered old VW that Sue drove and Ed would be able to claim the mileage on expenses. It smelled faintly of the Armani aftershave that Ed favoured, but mostly of something that was supposed to be 'good, old-fashioned English leather', thanks to an air freshener that dangled from the indicator stalk. When the car cornered, cardboard boxes filled with Ed's samples moved around in the boot and CD cases slid about in the passenger footwell. Nothing by Simply Red of course. Ed preferred music that had a little more 'edge', which meant that the most recent albums by Coldplay and Keane were currently on heavy rotation.

'I'm wiped out,' Sue said. 'We should have left an hour earlier.'

Ed grunted, thought. 'She *really* wanted us to stay longer, did you notice that? She didn't want people to go. You ask me, I don't reckon she's got a lot of friends. Either of them.'

'I don't think she's got very much to do.' Sue flicked on the car's main beam. They were on a short stretch of the M25 without lighting and there were no other cars in sight. 'That's all. Kids are old enough to look after themselves, she's a bit . . . lost.'

'*He's* hardly the best company in the world, is he?'

'I just think she's one of these people that needs to be busy. That needs something to get hold of.'

'Maybe that's why she's got this thing about the girl,' Ed said, turning to look at her. 'That business with the photos.'

'Actually, I encouraged her,' Sue said. 'I told her she should contact the police.'

'What the hell did you do that for?'

'I felt sorry for her.' A car on the opposite carriageway flashed, so she dipped her lights. 'Look, they won't take it seriously, or else they'll waste a couple of days trying to trace a few blokes by a swimming pool in the back of some holiday snaps. Not going to do any harm, is it?'

Ed said, 'I suppose not,' and they drove on in silence until the sign for Cobham services.

'I'm going to come off here for a bit,' Sue said.

Ed sniffed and smiled. 'See if you can find a quiet corner of the car park.'

She indicated and drifted across towards the slip road.

'Somewhere nice and dark,' he said. 'Then I can tell you just how sexy that expensive new hairstyle is.'

She looked at him. There was a thin sheen of sweat above his eyebrows, yellowish for a few seconds as they passed beneath a row of lights. 'I just want some coffee,' she said.

SEVENTEEN

Jeff Gardner walked downstairs and into the kitchen, where his wife was at the counter throwing a salad together. He watched her for a few seconds, enjoying the view, until she turned and saw him in the doorway.

'She gone down?'

'Finally,' he said.

'Dinner in five minutes, so make yourself useful.'

'Want me to set the table?'

'I was thinking about a good-sized glass of wine.'

'Coming up,' he said.

He walked to the fridge and took out the bottle, reached up for two glasses and started to pour. Truth be told, he needed one himself, *at least* good-sized, after a day during which the only time he had sat down was that twenty minutes by the pool at the Pelican Palms.

'Same story?'

'Excuse me?'

Michelle nodded up, towards their daughter's bedroom. 'She want the usual story?'

Gardner rolled his eyes. 'Yep. Stupid talking tiger.' One more reason he wanted that drink. His daughter was going through a phase of needing to hear the same bedtime story every night, read to her in exactly the same way, with nothing skipped and with the same voices for each character. If Gardner tried to change so much as a word—for no other reason than to keep himself interested—he was chastised in the comically severe tones that only a five-year-old princess can summon. He had mentioned it to his sergeant a few days before and the man, who had a daughter a few years older than Gardner's, had told him to grin and bear it. The time will come, he had said to Gardner, when she doesn't want to hear that story any more. When you *want* to read it to her, but she thinks it's stupid and babyish. It'll come sooner than you think and that's when you'll miss it.

Gardner saw the sense in that, so he kept on reading the story.

He took a sip of wine then handed a glass to his wife. She leaned forward to kiss him, glass in one hand, knife in the other, and said, '*Now* you can set the table.'

They ate outside, beneath the lanai. The fan overhead was jacked up to the maximum, but even at eight o'clock in the evening the temperature was in the mid-seventies. Gardner had changed out of his work clothes within minutes of walking through the door, had felt the stresses of the day begin to recede just a little as he climbed into baggy shorts and put on an old Tampa Bay Rays T-shirt. There were inflatables floating in the small pool: a green dragon; a multi-coloured ring; a ride-on turtle. There were wet towels draped across one of the loungers and the deck was still slick with water.

'I swear she was in there nearly all day,' Michelle said. 'Didn't want to come out. I couldn't get anything done because I had to watch her all the time, you know? Rushing whenever I had to go to the bathroom.'

'You left her in the water when you went to the bathroom?'

She set her fork down. 'I was inside for like, one minute and she had her swim-bands on, plus I can see her with the bathroom door open.'

'OK, just . . .'

114

'Just what? Listen, I'm the one that's with her all day.'

His wife had not raised her voice and when he glanced up he could see that she was smiling, but still Gardner knew his wife well enough to see that he was better off leaving it alone. He said, 'Good to know she's going to be a swimmer.'

When they had finished eating, he carried the plates inside and Michelle took their wine glasses through into the living room. She turned on the television and a few minutes later he joined her on the couch. He said how much he'd enjoyed the meal and she asked if he'd had enough to eat.

'I had a big lunch.'

'Let me guess . . .'

'The place is convenient.'

'You're going to look like a stupid sub,' she said.

The local news anchor announced that there were still no leads in the hunt for the killers of two elderly French tourists. He talked over clips of SPD officers—a couple of whom Gardner knew—interviewing people at the murder scene. Then, in an oddly upbeat voice, the female co-presenter introduced footage of the murdered couple's grown-up children arriving in the city. A pair of grim-faced young men shook hands with the Chief of Police, who kept his best side to the cameras and, in a tone of voice reserved for stupid people and foreigners, assured his visitors that everything possible was being done to apprehend their parents' killers.

When they switched to a story about a local fruit festival, Michelle began channel-surfing. She reached for her wine and said, 'So, is she going home? Patti Lee Wilson?'

'I think so,' Gardner said. 'She told me she'd think about it.'

'She's basically in denial, right?'

'I guess so.'

'That's not good. You have to face up to these things.'

'I guess.'

'Listen, don't get me wrong, I have sympathy for her. I mean how could anyone *not*? But, you know . . .'

Gardner nodded, but he was thinking that the manager of the Pelican Palms had said more or less the same thing. He tried to remember the man's exact words.

Some shit about passing the hat.

Michelle was a sucker for old-fashioned British mysteries, and they settled for an episode of *Poirot*. The one on the fancy train. After fifteen minutes or so, she turned to him and asked what the matter was.

'Amber-Marie Wilson would have had a story that she wanted to hear over and over again,' Gardner said. 'Same as any other kid, right? She had a favourite story and a favourite toy and a TV show she loved. God willing, we'll have all those things to remember and laugh about or whatever and we'll *still* have our girl. But now, all Patti has is those memories. How can that ever be enough?'

Michelle put her head on his shoulder, rubbed his arm.

'I don't want to let her down, that's all.'

'How could you let her down?'

'I made a promise to her today,' he said.

She raised her head. 'What did you do that for?'

'I'm not sure.'

Michelle nodded towards the TV. 'You want to leave that kind of thing to your boss. He's the politician.'

'This wasn't about trying to say the right thing or whatever,' he said. 'I meant it.' He thought about those French boys whose parents had been murdered. It was terrible, but it was the right way round.

How the hell did you bury a child?

He'd thought about that a great deal, not just since he'd been working on the Wilson case but since the first time he'd ever investigated the death of a young person. It was a question he'd asked himself a good many times after that. Once, sitting up late with a bottle in front of him, he'd typed it into Google. Wasn't that how everyone found the answers to tough questions these days? All he found were a lot of adverts for 'quality urns and caskets' and for 'memorial jewellery' companies offering to turn your loved one's ashes into diamonds.

He'd begun to feel queasy and had closed the website down.

'Jeff . . .?'

He took his wife's hand. On the television, the fat detective with the silly moustache was questioning a suspect. Gardner knew that in an hour or so he'd have the crime solved and the killer put away, that justice would be done.

He relaxed back into the couch.

Right now, it was just what he needed.

EIGHTEEN

They drive back from the Bonefish Grill in two taxis: Ed, Sue and Marina in one car, Angie, Barry and Dave in the other. It's only a ten-minute journey to the Pelican Palms and the cabs stay together all the way. Arriving in the village, there's a little good-natured argy-bargy about who is paying the fare, then once the cabs have left, the three couples walk slowly back into the resort, none of them seemingly keen for the evening to end.

Though there is no sign of any officers, there are three police vehicles in the car park.

'Wonder if there's any news?' Angie asks.

'Nothing good,' Dave says. He takes Marina's hand and nods towards the police cruisers. 'Or they wouldn't still be here.'

Ed says that they should have gone on to a bar somewhere, last night of the holiday and all that, but Sue reminds him that they have a long trip home the following day and they still have some packing to do. Angie confesses that she started packing two days earlier. Marina claims that she and Dave have done nothing and are just planning to throw their stuff into cases right before they're due to leave.

'I wish I could be that casual,' Angie says.

'It's not casual,' Marina says, 'so much as being disorganised.'

'Right then . . .' Sue says.

There are hugs between the three women, and between the women and men. Barry and Dave shake hands, then are both pulled into an embrace by Ed, who tells them that they need to relax and get in touch with their feminine sides.

'Or latent homosexuality,' he says, winking at Dave.

They start to separate, then, as the goodnights drag on, they drift back together and talk briefly about plans for the following day. There is some suggestion of seeing each other the next morning, grabbing a final hour or so by the pool, though nothing definite is arranged. Each couple has a hire car to return and some are planning to set off for Tampa airport earlier than others, but there is general agreement that they will all see each other in the departure lounge before the flight home.

'Definitely,' Angie says. 'Don't forget we need to swap those email addresses.'

Half an hour later, one of the couples is in bed and both he and she are reading: a novel that was discussed on a television book club and the autobiography of a northern comedian. Another couple is making love, and, although the cabins are detached, the walls are thin and on a still night such as this one the sound carries easily from one to another, so they take care to keep the noise down.

The third couple is arguing.

'Why did you lie? In the restaurant.'

'It was what I told the police, so—'

'That's what I mean. Why did you lie to the police in the first place?'

There is anger, plenty of it, but the volume is deliberately muted. Like the couple making love in the cabin just behind their own, they are making sure that they are not overheard.

'You know why.'

'I *know* that because of you *I* had to lie as well.'

'It was sensible, all right?'

'*Sensible?*'

'You know what the police are like, you know the way they think. They're the same all over the world. It just felt like the simplest way of getting crossed off the list or whatever and making sure we could get out of here tomorrow without being held up.'

'It was stupid.'

'Keep it down.'

'It was *stupid* because it's easy enough to check.'

'I don't see—'

'For heaven's sake, cameras, a witness, *anything.*'

For half a minute, neither of them says anything. One of them sits on the edge of the bed, working with clippers at their toenails. The other walks around, from one side of the bed to the other and back.

'Look, it doesn't really matter, does it?'

'No?'

'It was nothing important, it was just a detail.'

'We'll have to see. It depends if they find that girl, doesn't it? And what state she's in if they do . . .'

PART TWO

SUE AND ED

NINETEEN

Pete and Andy pushed their rented kayaks into the water just before 8.00 a.m. They had flown down from New York for a week's R&R away from college; seven days of sun and beer and hot Florida girls and so far things had been going pretty well on at least two of the three fronts.

Andy had not been overly keen on the kayak trip, preferring to spend his days sleeping—in bed or by a pool, he wasn't choosy—but Pete had finally convinced him that this was a good way to keep that chest of his nicely toned, which would surely increase his chances of scoring later on.

'Let's face it, you need all the help you can get,' Pete had said. 'Besides, the wildlife's awesome out there. We might even see a manatee.'

'Great,' Andy had said. 'That's all we need, getting the frigging canoe turned over . . . and there's alligators, right?'

'This isn't the Everglades, you moron. And it's a kayak, not a canoe.'

Following the map provided by the rental company, they paddled south into Blind Pass, the channel no more than seventy-five feet wide for the first ten minutes or so. There were houses on either side.

Apartment blocks or pricier, detached places, all with wooden docks alongside and boats of various sizes raised up out of the water.

They passed a sign in the water that said MANATEE ZONE, and Pete said, 'Told you.'

'What the hell are they anyway?' Andy asked, already out of breath in the kayak behind him. 'Giant seals or something?'

The day was bright and warm, same as every other day had been since they'd arrived. It would get even hotter as the morning wore on, so they each had bottles of water and cans of beer in their boat, along with tubes of sunblock in plastic bags next to their cameras and wallets.

'Just an hour, right?' Andy shouted. 'Then breakfast.'

'Yeah, yeah . . .'

They made steady progress through the shallow brown water, thick with weed. There were birds everywhere: blue herons, spoonbills and cormorants; snowy egrets in the branches of the trees on either side and the occasional osprey looking down on them from higher up, or perched on the signs reading *Slow Down* or *No Wake*. After twenty minutes or so, Pete pointed to the shoreline on their right and they paddled across. They hauled the kayaks up on to the shore, grabbed towels and walked over a ridge and down on to Turtle Beach. They drank their beer and swam for a while, the ocean calm enough that they were able to watch a group of dolphins breaching, black against the horizon a hundred yards away from them.

Even Andy was forced to concede that it was pretty cool.

Back in their kayaks, they paddled out towards Casey Key, where the channel widened and there were a few big boats moving around and the shoreline was nothing but mangroves on either side of them.

Pete pointed to a house in the distance, its flat grey roof just visible above the treeline. 'I think that's Stephen King's place,' he said.

'Wow, really?'

'It's round here somewhere.'

Andy looked and shrugged. 'Looks pretty ordinary.'

'What were you expecting? The Munster house?'

They paddled around a narrow spit of land and back on themselves into a small inlet, no more than fifty feet across. It was suddenly very quiet and they drifted for a while, birds occasionally taking flight as they passed and fish jumping all around them.

'That means something's after them,' Andy said.

The only sounds were the splashes as Pete paddled across to the furthest corner where a narrow channel was all but obscured by low branches.

'Come on, let's go into the tunnels,' he said.

Andy looked towards the scattering of narrow, overgrown inlets that snaked away into the trees. 'Are you kidding? How are we going to get in there?'

Pete reached up with his paddle and pushed the branches out of the way, lying low in his kayak and easing himself in. The mangrove roots twisted into the water all around them. Looking up, they could see enormous spiders waiting to eat on webs spun from tree to tree and translucent crabs scurried across the mud just inches away on either side. After only a few feet, Andy was complaining, saying that there were probably snakes. Insisting that it would be impossible to turn round, that they were going to get trapped and there was *no way* he was getting out of the boat.

The channel narrowed still further until it was barely wider than the kayaks themselves. 'This is stupid,' Andy said.

'Come on.'

'Jesus, what's that stink?'

There was a smell like rotten eggs as their paddles dug into the black, sulphurous sludge. Andy's kayak got tangled, hard to the bank, and, irritated, he told Pete to wait up. Pete paddled on. 'Don't be such a pussy,' he shouted.

A few yards ahead, Pete saw something wedged against the bank to his right, just below the waterline. A black mass of crap held fast in the tangle of roots. He pushed himself towards it, reaching up to keep the branches off his face. When he was close enough, he nudged tentatively at the black shape with the tip of his paddle. It felt like rubber. He saw

125

that whatever it was had been wrapped in trash bags. The plastic was torn in places and he glimpsed a flash of red below the water. A sliver of something else: mottled, like a dead fish.

He leaned out of his boat and wrestled the package until it was released from the cage of mangrove roots and floated free. Sweating from the effort, he dragged it to the side of his kayak.

'Andy, come here . . .'

He prodded at it and felt something give. He pulled his hand away.

'Andy.'

Using his paddle, he pushed the blade into one of the tattered holes in the plastic and shifted it hard from side to side. He watched a crab scuttle out of the hole, saw the pale mass it had left behind. Stared at what was left of a foot.

Pete shouted. Screamed.

Behind him, his friend—still desperately trying to release his kayak from the mess of roots and branches—shouted back.

'What is it, man? A 'gator? I fucking told you—'

From: Angela Finnegan angiebaz@demon.co.uk
Date: 25 June 11:17:09 BST
To: Susan Dunning <susan.dunning1@gmail.com>
Edward Dunning <Edduns@gmail.com >
Marina Green marinagreen1979@btinternet.com
Subject: Amber-Marie

Hi Everyone,

Not sure if any of you have been keeping up with this on the web, but just seen that they found that poor girl's body last week. Here's a couple of the stories I found online if anyone is interested.

http://www.mysuncoast.com/news/local/story/missing-girl-found-in-mangroves/PbuFJfJgJOoyA.cspx

http://bradentonsarasota.com/content/amber-marie-body-discovered

Probably been in the water since the day she went missing, that's what they reckon. Now I can't stop thinking about that woman and what she must be going through. There but for the grace of God etc etc.

See you all in a couple of weeks at Sue and Ed's. Sue, are you sure there's nothing I can bring? Happy to knock up a starter or a pudding or something.

Love to all,

Angie xx

TWENTY

Jenny Quinlan started slightly as a healthy stack of paperwork was dropped on to the desk she shared with another TDC, and as she smoothed her skirt and caught her breath, she looked up to see Detective Sergeant Adam Simmons grinning down at her.

'Here you go, *Trainee Detective Constable* Quinlan.'

Simmons parked his sizeable backside on the corner of the desk. Jenny slid her chair back a few inches and nudged the Tupperware container that held her lunch out of harm's way.

'Right up your street, this one.'

Jenny turned back to her computer screen. 'Really?' Simmons said much the same thing every time he palmed off some tedious or menial job on her.

'Don't worry,' he said.

'Who's worried?'

'Piece of piss, this one, I promise.'

'Meaning it's something you can't be arsed with.'

'Spot on.'

'Great . . .'

Jenny glanced up to see that Simmons was grinning again and, not for the first time, she wondered if the attention she was being paid was because her self-styled mentor had taken something of a shine to her. It was hardly flattering—the man could not be less sexy if he worked as a Jeremy Clarkson lookalike—but whether he was taking the piss or simply taking advantage, it made his presence fractionally less annoying.

It wasn't as though she was beating off admirers with a stick.

'Come on, Jen, you know that this is all part of the training. Sucking up to your sergeant.'

She knew well enough, having spent five months based in the CID room at Lewisham station. The weekly sessions attending court and observing post-mortems, the training in interviewing prisoners and handling evidence had gone hand in hand with those equally important modules that were not to be found in any Met Police prospectus or TDC handbook. The nod and the wink as favours were done and earned. The pulling of rank and the passing of bucks. The banter and the bullshit.

'As long as it's only sucking *up*,' she said.

She was delighted to see Simmons blush. This was the first time she had given him anything back—anything *like* that at any rate—and it was thrilling to see that it made him so uncomfortable. She remembered one of the female DIs in the pub one night, leaning across and whispering, 'Plenty like him around. All gob and no truncheon . . .'

Simmons eased himself away from the desk and slapped the flat of his hand down on the pile of papers he had delivered. 'Anyway, just as long as we're clear,' he said. 'Anything comes of this, any testifying needs doing and I'm the one who gets to go to Florida.'

'Eh?'

Jenny reached across and took the top sheet of paper. She recognised the seal of the US government and glancing down she saw that the covering letter had been sent from the office of the embassy's assistant legal attaché. She looked at Simmons.

'Don't get excited,' he said. 'It's just a couple of interviews, nothing too far away.'

Jenny was starting to get very excited, but did her best to hide it. She flicked through the pages, shaking her head and puffing out her cheeks as she looked at the names and addresses. 'I'll try not to get too carried away with the glamour,' she said.

'Just ask the questions and write it up.'

'Then you put your name on it?'

'Only if you've done a good job,' Simmons said. 'If you haven't, I tell them I trusted you with something but you obviously weren't up to it.'

'I think I can manage to ask a few questions,' Jenny said.

'I'm sure you can, love.'

'*Here's* a question . . .' Simmons had turned away, but now he turned back and leaned down towards her; up for the banter, for the *craic*. It was fine because, for once, she wanted him close. 'How much aftershave can one man wear before it actually becomes an arrestable offence?'

The expression on the sergeant's face—the attempt to look as though he had found it funny, the nodding and that eyes-closed smile—would be the second-best moment of Jenny Quinlan's day.

Reading through the documentation over the next hour or so, it was easy enough to follow the paper trail. The request, made almost a week earlier, had been fielded initially by staff at the US Embassy's legal department and passed on to New Scotland Yard. Jenny could only surmise that it had finally filtered down through assorted Territorial Policing units to CID at Lewisham because of the station's proximity to one of the three addresses on the original request form from the US.

Sarasota Police Department. The Crimes Against Persons Unit.

'Coffee would be great, if you're making . . .'

Jenny looked up. Two detective constables, a man and a woman, had just come back into the office; the woman doing the asking ever so nicely. This was part of it too, the glorified fagging, and Jenny swore to herself that when she became one of them, she would not do the same to whoever was in her position.

She laid the paperwork to one side. Said, 'Yeah, not a problem.'

She smiled at the two DCs as she walked across to the coffee machine, only too aware that they had probably sworn the very same thing to themselves once upon a time.

'Black with one sugar and white without,' the man said.

'Right,' Jenny said, but she did not need to be told. She could manage to ask a few questions and she could remember coffee orders.

As she waited for the ancient, grumbling machine to do its work, she thought back to the exchange with Simmons an hour or so before. The crack about his aftershave. Pleased with herself as she had been, her leg had been trembling as she'd said it and, even now, just thinking about him slowly rolling his head around before walking back to his desk, she could feel something tighten in her stomach.

'Funny, love,' he had said. 'That's funny.'

She looked across, but Simmons was engrossed in something on his screen. Instead, she caught the eye of the male DC, who nodded and smiled. Now, he *was* sexy, but like most men with any standards or a modicum of self-esteem he had never shown the remotest interest in her and Jenny turned quickly back to stare at the machine before the blood had a chance to reach her cheeks.

She could hear her friend Steph giving her a good telling-off, asking her why she never believed any man could be interested. Why she thought so little of herself. Easy enough for Steph, who looked like Courteney Cox pre-surgery and who'd had a boyfriend since they were in junior school, for God's sake.

'You do *tell* them you're not a lesbian,' Steph had said once. 'Don't you?'

It was true that a lot of people assumed Jenny was gay, believed that any woman who wanted to be a police officer had to be. She had argued with a man about it once, a friend of a friend of Steph's she'd quite fancied and she could still remember how . . . desperate she had sounded, with a drink or three inside her, trying to explain to him that

132

she honestly *wasn't* gay. At least that's how it had seemed afterwards and she had not bothered explaining it to anyone since, deciding any bloke that ignorant was not worth chasing, however tight his arse was.

'Very high and mighty,' Steph had said. 'But how long since you've had a decent shag?'

Jenny delivered the coffees and got no more than muttered thanks. She spent five minutes in the ladies, imagined exchanges with Steph, Simmons and the tasty DC rattling around inside her head, then walked slowly back to her desk. She still had three dummy crime reports to finish and a hypothetical anti-drug operation to plan for her workbook.

It wasn't like she had a lot of time to go looking for a bloke, was it?

She picked up the documentation Simmons had given her and began flicking through it. Three interviews to conduct and write up. Piece of piss or not, it looked as though she was just about to get even busier.

She read through the request from Sarasota Police Department one more time, looked at the world clock on her computer, then checked her watch. They were five hours behind in Florida and in less-than-sunny Lewisham it wasn't even twelve-thirty yet. She would try to get at least one of the reports finished, put a coat on and eat her sandwiches in the park, then call Detective Jeffrey Gardner after lunch.

She wasn't sure what a Florida accent was like anyway, but to her he just sounded like Elvis. His voice was lazy and chocolate brown and when he answered the phone he called her ma'am. She imagined him in a busy office with the first coffee of the day.

Doughnuts, maybe, and photos of the dead girl laid out on his desk.

Jenny introduced herself as a detective constable. Most TDCs did the same thing every now and again, besides which she told herself that Adam Simmons would almost certainly not want anyone to know he had palmed the job off on a trainee. The way she saw it, she was saving everyone unnecessary time and pointless explanations.

She felt bad for a minute or so.

Then she forgot about it.

133

'What can I do for you?' Gardner asked.

Jenny explained that she had read through all the documentation supporting his request for follow-up interviews with the three British couples. She said that she would try and get the interviews done as quickly as possible. He told her he was grateful for her help, how much he appreciated the support and co-operation the Met was giving his department on a difficult case.

She called him Detective Gardner. He told her to call him Jeff.

She thought about telling him to call her Jenny but decided it might make her sound less professional. Instead, she said, 'There were a few more things I wondered if you could send me. Just so I'm fully up to speed with everything.'

'A few more things?'

'Well, I know that all the couples were originally interviewed on the day that Amber-Marie went missing.'

'Just a couple of routine questions from patrolmen at the scene.'

'Would it be possible to see the transcripts of those?'

'Yeah, it's . . . possible. But this is just basic follow-up stuff I need you to do, you know? I sent a list of questions over, you got that, right?'

Jenny flicked through the pages on her desk until she found the list Gardner was talking about. She had already picked out several of the questions with a pink highlighter. 'Yes, I've got them in front of me—'

'I'm just making sure all my ducks are in a row here, that's all.'

'I understand, but I do think it would help to see what was originally said.'

There was a sigh. 'Sure. I'll get the relevant pages from the patrolmen's notebooks faxed over to you.'

'Thank you, Jeff.'

'A few things, you said.'

'Well, I was hoping you might send me some pictures of Amber-Marie.'

'Pictures?'

Jenny looked around. Simmons was deep in conversation with someone on the far side of the office who was pretending to find whatever he had to say funny. 'Well, anything you have really. Photos of the body obviously, and a copy of the PM report would be useful.'

There were a few seconds filled with background chatter before Gardner said, 'You're just supposed to be asking a few questions.'

Jenny lowered her voice. 'I know this is just routine, and I'm sorry to put you to any extra trouble, but I don't really believe in doing anything without being armed with as much information as possible. Least of all when we're talking about a murder inquiry. The more of it the better.' These were the things she trained for, after all; the boxes that needed ticking in her workbook before she was assessed and signed off. She had to 'demonstrate competence' in planning an operation. She had to show that she could organise and that she could take personal responsibility. 'It's your decision, obviously, but I genuinely believe that as far as getting your ducks in a row goes, all this will help me do that job properly . . .'

She had to show initiative.

The American told her to hang on, and the change in sound made it clear that he had put his hand over the mouthpiece. There was a minute or more of muffled conversation with someone—the tone of both voices even, some laughter in there at the end—until Gardner came back on the line.

'OK, Detective Constable,' he said. 'Let me have your fax number and email address . . .'

TWENTY-ONE

Sue found the boy towards the end of the lunch break. He was behind the chapel, crouched against a wall; his face glistening and snot-smeared like he'd been crying for a while. He was a Year Eight kid, twelve or thirteen, and she knew it was a couple of younger lads who had been giving him a hard time. She'd caught them at it before.

'Come on,' she said. 'Let's get you sorted out.'

Avoiding the playground, she walked the boy to an empty classroom, gave him some tissues, tried to calm him down. The urge to cuddle the poor little bugger was overwhelming, but she knew she had better not. She had seen one colleague's career go down the toilet after comforting a fifteen-year-old child in his class. Admittedly, that had been a male teacher and a female pupil, but still.

Bloody ridiculous . . .

The Head of Sport glanced in through the classroom window and came in for a few minutes. He leaned against the edge of a desk and folded his arms. He told the boy he needed to toughen up a little, that if he stood up to the 'little shits' who were tormenting him just the once, they'd get bored and find someone else to pick on. Behind his glasses, the boy's eyes began to fill again. The Head of Sport shook his head and said, 'I'll leave him to you.'

Sue wondered if the man had been bully or victim at school; it had clearly been one or the other. Once upon a time she thought that the world could be divided neatly into bullies and victims, but that was before long hours on playground duty where she had learned to recognise those other types who watched from the shadows or lingered around the fringes. Those who cajoled the bullies into action, winding them up like a child poking a dog with a stick until it bit. Those who liked to be part of the audience and to see a little blood and those who simply longed to run and tell; the ones that got their jollies vicariously. It took all sorts to make a world, her mother had told her that often enough. Even within the two main categories there were sub-groups. Many who bullied did so because they had once been on the receiving end and, as far as the victims went, she had known more than a few—long past childhood, all of them—who could not get through life any other way.

The ones who needed their victimhood. Who were defined by it, and would always find someone happy to oblige.

The boy sniffed, and asked in a quiet, high voice if Sue was going to say anything to anyone about what had happened. She looked at him, her sympathy waning just a little. His slack mouth and crooked fringe. She knew he might turn out to be one of those destined to suffer at the hands of the few who could see him for what he was.

That 'V' for Victim inked invisibly on to his forehead.

She thought about the most recent email from Angie.

Not sure if any of you have been keeping up with this on the web . . .

Sue almost smiled, thinking about Angie surfing the net deep into the night while Barry snored upstairs. She already had her marked down as a social network addict, happily tweeting and poking the hundreds of friends she had never met. Sue herself had never seen the point of all that, though Ed dabbled on some of those sites now and again, did stuff on his BlackBerry. She let him get on with it. She had looked at his Facebook page once or twice early on, but now she was happy to remain as ignorant about some of his female 'friends' as she was about the overnight sales trips—to the north, to Amsterdam, Barcelona and Dublin—which were seemingly every bit as necessary as they always had been, despite the orders starting to dry up.

Here's a couple of the stories I found online if anyone is interested . . .

'I'm OK now, miss,' the boy said. 'I don't want to be late for my next lesson.'

Sue wondered if Amber-Marie Wilson had a Facebook page and guessed that, if she did, it would now be getting very popular. She had seen a few of those. Virtual wreaths and smiley faces and messages of condolence left for the deceased as if they were still around to pick them up.

Miss u always

RIP babes

Thinking of you, never b forgotten x

Stupid. As though grieving itself was simply not enough. As though you had to be *seen* to be grieving.

'Mrs Dunning? Can I go back to my class now . . .?'

Sue asked the boy if he was sure he was all right. He nodded and she gently brushed brick dust from the shoulder of his blazer. She asked him if he wanted her to say anything to his mum. He shook his head and Sue thought, you should tell your mother everything, young man, because I've got a horrible feeling you're going to need all the friends you can get.

Ed drove into the pub car park, sat there for a few minutes with the radio on, then went inside and ordered a pint. He carried his beer out into the garden and lit a cigarette. There was a man, same kind of age as he was, sitting at one of the wooden tables a few feet away. Ed caught his eye and the other bloke nodded and raised his glass an inch or two off the table in greeting. Ed found himself wondering if this other man was doing the same sort of thing that he was. He thought about going over to join him, sharing a pint or two and a few jokes about what they were up to on the sly. Killing some time. He was about to say something when a woman came out of the pub to join the man at the table, who had obviously been waiting for her, so Ed nodded back then turned away.

He spent the next few minutes concocting an elaborate fantasy in which a second woman came out of the pub—this one twice as attractive and with nobody waiting for her—and sat down at the table next to his. Her legs made a sexy kind of *shushing* noise when she crossed them. She asked him if he had a spare cigarette, and it went from there.

'You waiting for anyone?'

'You, I think . . .'

'That works for me.' She smiled and blew smoke into his face, which he'd always thought was a come-on. 'You know this place has rooms, don't you?'

His dialogue could be a bit cheesy sometimes, he knew that, but he put plenty of work into the physical detail, which was what mattered to him the most. The glimpse of a white, lacy bra-strap when she leaned forward. A gap between her front teeth. Pink, painted toenails.

'So, why don't we have a few drinks and see what happens?'

A middle-aged couple with a dog wandered across and sat at the nearest table, which pretty much killed things, but Ed was happy enough. He had plenty to work with later on. Alone, or with Sue, depending on her mood.

Ed glanced across and saw that the man who was drinking with his girlfriend was watching him. He suddenly had the mad idea that the bloke knew exactly what he'd been thinking, or at the very least knew exactly what he was doing there, sitting on his own like Billy No-Mates. Maybe he would finish his drink and move on to somewhere else, before he started to look like too much of a loser.

Pink, painted toenails . . .

He reached beneath the table, slipped his hand into his pocket and made a few necessary adjustments.

He had been doing a lot more of this the last six months or so, as business had started to tail off. On a day like today, when Sue was at work, he could always go home for a few hours in the middle of the day. It wasn't possible during the school holidays of course, though they were only a few days away, and Sue had found out once when one of the neighbours had said something. Besides which, the truth was that he preferred being out and about.

He got restless sitting on his backside.

He had always covered a decent-sized sales territory. He liked to drive, to get around and see different bits of the country. It wasn't a sightseeing thing, nothing like that. He just enjoyed covering ground. The cost of petrol had become something of an issue lately though, so these days he was as likely to kill a few hours sitting in a country pub somewhere in Hertfordshire as he was batting up and down the M1 and seeing what he could find to do for fun in Leeds or Sheffield.

Fun was still important to him. The day it wasn't, he wouldn't care if he turned up his toes. He just had to work a little harder to find it these days.

His phone chirruped and when he picked it up there was a text message from Dave Cullen, asking if he fancied a lunchtime drink some time. They had swapped numbers back in Florida, but this was the first time Ed had received a text. He read it through a couple of times. He wondered if the same message had been sent to Barry. He'd be seeing them both anyway in under a fortnight when they all got together for dinner, but he supposed that a drink couldn't hurt.

Might be fun.

He texted back: *Sounds good, mate. Up to my eyeballs with work, but why don't we try and organise something next week? Clear the afternoon and make a session of it!*

Then he finished his drink and sent a text to Sue.

Buy some pink nail varnish.

When Ed walked into the kitchen, Sue was at the cooker, stirring something. The radio was on, a woman talking about a film or a play she hated, and Ed walked across and turned the volume down. Sue asked about his day and he told her he was knackered, that he'd been tearing about like a blue-arsed fly. There weren't enough hours in the day, he said. He asked about school and she told him it had been much the same as ever, going into no more detail than he had done; both saying 'you know' because the other one did know, both seemingly keen to leave work behind them and relax.

'What was that text all about?' she asked.

'Did you get the nail varnish?'

'I got it, but I really don't think pink's going to suit you.'

He laughed and moved up close behind her. He leaned into her and she had to steady herself momentarily against the cooker. He stayed pressed against her for half a minute or so—she with a wooden spoon dripping above a pan—then he blew softly, just once, on the back of her neck and turned to the fridge in search of wine.

'I fancy Indian,' he said.

Sue turned. Said, 'I'm making spaghetti Bolognese.'

'I'm really in the mood for a good curry.' He opened the fridge and took out a bottle. 'I've been thinking about it all the way home.'

'What about this?' Sue asked, waving the spoon over the pan.

'We can freeze it.'

'It's almost ready though.'

'I fancy Indian.'

Ed poured himself a glass of wine, then opened a drawer and began searching inside. Sue continued to stir her sauce. On the radio, the woman was saying something about the leading actor in the film or play she had seen, but Sue could not hear it properly.

When the phone rang, neither of them moved to answer it.

'Can you get that?' Sue asked eventually.

'I'm trying to find that bloody takeaway menu,' Ed said.

Sue took the pan off the heat and walked across to the phone, picking up a tea towel and wiping her hands as she went. She answered the phone and gave her name. A few seconds later, she said, 'Oh . . .'

Ed stopped searching for the menu.

'No, I don't think that will be a problem,' she said. 'Are you talking to everyone? To the Finnegans and—'

Ed moved into her eyeline. He raised his hands and mouthed a 'What?'

'I suppose so,' Sue said, after listening for a minute. 'It'll have to be after four-thirty though, because I don't get home from work until then, so . . .' She hummed agreement a couple of times and then said, 'We'll see you on Wednesday.'

When she had hung up, she looked at Ed and shrugged and said, 'Police.'

'Eh?'

'They want to talk to us about Florida.'

'What about Florida?'

'What happened to the girl.'

'Just us?'

'Everyone, I think,' Sue said. 'She didn't really want to say, but that was the impression I got.' She moved past Ed to the open drawer and after a few seconds' searching she produced the menu he had been looking for. She handed it to him and said, 'Don't over-order.' She turned and walked back towards the cooker. 'You always over-order.'

TWENTY-TWO

Barry and Angela were arguing about a missing vacuum cleaner, and what to do about it.

'She's got the sodding thing, I'm telling you,' Barry said.

'You reckon?'

'*Definitely.*'

Angie was holding the phone. She clutched it to her chest. 'She wouldn't, would she?'

'You got any other explanations?'

The Finnegans lived at number 12, but at the end of their relatively small road, on the corner where it met a much busier one, there was a second number 12. When it came to deliveries or giving directions, this had led to a certain amount of confusion over the years. In fact, Angie had taken care to let Ed, Sue, Dave and Marina know what was what three weeks earlier, on the night they had all come over for dinner.

'Ours is the bigger one,' she had told them. 'On the smaller road. The one with the two cars outside.'

'Well?' Barry asked.

Angie shrugged. She had no other explanations.

Two days earlier, she had ordered an expensive vacuum cleaner online, one so pricey that stumping up the extra twenty-five pounds to guarantee next day delivery had seemed neither here nor there. She had waited in expectantly, but the package had not arrived. Nothing having arrived today either, she had spent the last forty minutes being passed from one person to another at the delivery company, until she had eventually been politely assured that the vacuum cleaner *had* in fact been delivered, as promised, the previous afternoon.

'No,' she told the woman. 'It wasn't.'

'I'm not trying to be rude, madam,' the woman said, 'but we have a confirmation of delivery on our system.'

'I don't care what you've got,' Angie said.

'Let me make some more enquiries and I'll call you back . . .'

Neither Angie nor Barry had ever spoken to the elderly woman who lived at the other number 12. No more than a grunted 'hello', anyway. They saw her slowly walking her ratty-looking terrier, which on more than one occasion she had allowed to do its business on the pavement outside their house. They saw her at her window, peering out at the world from behind grubby lace curtains. Several times over the years, Angie had played the good neighbour and walked round to the other number 12 with post that had been delivered to her house by mistake. The old woman, if she bothered to answer the door, took her missing letters without a word of thanks and had never done the same thing for the Finnegans, despite several items of mail mysteriously failing to show up.

'I reckon she just chucks our post away,' Barry had said many times.

Nothing as valuable as a vacuum cleaner had ever gone missing before.

'Well, she won't be chucking this away,' Angie said. 'Will she?'

'We can't let her get away with it,' Barry said.

'We can't prove she's got it though, can we?' Angie put the phone back on its cradle. Picked up the coffee she was drinking. 'Maybe we can claim it on the insurance.'

'Right,' Barry said. 'So the old cow nicks our sodding Hoover *and* puts our premiums up. Sod that.'

Angie's mobile and the landline both began to ring within a few seconds of one another. Angie picked her mobile up from the worktop and looked at the screen. 'Sue,' she said. She nodded at the house phone. 'Can you get that? It's probably the delivery company . . .'

Angie stayed in the kitchen, while Barry wandered into the extension and took his call staring out into the garden. Listening to the woman from the delivery company, he watched a squirrel dart up on to the ornate stone bird table and begin filching bread Barry had put out that morning. He banged on the window, but the squirrel ignored him.

'You're joking,' Barry said, when the woman on the phone had finished. 'That's taking the piss, excuse my French.' He turned to look at Angie, but she was absorbed in the conversation she was having with Sue.

'You're kidding me,' Angie said. 'Was she British or American?'

'Unbelievable,' Barry said. 'I mean, that's our proof, isn't it?'

They hung up within half a minute of one another. Barry walked back into the kitchen and waited for Angie to finish. When she had ended her call, he said, 'You're not going to believe this.' Angie looked a little stunned, as though still trying to process whatever she'd been told. 'What?' Barry asked.

Angie shook her head. 'No, go on . . .'

'She signed for it,' Barry said. 'Can you believe that? They've found a copy of the delivery slip and she actually signed for it. She signed your name, the cheeky bitch . . .'

Angie nodded. 'That was Sue.'

'Yeah, I know,' Barry said. 'What?'

She walked past him, into the extension. 'They've had the police on the phone wanting to talk to them about that murdered girl in Florida. The *British* police, so it's obviously . . . what do you call it, an international operation. She reckons they'll be talking to all of us.' She leaned against the table, stared out into the garden then turned suddenly, excited. 'Oh my God, I bet it's because of those photos. That's got to be it. It's all because I emailed those photos to the police in Sarasota. Maybe they found something.'

Barry shrugged.

'I *told* you it was a good idea.' She turned away again, moved to the window, nodding to herself. Outside, the squirrel was still feasting on bread meant for the birds, but Angie seemed somewhat less concerned than Barry had been. She heard him walking out of the kitchen, but jumped when the front door slammed. She ran to the door, opened it and shouted after him as he stomped down the driveway.

'Where are you going?'

'Get our Hoover back,' Barry said, without turning.

Angie grabbed her keys from the table, pulled the front door shut behind her and followed him. She had on the training shoes she had worn for a Pilates class earlier in the day, but still struggled to gain ground on Barry, who for a big man had always moved surprisingly fast when the mood took him. By the time she did catch up with him, he was halfway up the old woman's front path.

'You need to calm down,' she said.

Barry ignored her, marched straight up to the front door and began hammering at it with both fists. 'Open this bloody door,' he shouted. 'I know damn well you're in there and I know you've got our property in there with you.' He hammered faster, leaning close to the wood which threatened to splinter at any moment and screaming, 'Listen, don't make me kick this piece-of-shit door off its fucking hinges, because if I have to come in there, I'm going to sort you *and* your stupid little dog out. Are you listening to me . . .?'

Angie moved up behind him and laid a hand on his arm. He shook it off, and, without looking at her, used his own hand to hold her back. Having lost the use of a fist, he replaced it with a boot, kicking at the base of the door and cracking it almost immediately.

'Do you hear me, you thieving bitch?'

Angie stepped away and said, 'Leave it, love.' She walked back to the gate, glanced up and saw the old woman peering nervously down from a first-floor room. She could see the bony fingers curled tight as they clutched at the thin material of the curtain; the old woman flinching at every curse and with each vicious blow and kick at her door.

'Come on, Barry,' Angie said. 'For God's sake.'

Marina walked back into the sitting room, tossed the phone on to a chair and flopped down on the sofa next to Dave.

'What did you tell her?'

'I told her we already knew,' Marina said. 'I told her that Sue had beaten her to it.'

Dave smiled. 'That's what you said? "She beat you to it"?'

'No . . . I just said that Sue had already called. Filled us in.' Marina reached down for a glass of wine on the floor next to the sofa. 'I think Angie was a bit miffed, actually. She was all excited about giving us the news, you know?'

'She's more of a drama queen than you are.'

'Oh, *much* more,' Marina said.

On a small side table next to the sofa, assorted remote controls were arranged in a row. Dave picked one up and muted the sound on the television. Before the first of the phone calls, they had been enjoying an episode of *The Wire*. They were working their way through a boxed set of the first series after Dave had suggested they try and catch up, so that they might have something to contribute when people talked about it. Killing the sound did not make too much difference, as they had been watching with the subtitles on. He put the remote back and picked up his inhaler. He shook it, puffed and said, 'So, any idea when?'

'They're talking to Sue and Ed on Wednesday,' Marina said. 'That's as much as I know. I should think they'll get in touch with us fairly soon though.'

'Do you think they'll talk to each couple together?'

'What do you mean?'

Dave let his head drop back. 'Or split them up?'

Marina slipped off her sandals, then swung her legs up and across Dave's lap. 'Does it matter?'

147

'If it was *me*, I'd split them up,' Dave said. 'That way you can be sure there isn't any collusion. Easier to catch people out.'

'Yeah, but only if you've got any reason to be suspicious about the people you're interviewing.'

He began rubbing her feet. 'Obviously.'

'Which isn't the case here.'

'Of course not,' Dave said. 'But you do have to wonder why they're talking to everybody.'

Marina shrugged. She closed her eyes and moaned as Dave applied a little more pressure to the soles of her feet. 'Nice,' she said.

'Man or woman?'

'Who?'

'The copper who's doing these interviews.'

'No idea,' Marina said. 'It was a woman who called Sue and Ed, but I don't know if she'll be the one that actually does the interviews.'

Dave nodded slowly, thinking. 'Again, if it was *me* . . . I'd send a couple to interview a couple. There's all sorts of tricks you can pull using that combination. The female cop could fix on the woman, try and bond with her over women's stuff or whatever, gain her confidence.'

'Women's stuff?'

'You know what I mean. *Or* . . . she could deliberately flirt with the man, and the male cop could flirt with the female interviewee. Create a bit of friction and catch people off guard. Like good cop bad cop, but with a bit of sexual tension thrown in.'

'You've obviously thought about this a lot.'

'I always thought I might have made a good policeman.'

'Except for the dealing with people bit,' Marina said. 'That's why you prefer working with machines.'

'It's a reliability issue,' Dave said. 'That's all.'

'Machines aren't always reliable.'

'They're easy enough to replace though, aren't they?' He shrugged and smiled. 'Anyway, I've got you to do the dealing with people. The chit-chat . . .'

'I'd quite like to *play* a copper.' Marina turned her head, stared towards the muted television. The main cop was sitting in a bar. The subtitles said that there was *music playing in the background*. 'A nice juicy part in a TV cop show can set you up for years.'

'Well, you'd better keep a close eye on whoever they send to grill us,' Dave said. He rubbed a hand up and down his girlfriend's bare shin, then reached for the remote control. 'See if you can pick up a few tips.'

Marina wiggled her toes. Said, 'I certainly will.'

TWENTY-THREE

Don't get me wrong, it's not like I was sitting on the flight home planning the next one or anything like that. It wasn't as if I watched the light go out in Amber-Marie's eyes, saw that amazing smile freeze and fade then immediately thought . . . *I want to do that again.*

That wasn't how it went, I promise you that.

It wasn't *too* long after I got home though.

Maybe it was because we'd all been talking about what had happened in Florida so much. Maybe it was in my head even more than it would have been otherwise. I started thinking, just generally, about how things might work, asking myself how easy it would be now I was back at home with family and friends. How long I should wait, wondering where to look for the right girl, all of that. Then one day I realised I'd decided to do it.

After that, it was easier to . . . relax into it. I could start to think a bit more specifically.

Those books I mentioned before, the ones with the blood-spattered covers that single blokes who still live with their mums and middle-aged women seem to like so much? This would be the part they'd probably refer to as 'getting a taste for it'. The monster's 'hunger' for killing . . . his 'dark compulsion', that sort of Christmas cracker clap-trap. It's nearly always a sexual thing of course, they like to bang on about that, throw in a few nasty pictures as well if they have them. The single blokes and the middle-aged women *love* those nasty pictures.

Nearly always a sexual thing . . .

I'm not even going to *discuss* that kind of rubbish.

All I will say is that it honestly never felt like a 'taste'. I don't think I've ever been 'compelled' to do anything in my life and even though I can't swear that I'll never do it again, I've certainly not been 'hungry' to kill since the business with the second girl.

I suppose it just began to feel like doing it again was the right thing to do. If I could, then I should . . . that sort of thing. Yes of course, I *wanted* to, I'm not denying that, but that's not *needed*, is it? That's not being driven by some stupid urge or an insatiable appetite.

I wanted to find another one of those amazing smiles, that's all.

This time round though, things would have to be organised a bit more carefully than they'd been back in Florida. That wouldn't be difficult of course, seeing as what happened between me and young Amber-Marie wasn't planned at all. It was still astonishing to me that I'd been able to do what I'd done out there and walk away clean as a whistle. My heart would start to go like the clappers just thinking about it and, looking back on the events of that afternoon, it was clear that I'd been pretty bloody lucky.

Nobody had seen her get into the car.

Nobody had seen what had happened when I'd stopped the car.

Nobody had seen me driving down to the water later on.

Well . . . OK, somebody almost certainly *did* see the girl get into the car and either forgot about it or neglected to mention it to the police. As far as not being spotted when I stopped to do what I needed to, I *had* taken care to find somewhere secluded. It wasn't like I just pulled up and strangled her at the traffic lights. All in all, the way I looked at it, I'd taken one or two risks and even though I'd not done anything massively stupid, fate had been nice and kind. No question about that.

To me, if not to poor Amber-Marie Wilson.

Luck runs out though, I was well aware of that and there was no way I could count on being anything *like* that jammy second time around. I kept that thought with me every day. All the time I was trying to sort things out for a second girl.

The first question, the big question, was *which* girl and where to find her. The answer was easy enough, of course. Turns out Google's handy for a lot more than finding out who played who in what movie or settling arguments at parties.

Finding the right kind of school took minutes, that's all.

I had a good look round every inch of the perfect park and play-ground without leaving the house.

Same thing when it came to planning the route . . .

There's plenty of sick stuff online we'd be a damn sight better off without, no question. However good Wikipedia or Facebook might be, kiddie porn isn't a price worth paying. And all this social networking isn't actually about meeting people, not when you stop and think about it. I mean, they're not really your 'friends', are they?

Still, what did we do before the internet? That's all I'm saying. It's hard to remember sometimes, isn't it?

TWENTY-FOUR

'Is this OK?' the wife asked.

'It's fine.'

'Are you sure you don't want tea or coffee or something?'

'Thanks, but this really shouldn't take too long . . .'

Jenny had been shown into the Dunnings' living room: stripped floorboards and off-white walls; sofas and wall-mounted plasma at one end, antique pine dining table at the other. They moved to the end looking out towards the garden and sat at the table. Jenny took her paperwork from her bag and laid it out carefully in front of her.

'Did you find us all right?' the husband asked.

Jenny nodded and continued to arrange her documents, happy to take her time, enjoying the apprehension she could sense in the couple sitting on the other side of the table. Thinking: I could get used to this.

'Right then,' she said, eventually. She flipped open a notebook and clicked the top of her pen. She drew a piece of paper towards her, scribbled one final note in the margin, then looked up and smiled. 'So, according to the statement you made to Patrolman Magenheim, you drove to the shopping mall on the afternoon Amber-Marie Wilson went missing.'

'We didn't know that was his name,' the husband said. 'He just asked us a couple of questions really. If we'd seen anything, that kind of thing.'

Jenny waited.

'Yes,' the wife said. 'The Westfield mall at Sarasota Square.'

'What time would that have been?'

'One o'clock-ish. Straight after lunch.'

'Where did you have lunch?' Jenny asked.

'In the cabin. We'd got a few bits and pieces in from the supermarket for sandwiches and what have you.'

Jenny nodded and wrote. 'It's a damn sight cheaper than eating out.'

'It wasn't a question of cheaper,' the wife said. 'You just get a bit fed up of the enormous portions after a while. The sauce they smother everything in.'

'Right,' Jenny said. Looking at the wife, she doubted that the woman had ever eaten an enormous portion of anything in her life. Following her to the table, Jenny had seen no backside to speak of and it looked as if she had breasts like a girl under her plain grey T-shirt. Jenny wondered what Susan Dunning's issues were, figuring that there had to be some.

That said, she couldn't think of too many skinny women she trusted very much.

'So you were at the mall for what, a couple of hours?'

'We were back about three,' the husband said. 'We dropped the shopping off in the cabin then went back to the pool and met up with the others.'

'The others being . . .?'

'Marina Green and Dave Cullen.'

'And the Finnegans,' the wife said. 'Barry and Angela.'

'You've all become friends by the sound of it,' Jenny said. 'I gather you've been meeting up since you got back from Florida.'

'Well, we've had dinner once,' the husband said. He had that laugh in his voice, which Jenny had noticed a few times already. He clearly thought he was being charming, but more often than not it sounded patronising. He was good-looking, no question about that, but he acted like he knew it. Like he knew that *you* knew it. He'd held eye contact a couple of seconds too long when shaking hands at the door and Jenny had seen his eyes flash to her chest a couple of times since. She knew there was plenty to see beneath the cream blouse she had chosen to wear with the sensible grey two-piece, though she guessed that as far as Ed Dunning was concerned, almost any breasts would seem enormous compared to his wife's.

'So, you got back to the Pelican Palms at three o'clock . . .'

'I couldn't tell you it was three exactly,' the wife said. 'But that's what time we reckoned it was when we were all talking about it later.'

'You talked about it?'

'Obviously,' the husband said. No laugh this time. 'It was pretty big news and we were all out having dinner together. We'd seen the girl and we'd spoken to her mother, so . . .'

'We were upset,' the wife said. 'Anyone would be.'

'What did you think of the girl?' Jenny asked.

The couple exchanged a look. The wife said, 'Sorry?'

Jenny looked at the husband. 'You'd spent some time with her.'

'Well, not really.'

'Spoken to her.'

'For a few minutes, that's all.'

'I don't see what this has got to do with anything,' the wife said.

'What do you mean, "think" of her?' The husband put the laugh back into his voice. 'She seemed like a nice enough girl. I don't know what else to say.'

'She had learning difficulties,' the wife said, nodding down at the paperwork Jenny had spread out. 'You do know that, don't you?'

'Of course.'

'She was very trusting. Not shy at all, you know? We were having dinner one night and she just walked right up and started talking to us.' She turned to her husband. 'Remember?'

'That night at the Oyster Bar?'

'There was a man,' the wife said. 'Talking to the girl's mother.'

155

'What man?' Jenny asked.

The wife leaned forward, animated suddenly. 'I remember pointing him out to Marina, or it might have been Angie. The girl was at our table and when I looked around for her mother, I could see her down on the street talking to this man. They looked like they were pretty friendly, you know? When I looked again a minute or so later, he wasn't there any more. I didn't think about it until now and I mean it's probably nothing . . .'

'Can you describe him?'

The wife described the man she claimed to have seen and Jenny wrote it all down, then read it back to the woman to make sure she had got everything right.

'Worth checking out, I would have thought,' the husband said.

'We'll check everything out,' Jenny said.

While Jenny was writing, the husband said, 'So, is this the first time you've worked with the American police?'

Jenny nodded, hummed a yes.

'It'll be funny when they get your reports,' he said. 'I mean, presumably they'll have to change all the spelling. Colour and grey or whatever. Plus it's "homicide" over there, isn't it? Homicide instead of murder.'

'We call it homicide too,' Jenny said.

'How much longer is this going to take?' the wife asked. 'I just need to know if I'll have time to get dinner sorted or if we should forget it and get a takeaway.'

'Sorry, I'll be out of your way in a minute,' Jenny said, smiling. She spent a few more seconds writing, then glanced up and said, 'What did you get, by the way?'

'What do you mean?' the wife asked.

Jenny was already writing again. She did not look up. 'At the West-field mall. What did you buy when you were shopping?'

The wife turned to her husband. He shrugged, then laughed and threw up his arms. 'Don't look at me,' he said. 'As a bloke I'm genetically programmed to forget *everything* where shopping's concerned.'

'I can barely remember myself,' the wife said. 'A couple of T-shirts, I think. A sweater. It wasn't the only time I was there, so I can't be sure what I got when.'

'Don't worry, it doesn't matter.' Jenny scribbled a final word or two and began to gather up the paperwork. 'Done,' she said. 'Sorry it's taken so long. I'll leave you a card with my number on, in case anything else comes back to you.'

Walking back to the front door, Jenny said, 'It's all a lot cheaper over there, isn't it? Clothes and stuff.'

'Way cheaper,' the wife said.

'Depends a bit on the exchange rate,' the husband added.

The wife leaned past him to open the front door for Jenny. 'Still less than over here though.'

'Well, that's because this bloody country's one big rip-off,' the husband said. 'Almost everything costs more than it should. Clothes, electrical gear, and don't get me started on the price of petrol.'

'Oh, that reminds me,' Jenny said. She fished in her bag and took out her notebook again. 'What car were you driving in Sarasota?'

The husband stared at her. 'Car?'

'Your hire car.'

'God, I don't know,' the wife said. 'It was a white one. Ed . . .?'

Jenny waited, stared back at the husband. 'We're just getting our ducks in a row, Mr Dunning, that's all.'

'It was a Chevy Impala,' the husband said. He saw Jenny hesitate, her pen poised. '*Chevrolet* Impala.' He smiled. 'You want me to spell it?'

'No, it's fine.'

'I wanted a Dodge Charger, but the rental company didn't have any left. Chevy's pretty good though . . .'

'Well, thanks for your time,' Jenny said. 'I'll let you know if I need anything else.' She shoved her notebook back into her bag, pushing aside the packet of tampons that was sitting near the top. She looked up, hoping that the husband hadn't seen it.

He was leaning against the door. 'Right. If you've got any more ducks that need straightening up.'

157

TWENTY-FIVE

As usual, at lunch they talked about anything but work—sports, music, the rumours about an affair between two of the detectives who were not there—but once the majority of his colleagues were on their way back across the road to the office, Gardner stepped outside the still noisy delicatessen, sat down at one of the tables and called Atlanta.

'Yeah . . .?'

'Patti, it's Jeff Gardner.'

She said, 'Yeah,' again, a little quieter this time, and in the pause that followed Gardner could hear the click of a lighter, the crackle of the cigarette as it met the flame. The first desperate inhalation.

'How's it going?'

Then the long breath out. 'Peachy,' she said.

Even with sunglasses on, Gardner had to squint a little against the brightness. He had taken off his jacket as soon as he had left the comfort of the deli's air-con behind, but already he could feel the hot sheen of sweat building across his face and neck. The day was a killer and this would be the worst part of it, in every sense.

'I just wanted to call to see how you were holding up,' he said. 'You know? Let you know what's happening here.'

158

'So, what's happening there, Jeff?'

'You mean with regard to the investigation? Or—?'

'With regard to getting Amber-Marie home.'

'Well, it shouldn't be too much longer. I'm afraid that's the best I can tell you, right now.'

'Was it really worth calling?' she said. 'Just to tell me that?'

Using his shoulder to hold the phone in place, Gardner began to roll up his sleeves. 'I'm sorry,' he said. When he was finished, he took the phone from his ear and quickly wiped the sweat from it. 'I'm doing everything I can to speed things up here.'

A little over two weeks now, since Amber-Marie's body—or what was left of it—had been found and recovered from the mangrove tunnels down near Casey Key. Gardner had taken the call. He had made sure he was on the spot as the body was lifted from the water. He had been there when it was transported to the morgue at Sarasota Memorial Hospital and had witnessed the post-mortem.

But he had let someone else tell Patti Lee Wilson.

Gardner had found himself something that urgently needed to be done when the moment came to make the call. He had walked away and let his sergeant tell Patti that they had found her daughter's body in the water. That they were sorry for her loss and that they would be happy to put her in touch with the appropriate counselling service.

The standard stuff.

He thought the guilt would ease off, but it had continued to bubble and burn. He had met Patti at the airport the following morning, when she had flown in to formally identify her daughter's body, and that evening he had driven her back to put her on the last flight home to Atlanta. By then there had been a deal of strong drink taken and, sitting in the lounge at the airport, she had leaned against him and wept while he kept his eyes on the departures board. Between sobs, she had talked about getting that call, told him she had known what was coming before she'd picked up the phone.

'Only thing is,' she had said, 'I always imagined it would be you.'

★

Now, if anything, he felt even worse. Making small talk when the truth was he could not even tell this woman when her daughter's body would be released for burial.

Burning with the guilt, because it was all just a question of paperwork.

The post-mortem showed that Amber-Marie Wilson had been strangled to death, but gleaning almost anything else had been impossible due to the state of the body. Those eight weeks in the water had provided plenty for crabs and fish to feast on, but had destroyed any forensic evidence there might have been. While Gardner and the rest of the team strongly suspected a sexual assault, there was nothing to support it. There was no trace of stranger DNA. They all knew perfectly well that, as things stood, Amber-Marie's remains would not reveal any more about how she had died or who might have killed her.

Now, it was just about a process. Moving through a system that was notoriously slow and which took no account of grief.

'I'm pushing them as hard as I can, Patti,' Gardner said. 'I swear to God.'

'I know you are. I didn't mean to be so sharp.'

'That's OK.'

'You want the truth,' she said. 'I ain't holding up any better or worse than I was the last time you called.'

Her words were starting to sound just a little slurred. Gardner was relieved that he had not left this until the end of the day. 'No worse has got to be good, right?'

'I guess. But we both know it can't get any better until I get my baby back.'

'I know.'

''Til I can say goodbye.'

'I'll keep at them,' he said. 'Make sure there's no hold-ups.'

'I know you will,' she said.

He felt that burn crank up another notch in his gut, the warm sweat running in ticklish trails between his shoulder blades and down from his chest to his belly. He needed to be back inside. 'Listen, Patti . . .'

'How are you holding up anyway, Jeff?'

Gardner pushed his chair back, turned and lifted his jacket from the back of it. 'It isn't about how I'm feeling,' he said.

After a few seconds of silence there was another long intake of breath, then a ragged, smoky laugh when it was released.

'Isn't it?'

Jenny worked on her report for three hours without a break and was still buzzing and not a little breathless by the time she had finished. She had been heady with excitement since leaving the Dunnings' place in Southgate just before five o'clock, by which time there had been no point in going all the way back to the station. Instead, she had travelled—via two different underground lines and a horribly crammed overground train—back to her flat. She had said hello and goodbye to her flatmate, carried tea and a packet of digestives through to her bedroom and got down to work.

By the time she looked up from her computer, it was almost nine-thirty. Jenny was shocked to see that it was dark outside, oddly thrilled that the time had gone so quickly. Half the packet of biscuits was gone too, but she was still starving.

She went out to the kitchen and stuck three slices of bread in the toaster.

She shared a flat in New Cross with a nursing student who, like Jenny, preferred to keep herself to herself. It was a convenient arrangement, not least financially and, though the pair of them might share a bottle of wine once a month, swapping gory tales and gossip from cop shop and hospital, they were not particularly close. Jenny was fine with that. She had Steph, and work was full-on and she certainly did not need any more friends.

Not more female friends, anyway.

When her toast was ready, she slathered Marmite on two of the slices, jam on the other—so it would count as pudding—and grabbed a can of Coke from the fridge. She wondered if that would be enough, then remembered that the biscuits were still on her desk. She took the hastily improvised supper back to her room and ate it quickly while reading through her report again.

Interview with Edward and Susan Dunning. 29 June, 17.00.

Jenny had exceeded the limits of her brief somewhat, she knew that very well, but she felt good about it. Better than good. It would have been easy enough to get in and out of the Dunning place in ten minutes; to get the dates and times, to tick only the boxes she had been told to get ticked and be curled up in front of *Desperate Housewives* by now, if that had been what she wanted.

That wasn't the kind of copper she was. Or ever wanted to be.

E.D. Superficially charming. Likes to be in control. Over-compensating for something??

S.D. Seems happy to play the little woman. Less concerned with being likeable. Poss anorexic??

There had of course been no need for Jenny to describe how she had *felt* about her interviewees, but however routine this particular job might be, she had been trained not to ignore these first impressions. Taught that almost anything could turn out to be important: an off-hand remark; a glance; a hesitation.

A joke.

All the information that *had* been requested was there of course, front and centre. Confirmation of exactly what the subjects had said when originally questioned. The required details. Required or not, when talking to those same subjects herself there were . . . other questions that had seemed to Jenny entirely appropriate. Now, seeing the answers in black and white in her draft report, she felt sure that she had done the right thing in asking them.

Chevrolet Impala (White).

Having read everything that Detective Gardner had sent across, it had become obvious to Jenny that Amber-Marie Wilson had got into a car with someone. How else could she have been spirited away into thin air so quickly? Asking for a make and model of car—and she fully intended to ask the other two couples the same question—made complete sense, surely. It was not information that anyone had instructed her to acquire, but that was not the point.

'Any idiot can be *organised*,' one of the DCs had said to her once. They were in a pub near the station. He had bought her a tomato juice and when he leaned in she could smell Stella and Polo Sport. 'You want to be a notch above "competent", you need to show a bit of initiative . . .'

Maybe if you'd shown a bit that night! That's what Steph would have said. *Then another copper wouldn't think you were a lesbian, would he?*

The sound from her flatmate's television was bleeding through the wall, so Jenny put on a CD to drown it out. An Adele album she knew every word of. She took one more biscuit and pushed the packet to the far side of the desk. She saved her report as *Wilson Homicide Interviews: 1,* then opened up Google.

She typed in *Jeffrey Gardner. Sarasota Police Department.*

There was no shortage of hits. The detective's name mentioned in connection with any number of cases. Robberies, rapes and murders. Halfway down the third page, there was a report about him winning some kind of bravery medal and when Jenny opened the page there was a picture of Gardner shaking hands with the Chief of Police.

She was surprised to see that Gardner was black, then surprised at herself for being surprised. For thinking, even for a moment, that he hadn't 'sounded' black. She knew she was being ridiculous, that she didn't 'sound' Irish, even if an odd accent tended to appear from nowhere when she was talking to her mother.

'*Jennifer Quinlan, I don't know* what *you think you sound like . . .*'

He looked like Denzel Washington, she thought, trying and failing to zoom in on the picture. A little bit heavier maybe, but he carried it just fine, and that voice seriously suited him. Sweet and deep like molasses in a mineshaft.

'*What can I do for you, ma'am?*'

Jenny pointed the remote and turned Adele up a notch or two. 'Someone Like You'. She opened up the next page of search results, then stretched across the table and helped herself to one last biscuit.

TWENTY-SIX

It had been good of Jeff Gardner to call. He was a great guy. With a lot of the cops, she felt like they were just saying shit they'd said too many times before and there was no real feeling in it, but he was different. Like it still meant something.

Patti sat on the floor, her back against the couch, some comedy show on the TV she didn't remember switching on turned up loud. The rain was coming down in sheets outside. Still plenty warm enough in the house because the ice in her martini pitcher was almost melted, though she could not be bothered to get off her ass and go to the refrigerator.

The photos were spread out on the rug between her legs.

There were a couple of old ones from back when Amber-Marie was a baby. Sleeping in her stroller or lying on her back in the grass and kicking those pudgy little legs for all she was worth. There were even one or two with her daddy in them, which must have been some kind of miracle, because the way Patti remembered it, that useless dick wasn't around more than five minutes after she was born.

Mostly it was just Amber-Marie though. Or the two of them.

She kept coming back to the pictures from Sarasota. Amber-Marie on the beach and in the ocean, pointing at stuff on the street. She could sulk with the best of them when she didn't get her own way, Patti knew that better than anyone, but there wasn't a single picture from that vacation where she wasn't smiling. Not those stupid awkward 'camera' smiles either.

Her baby had a different kind of smile.

There was a bunch of great shots with her and Amber-Marie around the pool at the Pelican Palms. One of those nice British guys had taken them, though she'd given up trying to remember his name. There were a couple of Amber-Marie on her own—sitting on the edge of the pool with her legs in the water—that he'd kindly snapped before giving Patti her camera back. He knew what he was doing for sure, they were really great pictures, but looking at them now she felt hot suddenly and a little sick. She was almost certain they had been taken on that last morning.

They might well have been the last photographs taken of Amber-Marie before she disappeared.

She reached for the plastic pitcher and poured herself another glass. A fair amount of martini ended up on the floor so, cursing to herself, she pushed the photos out of the way and leaned down to mop up the mess with the bottom of her T-shirt. She leaned back and clutched at the edge of the rug like it might stop her falling. Some fat idiot on the TV was arguing with his wife.

Patti took a drink and sucked on the sliver of ice until it was gone.

TWENTY-SEVEN

Jenny sat with the wife in the conservatory. The smell of furniture polish fought it out with the fresh flowers in the middle of the table and it was obvious that the woman of the house had been up since the crack of dawn, cleaning the place from top to bottom. Those who reached for the Cif if the police were paying a visit were not necessarily any nicer—certainly no less guilty—than those who made rather less effort, but it definitely made the process a little more enjoyable.

The week before, tagging along on a job with Adam Simmons, Jenny had sat in the corner of a room that reeked of feet and fried food and whose owner only looked up from his fifty-inch plasma screen to shout at the dog curling out a turd behind the sofa.

Afterwards, walking to the car, Simmons had said, 'That counts as being house-proud on this estate.'

'We'd been to Orlando,' the wife said. 'You know, done the whole theme park bit when the kids were younger.' Angela Finnegan had already described the building of their extension in a fair bit of detail, talked about the problems with local teenagers hanging about in the park over the road and made it clear just how handy the house was for Gatwick Airport. Now, though Jenny had yet to ask any of the questions she had

166

sat up preparing the night before, they were at least talking about the holiday that was the reason she was there in the first place. 'We'd never been to the other side of Florida though, so we thought we'd give it a try.'

Jenny glanced across at the collection of framed photographs on a side table. Two serious-looking children, a boy and a girl, in school uniform. In another picture, a different boy in a different uniform; a year or two older and trying his best to smile, but not quite pulling it off. 'You've got nice-looking kids,' she said.

The wife smiled and said, 'It's complicated.' She pointed to the photograph of the boy and the girl. 'Those two are mine,' she said. 'Laura's fourteen and Luke's a year and a bit older. Poor little bugger's up to his eyes in GCSEs at the moment.'

'They put them under so much pressure now, don't they?' Jenny said. 'It's ridiculous.' The wife pointed to the other photograph. 'That one's Nick. He's Barry's son from *his* first marriage.' She rolled her eyes. 'Like I said, it's a bit complicated.'

'Most modern families are,' Jenny said.

'I suppose so.'

'So you took the three of them to Disney?'

'No, just my two. Barry's ex was a bit touchy about all that when we first got together. Things are easier now.'

'Good.'

'You got kids?'

Jenny saw the woman glance down at her left hand. She lifted it without thinking and tugged at her earlobe. 'Not just yet,' she said. 'Career comes first.'

'Of course—'

'I'm kidding,' Jenny said, hoping she looked like she meant it. 'Just not got round to it.'

'Well, it's difficult, isn't it?' The wife nodded, serious. 'With what you do, I mean. It must be pretty full-on.'

Jenny looked at her watch. Said, 'Talking of which . . .'

'I'm really sorry,' the wife said. 'He promised me he'd be home by now.' There was an edge to her voice suddenly, angry or just

167

embarrassed, it was hard to tell. She got up and moved across to where she had put her handbag on a window ledge. She rummaged inside for her phone then walked away into the kitchen with it. 'Let me see where he is . . .'

It was a little after midday on a Thursday afternoon. When Jenny had spoken to the wife two days earlier to arrange the appointment, she had been assured that this was a convenient time for her and her husband. That they would both be available. Jenny had set off good and early to get there in time and ended up having to kill half an hour window-shopping.

'Where are you?' Jenny heard the wife say. Then: 'Oh, all right then, well, hurry up. We're waiting . . .'

'Is there a problem?'

The wife shook her head and slid her phone back into her bag. 'He's just pulling up outside,' she said. 'He got held up on site, I'm really sorry.'

'It's fine.' Jenny leaned down for her own bag and began arranging her papers on the nicely polished table.

It was a good job that the wife had apologised for her husband's lateness as he clearly had no intention of doing so himself. He walked in sighing and shaking his head, as though it were all the fault of far too many other people to mention. After tossing his car keys down on to the worktop, he walked across and dropped into a chair next to his wife without even bothering to take his jacket off.

'This is Detective Constable Quinlan,' the wife said.

The husband said, 'Hello.'

'Do you need a couple of minutes?' Jenny asked. 'I mean, if you want to get a drink or something, take your coat off . . .'

'I'm fine,' he said, folding his arms. 'Fire away.'

Jenny smiled and picked up her pen, thinking: suit yourself. It may just have been the result of a particularly shitty morning at work, or he may have been on edge for some other, more personal reason. Some people, Jenny knew very well, were uneasy talking to the police for no other reason than because they *were* talking to the police. It made them feel guilty, even if they hadn't done anything. Guiltier still, of course, if they had.

Whatever the reason for Barry Finnegan's discomfort, Jenny was enjoying it.

'You told the police in Sarasota that you were on the beach at the time Amber-Marie Wilson went missing.' She looked from one to the other. 'Is that right?'

'That's right,' the wife said. 'I mean, yes, that's where we were. It's *such* a gorgeous beach. We tried to get there as often as we could, didn't we?'

'Well, you like it more than I do,' the husband said.

'Barry gets bored. Plus he burns if he's not careful, so . . .'

'Can you remember what time you got to the beach?'

The wife thought for a few seconds. 'We were there from about twelve o'clock, I think. We got back to the resort about three.' She nodded. 'I think three hours is plenty, even in the shade.'

'So you had lunch on the beach?'

'We didn't have lunch at all,' the wife said. 'We got into the habit of skipping lunch whenever we could. The breakfasts over there are so enormous that you're not really hungry until dinner time anyway. On top of which, three meals a day over there is *not* very good when you're trying to watch your waistline.' She reached across and playfully patted her husband's belly. 'Which some of us are.'

Jenny watched the husband flinch and quickly move his wife's hand away. When he looked up and saw that Jenny was watching, he smiled and shook his head as though amused by what his wife had said. Jenny didn't think either of them was particularly big and had been pleased to see that the wife was clearly as fond of biscuits as she was. More than the Dunning woman, at any rate.

'So, did you talk to anyone when you were at the beach?'

'Not that I can remember,' the wife said. 'Barry?'

'No, I don't think so.'

'So what, you just read? Sunbathed, whatever?'

The wife nodded. 'Swam a bit to cool off . . . had a nap, I seem to remember. Oh, and Barry went off to buy some fags, didn't you, love?'

The husband turned quickly to look at her. He cleared his throat then started talking as he turned slowly back to Jenny. 'That's right, I was running low.' He nodded like it was all coming back to him. 'Getting through the duty-frees a bit quick . . .'

'So how long were you gone for?'

'Sorry?'

'Just a few minutes, or . . .?'

'More like an hour, wasn't it?' the wife said. 'At least forty-five minutes, anyway.' She looked at her husband. 'You drove back into the village, didn't you, love?'

The husband was still nodding, nice and slowly. Talking to the table-top. 'I went for a beer, if you must know. A couple of beers, and a few fags.' He looked up at Jenny, leaned forward. 'You can't smoke on that beach, and you can't even have a bottle of beer. Stupid, isn't it? I took a couple of bottles in a coolbox the first day and some old git told me I was breaking the law. On the beach, for God's sake. So . . . I went to buy a packet of fags from one of the places in the village and stayed for a drink. Watched the world go by for a bit.' He nodded towards his wife. 'She had her nose in her book and I was getting too bloody hot. So . . .'

'Can you remember the name of the bar?' Jenny asked.

He shook his head. 'Sorry.'

'They're all the same along there, aren't they?' the wife said. 'Decks and big umbrellas, plastic parrots, what have you.'

He nodded. 'That's right.'

Jenny shrugged and scribbled something. 'Did you see the girl?'

'Sorry?' Now it was the wife's turn.

'Well, chances are she walked along that main street through the village after she left the resort, and you know, you said you were just sitting and watching the world go by. I mean, I know it's a long shot . . .'

170

'Of course I didn't see the bloody girl,' the husband said. 'I would have said if I'd seen her, wouldn't I? I would have told the police at the time.'

'You *told* them you were at the beach,' Jenny said.

'Yes—'

'When you weren't.'

'Right . . . because the fact that I nipped into the village to buy some fags and have a swift pint is neither here nor there, for heaven's sake.' He was looking from his wife to Jenny and back; his voice rising in pitch and volume. 'I mean, *obviously* I would have said if I'd seen the girl. *"Did you see the girl?"* That's a stupid question.'

The wife reached towards him. 'All right, love—'

'Maybe they should start sending somebody with a bit more experience to do stuff like this. Somebody who knows what they're doing.' The husband pushed back his chair, stood up and braced himself against the table. After the smallest of nods towards his wife, he leaned down towards Jenny. 'What did she say you were? A detective *constable?*'

Jenny could feel the colour coming to her cheeks and hid it by looking down for a few seconds. Gathering her papers, and her thoughts. 'I'm sorry that you're so upset about this, Mr Finnegan, but at the end of the day that can't be helped. And the fact is it really doesn't matter what an officer's rank is, because if you want to get anywhere, you have to ask *both* sorts of questions.' She paused, then looked up at him and slid her card across the table. 'The clever ones and the stupid ones. Because you know what? Sometimes it's the stupid ones that get you the right answers.'

Fifteen minutes after the police officer had left, Angie carried two mugs of tea out into the garden. Barry was smoking. He was standing at the edge of the patio, looking out across the lawn that Angie had paid the gardener extra to come in and cut the day before. It was not a particularly warm afternoon, but there was no wind to speak of and Angie could just make out the low drone of traffic on the M23 as she laid Barry's tea down on the plastic table.

She said, 'There you go, love,' but he ignored her.

She sat at the table and drank her own tea. She took Quinlan's card out of her pocket and stared at it. 'Do you know, she never even mentioned those photographs I sent? Not once. I mean, even if nothing came of it and that wasn't why the police over there got in touch with the police over here, you'd think somebody might at least have said thank you. Don't you reckon? No wonder people don't bother trying to help the police when you get no thanks for it.'

Barry said nothing. She could see the tension in his shoulders.

'You all right?' she asked.

When he turned, it was clear that his mood had not got any better. He was smoking in the same way he always did when he was angry; like a market trader or a teenager trying to look hard. The cigarette cupped in his palm, pinched between thumb and second finger.

'Why the hell did you have to go and say that?'

'Say what?'

'That business about me going to buy fags, being gone for an hour.'

'What's the problem?'

'The *problem*? Jesus . . .'

'I just thought we should tell them exactly what happened,' Angie said. 'We didn't mention it when we were over there. That's all.'

Barry flicked his nub-end on to the grass. 'Have you any idea what you made me look like?'

'Don't be so bloody daft,' she said. 'I don't suppose she thought for a minute that you were lying about anything.'

He turned and stared at her. 'Who the hell said anything about lying?'

'Exactly . . . that's what I'm telling you.'

'I meant that you made me look stupid. *Stupid*, all right? Nothing to do with anybody lying.'

'Stop shouting.'

'We didn't mention it over there because nobody asked us.' He stepped towards her, started to point. 'We told them we went to the beach because that's what we did. Nobody asked us for a minute-by-minute breakdown, did they?'

'All right—'

'Now you come out with all *that* in front of a copper. How do you think that makes me look? It makes me look like a bloody idiot.'

Angie laid her mug down, none too carefully. 'Listen, stop shouting the odds, all right, because *I* wasn't the one who came marching in late with a face like fourpence, was I? I don't care how bad your morning was or what your twat of a brother's been up to. That woman was a police officer, for God's sake, not some punter moaning because you didn't put her roof on right.' She shook her head. Her eyes were narrow and the lines deepened around her mouth as it tightened. 'I can't believe the way you showed me up, talking to her like that . . .'

They said nothing for a minute. Barry lit another cigarette. He shifted slowly from foot to foot, then walked across and pulled out a chair at the table. 'Lying?' he said, the anger gone now. He sat down. 'For crying out loud, Ange, who's talking about anybody lying?'

TWENTY-EIGHT

Sue had been waiting nearly twenty minutes at a corner table in a wine and tapas bar just off the Strand. Though the waiter had enquired more than once, she insisted that she was 'fine for the moment' with the glass of tap water she had asked for when she'd arrived. She resented his persistence, the malevolent glances from behind the bar, almost as much as she resented being kept waiting.

Being made to look as though she had been stood up.

It was probably the teacher in her—her days conveniently marked out by timetables and the ringing of bells—but the truth was she'd always hated people who could not be bothered to turn up when they were supposed to. People could waste their own time if they wanted to, but it was rude and arrogant to waste somebody else's and she would never dream of doing it herself.

The courtesy of kings. Wasn't that what they called it?

Ten minutes later, after several more pitying looks from the waiter, she was on the point of leaving when Marina came rushing in, flapping and flustered. She said, 'I'm *so* sorry,' and '*Oh* my God,' and talked about delays on the trains coming north while she struggled out of her shabby-chic overcoat.

'It's fine,' Sue said. 'Let's have a drink.'

'Haven't you got one?'

'I didn't want to start without you.'

'Don't worry,' Marina said, sitting down. 'I would have caught up.'

'Shall we get some wine?'

'I think I'm going to have a *massive* gin and tonic, actually.'

'Sounds good to me,' Sue said. She signalled to the waiter who, as might have been predicted, took his time about coming across to take their order. When he had finally turned away from the table, Sue said, 'You look fantastic.'

'Thanks, so do you.'

'Oh . . .'

'What?'

Sue pointed. 'Your bag . . .'

Marina lifted up her red leather handbag and smiled. 'What about it?'

'I've got the identical bag,' Sue said. 'You've seen it.' Marina looked confused. 'I had it with me the night we all went for dinner at Angie and Barry's. Don't you remember, you were talking about it, saying that you liked it or something?'

Marina shook her head. 'That must have been Angie,' she said. She shrugged and placed the bag back on the floor. 'I've had this ages.'

The waiter brought their drinks across and left menus which they seemed happy enough to ignore for the time being. The compulsory background music—some kind of tango-meets-electronica thing—was coming from speakers nearby, but it wasn't so intrusive that they had to shout across the table to make themselves heard. It was one of the reasons Sue had chosen the place.

'Talking about Angie,' Marina said. She leaned forward and lowered her voice conspiratorially, as though Angie, or someone who knew her, might be sitting nearby. 'Why didn't you ask her?'

'No big mystery,' Sue said. 'I thought it might be a long way for her to come, that's all.'

'Oh, right.' Marina looked a little disappointed.

175

'Easier with just the two of us.' Sue took a sip of her drink. 'Probably best not to mention it when we see her though. I don't want to upset her.'

'Course not.'

'You and Dave still all right for next week?'

'Wouldn't miss it,' Marina said. She leaned forward again. 'So, come on, I'm dying to hear all about your visit from the boys in blue.'

'It was a bit strange, to tell you the truth.'

'Really?' Her eyes were wide. 'How many of them were there? Men, women?'

'Just one woman,' Sue said. 'Quite young, but very serious.' She flicked a fingernail against the side of her glass. 'She asked us what we thought about the girl.'

Marina was drinking. She swallowed fast. 'The girl who went *missing*?'

'The dead girl.'

'Why the hell did she want to know that?'

'That's what Ed said. We thought it was just going to be a few quick questions. When we'd last seen her, if we'd noticed anyone suspicious, that kind of thing.'

'That's exactly what she told us too,' Marina said. 'When she rang. A few questions. Bloody hell . . .'

'I told her about the man we saw.'

'What man?'

'That time at the Oyster Bar. We saw a man talking to the girl's mother, down on the pavement, remember?'

'Yeah, vaguely . . .'

'So they'll probably ask you about that, ask you for a description or whatever. You remember? He was tall, fit-looking. Short dark hair and tattoos on his arms . . .'

Marina was nodding, but she still looked shocked. '"What did you think of the girl"? What on earth did you say? I mean, what did she *expect* you to say, for God's sake?'

'We were both a bit thrown, to be honest,' Sue said.

'I'm not surprised.'

'Actually, I don't think she liked Ed very much.'

Marina took a second. 'Really?'

'I might have imagined it, but there was a bit of an edge, you know?'

'Maybe she fancied him,' Marina said. 'Some women can get like that.'

Sue shook her head. 'I can usually tell.'

Marina smiled and drained her glass.

'So, when's *your* interview?' Sue asked.

'Tomorrow,' Marina said. 'I'd better warn Dave that we're in for a grilling.'

'I'm sure it'll be fine—' Sue's mobile began to ring and she dug it out of her bag. She glanced at the screen, looked up and said, 'Angie. Her interview was today, so I'm sure she's desperate to tell me how it went.' She pressed the key to drop the call. 'I'll ring her back tomorrow. I wouldn't mind betting she calls you in a minute . . .'

Marina took her own phone out and put it on the table. They stared at it for a few seconds, but it didn't ring. They laughed and decided to get a bottle of wine and, when the waiter came over, they ordered bread and a few plates to share: olives and manchego cheese, chorizo in cider, artichoke hearts.

'If we're going to keep drinking,' Marina said, 'we'd better eat something.'

When Marina stood up to go to the ladies, Sue said, 'You changed your hair again.'

Marina's hands moved to her hair, and as she clawed fingers through it she turned to look at herself in the ornate mirror on the wall above their table. 'I wasn't sure about the blonde bits in the end,' she said. 'Went back to the red.'

'You've lost some weight too.'

'I've been going to the gym,' Marina said, a hand dropping to her stomach.

'Looks good.'

'Well, I need to put the work in if I'm going to keep up with you.'

Sue laughed and when Marina asked why, she explained how Ed was always banging on about the way women compliment one another. 'It's one of the *funny* routines he trots out now and again,' she said, rolling her eyes. 'How blokes never do it, you know? How you'll never catch a hairy-arsed bloke saying to his mate, "You look great in that", or "Have you been working out?" whereas women do it all the time.'

'Because *we're* not petrified in case someone thinks we're gay.'

'Right, but Ed says women deliberately play up to that. You know, the way they dance together in clubs, pretending to be lesbians when they're not.'

Marina laughed. 'I bet he likes to watch though, doesn't he?'

'Don't all men like watching two women?' Sue looked up at Marina and smiled. 'Have you checked out the history on Dave's internet browser lately?'

'God, no,' Marina said. 'First, he'd know exactly how to hide it and even if he didn't, I don't really think I want to know.'

'Probably very sensible.'

'What about Ed?'

'Well, he's not quite as careful as Dave, put it that way.'

'Really?' Marina raised her eyebrows, but Sue showed no inclination to say any more on the subject.

The waiter was hovering with the wine. Marina asked him where the toilets were and he waved vaguely towards a staircase at the back of the restaurant. When she stepped away from the table, Sue nodded at the red leather handbag and said, 'I still can't believe that.'

Marina took a final glance at herself in the mirror. 'Great minds,' she said.

Jenny was taking her time over the first draft of *Wilson Homicide Interviews: 2*. She was thinking hard about how best to describe that day's interviewees, their demeanours, their reactions. While all her questions had been answered eventually, she was in no doubt that both of them had been distinctly rattled at various points during the questioning, even if the husband had not been as good as his wife at hiding it.

Barry Finnegan certainly had quite a temper on him.

Sitting there while he ranted and raved, Jenny felt a quiet thrill that had stayed with her the rest of the day. She must have been doing something right, she knew that, to have got under his skin to that degree. On top of all that, she was pleased that she had not reacted to his jibes about her lack of experience, the taunts about her stupid questions.

'*You want to be at the sharp end*,' Simmons had said to her once, '*you'd better get used to plenty of abuse.*'

She was used to it, to taking it and showing nothing. You couldn't let them in, not for a second, couldn't show them any chink. So, she had sat there quietly, loving every moment of it, while Barry Finnegan sweated and spat like a balding bull terrier.

Thinking: all day long, mate. All day long . . .

As it happened, Angela Finnegan had succeeded in calming her old man down eventually, to the point where Jenny had been able to ask a few more questions. He had listened and answered like a good boy. He had made no comment as to whether he found the questions stupid or not.

Yes, they had talked about the girl's disappearance with the other couples.

No, they did not remember seeing Patti Lee Wilson talking to any man.

They had been driving a red Nissan Altima.

Jenny saved the document and sat listening to the noise coming from the living room. The nursing student had invited a couple of friends round for dinner. She had told Jenny she was more than welcome to join them, but with an expression that said she'd be happier if Jenny declined the offer. Now, Jenny wondered if she could maybe go out and have a last drink with them or something. She looked at her watch. It was nearly eleven o'clock and she had the final interview tomorrow.

It had been a long day.

In the living room, one of the girls began laughing and someone clapped.

Jenny undressed quickly and slipped into bed; blissful between the clean sheets she had put on before leaving for work. She lay there thinking that if she *did* get a chance to go to Florida, to work on the case with Detective Jeff Gardner . . . as a consultant for the Met or even as his partner . . . that she fancied driving a Mustang . . .

TWENTY-NINE

A momentary lapse, that business in Sarasota.

A weird one-off, something to do with the heat maybe . . .

All of which *might* be trotted out by a desperate defence brief with his back to the wall, none of which would cut any ice with even the stupidest jury and certainly not after the business eleven weeks later in Kent.

No excuses, second time around.

It's strange, but despite how fast everything happened that afternoon in Siesta Village, and it was certainly quick, I sometimes reimagine it in slow motion. You know, the way they'd show the key moments if they ever made the film? The way they *have* shown them in a dozen films about a dozen people who've done what I did.

A heart starting to race, that's the usual soundtrack, isn't it?

The blur of bars and shopfronts that comes into focus as I slow up and come abreast of the girl. Her face when she sees me. Her face as she walks to the window when I wave her over. The water that sloshes in the bottle when I lift it up to show her. The hand reaching for the door handle and pushing the door open from inside. The backside that settles into the seat and, of course, the smile. Big, slow zoom in on that. The girl might have been missing a few bits and pieces when brains were handed out, but her teeth were bloody perfect . . .

What was said, too. I go over that a fair bit. I can't swear it's absolutely the authentic dialogue, but it's as accurate as I can remember.

'*So, where are you off to?*'

'*I want to get the egg.*'

'*Does your mum know where you are?*'

'*Can you give me the money to get it?*'

'*What kind of egg?*'

'*A big egg. A chocolate egg wrapped in red . . .*'

'*It's too hot to be walking, so why don't I give you a lift and maybe when we get there I can buy you the egg. How's that?*'

'*It's not far. Walking's good for you.*'

'*Yes it is, but today's far too hot to be out in the sun. Come on, I've got some water. Look . . .*'

Driving through drizzle, past Chislehurst and Swanley, I wondered what the conversation might be like this time. How much going round in circles there might be. How much persuasion it would take. I hadn't needed to work very hard with Amber-Marie, which was why I was looking for the particular school whose postcode I'd programmed into the sat-nav before setting off. The park where I knew those parents would be likely to take their kids at the end of the day.

Those particular kids.

Shitty weather or not, that first day I drove out to take a look at the place I was struck by how nice the countryside was. There are plenty of places like the one I was after in London of course. There are plenty of those sorts of kids being taught in bog-standard, inner-city schools, but it must be nicer for them where there's a bit more green space than you can find in Hackney or Walthamstow. A bit more calming, a lot less noisy and stressful, and that's got to be good when you're a child with these sorts of problems.

Less busy too of course, which made it a whole lot handier for me.

I parked within sight of the exit and watched them come out at half past three. Lots of parents, but I was expecting that. Not too many of

181

these kids would be trusted to get the bus home. Then, even though the weather wasn't great, I followed a gaggle of mums—mostly mums, of course—and their children across to the park.

They're just like any other group of parents and kids in the end. The mums start to talk. They're desperate for a bit of adult conversation and who can blame them, the lives they've got? So they sit on benches and natter, they stand in clusters smoking, they grab a few minutes' peace while the kids entertain themselves.

While they run and climb and shout and stare and laugh.

While the odd one drifts a bit too close to the line of trees or wanders towards the very edge of the adventure playground.

Driving home, I decided that when it came to what I was going to say, I should probably just play it by ear. Something would come to me. If you plan *everything*, you run the risk of what you say sounding . . . rehearsed, and I think a child can sense that. That first impression is crucial, same as when you meet anyone really.

It's all about what they see in your face.

Thinking back . . . nice and slow with that thumping-heart soundtrack . . . the electric window going down and her turning, eyes wide when I call to her, I reckon Amber-Marie reacted to my smile every bit as much as I reacted to hers.

THIRTY

You learned about people from talking to them in their homes. The way they lived told you a lot. Clutter and mess rarely went hand in hand with an organised mind, for example, while someone who cleaned and tidied to a ludicrous degree might well have something to hide. Basic stuff that might prove useful. Still, Jenny believed there were things to be learned in all sorts of places and felt it could do no harm to ring the changes. So, she asked Marina Green and Dave Cullen into Lewisham Police Station to conduct their interview.

They were, she decided almost immediately, a bloody strange couple.

The girlfriend would clearly have been glamorous without make-up and wearing a sack, but nevertheless looked to have made something of an effort with her appearance. She wore a multi-coloured Western-style shirt over black leggings—or were they jeggings? Jenny was not sure—with patent leather Doc Marten boots. Jenny wondered if that was the sort of outfit she wore as a dental receptionist, and if she had to take the diamond stud out of her nose.

'I love your hair,' she said.

The woman thanked her, laughing.

'What?'

'Just a conversation I was having with a friend,' the girlfriend said. When she saw that Jenny was happy for her to explain, she said, 'The way women say nice things like that, but men don't.'

'*I* told you how great your hair was,' the boyfriend said. He was somewhat less well groomed than his other half, in stained jeans that were saggy around his arse and a shapeless brown jacket. He had the sort of scraggly beard Jenny saw on some of the schoolboys at her bus stop in the mornings and looked as though he'd probably have trouble arm-wrestling any one of them. Clearly Dave Cullen wasn't too bothered how he looked, which Jenny admired to a degree, but still . . . he was definitely what Steph—who was fond of using football terminology to measure this kind of thing—would have called non-league material.

'To other men, I mean.' The girlfriend—who was probably Chelsea or Man United, Liverpool certainly—smiled at Jenny. 'Idiot . . .'

The boyfriend shrugged, twitched like he'd been given a tiny shock. He had been a bundle of nervous energy since they had arrived; seemingly over-excited to be there, nodding like a kid in a sweet shop and puffing away on his inhaler, firing off questions as Jenny led the two of them through the station.

'*Where are the CID offices?*'

'*Do you not get on with the coppers in uniform or is that just a myth?*'

'*Does this station have a custody suite?*'

They were sitting in a bog-standard interview room. Jenny on one side of the scarred wooden table, the couple on the other in nice uncomfortable plastic chairs. There was no other furniture in the room. A box of tissues that Jenny guessed was left over from an earlier interview was sitting on the table. The place smelled of pine air-freshener and the sweat it was not quite able to mask.

'Thanks for giving up your time to come in,' Jenny said. 'I know you've both taken time off work, so I'll try not to keep you too long.'

The boyfriend nodded towards the heavy-duty twin CD recorders built into the wall. 'You recording this?' Jenny shook her head. He nodded up towards the camera high in the corner. 'They normally video these things as well now, don't they?'

'This really isn't that kind of interview,' Jenny said.

'Normally though, right? And you wouldn't usually interview anyone on your own, would you? In fact, is that actually allowed?'

'Like I said, it's just a chat.'

'Police and Criminal Evidence Act, right? PACE, right?'

'You seem to know a lot about it.'

'He watches all the shows,' the girlfriend said. 'Reads endless books about it. True crime stuff.'

The boyfriend shrugged again, looking pleased with himself. The girlfriend's hand was clutched tightly in his.

Jenny thought she knew the type. At the extreme end of the spectrum were the nerds who constantly applied to join the police and were always knocked back, usually with very good reason. Many ended up as traffic wardens or working as civilian support staff.

'You should apply for a job,' Jenny said, smiling. 'The Met's always on the lookout for good IT staff.'

He blinked slowly. 'I design games,' he said. He spoke quietly, sounding rather less excited suddenly. 'It's a bit more creative than IT. Pays a damn sight better too.'

Jenny looked down at her notes. 'According to the short statement you gave in Sarasota, you were having lunch when Amber-Marie Wilson went missing from the Pelican Palms.'

'One of those bars in the village,' the girlfriend said. 'I think we were there from about one until three o'clock-ish.'

'I couldn't swear to it, but it might have been Gilligans, or maybe The Daiquiri Deck.' The boyfriend thought for a few seconds then shook his head. '*Might* have been. Mind you, whichever one it was, I'm not sure our waiter would remember us now.'

'It doesn't matter,' Jenny said.

'Not exactly cast-iron in alibi terms though, is it?' The boyfriend winked at the girlfriend. 'The pair of us vouching for each other.'

'So, you were there together, all that time?'

The boyfriend smiled. 'I might have gone to the toilet . . .'

'I don't suppose you saw the girl.'

185

'No,' the girlfriend said. Calm, straightforward.

'I'm afraid not,' the boyfriend said.

Jenny wrote for a few seconds. 'Thanks for staying calm, by the way.' She looked up at them. 'Mr Finnegan got rather emotional when I asked him the same question.'

The girlfriend said, 'Oh.'

'Why did you need to ask Barry?' the boyfriend asked. 'They were at the beach, weren't they?'

'We found out that Mr Finnegan went back into the village and spent some time drinking at one of the bars.'

The girlfriend said, 'Oh,' again.

'Did you see him?'

'Like Dave just said, we thought they were at the beach.'

'He was driving a red Nissan Altima if that helps.'

The boyfriend shook his head. 'I'm sorry, no.'

'What car did you and Miss Green have while you were out there? That's one of the questions on my list, so . . .'

They exchanged a look. 'A Neon or something,' the boyfriend said. 'A Dodge Neon? A silver one. I don't know a lot about cars, but we only wanted a small one. Something low on emissions, you know?'

'There's only the two of us,' the girlfriend said. 'No point in getting some big gas guzzler, is there?'

Jenny shook her head and said, 'I suppose not.' She put her pen down and looked at the boyfriend. 'So, as someone who knows a bit about these things, as an . . . enthusiast, what do *you* think happened to the girl?'

'Pardon me?'

'I'm just interested in your opinion,' Jenny said. 'I mean you must have thought about it and sometimes it helps to get another perspective, you know?'

He glanced up at the camera as though he were being filmed then sat back and folded his arms. 'Well, whoever took her had to have been driving a car or a truck or whatever.'

'Obviously.'

He smiled. 'I can see why you had to ask about the car.'

Jenny smiled back. 'Go on . . .'

'I think she was probably taken somewhere and killed fairly quickly.' He nodded. 'In almost all these cases the victim is killed within hours of being abducted. They don't tend to keep them for long. I mean, it's been known of course, there's plenty of documented cases, but overall it's pretty rare. If I was a betting man, I'd say he killed her straight away.'

'*He* killed her?'

'Well, no, not necessarily a man of course. No, you're right. Especially not when there's children involved.'

'What about a he *and* a she?'

'That's been known too, of course, God yes. Fred and Rose West. Brady and Hindley, obviously. A woman enticing the victim into the car and driving to where her partner's waiting. Yeah, that's possible . . .'

'Easier to get a child's trust in some ways, I would have thought,' Jenny said. 'Something familiar about the *shape* of a couple. Like their own parents, if they've got parents, of course.'

'Statistically more likely to be a lone killer though,' he said.

Jenny shook her head. 'Can't argue with statistics.' She glanced at the girlfriend who was looking a little bored with proceedings, picking at a painted fingernail. 'They run our lives, don't they?'

'Well, to a degree,' the boyfriend said. 'But don't forget, lies, damned lies and all that.'

Jenny nodded, though she did not know what he was referring to. 'So, *statistically*,' she said, 'what are our chances of catching him?'

He pushed out his bottom lip, chewed on his top one while he thought about it. 'Well, there's not really a simple answer to that,' he said. 'There are a lot of variables. Stranger murder is a lot harder to solve than a domestic killing, for a start, and are we basing this on British or American rates of homicide clearance?'

'Either,' Jenny said.

'We solve a higher percentage of murders here than they do over there.'

'So, average it out.'

'A lot depends on how high-profile the murder is, of course. If it gets a lot of publicity, which I don't think this one did particularly. If there's any political pressure on the police—'

'An estimate will do, Mr Cullen.'

The girlfriend was looking a little agitated. 'I could really do with getting back to work,' she said. 'Are we about finished?'

The boyfriend seemed perfectly content, however. He considered the question for a few more seconds then said, 'Sixty-five per cent maybe. Yeah, there or thereabouts. A sixty-five per cent chance of catching him.'

'I'd take those odds,' Jenny said.

Without taking his eyes off Jenny, the boyfriend reached into a pocket for his inhaler. He gave it a shake and said, 'I'm guessing that so would your killer.'

THIRTY-ONE

It felt like a tooth that was starting to go rotten. It was OK as long as you remembered not to bite down on it or made sure to eat in a certain way, but a few times every day the pain would remind you that things weren't getting any better. Detective Jeffrey Gardner knew it was hardly unique. Looking around the office, he knew that each of his colleagues had rotten-tooth cases like the Amber-Marie Wilson murder that snuck up and made them wince just when they thought they'd forgotten them. Files sitting in a drawer somewhere or stashed away on their desks, buried beneath the paperwork on other jobs.

Newer cases they might at least have a chance of solving.

Once or twice a day he followed up on his promise to Patti Lee Wilson and chased whoever needed chasing to get her daughter's body released for burial. Once or twice a day he was told that things were in hand, that they didn't need telling how to do their jobs and he would be the first to know when they had finished with it.

'*It can't get any better until I get my baby back . . .*'

As far as the case itself went though, there was a good reason why the urgency had gone out of the investigation. Brick wall, dead end, whatever damned cliché you chose to signify the lack of progress, they

189

had run into it good and hard. Gardner was as fired up as he had been on day one—since Amber-Marie's body had finally surfaced, bloodless and bloated in the mangrove tunnels—but when it came to prioritising, his lieutenant had a job to do, same as the detectives did. That rotten tooth had stung like a bitch, the day Gardner had been told to move the paperwork on the Wilson murder from a red file to a grey one.

In bed that night, Michelle had sighed and said, 'It's not like there haven't been cases like this before, honey. Why is this one getting to you so much?'

It wasn't anything Gardner could put into words, so he just said, 'I know, you're right,' and lay back and let her try to take his mind off a dead girl the best way she knew how.

He was working through witness statements on a stabbing outside a bar on Main Street and thinking about getting lunch when his phone rang and the operator put through a call from the Metropolitan Police.

'It's Jenny Quinlan here, Detective.'

'Oh, hi . . .'

'From London,' she added, just in case Gardner needed reminding where the Metropolitan Police were based.

'Yes, I remember,' Gardner said. A skinny, white detective named Whitlow was grinning at him from the desk opposite. 'What can I do for you today?'

'I wanted to give you an update, really. I'm just finishing writing up my report on the last interview session . . . the one with Marina Green and Dave Cullen? Anyway, one or two things have come up over the course of the three interviews I thought you should know about.'

'Interviews?'

'With the three couples. You wanted—'

'Well, it was just a few things we needed confirming.'

'Yes, of course, but I presumed you would want these things done properly.'

Gardner fought the urge to yawn. 'Absolutely.' Whitlow was still grinning. Gardner grinned back and rolled his eyes. 'I'm listening.'

'Sorry?'

'What exactly has "come up"?'

'Well for a kick-off, none of the couples was completely honest when they accounted for their whereabouts when the girl went missing.' He could hear the sound of papers being riffled through. 'Or at the very least they were being a bit forgetful.'

Gardner reached for a pen, said, 'Go on . . .' He listened while the woman told him that the first couple—the Dunnings—had confirmed that they had been shopping, but that they had not been able to say what they had bought at the mall. He cut her off without writing anything down. 'I'm not sure I see your point,' he said. 'It was almost ten weeks ago. Listen, when I go shopping with my wife I've forgotten what we bought almost as soon as we've bought it. It's a defence mechanism.'

She didn't seem to find his comment very funny. 'I thought it was odd, that's all.' When Gardner did not respond, she told him that Barry Finnegan had not stayed on the beach with his wife as had been thought, but had instead driven back into Siesta Village. 'To buy cigarettes, he said, and he could have been gone for anything up to an hour. Enough time, I would have thought.'

'Enough time for what?'

'Well, if he saw the girl . . .'

'I think perhaps you're getting a little ahead of yourself here.'

'He was very edgy,' she said. 'He got aggressive when I pushed him about it.'

'I don't quite get why you were *pushing* anybody.'

'So was Dave Cullen, come to that. He was acting very strangely, plus he and his girlfriend couldn't tell me the name of the bar where they claimed to be having lunch.'

'I'll say it again. This was ten weeks ago.'

'Even so—'

'I can't remember the name of the bar I was in last night and, more to the point, you were just supposed to be gathering information. Basic timeframes. Anything these people might have remembered and so on.'

'I've got the makes of car they were all driving.'

191

'You've got what?'

'I thought it would be useful information,' she said. 'I mean there must have been a vehicle involved.'

'Yeah, we'd worked that much out.'

'At the very least you need to eliminate people from the inquiry, don't you?'

'OK, tell me about the cars,' Gardner said, doing his best not to raise his voice. There was more shuffling of papers until the woman found what she was looking for. He scribbled down the three makes of car. Said, 'Thank you.'

'There's something else.'

Whitlow had been joined by another detective, a woman he might or might not have slept with once after a party. The pair of them were looking over at him and chuckling. Gardner looked down at his notebook where he was drawing squiggles around the few words he had jotted down. 'I really need to get on,' he said.

'This is important,' Quinlan said. 'Something they remembered.'

Gardner leaned back in his chair. 'Go ahead.'

'They saw a man with the girl's mother.'

'Who did?'

'A couple of them saw him, one night when they were all out for dinner. They saw a man talking to Patti Lee Wilson on the street. I've got a description . . .'

She described the man with tattoos that Susan Dunning had told her about and Gardner wrote down the details. He asked her if any of them had seen the man again, but she was not able to tell him. She apologised profusely for not having asked and offered to re-interview the couples concerned, but he told her politely but firmly that it would not be necessary.

'Got to be worth looking into, I would have thought,' she said.

'I'll check it out,' Gardner said.

'Well, let me know how you get on. You've got my email address?'

Gardner wasn't sure that he did, or that he needed it, but said, 'I think so,' anyway. She promised to send through the completed reports in the next day or two, told him that he would then definitely have her email address. He said, 'Great.' She told him she was happy to help and not to hesitate if he needed anything else.

He thanked him and hung up.

In less than a minute, Whitlow's bony rear end was firmly planted on the edge of Gardner's desk. 'That your Miss Marple?'

'She's a little over-enthusiastic is all,' Gardner said.

Whitlow looked at him. He could clearly see something other than annoyance etched across Gardner's face. 'Listen, how about we get a few after work? Blow some cobwebs off. Maybe we can hit a bar you won't remember the name of tomorrow.'

Gardner smiled. It was also clear that his friend had been listening in. 'Maybe,' he said.

'Nothing sorts out a toothache like beer,' Whitlow said.

Gardner looked down at the notes he had scribbled during the call from Quinlan. Three cars and a man with tattoos. He thought that in the absence of anything better, Whitlow was probably right.

There was rain coming, so Jenny walked quickly towards Lewisham station. Thinking back, line by line, through the call to Florida. The things she had said and the way he had reacted.

Going over her performance.

It was obvious that Detective Gardner had been pushed for time and that was understandable with a major murder investigation to run, but all the same she was fairly pleased with the way she had handled herself. Confident and assertive, without being stupid about it or overstepping the mark. She had actually surprised herself with just how forthright she had been when he'd been slightly dismissive or had tried to suggest that she was getting carried away.

Plenty of room for improvement though. No point in kidding herself.

Getting a little ahead of yourself here. That had stung, still did if she were being honest, but she hadn't let it get to her and it wasn't as bad as getting caught out about the man Sue Dunning had seen with the girl's mother.

Why the hell hadn't she thought to ask if anyone had seen the man again?

It was such a basic mistake, neglecting to ask the obvious follow-up question. She kicked out at a plastic bag on the pavement and felt a little better, a little more determined. Jenny was nothing if not a quick learner and she would not screw up like that again.

She went out of her way to make a good impression on anyone useful, but she *really* wanted to impress Jeff Gardner.

If she were being critical of herself—and there was no point being otherwise—she had perhaps not stated strongly enough just how suspicious she was about the people she had interviewed. She had disliked each couple a little more than the one before and was not sure that she trusted any of them. Barry Finnegan was clearly capable of snapping without much provocation. Ed Dunning was a sleazebag and Dave Cullen was just downright creepy. She had fought shy of suggesting that all three couples might be in it together, but she wished she had at least voiced her suspicion that there was some covering of tracks going on. That one of them, and perhaps more than one, was trying to protect someone else.

She should definitely have said something to Gardner. Maybe she'd mention it when she emailed the report across. How the hell would anyone know she had come up with all this stuff if she didn't speak up?

Jenny wanted the killer caught, of course, but there was always a question of credit being given where it was due. She'd learned that much while she was still a cadet, for God's sake. Thinking about it, she decided that Jeff Gardner was definitely the sort she could trust, someone who would make sure the work she had done on the case was acknowledged properly.

He seemed like one of the good guys.

Looking at the darkening sky and picking up her pace a little, she fantasised again—just for a minute or two—about herself and Jeff Gardner working the next case together. In truth she would happily have settled for a quick rise through the ranks in south London . . . DI in five years, something like that . . . but it never hurt to aim high, did it?

194

You heard about Quinlan? Jammy cow's been transferred to Florida . . .

She would finish off the report on the Cullen/Green interview as soon as she got home. She would open a bottle of red wine and curl up in front of something on the TV. One of those US cop shows she loved so much. Something gory and action-packed, with a string of caring, sensitive cops whose wives didn't understand them and could never really appreciate the pressures of the job. One cop in particular, who blurted all that out over a beer at the end of a tough day, then fell into the arms of his gorgeous female partner.

We shouldn't be doing this. It's wrong . . .

A few fat raindrops were spattering the pavement by the time she reached the station. At the entrance, a man with hollow cheeks and blood around his mouth was selling copies of the *Big Issue*. He didn't seem bothered about the rain. Jenny cheerfully tossed a handful of loose change into his cap, took a copy of the magazine and hurried towards the platform.

THIRTY-TWO

'I'll get them in,' Ed said.

Dave swallowed fast. 'Hang on, I haven't finished this one yet.'

'We can't help it if you can't keep up.' Ed laughed and shook his head. 'Right, Barry?'

'Just have a half,' Barry said.

'No, I'll have one,' Dave said. He took another mouthful and, even though he still had over half a pint left, he held up his glass, shouted after Ed as he weaved his way towards the bar. 'I'm fine . . .'

The Sussex on Long Acre was as crowded as you might expect on a Saturday evening and they had been standing for a quarter of an hour before they'd been lucky enough to snag a small table in the corner. Leaning heads in to talk, they were no more than inches apart, but they still had to raise their voices to make themselves heard above the chatter and the ambient soft rock. It took Ed the best part of five minutes to get back with the drinks, during which time Dave looked around and said, 'Reminds me why I don't come into the West End if I can avoid it,' and Barry said, 'Right.' They both looked around some more, then Barry took the opportunity to visit the gents while Dave made what headway he could with what was left of his drink.

Back at the table, Ed tossed packets of crisps over then raised his pint. The three of them clinked glasses. Ed craned his neck to look at the group of young women squeezed round an adjacent table then turned back to make some comment and saw something on Dave's face.

'What?'

'Nothing.' Dave smiled and took a sip. 'I was just thinking about our last night in Sarasota, that's all. When we drank to that girl and none of us knew what her name was.'

'The Bonefish Grill,' Barry said, nodding. 'You remember how blinding that fish and chips was?'

'Yeah, well.' Ed downed a third of his drink in one go. 'We're hardly likely to forget her name now, are we? Not now we've all been questioned by the Met's finest.'

'Right silly cow *she* was,' Barry snarled. 'Firing off stupid questions left, right and centre.'

'What questions?' Ed asked.

'Same ones she asked you, I suppose.'

'Yeah, course, but what were the *really* stupid ones?'

'Oh I don't know, stuff about the girl. Had I seen her, for Christ's sake.'

'We'd all seen her,' Ed said, shaking his head and looking at Dave. 'After she went missing, I mean.'

Dave nodded. 'Right, yeah. She mentioned that business about you not being at the beach or whatever when she talked to me and Maz. About you going to buy cigarettes or something . . .?'

Barry turned to him. 'She told you what we said in our interview? Isn't that a breach of . . . I don't know, privacy or whatever?'

'I don't think so,' Dave said.

'That's definitely out of order,' Barry said. 'I've a good mind to ring up her boss or something. I'm sure they aren't allowed to do that. I mean you've got rights, haven't you, that sort of thing?' He saw that Ed was stifling a laugh and held out his hands. 'What's funny?'

'Nothing.' Ed winked at Dave. 'Just looks like somebody's pissed off because they got caught out telling porkies, that's all.'

'Bollocks,' Barry said.

'Sure you didn't nip back into the village to hook up with one of those waitresses at the Oyster Bar?'

'Yeah, well.' Dave nudged Barry and nodded towards Ed. 'You should have heard what she told us about *you*.'

'What?' Ed asked.

Dave shrugged. 'That would be telling, wouldn't it?'

Ed stared at him, unsure for a moment or two, before he broke into a grin and said, 'Piss off.' He reached across to push clumsily at Dave's shoulder.

'Boot's on the other foot now, mate,' Barry said, laughing.

Ed stayed leaning in and after signalling to the others to do the same, he inclined his head towards the girls at the adjacent table. 'West End's heaving with that sort on a Saturday night,' he said. 'Office girls out on the sniff.'

Barry had a good look, making no attempt to hide the fact. 'I don't think they're on the sniff for old men like you though.'

'You'd be surprised.'

'You're twenty years too old, mate.'

'I can't see any white sticks either,' Dave said. 'So I reckon you're out of luck.'

Ed flashed a sarcastic smile, then sat back shaking his head. 'You pair are unbelievable,' he said. 'You seriously telling me you'd say no, given the chance?'

'Not interested,' Barry said. 'Know which side my bread's buttered.'

'You've never played away from home?'

Barry kept shaking his head, lowered it towards his glass.

'Dave?' Ed waited. 'I mean, I know *you've* got no reason to want to . . .'

Barry flashed Ed a hard look, but Ed ignored it.

'No way,' Dave said. 'I'm a good boy.'

'*Seriously?*'

Dave looked across at the girls. One of them caught him looking and he reddened slightly before turning back and grinning at Ed.

'Well . . . I suppose it doesn't do any harm to go window-shopping now and again, does it?'

Barry laughed like he was unconvinced. Dave looked at him and Barry shook his head. Said, 'Whatever.'

'Well, the night is young,' Ed said, rubbing his hands together. 'And even if *we* aren't, some of us aren't quite dead below the waist yet. So drink up and let's move on.'

Barry looked at his watch.

Ed was already out of his seat and downing what was left of his beer. A young couple, keen to grab the table, moved up to hover alongside him and he gave them the nod.

'I can't be *too* late,' Dave said.

Ed said, 'Lightweights,' and turned towards the door.

The Imperial should only have been five minutes' walk away, though it took somewhat longer than that to negotiate the crowds thronging Leicester Square and pushing towards Piccadilly Circus. Close as it was, the pub, tucked away on a side street, was a lot quieter than the Sussex had been and despite the occasional siren outside and the roars from passing stag nights, they could communicate without shouting or the need for exaggerated hand gestures.

By ten o'clock they were five pints in apiece, though only Dave and Ed showed any real sign of it. Ed's voice had become a little louder and the Midlands accent that bit more noticeable. Dave had grown quieter, pint on pint, while the smile—which sometimes seemed knowing and sometimes wholly innocent—had become more or less permanent.

Barry just kept on drinking, his face perhaps a fraction more flushed than before. Seemingly happy enough to watch and chip in.

'So what sort of season are United going to have then, Dave?' Ed nodded to Barry, bringing him into it. 'They bought wisely, you reckon?'

'Can we talk about something else?' Dave asked.

Ed laughed and Barry helped him out. They had been ribbing Dave about his distinctly part-time support for Manchester United, picking up where they had left off at Barry and Angie's dinner party.

199

Dave seemed to take it well enough, but he had clearly run out of comebacks.

'We can always go back to talking about women,' Ed said. 'You're obviously a bit more comfortable with that.'

'What about politics or movies or something?' Dave tilted his glass towards Ed. 'What about *books*?'

Ed ignored the question, looking around the bar. 'Not quite as much talent in here, mind you.'

'You're totally cunt-struck,' Barry said. 'You know that?'

Ed seemed happy enough with the description. 'You say that like it's a bad thing.'

'How's Sue feel about it?'

'Keeps things interesting.' Ed paused, like he wanted them to think about that, then leaned in. 'I hope I don't need to remind you two that what gets said on a boys' night out stays on a boys' night out.'

Barry muttered, 'Fine with me,' and Dave nodded. 'I wonder what the girls talked about the other night,' he said.

'I think they were too busy putting the white wine away to talk about much of anything,' Ed said. 'Sue was totally hammered when she got back.'

'When was this?' Barry asked.

'Yeah, Marina was pretty pissed as well,' Dave said.

Ed grinned. 'Got lucky, did you?'

Barry shook his head, confused. 'When did the girls go out?'

'When was it?' Ed said. 'Thursday?'

'First I've heard of it,' Barry said.

'Maybe Angie couldn't make it or something,' Dave suggested. He looked at Ed and both reached simultaneously for their glasses to cover the awkward pause.

'Or maybe she's keeping secrets,' Ed said, when he'd put his glass down.

Barry looked at him. Said, 'We don't work like that.'

There was another pause.

'Anyway, you all still on for dinner next Saturday?'

'Looking forward to it,' Dave said.

'Yeah,' Barry said, quietly.

'And let's try not to spend the *whole* night talking about dead girls, shall we? Life goes on, you know?' Ed looked at Barry. 'I mean, no disrespect, but your missus seems a bit obsessed by it. Those pictures, what have you.'

'She just wanted to help, that's all.'

'I'm just saying.'

'I think I need to eat something,' Dave said. 'I didn't have time for lunch.'

'Let's have one more in here,' Ed said. 'Then we can go and get some food.'

Barry stood up to get the round in. He and Dave had been on lager all night, while Ed had been drinking Guinness. This time, Dave announced that he would have a pint of Guinness too.

'You don't need to do that,' Barry said.

'Do what?'

Barry nodded towards Ed. 'Have that just because he's having it.'

Dave reached for a beermat and began turning it over and over. His face was almost as red as Barry's. 'I fancy Guinness,' he said.

Barry took a step towards the bar and bumped into a teenager whose beer slopped on to the floor between them. Barry said, 'Oi,' and the teenager backed away, a hand raised.

Ed raised his eyebrows at Dave and said, 'Remind me not to piss him off too much, will you?'

In the Maharajah on Rupert Street, Ed said, 'I've always wanted to sleep with a black woman.'

'I didn't think you were choosy,' Barry said.

Ed ignored the comment and carried on looking at Dave. They had almost finished eating, but there was still food left in the serving dishes and fresh pints of Kingfisher in front of them. There was only one other table in the place occupied—three men in suits and ties eating in virtual silence—and the waiters hovered near the kitchen, as though waiting for all of them to leave.

'I mean, I know Marina isn't *completely* black.'

'Mixed race,' Dave said, chewing. He tore off a chunk of nan bread and dunked it in what he had left of the extra hot lamb jalfrezi he had insisted on ordering. 'Her mum's black.'

'That's the thing though. Even if it's fifty-fifty, they're always more black than white, aren't they? They never think of themselves as white.'

Dave shrugged and chewed.

'So, come on then?' Ed said.

'What?'

'You know what I'm talking about. They're supposed to be better in the sack, aren't they? More imaginative, whatever.'

'Fuck's sake,' Barry said.

'Noisier, too, that's what I've heard.'

For a few seconds, nobody said anything. The low-level Indian music that had been playing on repeat since they had arrived sounded suspiciously like a sitar version of 'When You're Smiling'. Ed had pointed this out when they sat down and he and Dave had pissed themselves laughing about it for almost a minute. Dave had been doing a lot more laughing in the last hour or so, had needed a puff from his inhaler on one occasion.

Barry had not said very much.

'Come on,' Ed said. 'Just between us . . .'

'What gets said on a boys' night out,' Barry muttered.

'Exactly.'

Dave washed down his mouthful of food with a noisy slurp of beer. He wiped his mouth with the back of his hand and sat back, grinning. He waited, enjoying the moment, then said, 'Well, what can I tell you? They're not wrong.'

'I knew it,' Ed said, clapping his hands together. 'You jammy bastard.'

Dave held up his hands. 'I'll say no more than that.'

One of the hovering waiters came to the table and, without asking if they were finished, began clearing the plates away. All the time, aside from the occasional hiccup, Dave was still smiling and nodding, pleased with himself at having revealed something so apparently impressive.

When the waiter had left, he said, 'I'll tell you something else. When that copper was interviewing us about the Sarasota business, she asked me what I thought had happened to the girl.'

'Come again?' Barry said.

'She asked my opinion.' He shrugged like it was no big deal. 'You know, what my theory was.'

'So, what is it?' Ed asked.

'That the killer took her in a car . . . pretty obvious.' He had started off brightly enough, but he paused for a few seconds after taking a deep breath and finished his speech slowly, as though determined not to stumble over his words. 'That he probably killed her straight away, because you know, that's how it usually works. Not always, of course, but more often than not. Then we just bounced a few ideas off each other . . . the possibility that there might have been more than one person involved, a man and a woman working together even. That kind of thing.'

Ed looked into his glass for a few seconds. Said, 'All a bit far-fetched if you ask me.'

'Why on earth'd you say all that?' Barry asked.

'She asked me,' Dave said.

'Why you though?' Ed asked. He smiled thinly then answered his own question. 'They probably had you pegged as a bit of a weirdo.'

Dave's smile was even thinner. 'Or someone who knew what he was talking about.'

'Exactly,' Ed said.

Barry turned in his seat. 'Why did you come out with all *that* shit?'

'Who says it's shit?' Dave said.

'You start spouting that stuff. I mean, where does that leave the rest of us?'

'It's got nothing to do with you.'

Barry puffed out his cheeks and shook his head. He looked at Ed. 'I'm done.'

'We were just talking, that's all,' Dave said. He opened his mouth to say something else, but Ed was already turning away from him, waving towards the waiters and scribbling in the air.

THIRTY-THREE

Sue had booked a hair appointment good and early. The best part of two hours to style and get rid of the grey. In the forty-five minutes reading the magazines and waiting for the colour to take, she had been able to lose herself easily in the mindless tales of celebrities' plastic surgery nightmares and reality TV tittle-tattle. Later though, her head back and the assistant stylist's fingers working rhythmically at her scalp, she had closed her eyes and suddenly found herself thinking about the girl: her body bobbing in a cage of mangrove roots, tangled in weed, moving with the current.

'Is this pressure all right for you?'

Sue had grunted a yes.

She had asked herself how accurate her imaginings were and decided that the pictures in her head were probably too . . . dreamy. There would be photographs somewhere and she even wondered if that was the sort of thing that eventually surfaced on the internet. She'd heard stories about the victims of car crashes and executions. If not, there would be descriptions out there, almost certainly. Hadn't the body been discovered by somebody out kayaking or something? He would have given a statement of course, spoken to the press too, she imagined, and the TV people. If there were, then she guessed that Angie would have tracked them down online. Would have printed them out most likely and filed them away in a big, brightly coloured ring-binder with her collection of newspaper reports and duplicates of the holiday snaps she had sent to the police.

Sue would not have been surprised to see Angie turn up later on with a bottle of wine in one hand and nicely bound copies for each of them in the other.

'Water temperature OK for you . . .?'

Now, walking from the salon to the supermarket, she told herself that her curiosity about how the girl had looked was only natural, however morbid it might sound if she voiced it. Curiosity about the whole case—the disappearance and the investigation—was only to be expected and she was certainly not judging Angie Finnegan. It was odd though, she thought, that Marina had not said too much about it. Despite believing that she was a pretty good judge of character, Sue had yet to get a handle on that woman at all.

Even when they'd been out together, after a few hours drinking and talking ten to the dozen, Sue couldn't say what she really thought of her. Even after a few glasses of wine she had not felt able to tell her about Emma. She wondered if she might feel ready to tell her tonight, to tell any of them. She would have to wait and see if the opportunity presented itself. She enjoyed telling people, ached to do it, but obviously she needed to pick her moment.

Ed . . .

Walking on, she wondered how his tennis match had gone and what kind of mood he would be in later on. She was hopeful, as he was far more relaxed at weekends. She knew why of course, knew perfectly well what he was up to during the week. She'd begun to suspect as much anyway, but when the woman two doors up had told her that Ed had been coming home an hour or two after Sue had left for work, she had quickly figured out what was happening. She didn't blame him particularly, but she was certainly not going to let on that she knew. She would wait for him to confide in her. That was what couples did, wasn't it.

Up to a point, of course.

She walked past a small parade of shops set back from the main road, trying to decide what to buy for dinner. There had to be something other than pasta she could manage. Why hadn't her mother taught her to cook, for God's sake? Why hadn't she done a lot of things, come to that?

Just shy of the supermarket entrance, she caught her reflection in a plate-glass window and stopped. She turned side on to admire her newly coloured hair. She ran fingers through it and while she stared at the blur of reflected traffic crawling past behind her, she saw the girl again.

She saw her open face and fat, wet lips.

She saw the snot-smeared face of the boy she had found crying at school a few weeks before.

Eyes filled with tears and relief.

Eyes wide and trusting.

Shaking the images away, she stepped towards the supermarket. She yanked a trolley free of its chain and marched inside. They would eat spaghetti carbonara and damn well like it.

It was a warm day with no wind, and the club was busy, even for a Saturday morning. Ed sat at the bar finishing a pint of orange juice and lemonade, thinking through the doubles match he had just lost; reliving the vital rallies, the silly points that had cost him and his partner the game. He had been over-hitting his ground strokes and been atypically indecisive at the net. He told himself it was just an off day and that his partner had not played particularly well either, but Ed knew they had lost because his mind had not really been on the game.

'Never mind, mate.'

He turned as his doubles partner came out of the shower room and walked towards the clubhouse door. Ed wasn't going to go as far as saying sorry, but he managed a shared shrug of resignation and they hastily agreed to arrange another game early the following week. When he turned back to the bar, the club manager asked him if he wanted anything else. Ed was no longer thirsty, but said, 'Sod it,' and ordered a bottle of beer.

'More like it,' the manager said.

It was good to be relaxing without that niggle of guilt he felt during the week when he found himself sitting on his backside. No more than a niggle though. What the hell else was he supposed to do, things being the way they were? Drive for an hour to Slough or Maidenhead so he could try and fail to flog a set of atlases to some sour-faced bookseller? A poxy set of medical textbooks?

'Here you go.' The manager set his bottle on the bar. 'Drown your sorrows.'

Ed blinked, then realised the man was talking about the tennis match.

He hadn't drunk anything since his night out with Dave Cullen and Barry Finnegan a week before. Since he had reeled in just before midnight, been berated by Sue for waking her up and been called a 'pisshead'. The truth was, he could not remember the last time he'd drunk so much, and booze was something he had no problem going without, so he didn't think it did any harm to have a blowout now and again. Sue probably drank more than he did, when you added it all up.

He had never been one of those drinkers blessed with the ability to forget the rubbish they came out with after one too many. Or six. Not that he hadn't meant everything he'd said that night. *In vino veritas*, all that. What he really cared about was that they hadn't *thought* he was talking rubbish.

That they thought he was a good bloke.

He'd decided, thinking back through their mini pub-crawl, that Dave was actually a pretty good bloke himself; that he wasn't quite as geeky or superior as Ed had first thought. Barry was another matter, though. What the hell was his problem? Maybe he just wasn't bright enough to keep up, but Ed didn't have time for anyone who didn't laugh at a decent joke, or wasn't able to take one. Who refused to contribute.

What gets said on a boys' night out . . .

Obviously he hadn't told Sue very much.

It was fine as it turned out, because the next morning all she'd done was make snide comments about needing to keep her voice down and how men never really talked about anything important. How she could get more out of someone she'd just met in ten minutes than Ed could get out of his oldest friend in an entire evening. You're right, he'd said. It was just football and old TV shows. He certainly hadn't told her that he'd put his size ten in it about Angie not being invited when Sue went out with Marina. And of course he hadn't said a dickie-bird about Dave's conversation with that policewoman. The various 'ideas' they had 'bounced' around. His tin-pot theories.

He didn't want to talk about that stuff. Simple as that.

He jumped when a club member he'd played with a couple of times slapped him on the back. A bumptious tosser who brought three rackets on to the court when he couldn't hit a winner if his life depended on it.

'So, how's business, Ed?'

One of those pricks who only asked so he could tell you just how well he was doing, as if the new Mercedes in the car park had not made that obvious enough.

'Yeah, not bad,' Ed said.

'Pleased to hear it.' For once, Ed was spared a detailed report on the commercial property boom and instead the prick said, 'What are you and Sue doing later? We thought we might try that new Thai place in Enfield.'

'Sorry, mate, we're having people over,' Ed said.

'Anyone I know?'

Ed resisted telling the man that they were unlikely to have any friends in common. 'Just two couples we met on holiday.'

'Uh-oh.'

'Yeah, you know how that goes.'

'Good luck with that,' the man said, pulling a face. He waited as though expecting to be offered a drink then saw someone else he was keen to impress and drifted to the other end of the bar.

209

Ed lifted up his beer. That was something else he'd meant when he was out with Barry and Dave. He definitely did not want to spend the whole evening talking about Amber-Marie Wilson. Laughing and joking one minute, murdered girls the next.

He knew it would probably be an uphill battle.

THIRTY-FOUR

Gardner caught a flight just after 8.00 a.m. and was touching down in Atlanta ninety minutes later. He waited with Patti Lee Wilson as the transport casket was carried slowly off the plane. He stood firm when she leaned against him while it was loaded into the back of the white Cadillac Statesman which had been given permission to drive on to the tarmac.

White for a child, Gardner guessed.

She did not cry. He figured that she was cried out, for the time being at least. The guy from the funeral home nodded to him before he shut the car door and drove away. They watched it leave and Gardner waited for the noise of a 747 roaring into the air from the next runway to die down before he spoke to her.

'They'll look after her now,' he said.

'Better than I ever did,' she said.

He laid a hand on her shoulder and shook his head, told her not to talk nonsense. They turned and walked back towards the terminal together. One of the mechanics working at some steps near the apron took off his cap as they walked past and Gardner gave him a small nod.

'You want to get a drink?' Patti asked. 'I want to get a drink.'

'Can we have one back at your place?' Gardner said. He reached past to open the door for her. 'There's something I need to talk to you about.'

'Fine by me,' she said. 'Liquor's cheaper at my place.'

She lived in a brown and white, two-bedroom condo in Decatur. The place was neat and clean; neater and cleaner than Gardner had expected and it shamed him a little to admit this to himself.

They sat sweating in the living room, a plastic fan creaking and clicking as it spun overhead. Each of them had a beer and Patti had poured chips into a large bowl, which sat between them on the vinyl couch.

'Air-con's playing up,' she said. 'I've got a service contract, but I'm a bit behind with it. Things got away from me these last few weeks, you know?'

'It's fine,' Gardner said. 'Beer's cold.'

She held the bottle to her forehead. 'Right.'

'A witness told us you were talking to some guy,' he said. 'A few days before Amber-Marie went missing. You remember that?'

She thought about it.

'You were outside one of the bars in the village. She was inside talking to the three British couples?'

That appeared to jog her memory. 'Right,' she said. 'Yeah, some guy.'

'Dark hair, pumped up, tattoos on his arms?'

'That's him.'

'Who was he?'

'Just some guy hitting on me,' she said. 'We were both having a cigarette and we got talking, that was all.' She drank. 'You know, tell you the truth, I might actually have been hitting on *him*.'

'Did you see him again?'

'No.'

'Did you tell him where you were staying?'

'I don't think so,' she said. 'I mean I might have done.'

'OK, so do you think he might have seen Amber-Marie?'

212

She shrugged. 'I guess it's possible. I can't remember if she was still with me when we got talking. I can't say for sure.' She looked at him. 'You think he might have been the one?'

'I'm not saying that.'

'But he might have been, right?'

'We have to look at every possibility,' Gardner said. He could see from her pained expression that she was already thinking the man with tattoos *was* the one. That her attempt to pick up a good-looking stranger on the street had led directly to her daughter's abduction and murder. Confirming what she already believed; that it was all her fault.

Gardner's cell buzzed in his jacket pocket and he took it out. There was no number displayed.

He flipped it open and gave his name.

When the caller had identified herself, Gardner said, 'How'd you get this number?'

'Your office gave it to me,' Jenny Quinlan said.

Silently cursing Whitlow or whoever else had passed on his cellphone number, Gardner pressed the handset to his chest and told Patti that he needed to take the call. He told her a second time. Her face still creased with unpleasant thoughts, she waved a hand and told him to go ahead. He stepped outside the door into a front yard that was irregularly divided into patches of dried mud and crabgrass. There was a rusty swing in the far corner. On the sidewalk opposite, a boy on a bike was being pulled along by a toffee-coloured retriever.

'I'm a little busy,' he told Quinlan.

'Yes, of course.'

'So you'll need to be quick.'

'Well I sent you the interview reports a week ago and I hadn't heard anything back, so . . .'

'This is not the only case I'm working, you know.'

'You didn't get back to me, that's all.'

'I would have done so if I'd needed to,' Gardner said. He heard the intake of breath and immediately felt bad for snapping. 'The department budget doesn't stretch to too many transatlantic phone calls.'

213

She laughed rather more than was necessary. 'I know what that's like,' she said. 'We haven't even got a kettle that works properly in the Incident Room. The computers are steam-powered!'

Gardner breathed in. Hot asphalt and a whiff of dog-shit. 'So . . .'

'So, have you had a chance to follow up on anything I told you about?'

'As it happens, I'm doing that right now.'

'Oh, how's it going?' Her voice was a little higher suddenly. 'Anything useful? Any . . . breaks?'

'Not as yet, I'm afraid.' He pressed on quickly, before the woman could ask any more pointless questions. 'But we will follow up on anything we think worth following up, OK?'

'Well, you know where I am,' she said.

'I know where you are.' Gardner snapped the phone shut and slipped it back into his pocket. Cute accent or not, the woman was fast becoming a royal pain in the ass, and on reflection he wished he had been a little tougher on her.

When he came back inside, Patti was sitting on the couch with a fresh beer. She reached down to the side of the couch for another bottle and held it towards him. He could feel a headache kicking in and did not want another, but he took it anyway.

'You staying for the funeral?' she asked.

Gardner picked at the label on his bottle.

'You're welcome to stay over here.'

'I'd like to,' he lied. 'I really have to get back.'

She raised her arms and barked out a dry laugh. Gardner could see that she wasn't cried out at all. 'Suddenly, I've got a spare room.'

THIRTY-FIVE

It wasn't as though she *never* worked on Saturdays. Still, Jenny had decided it would not be a good idea to let on that today she was actually calling from home, on her own time. On her own dime, as he might have said.

She lay back on her bed, thinking things through.

That crack about transatlantic phone calls. Laughing and joking with her like any other colleague. Maybe a bit flirty too, if that wasn't her imagination running riot with her.

'He looks sod all like Denzel Washington,' Steph had said, when Jenny had shown her Gardner's picture. 'Well, maybe if Denzel Washington had spent a fortnight eating nothing but doughnuts.'

'He's got this amazing voice.'

'You can't shag a voice . . .'

It was incredible timing, Jenny thought, to have called just when he was running down one of the leads she had given him. He clearly hadn't wanted to say too much about it though, so maybe he'd been unable to speak freely. Perhaps he'd been talking to someone he didn't want listening in on their conversation.

Cop talk.

She flicked the television on, then flopped back on to the bed, trying to decide what to do with the rest of her Saturday. Steph was busy, but that didn't matter. She might go and see a film, she thought, or there were two or three novels she'd picked up and put down again. She might even just stay in and watch whatever the hell she wanted on TV, which was after all one of the advantages of being single. Everyone was always banging on about being with somebody, but that didn't always turn out for the best, did it, even when you stayed together? Thinking about the likes of the Finnegans and the Dunnings and that other weird pair, Jenny decided that being in a couple was not all it was cracked up to be.

You could have way more fun on your own.

THIRTY-SIX

Behind the counter, Devon or Deron poured out hot milk and said, 'You're usually in a bit earlier than this.'

Dave said, 'Yeah, my girlfriend normally does the morning class at the theatre.' He pointed back towards the Brixton Road. 'She's doing something a bit different today, that's all.'

'She an actress or something?'

'Trying to be.'

'Have I seen her in anything?'

'She's just starting out,' Dave said. 'It's a tough business to get into.'

The barista nodded. 'I'm really a guitarist . . .'

Dave took his coffee across to a table in the window and spread out his *Guardian*. Having admitted defeat with the espresso, he had decided to persevere a little longer with broadsheet newspapers.

He turned the pages slowly.

He should probably have just said, 'Yes,' to the bloke behind the counter and not 'Trying to be,' but still, asking if he'd seen her in anything after that was pretty stupid. The truth was, he was never very comfortable talking about Marina to anyone. He'd shown Kevin a picture at work, of course, because he'd wanted him to know how gorgeous she was, but he tried to avoid any further discussion. He wanted to keep his private life private.

He wanted to keep her to himself.

He took a sip of coffee and felt his chest tighten as he remembered some of the things he'd said when he was out with Ed and Barry. Things about him and Marina, personal stuff. He was not a drinker. He was only grateful that he hadn't blurted out anything else, that he hadn't said too much. When Marina had asked how the evening had been, Dave had told her that Ed had been showing off as usual, that Barry had been a bit surly. She had nodded as though expecting nothing else, still she knew how much he'd been drinking so she had been wearing the expression that clouded her face if there was even a fraction of doubt. Wanting to make sure there was ground he had not been stupid enough to cover. Up close, looking him in the eye and checking for a reaction.

'Don't be silly,' he had told her. 'They're idiots. I just listened to them talk rubbish all night.'

In spite of himself, he was still wondering what Ed had meant in the Indian restaurant. Calling him a weirdo, saying 'exactly' the way he had. Dave had struggled to keep his anger in check, to control his breathing, but he desperately wanted to know what Ed Dunning thought of him; what all of them said about him and Marina behind their backs. Obviously nobody ever really knew what anyone else was thinking and, on balance, that was probably a good thing. Like that film where the hero tells everyone exactly what's on his mind and his life falls apart very bloody quickly. But when it came to what people said and what they actually thought, Dave considered himself more finely attuned to that everyday deceit than other people. More of an expert. He told himself that he could see the yawning gap between the public and the private face; the breadth and the blackness of it.

He drank his coffee, remembering a line from some book or film he'd seen somewhere.

Who knows what evil lurks in men's hearts?

He smiled, thinking that in Ed Dunning's case there was probably nothing lurking apart from the next shit joke and something about the size of a woman's tits.

Devon—yes he was sure it was Devon—wandered across and put a plate down in front of him. 'Cheesecake,' he said. 'On the house because you're a good customer. My sister makes it . . .'

Dave said thanks and helped himself to a forkful. Sweet as it was, a sour taste came up in his throat as he thought about dinner at the Dunnings' place that evening.

Smiling and trying to keep that gap nice and wide. Then Ed making some crack about what he and Marina got up to in bed.

The hell there would be to pay.

Marina shifted in the hard seat of the plastic chair. She crossed her legs, uncrossed them again. She held on to the sides of the chair.

Philip was looking up at her from the front row of the auditorium. 'This exercise is called the "hot seat",' he said. 'It's about staying in character, no matter what's thrown at you . . . but it's also about using what's inside you, tapping into your own feelings so that you can pass them on to your character. You OK with that?'

Marina said that she was.

'I've been working on a character for you—'

'What's she called?'

He waved the question away. 'We'll find out. It's who she *is* that matters, what she's feeling. The way things are shaping up in my head, there's definitely going to be a sadness in her and maybe that's because of something I see in you, and that's what I want to get to this afternoon. You ready? You clear how this works?'

She nodded.

Philip took a few seconds, then sat back and folded his arms. 'What's your name?'

'Kelly,' Marina said, quickly.

'You live round here?'

'Camberwell.'

'And what do you do for a living?'

'I'm a sex worker,' she said. She gave her character a far more pronounced London accent than she had herself. She thought it sounded pretty good. 'A prostitute.'

He nodded, thought about it. 'Are you happy doing that?'

'Happy as you can be.'

'What's that mean?'

'What does "happy" mean anyway?'

'I think *I'm* pretty happy . . .'

'Well, I wouldn't still be tossing off old men if I won the lottery tomorrow, put it that way.' She was thrilled to see him smile at that and had to control the urge to smile herself.

'You got any kids?'

'A boy and a girl.' She was trying to think of names when he asked the next question.

'You doing this for them, Kelly?'

'Yeah, and to pay for what I need.'

'You mean drugs.'

'Would *you* do this unless you were completely out of it?'

He smiled again and held up his hand. 'OK, that's great, now stay in character please, hold on to that and stay focused, all right.'

She nodded. She was still Kelly. She imagined herself walking up to the side of a car, leaning down to the window. The excitement, the fear . . .

'I love the way she's making jokes to mask the sadness I was talking about,' he said. 'That's great. But I want to go deeper. I want to *expose* it. Once we've done that we can put it back in its box, but we need to bring it out into the light and see it for what it is . . .'

She had a short leather skirt on, a denim jacket, fuck-me heels.

'Just close your eyes and get centred,' Philip said. 'I want you to think of something that makes you sad . . . maybe it makes you angry . . . just focus on whatever that is. If it's a person, focus on his face, on every detail you can remember . . .'

She shook her head, but her very reluctance seemed to make Philip even more excited. He stood up and his voice moved from a quasi-hypnotic drone to something rather harsher.

'Focus on it. *Use* it . . .'

It was easy. Uncle Ian. Her dad's best friend who was not really an uncle and who was not the man her father thought he was. The smell of fags and barley wine on him and the turn of her stomach and the blankets pulled up tight to her chin when the door squeaked and the light spilled into her bedroom and Uncle Ian stepped inside.

Her breath caught.

Philip said something but she couldn't make it out. He raised his voice and said, 'Tell me where you are?'

Light blue wallpaper with small yellow flowers on it. The lamp with a tear in its shade. A shelf above her bed with all her books and animals and a metal money-bank like a miniature red pillar box.

She said, 'I don't want to.'

'Tell me who's there, Kelly.'

She wasn't Kelly and she couldn't do this. Why was he making her do this? What was wrong with what she'd been doing? Making things up and thinking about how she looked and doing the London accent. That was good, wasn't it? That felt like acting.

She couldn't do this. She couldn't do this . . .

Dave was the only person she had ever told. It was what had brought them together in the first place. That shared experience. She remembered him finding her crying in the corner at that stupid party. Thinking she was drunk until they'd started talking and it had all come pouring out of her. He'd made it clear that he understood, that he knew what she had gone through. He'd told her that none of it was her fault, none of it.

They had talked all night and then, as usual, she'd fucked the pain away.

221

She opened her eyes. Philip was walking towards the stage and rummaging in his pocket.

He thrust a tissue towards her and said, 'Let it out, OK. It's all useful. Come on, let's go and talk about it.'

In the dressing room, Philip produced a tobacco tin and took out a ready-rolled joint. 'Do you want some of this?' he asked.

'People will smell it,' she said.

He lit the joint. 'I'm not scared of a few geriatric tap dancers.'

It was strong stuff—skunk, he told her—and her head was starting to spin after just a couple of tokes. Philip was waving his arms and talking about the play he was writing for them all, how the part he had in mind for her was definitely the most important.

She nodded along and tried to follow what he was saying.

At some point he started talking about his wife and kids. He said something about how his students were like children, like older children and how he hated to see them upset.

Then he leaned in to kiss her, and she let him.

THIRTY-SEVEN

Barry had started to lose it from the moment his ex-wife picked up the phone. Something to do with just hearing her voice, like those dogs in that experiment, didn't matter what sort of mood she was in. Still, better her than that arsehole accountant she was shacked up with, who cycled everywhere and had bought his son a fucking Chelsea strip for crying out loud. Now he *really* knew how to wind Barry up.

Hiya, Barry. How's it hanging, mate? Let me put her on . . .

Not that winding him up was particularly difficult these days. He wasn't stupid, he knew he'd been flying off the handle a lot lately, that almost anything was liable to set him off.

Like walking on eggshells, Angie kept saying.

Two minutes, that's all the time the miserable bitch had given him on the phone with Nick. Barely time to get beyond hello, for Christ's sake. 'Why d'you keep doing this?' he asked. 'Why can't I talk to my own son on the phone for more than two bloody minutes?'

'He's got homework to do,' she said.

'Come on, it's Saturday.' She said nothing. 'I've got rights.'

'You've got no rights,' she said.

He recognised the signs, but as per usual, by the time he did it was too late to do anything about it. The prickle of sweat across his chest, the ache in his jaw from grinding his teeth.

He had all but ground the buggers to dust that night on the piss with Ed the smartarse and Dave the dickhead. It was general things, like the fact that he was actually younger than Ed Dunning but somehow felt years older. The way Ed and Dave had shared looks, like he wasn't quite bright enough to appreciate their double act as much as he should. More specific stuff too, like Ed's pathetic leering at anything with knockers and thinking he was Mr Entertainment, or Dave sucking up to him like the weedy kid in the playground and talking about what had happened back in Florida when he really didn't know the first thing about it.

Neither of them would know a solid piece of four-by-two from the holes in their arses. Neither of them knew how smart he was and *neither* of them had the first idea what had happened to that girl.

His ex-wife was talking. Lecturing him. He had to concentrate to make it out above the hiss that might have been on the line or in his head.

'I need to talk to you about maintenance,' she said.

The prickle of sweat was spreading. 'Look, I know.'

'You're behind and I don't want to go to my solicitor about it, but I will if I have to.'

'You don't have to do that.'

'So, don't make me.'

Why the hell was she being like this? Why was everybody doing their level best to screw his life up? He felt like he was being punched and punched.

'We've lost a couple of big jobs lately,' he said. 'That's all.'

'Not my problem, Barry.'

'Things'll pick up.' He was squeezing the phone so hard that his knuckles had whitened and his arm was locked solid. 'I just need—'

'You could get a loan,' she said.

'Come on.'

'Borrow some cash off your brother.'

'Why don't you—?'

'He's always been better than you at managing his money.'

'. . . just go and fuck yourself!'

She hung up and he shouted out the last two words again as he smashed the phone back on to its cradle.

Angie had called up to tell him that tea was ready and was just setting his Arsenal mug on the counter when Barry came into the kitchen.

'What the hell have you done to yourself?' she asked.

He looked down at his fist and tightened the bloodied wad of toilet paper that was wrapped around it. 'Stupid,' he said. 'I broke one of the windows in the bedroom.'

'You all right, love?'

'I cut myself trying to board it up, that's all.'

Angie passed Barry his tea and told him it didn't matter. She did not need to listen to some half-arsed explanation. She knew that he had gone upstairs to phone his ex.

'I'll get one of the lads to come round and sort it out tomorrow,' he said.

They sat at the island and drank their tea. Angie fetched the biscuit barrel and they both dug in.

'I've still got a good mind not to go tonight,' Angie said.

Barry dunked his biscuit. 'Suits me.'

'I mean, I almost certainly wouldn't have gone for that stupid drink anyway, I've got too much to do with the kids, but it's nice to be asked, isn't it? Especially when I was the one that got the ball rolling, when it was me that got everyone together in the first place. Plain bloody rude, that's what it is.'

'Maybe you missed an email or something,' Barry suggested.

She shook her head. She hadn't missed anything. It was no great mystery to her because she'd been through the same thing plenty of times at school and knew exactly what was going on. The cool, skinny bitches who did not want to be seen hanging around with the fat girl. Even back then, much as she had cried about it and wished that things were different, she had felt a small, warm glow of satisfaction, sitting on her own in the corner of the playground or playing on her own. She knew that she was better than them because she was nicer. She would not grow up and hate herself because of the way she had behaved.

She had comforted herself with that thought back then, sitting at the edge of the playing field or bouncing a ball alone and thinking of all the horrible things she wanted to do to them.

'Well, stuff them,' she said.

Barry let out a long sigh. 'I wish I hadn't mentioned it now . . .'

'No. Stuff them because we *are* going to go and *we'll* be the ones with the moral high ground, right, love? We can sit there and look at their smug faces and they won't know that we know.'

'Well, they'll probably work out that I've told you.'

'They won't know for certain though, will they?' Angie said, smiling. 'And it suits me just fine to let them think they've got away with it.'

'Whatever,' Barry said.

When the tea was finished, Angie told Barry to put the biscuit tin away, to 'put a padlock on the bloody thing'. She watched him slouch across to the cupboard; the small steps and the rounded shoulders like he was carrying the weight of the world, and said, 'You really don't want to go tonight, do you?'

'They're not our sort, are they, Ange? Or at least . . . they don't think we're their sort.'

'I thought you had an OK time,' Angie said. 'When you went out with Ed and Dave. I mean, I know Ed can be a bit of a pillock . . .'

'It's Dave I really can't work out,' Barry said. 'Who the hell he is, I mean.' He came back to the central island and sat down. 'It's like he's just trying to please everyone or something, like he . . . adapts. He's Jack the Lad with Ed, talking about birds or whatever, "I'll have what he's having," all that. Then with his missus he's all meek and sensitive. Like whatever you call it . . . a new man.'

Angie nodded. She had noticed something similar herself, thought Marina was exactly the same, that the two of them were probably very well matched. 'I know, but isn't everyone a bit like that? Trying to fit in.'

'Not me, mate,' Barry said. He slapped his hand on the granite. 'What you see is what you get.'

'Unfortunately.'

'What?'

'I'm joking,' Angie said, reaching across to rub the back of his hand.

And she was. She knew that her silly sod of an old man would do almost anything for a quiet life and yes, there were certainly things she would change, top of the list being lengthening that short fuse of his. But as much as she believed anything, Angie believed that Barry was fundamentally honest and decent.

Whatever that stupid cow of a copper might have thought.

THE SECOND
DINNER

THIRTY-EIGHT

There were the usual pleasantries exchanged at the Dunnings' front door. Kisses were given, some of which actually made contact with skin. Wine and flowers were handed over and gratefully received. The visitors made admiring comments about the hallway's original features: the black and white Victorian tiles on the floor; the elaborate coving; the dado rail.

Barry nodded and said, 'You'd be amazed how many times people have paid me to rip stuff like this out.'

'People are idiots,' Ed said.

'Barry's got a nice little sideline selling that stuff on to reclamation yards,' Angie said. 'Haven't you, love?'

They moved through to a sitting room that was actually two rooms divided by floor-to-ceiling doors, which had been opened for the evening. The dining table had been laid at the end of the room that was nearest the garden.

'This is gorgeous,' Marina said.

Sue shook her head. 'Thanks, but I'd love to have a kitchen that was big enough to eat in,' she said. 'One of these days we might be able to get something like Barry and Angie have got.'

'Well you know where to come,' Angie said, nudging Barry.

Dave looked at Ed. 'I reckon you need to sell a few more books.'

Ed said nothing and instead made a show of opening a bottle of Cava while Sue fetched glasses. Angie did not see the label and said, 'Blimey, champagne. Someone's pushing the boat out.'

Marina poked Dave in the side and said, 'You're driving . . .'

While the glasses were filled, they talked about their respective journeys to Southgate. Though the M23 had been busy, Angie and Barry had still managed to get there from Crawley in about the same time as Marina and Dave had driven up from Forest Hill.

'I don't get into London very often,' Angie said. She exchanged a look with Barry. 'I always forget how bad the traffic is.'

They moaned about London for a while. It was dirty and expensive and the crime had reached ridiculous proportions. Sue and Ed tried to defend their decision to live where they did, but admitted to having been burgled three times in five years. Marina and Dave had only been done once, but it had been messy, Marina said, pulling a face.

'Why do people do that?' Ed asked. 'Why don't they just take what they want then bugger off and buy their drugs? Why do they have to piss on your bed, or whatever?'

'Maybe they're on drugs when they do it,' Marina said.

'Still, not as bad as in America,' Angie said. 'All that shooting and what have you.'

They all nodded, looked at their glasses.

What have you . . .

'To good friends,' Ed said, raising his glass.

They drank and there were a few seconds of awkward silence afterwards.

'So, what's the latest?' Sue asked.

Angie saw that Sue was looking at her and pointed at herself. 'Me?'

'I just thought you were looking out for news on the internet. We count on you to keep us up to date.'

'Oh . . . well, nothing new,' Angie said.

'And we've not heard any more from that woman,' Dave said. 'Have you? What was her name?'

Angie, Barry and Sue shook their heads.

'Quinlan,' Ed said.

'Oh well, it looks like we're all off the hook,' Angie said, laughing.

Marina had drifted across to the built-in bookshelves either side of the fireplace and was scanning the titles, her head cocked. 'Dave and I would love to get somewhere a bit more like this,' she said. She turned back to Sue with a cheeky grin. 'Any chance we could see the rest of the place?'

'Help yourself,' Sue said. 'I just need to keep an eye on dinner.'

'You sure?'

'It's nothing fancy by the way. Not in Angie's league.'

'I'm sure it'll be lovely,' Angie said.

'I'll do it,' Ed said. His hand was on Sue's backside. 'Even I can manage to chuck some spaghetti in a pan.' He gave her a little push towards the door. 'You show Marina and Angie upstairs.'

In the kitchen, Dave and Barry stood with their drinks watching Ed grate cheese and chop bacon.

'We'll make a new man of you yet,' Dave said.

Barry laughed, then said, 'I told Angie about the girls' night out. The one she wasn't invited to.'

Ed stood there with the knife in his hand. 'Nothing to do with me, mate.'

'I know. I just thought you should know that she knows.'

'Great.' Ed went back to his chopping.

'She won't say anything.' Barry stepped closer to him. 'You know, she's got better things to worry about. I mean obviously she's *far* too busy on the internet all day long.'

Ed turned round again. Looked at Dave.

'I don't think Sue meant anything by that,' Dave said.

Barry was still looking at Ed. 'Well, it sounded to me like she was suggesting Angie sits there glued to the internet like some sad old mare, looking for stuff about dead girls or whatever because it's so much more interesting than the life she's got at home. You know, that's what it sounded like . . .'

'She didn't mean that,' Ed said.

'I definitely didn't get that impression,' Dave said.

'Sue hasn't got a bad bone in her body,' Ed said. 'And trust me, I've tried to find it.'

'*I* thought she was trying to be nice,' Dave said.

Barry downed what was left of his wine. He nodded slowly and said, 'Yeah, sorry. Not had a great day, that's all.'

Dave pointed at the plaster on Barry's hand. 'Yeah, what the hell have you been doing to yourself?'

'Good question.' Ed wiped his hands on the back of his jeans. 'My money's on some sort of extreme wanking accident.'

Barry's spluttered laughter was all the more explosive as he was clearly doing his best not to react. He gave Ed a thumbs-up and asked if he could have a beer.

The girls were in Sue and Ed's bedroom.

Marina and Angie made it clear how much they admired the arrangement of cushions on the bed and the painted shutters at the window. They both said how much they adored the small walk-in wardrobe; Ed's shirts all hung in a row and arranged by colour, Sue's bags and shoes laid out neatly on shelves.

They walked across to study a display of framed photographs arranged on a dressing table. There were pictures of two older couples they presumed were Ed and Sue's parents. There were pictures of Ed posing with a trophy in his tennis gear, of Sue and a group of children in uniform. There were several of Ed on beaches or lounging in a sunny garden, showing off the body they had got used to seeing around the pool at the Pelican Palms Resort.

'Lovely photos,' Angie said.

Behind them, Sue opened a drawer in her bedside table and when Marina and Angie turned around, she was holding a small silver frame with another photograph inside.

She passed it to Marina.

A young girl with long blonde hair and an awkward smile.

'That's Emma,' Sue said. 'My daughter.'

They both looked at her, eyes fixed as though knowing they had to avoid looking at one another. 'I didn't know you had any children,' Angie said.

'She died,' Sue said. Nice and simple. 'Six years ago . . . nearly seven. She was thirteen.'

'God, I'm sorry,' Marina said.

'There's no need.'

Angie shook her head. 'How . . .?'

'Leukaemia.' Sue saw Angie look past her at the drawer from which she had taken the picture. 'Ed can't bear having any photos around.' She sat down on the edge of the bed. 'I think . . . for some people a photo reminds them of what they had, but for others . . . for Ed, it's all about what they've lost. He still can't come to terms with it, not really. That's why he breezes through life telling his stupid jokes and showing off, but he still wakes up in tears sometimes. Or I hear him, from another room. They were very close. That whole daddy–daughter thing . . .'

Angie sat down on the bed beside her. 'Did you not try and have any more kids?'

'Yes, we tried.' Nice and simple again. 'But you take what's given you, don't you.' She took the photograph back from Marina and looked at it. 'She was really sporty, just like Ed, and outgoing. I know no parent ever says anything bad about their own child. You never hear anyone saying, "She was thick as a plank" or whatever, but I honestly believe she was a special kid.'

'I'm sure she was,' Angie said.

'Maybe it's the special ones that get taken early.' She turned and stared at Angie, serious. 'Don't waste a day with your kids, not even a second.' She glanced up at Marina. 'You too, because I know that you and Dave are going to have some.' She sniffed. 'God, look at me. I haven't cried over Emma for ages . . .'

She stood up, placed the picture carefully back in the drawer and took a tissue from a box on top of the bedside table. 'Please don't say anything to Ed.'

'Don't be daft,' Marina said.

She hugged each of them and said, 'I'm really glad we were all there at the same time. In Florida, I mean. I think we were *so* lucky. You never know, do you, when you meet people like that, on holiday. It's a lottery, isn't it?' She laughed and said, 'They might turn out to be your worst nightmare.' She looked from one to the other then nodded and reached for the door. 'Right, come on. Let's go and see what kind of a pig's ear Ed's made of dinner.'

The spaghetti carbonara was a big hit and there were cheers when Sue brought dessert out.

'I bloody love tiramisu,' Marina said. 'Not too good for my waistline, mind you, but what the hell.' She smiled when Dave leaned across and began to stroke the back of her neck.

'Before anyone asks, it's from the supermarket,' Sue said. She began serving it into bowls. 'I put it into this dish and I *thought* about lying, but I'm not sure I'd have got away with it.'

'I wouldn't have said anything anyway,' Angie said.

'It literally means "pick me up",' Dave announced, taking his bowl.

'What?' Barry asked.

'In Italian. That's what "tiramisu" means. I think it's because of the booze, which is usually Marsala wine, but you can also use rum or cognac.'

'Where d'you learn all this stuff?'

'I don't know.' Dave started eating. 'Just know it.'

There were grunts of approval as everyone tucked in. Ed was busy refilling glasses where needed. They had already put away three bottles of wine and this despite the fact that Sue and Dave were barely drinking. They began talking about a sex scandal involving a politician who had resigned to spend more time with his family. Ed said that was the excuse they always gave.

'Maybe it's true,' Marina said.

'No smoke without fire,' Ed said.

Sue got up to fetch another bottle and, as she passed his chair, Ed slid an arm around her waist and asked her to see if she could dig out 'a cheeky little number' from the 'cellar'.

That made Angie laugh. 'I like cheeky numbers,' she said.

Barry had been staring at Dave ever since the lecture on Italian cuisine and language. 'Come on then. Why don't you tell everyone what you told that copper?'

'Oh, come on, mate,' Ed said. 'We don't want to get into all that.'

'Seeing as you seem to know so much,' Barry said.

'All what?' Angie asked.

'Oh, Dave here has got all these theories about what happened to that girl, what the killer did to her, all that.'

'I never talked about anything like that,' Dave said.

'He really didn't,' Marina said.

Ed pushed his empty bowl away and threw up his hands. 'Why can't we just stick with the pervy politician?'

'What do you mean, talking to that copper?' Angie asked.

'He reckons she was asking him what he thought,' Barry said. 'Like he was some kind of police consultant or something.'

'Go on then,' Angie said.

'Please don't get him started on all that.' Marina shook her head.

'I'd like to hear it.'

'I just said . . .' Dave put his spoon down. 'I just said that I thought she was abducted in a car and that she was probably killed quickly.'

'Why quickly?' Angie asked.

'It's more likely, that's all.'

Sue came back in with the wine. 'What have I missed?'

Ed nodded to Dave. 'Detective Dave's on the case,' he said. 'Giving us his theories.'

'They're talking about Amber-Marie,' Angie said, as Sue sat down.

'All right then,' Sue said.

'So, why wouldn't he keep her for a while?' Ed asked. 'You know, have some fun with her?'

Marina said, '*Fun?*'

Ed shrugged. 'I'm just trying to think like the killer.' Sue looked at him and he pointed at Dave. 'Listen, he started this.'

'Even so,' Sue said.

'I'll do what I want,' Ed said. 'All right?'

Sue smiled.

'I never suggested talking about this,' Dave said. 'I'm perfectly happy not to.'

Angie leaned towards him. Said, 'Isn't it usually some kind of sex thing?'

'The police could tell,' Barry said. 'DNA or whatever.'

'No.' Dave shook his head. 'She was in the water for weeks, so there wouldn't have been any forensic evidence worth talking about.'

'Surely they could get something,' Angie said. 'Like on CSI, I mean they've got all this amazing equipment these days, haven't they?'

'That's just a TV show,' Dave said. 'All that time in the water, there wouldn't have been much of her worth testing. You'd be amazed at what water can do to a body, what it looks like afterwards. Plus there's all the wildlife out there. Crabs and possums and all that. Insects and scavengers helping themselves to what was left of her.' He saw the look on Marina's face. 'They asked me . . .'

'So, if it wasn't sexual,' Sue said, 'why was she taken? What was the motive?'

Dave shrugged. 'Sixty-four-thousand-dollar question.'

'What's that in English money?' Ed asked, grinning. 'About forty grand?'

'Not knowing the motive's what makes him difficult to catch,' Dave said.

'So, is he a serial killer then?' Angie asked. 'Somebody who's done this thing before?'

'I reckon so.' Dave sniffed. 'And somebody who's likely to do it again.'

'He'll make a mistake,' Marina said. 'They always do.'

Dave shook his head again. 'Yeah, in films, but there's loads who never get caught or else get away with it for years. It's always the ones you least expect, as well. Your best mate or the bloke next door who looks like he wouldn't say boo to a goose.'

Angie gave a theatrical shudder. 'Makes you think, doesn't it? I mean, nobody knows anyone really, do they?'

'I know one thing,' Ed said. He turned towards Sue. 'Somebody's going to get a smacked backside if they don't go and put a pot of coffee on.'

'Your wish is my command,' Sue said, pushing her chair back. 'Anybody else?'

'We should hit the road,' Dave said.

'Actually, I wouldn't mind a coffee,' Marina said. 'D'you mind, babe?'

'Any chance of a cappuccino?' Angie asked.

'Sorry, we keep meaning to get one of those bloody machines,' Sue said.

Ed looked at Sue, like it was all her fault. 'Shame, I fancy one of those too.'

'Never mind,' Angie said. 'If you can find me a straw, I'll blow bubbles into it for you.'

'You hear that, Barry?' Ed said. 'Your wife's offering to give me a blow job.'

Barry's spoon clattered into his bowl so loudly that Marina jumped a little and let out a gasp. He looked at Ed for a few seconds, then pushed his chair back hard and stood up fast. Ed flinched as Barry lunged towards him, and managed a weak laugh when Barry did no more than playfully slap him on the cheek.

'Bloody hell,' Ed said, when he had recovered himself. He was laughing a little more now. 'I thought he was going to deck me.'

Barry smiled. Said, 'I still might.'

'You see?' Angie said. 'What did I tell you? Nobody really knows anyone.'

THIRTY-NINE

Jeff Gardner called his wife from a motel near Hartsfield-Jackson airport in Atlanta.

'How was it?' she asked.

'She did pretty well, considering,' Gardner said.

'That's good.'

'I know she's putting on a show though.'

'Of course. I can't imagine . . .'

Gardner did not tell his wife that *he* could. Because he'd stood sweating on that hot tarmac as the casket had been lifted down from the hold and imagined that it was his little girl inside. *Their* little girl. He did not tell her that he had a pretty good idea what that hole inside yourself felt like when you lost a child. That for Patti Lee Wilson it seemed as though she would never be a complete person again, as though every time she laughed or talked about something ordinary it would be no more than a trick she had taught herself.

'Wait, shouldn't you be on the plane already?'

'She wants me to stay for the funeral tomorrow,' he said.

'Oh.'

'I told her I needed to get back.'

'Right, we're supposed to be seeing my mom and dad tonight.'

'I think I should though,' he said. 'Stay, I mean.'

Michelle said nothing.

'I've found a cheap place near the airport and there's a flight I can get right after the service. Honey . . .?'

Michelle said OK, and that she understood, but he knew that she really didn't. He asked about their daughter and his wife's voice was colourless when she told him that she was doing fine. She asked, 'Who's going to read her the tiger story tonight?'

'Look, I'm sorry.'

'You know she's only happy if you do it.'

'It's one night.'

'I can't do all the voices the way you can.'

Gardner did not know if there had been a story Patti Lee had liked to read for Amber-Marie, if she had done voices. But there would have been rituals and shared moments, silly things that the woman would certainly be thinking about the following day when she finally said goodbye.

'I need to be there,' he said.

'You're not her friend, Jeff.'

'For me as much as her, OK? I feel like I've let her down.'

'That's ridiculous.'

'I think she's been let down too many times in her life,' he said. 'And this is something I can do. It's really not such a big deal, we can rearrange with your parents . . .' He told her that he loved her and to give his little girl a big kiss. He told her that he would probably get something to eat at the motel and that he would call her in the morning.

He said, 'We've got a lot to be thankful for.'

When he had hung up, he lay back on the thin mattress and turned the pages of the laminated motel services guide. Thinking about trying to find a decent bar and the look on Patti Lee Wilson's face when he told her that he would be coming to the funeral.

241

'Appreciate it,' she said. 'Really, I do.'

The decision made, he had taken another beer from her and they had talked for another hour or so. From what she told him, just having one more person inside that little church was going to make a real difference.

In the end, Jenny had decided to stay in. Her flatmate was out on the razzle which made the decision easier, but she was happy enough with a few glasses of wine and the TV, even though there had been nothing on but reality shows and chick-flicks and she had eaten rather more of what was in the fridge than she would have liked.

A lot more, in fact.

She got into bed with one of those crime novels whose disregard for even the most basic elements of police procedure drove her crazy. She was keeping a note of all the inaccuracies and one day she fully intended to contact the writer and let him know. After only ten minutes of reading, her eyes felt scratchy and she had read the same paragraph three times, so she turned off the light.

She lay there, struggling to get comfortable and unable to sleep despite her exhaustion, knowing that her flatmate would probably wake her up when she came back in. Cackling with girlfriends or with some horny junior doctor.

They were what, five hours behind in Florida? She imagined Detective Jeff Gardner getting home from work about now. Taking off his gun and settling down to dinner with his wife.

Was he married?

For a few moments she considered getting up to see if she could find any clues on the internet. Perhaps if she blew up that picture she had found, she might be able to see if there was a wedding ring or not.

She could imagine what Steph would say, and stayed where she was.

If he *was* married, she wondered if he had mentioned her to his wife. She wondered if he had bothered looking *her* up; he would probably have done so out of curiosity if nothing else.

She finally drifted away, asking herself if there were any pictures of her floating around out there in cyberspace, and when she was woken by music from the living room, a glance at her bedside clock told her that she had only been asleep for forty minutes.

She listened. Mumford & Sons . . . laughter . . . the low notes of a man's voice.

The horny junior doctor.

Bitch!

FORTY

They were both well over the limit, but as Angie had drunk marginally less than Barry, she had been the one to take the keys to the Range Rover when they left the Dunnings' in Southgate. Despite Barry's insistence that driving slowly was even more suspicious than weaving all over the road, she stuck to a steady sixty miles an hour, even on an all-but-deserted stretch of the M25.

When he wasn't moaning about how long the drive home was taking, he was bitching about the last few hours he was 'never going to get back'.

'There's definitely something off about that pair,' he said.

'Which pair are we talking about?'

'Yeah, well, could be either of them, but I was talking about Sue and Ed.'

'Go on . . .'

'Did you notice that when he told her off . . . I can't remember what it was about exactly, but she seemed to *like* it. And all that slapping her on the arse.' He stared out of the window. 'You reckon they might be into, what do you call it, S&M? Whips and chains and all that?'

'I never had her down as the kinky sort,' Angie said. 'It's like I said back there—'

'Do you reckon he puts a dog collar on her?'

'Haven't got a clue,' Angie said. 'Who knows what people get up to when the bedroom door closes?'

Barry said nothing for a while and Angie knew she had said the wrong thing. After all, aside from nodding off with a good book and some heavy snoring, there was nothing at all going on once she and Barry had closed *their* bedroom door.

Still a very sore point.

'I just mean it's not really our business, is it?' she said.

'Well, there's definitely something funny going on.'

'She's got problems,' Angie said.

'What?'

She told him about Sue's daughter, the conversation in her bedroom.

'Jesus,' Barry said.

'I know, can you imagine what it's like to lose a child?'

They drove on in silence for a minute, until Barry said, 'Yeah, well good as lost mine already, haven't I?'

'It's hardly the same, love.'

Barry's head was back, his eyes closed. 'I think in a way it's actually worse. I mean, if they're gone, they're gone, aren't they? But with Nick . . . it's like all I can do is imagine all the stuff he's doing without me. It doesn't make any sense . . .'

'Don't you think losing a child at thirteen is senseless? Doesn't matter if it's an illness or a car accident or if it's what happened to that girl in Florida.'

'Talking of which,' Barry said, 'how bloody odd is that Dave? How bloody odd is his other half, come to that?'

'Well, she's a bit . . . theatrical, maybe.'

'They're always *touching* each other,' Barry said. 'You noticed that?'

'Nothing wrong with that, is there?'

'Always got their hands all over each other. Like bloody kids.'

245

'I think it's nice,' Angie said.

'All that crap he was coming out with.' Barry leaned forward and looked at her. 'And while we're on the subject, what was that about "At least we're off the hook"? What the hell was that supposed to mean?'

'It was a joke, Barry. I was joking.'

'So, do you think they actually thought we might have had something to do with it? Is that what you think?'

'I don't know about "we",' Angie said. 'I think it was that business of you driving off to buy fags or whatever that was the issue.'

'*Or whatever?* What's that mean?'

'It doesn't *mean* anything. I'm just saying.' She cursed herself for saying anything at all. The last thing she wanted from here to Crawley was Barry ranting about how the world and his wife were out to wind him up. Pushing his buttons. How everyone was against him.

She asked him what he'd thought of the food, talked about making them both a nice cup of tea when they got in, and nudged her speed up to sixty-five in an effort to keep him happy.

This time of night, Dave and Marina had elected to drive home straight through town and were only ten minutes from Forest Hill. They had talked all the way about what Sue had told Marina and Angie in her bedroom. Or rather Dave had talked, and Marina had chipped in when she had the chance.

'It explains a lot,' Dave said. 'I mean the whole eating disorder thing for a kick-off.'

'She eats as much as I do,' Marina said. 'Some women are jammy like that, have the right metabolism.'

'Well, I think you're wrong, but let's leave it. It does explain why she lets her husband treat her like dirt.' He looked at her, clearly with a lot more to say. Marina shrugged. Go ahead. 'Well, it's all about guilt, isn't it? I know she had nothing to do with what happened to her daughter, but the mind doesn't work like that. It isn't always logical. Somewhere, she might well feel like she was responsible in some way, like it was a genetic thing that was her fault or that there was something she could have done to prevent it. Or maybe it's just that she feels bad for not being a better mother when her daughter was alive.'

'How can you possibly know that?'

'I can't, but like I say, the mind plays strange tricks. I just think it might be the reason why she lets Ed get away with that stuff, why she lets him bully her like that. Because perhaps, deep down, she feels as if she deserves it. To be punished, you know?' He looked across at Marina. 'It's just a theory.'

'You've got plenty of theories,' she said.

He smiled. 'That stuff about the girl, you mean?'

'I don't know why you felt the need—'

'I didn't,' Dave said. 'I mean why the hell would I? Barry clearly had a bee in his bonnet, so I told him what he wanted to hear, that's all.'

Turning off the roundabout at the Elephant and Castle, Marina said, 'I think they both had bees in their bonnets. She definitely knew about that drink Sue and I had. Did you not see the face she had on her when she got there? That comment about not getting into London very much.'

'Over my head,' Dave said.

'Did you say anything?'

'About what?'

'About me and Sue meeting up?'

He shook his head. 'Ed mentioned something when we went out. I think Barry might have picked up on it . . .'

Marina drummed her fingers on the armrest for half a minute. 'Well, thank God *someone* can keep a secret.'

Sue was already in bed, while Ed was taking his time as usual in the bathroom. She shouted through the open door to him. 'Did you see the dress Marina was wearing?'

He shouted back. 'What about it?'

'I've got almost exactly the same dress.'

'Good job you weren't wearing it then.'

Sue squeezed moisturising cream into her palm, put the tube back on the bedside table and began rubbing it in. 'She has the same handbag as me too. She had it with her when we met up for a drink. She said she'd had it for ages, but I don't know.'

'You think she's copying you?'

'I don't know what to think,' Sue said. 'It's a bit freaky.'

'You should be flattered she thinks you have such good taste . . .'

Sue counted to ten in her head, then said, 'I told her and Angie about Emma.'

After a few seconds, Ed emerged into the hall and walked through the open door into the bedroom. He was wearing underpants, with a towel draped across his shoulder. He was still brushing his teeth, though very slowly. He looked at Sue for a few moments then turned and walked back to the bathroom, closing the door hard behind him.

Sue switched her bedside light off and turned on to her side. She reached across to open the drawer and took out the photograph. She looked at it. She wiped it carefully with the edge of the sheet and said, 'I don't care.'

A couple of minutes later, Ed came back in, heavy on his feet. 'What the hell did you do that for?' He saw what she was holding. 'Sue . . .'

'Sue *what*?' She adjusted the pillow she had propped up behind her. 'Sue, don't be stupid? Sue, put that back?'

'You need to stop it.'

'When was the last time we even talked about her?'

'I'm not doing this.'

'Not since her birthday.'

'It's ridiculous.'

'We're not the same,' Sue said. 'You don't feel it in *here*.' She slapped at the duvet across her belly. 'You don't feel anything that isn't giving you a hard-on.' She stared at him. 'And I don't *think* Emma fell into that category.'

'You've seriously fucking lost it, you know that?'

She turned the picture frame around and held it towards him. 'Ring any bells?'

'Don't push it.'

'Emma Dunning? She used to live with us . . .'

248

Ed still had the towel. He threw it towards the laundry basket in the corner. He took off his shorts and did the same with them, then walked around the bed and sat on the edge of it, his back to her.

'Pretty girl, she was,' Sue said. 'I mean this isn't even a particularly good picture of her.' Although she knew Ed could no longer see it, she continued to brandish the photograph at him. 'Anything at all?' She watched the muscles tense across his shoulders and swallowed, dry mouthed. 'Anything *stirring*?'

He reached across and began to adjust the digital clock on his bedside table. 'I'm playing tennis in the morning,' he said.

'Ed—'

'I'm not sure what time I'll be back, so don't bother about lunch.'

'Please . . .'

He lifted himself off the duvet and slipped beneath it. He reached for his light and said, 'Put the picture back.'

FORTY-ONE

I was grateful for good weather, the day I drove out to take the girl.

Rain would have seriously hampered my chances and though sunshine meant there would be more people out and about, it also gave me a bit more choice. On top of which, there's nothing like decent weather to encourage wandering about and to make people a bit more carefree.

Careless.

I parked in the pre-selected spot—on a side road out of sight of any buildings—and walked across the small park towards the playground. I could hear children's voices and music from a radio. I was carrying a kids' plastic lunchbox and I tried to look slightly annoyed, as if waiting for a child was making me late for something or messing up my plans. There were kids of all ages milling around and even though there was plenty of equipment aimed at the older kids—a wooden bridge, jungle climbers and nets—a lot of them still chose to play on swings and in the sandpit.

These were the ones I was here for.

The parents hung around in groups, smoking here, gossiping there, and there was plenty of cover in the trees, which was handy. Benches and tree-stumps to sit on, my head in a paperback. I nodded to a man as he jogged past, lost in whatever music he was plugged into. I had a dog lead in my pocket and I took it out when a stroppy-looking dog owner came close. He was losing his rag with a golden retriever who kept disappearing and I promised him I'd keep an eye out for it, told him that my own dog—I decided I had a Jack Russell—was doing much the same with me.

After about twenty minutes, I watched a girl come wandering out of the playground after a small dog. She was the right sort of age and the uniform told me she was the right kind of child. As she got closer to me, out of sight of whoever was supposed to be watching her, I started calling out, like someone searching for a lost child. Not loud enough for anyone other than the girl to hear, not loud enough to cause any sort of alarm.

I picked the name Charlie.

I looked up like I was surprised, and asked her if she'd seen a five-year-old boy. Told her there was probably a Jack Russell dog with him.

She shook her head. Nice and slow.

'I need to find him because we're going to go and buy something.'

She studied me. 'What are you going to buy?'

Like I said before, I'd decided to play it by ear and it felt pretty inspired at the time, if I say so myself.

'An egg,' I told her. 'A big chocolate egg, wrapped in red.'

'I like chocolate,' she said.

I laughed. 'Doesn't everyone like chocolate? Charlie loves it . . .'

She nodded, waggling her fingers at her dog, who was sniffing around a few feet away. 'I *really* like it.'

I said, 'Do you want to come with us? I could probably afford to buy you an egg as well.' I saw her look back towards the playground. 'Oh, actually I'd better ask your mum, because she might not want you to have all that chocolate.'

'She won't mind,' the girl said, and I knew I was going to be all right.

'Well, maybe you should save some for her,' I said.

'OK,' she said. 'Just a bit though because she doesn't want to get fat.'

'Of course not,' I said.

She shook her head. 'Of course not.'

'Come on then,' I said. 'I think Charlie's probably back at the car.'

'What about your dog?'

'Charlie will have found him by now.' I took a few steps. 'We'll have to keep the dog away from the chocolate egg though. It's bad for dogs, did you know that?'

She took a few steps after me. 'Not bad for people though.'

'No, course it isn't . . .'

Even though I wanted to, I was careful not to take her hand as we walked away. I let her follow me, that was all. Her dog started to do the same, so I picked up a stick and chucked it as far as I could into the trees and the girl didn't seem to care as the dog chased after it. 'We don't want him getting any of our chocolate, do we?' I said.

She smiled.

It wasn't quite as heart-stopping as Amber-Marie's. I'd be lying if I said it was.

A small lie in the scheme of things, obviously, but I don't want anyone to think I've been lying all the time. I want to be nice and clear about that. Lying's played its part in all this, no question about it. One lie leading to another, which is why it all happened the way it did.

You also need to remember one other thing.

I wasn't the only one who was lying.

PART THREE

MARINA and DAVE

From: Jennifer Quinlan <Jennifer.Quinlan@met.police.uk>
Date: 13 July 09:16:32 BST
To: Jeffrey Gardner <j.gardner@sarasotapd.org>
Subject: Missing Girl In UK

Detective Gardner,
If you have not heard about this already, the following articles should prove very interesting . . .

http://www.thisislondon.co.uk/standard/article-2395632-family-fear-for-missing-girl-as-police-search-woodland.do

http://www.telegraph.co.uk/news/158724/missing-girl-police-appeal.html

http://www.thisiskent.co.uk/fears-for-missing-sevenoaks-girl/story-13342751-detail/story.html

The girl went missing from Sevenoaks in Kent (one hour from central London) two days ago. Her name is Samantha Gold. She is thirteen years old with long blonde hair, and disappeared from a playground in a small park near her school. **This school teaches children who have learning difficulties! Samantha Gold could be Amber-Marie Wilson!** I am attaching contact details for the officers in charge of the investigation should you wish to liaise with them. Obviously if there is anything I can do, please do not hesitate to get in touch.
All the best,
DC Jenny Quinlan

FORTY-TWO

Two days after Jenny sent the email, Gardner called. Friday afternoon, she was an hour into a tedious report on some ongoing domestic
that was threatening to turn nasty and reached for the phone without
thinking, in the same way she might reach for a biscuit while flicking
through a magazine. She said her name and fought the temptation to
whoop like some piece of pond-life on *Jerry Springer* when that familiar
velvety voice said his.

'So, Jenny, you busy?' he asked.

She had presumed that she was well and truly out of the loop, now
that the Sevenoaks case seemed to have become tied into the Florida
investigation and Gardner's team in Sarasota was officially liaising with
both Kent police and the Met. All the same, she had been following
the case from a distance, calling in favours from the most tenuous of
contacts anywhere near the inquiry, studying reports, keeping her
ear to the ground. Five days after she had gone missing, there was
almost nothing Jenny Quinlan did not know about Samantha Gold's
disappearance.

Apart from who had taken her.

Gardner said, 'I need to put you back to work.'

'Oh,' Jenny said. Thinking, *now* you do. Now you're taking me a bit more seriously. 'So my email was helpful, then?'

'Absolutely,' Gardner said. 'Well . . . because we get so many tourists, when something like the Wilson murder comes along we try and reach out to those places the majority of visitors come from, you know? All over the US, most of Europe . . . so anything with a similar MO is going to be on our radar. So the fact is, we knew about your missing girl pretty fast. Thanks for the heads-up though . . .'

Jenny tried to keep the disappointment from her voice. 'No problem.'

'Anyway, I've been looking through the reports you sent.'

'OK.'

'Good job, by the way.'

'Thank you.' Jenny inched her chair closer to the desk and looked round quickly to see if anyone was listening. To make sure nobody could see her blush.

'We've done some checking and there are certain . . . inconsistencies, shall we say, in one or two of your witness statements.'

'They've been lying?'

Gardner paused for a second or two. 'Yeah, they've been lying.'

'Who?'

'We checked video surveillance at the mall that Edward and Susan Dunning claim they visited on the afternoon that Amber-Marie Wilson was taken. A lot of the stores have already wiped the tapes, but we've managed to find Mrs Dunning in four different outlets.'

'So . . .'

'*Just* Mrs Dunning.' Gardner paused again and Jenny heard him take a drink of something. 'No sign of her husband on any cameras. There's no video surveillance in the parking lot unfortunately, but based on what we've got so far there's nothing to confirm he was ever there.'

'Well, they both had the same story,' Jenny said. She was trying to keep her voice down, but it was hard, the flutter in her chest. 'So, if he's lying, she's covering up for him.'

'Right,' Gardner said.

'You want me talk to them again?'

258

'I want you to talk to *all* of them again. I want to know why it took Barry Finnegan an hour to buy cigarettes and why that other couple are so vague about the bar they claim to have eaten lunch in. That guy, Dave Cullen? Something a little off about him, at least that's what came across in your report . . .'

'He's definitely a bit strange,' Jenny said. 'Sort of intense, you know? And he seemed a bit too interested in the case if you ask me—'

'Well, make sure he knows *we're* interested in *him*. See what you can shake loose. You might want to start with what they were doing the day Samantha Gold disappeared.' He waited for a response and when he didn't get one, Gardner said, 'You OK with this?'

'I might need to clear a few things with my boss, that's all.'

'Already done,' Gardner said. 'I spoke with your . . . what? Your lieutenant?'

'DCI,' Jenny said. 'Detective chief inspector.'

'Right. I told him what a great job you'd done so far and that if it was acceptable to him I'd like you to stay on it.'

'He said that was OK?'

'Well, to begin with, he was a little surprised that you'd done quite as much work as you had.'

'Shit.' Jenny had said it before she could stop herself. A muttered hiss of panic, anticipating the dressing-down she would get for over-stepping her boundaries, for failing to keep her superiors informed.

Gardner chuckled softly. 'It's fine,' he said. 'I just gave him all the "hands across the ocean" stuff. Told him what a great job he was doing in bringing on officers who were prepared to go the extra mile, you know? Who used their initiative.'

'Thanks.'

'Obviously, I didn't tell him you hadn't exactly been straight with me, but as long as we're clear about how we proceed from here, I'm willing to overlook that, *Trainee* Detective Constable . . .'

When she had hung up, Jenny rummaged in her bag and fished out the memory stick that held the reports she had written up for Jeff Gardner. She loaded the files on to her computer and began reading through her notes on the conversations with the Dunnings, the Finnegans, Dave Cullen and Marina Green. Behind her, someone began to complain loudly about being thirsty. Somebody else laughed. She turned and saw a balding DS who fancied himself as the office comedian waving an empty mug in her direction and nodding towards the coffee machine.

She told him to make it himself.

FORTY-THREE

That indefinable, oddly soporific time between late Saturday afternoon and early Saturday evening and Angie had already taken up her regular position in front of the television. She had a bottle of white wine open and her legs up beneath her on the sofa. She wore grey velour tracksuit bottoms and a DKNY T-shirt and the menu for a local Chinese delivery place lay on top of the *TV Times*, next to a dog-eared book of Sudoku puzzles on the table she had pulled across from the nest beneath the window.

Perfect . . .

King prawn and mushroom with egg-fried rice and some of those sesame prawn toast things. *Harry Hill* then *The X Factor* and maybe that Matt Damon film where he was a spy without knowing it, if she wasn't already asleep by then. Barry shaking her awake; opening a beer and taking her place on the sofa to watch *Match of the Day*. Or maybe even following her up, his hands on her backside as she climbed the stairs, naked in the hall when she came out of the bathroom, with his knob in his hand and that big stupid grin.

Not that Angie could remember the last time there'd been any of that.

She picked up the remote and started flicking through the channels as soon as the ITV news came on. It would only be the same terrible stuff as always, after all. Bombings in Afghanistan or Iraq or wherever, job losses and the football results. Never anything *nice*, never anything that made her smile. They'd even stopped doing those funny little stories at the end about cats that got reunited with their owners after umpteen years or nutters seeing Jesus in a piece of toast.

Was there no point even *trying* to cheer anybody up any more? When had the world become so bloody miserable?

Nothing on as yet that took her fancy, she flicked back to ITV and reached for her mobile to make sure she hadn't missed a message from either of the kids. Laura and Luke were both out with friends. Each had a social life far busier than hers or Barry's: parties and Pizza Hut and trips to the cinema at fifteen quid a pop; gatherings outside the local shopping centre where—if Laura and Luke were to be believed—everyone *but* them would be smoking and drinking cheap cider.

For God's sake, don't you trust us . . .?

In a few hours the text messages would come through, the pair of them demanding to be picked up from God knows where. She'd be in bed with the latest Lee Child by then, leaving Barry to pull his sheep-skin on and stalk out to the Range Rover. Moaning about not being able to have a drink, being nothing but a 'glorified bloody taxi service'.

On the screen, a man and a woman walked slowly up on to a small stage and sat behind a table.

Angie put her phone down.

They both looked tired and very serious, washed out.

They were holding hands.

Angie turned up the volume as a man in a smart suit—a police officer, she quickly realised—made the introductions. She could hear the whirr and click of cameras as he spoke. A short statement, he said. No questions. He gently nudged a small microphone a little closer to the woman, who smiled a thank you and unfolded a piece of paper.

'If anyone out there has any information at all about our daughter, please come forward and pass it on to the police.' The woman's voice was surprisingly loud. The police officer moved the microphone away again and the woman grasped it nervously. 'If anyone watching this is holding our daughter . . .' She looked up from her notes, stared into the camera for a few seconds then flinched as a flash went off. 'If you've got Sam, we're begging you not to hurt her.' She raised a hand to her face and her husband laid a hand on her arm. 'We're begging you to let her come home. Please . . . she needs to come home.' She nodded across to the police officer then folded up her sheet of paper, kept folding until it was nice and small.

The police officer nodded back. Mouthed, 'Well done.'

The husband leaned towards the microphone and said, 'We miss you, Sam, and we love you . . . very much.'

'I reckon it was him.'

Angie turned to see Barry standing in the doorway. '*What?*'

He pointed to the television. 'It's always the dad.'

'Oh, that's rubbish.'

'Look at him.' Barry ambled in and sat down on the edge of the sofa. 'He looks like he's trying too hard, you ask me.'

'You're wicked,' Angie said. They watched as the police officer read out a final statement and a number appeared at the bottom of the screen over a picture of the missing girl. 'No way. Never . . .'

'Oh, listen,' Barry said. 'I was thinking I might ask a few of the lads over next Saturday, watch the Arsenal–Spurs game. Fair enough?'

'You asked your brother?' Angie looked at him. 'Might be a good chance for you and him to have a natter, you know.'

Barry kept his eyes on the screen. 'Just the lads,' he said.

'Well, make sure you've got rid of them by this time.'

'Why?'

'We've got dinner round at Dave and Marina's and I'll need to get ready.'

Barry slumped back on the sofa. 'Oh, Christ, do we have to?'

'Well, we don't *have* to, but it's their turn and we've said we're going now, so . . .'

'*You* said.'

'Don't be so miserable.'

'It was hardly a laugh a minute last time, was it? People getting chopsy and kicking off.'

263

'That was you, if I remember rightly.'

'Yeah, well.'

'I'm looking forward to it,' Angie said.

They watched as the parents of the missing girl were led off the stage amid an explosion of camera flashes and the reporter at the press conference handed back to the studio. 'Yeah, definitely the dad,' Barry said. 'Definitely him, if you ask me.'

Angie hauled herself up off the sofa. 'Nobody's asking you.'

Just before she left the room, Barry said, 'I'll have tea if you're making some . . .'

When Ed came in, Sue was at the small table in the kitchen, sharing a bottle of wine with a colleague from school. Graham Foot was the teacher she was closest to, the only one she truly considered a friend, and a much-needed ally when it came to some of the battles with a head teacher who clearly did not like children over much and whose head was usually halfway up the arse of an Ofsted inspector.

She could relax with Graham, open up to him—as far as she ever did with anyone—and she knew very well that this closeness was not unconnected with her friend's sexuality.

Graham was a gay man.

Childless.

Graham turned when Ed came in and held up the bottle.

'Want one?'

Ed looked at Sue. 'I'm going to have a shower.'

Sue said, 'There's some pasta left if you fancy some . . .'

Ten minutes later, Ed was drying himself, and hoping that Graham was not going to overstay his welcome. At the mirror, he wiped away a circle of steam and moved a blob of styling wax carefully through his hair. Graham was all right, as far as it went and it wasn't as though Ed had anything against poofs. He'd met plenty of that sort over the years through work and there was even one they played with regularly at the tennis club. It was never an issue and all of them, even the player concerned, enjoyed a laugh and a joke about it.

'*No wonder you can't volley with a wrist as limp as that . . .*'

'*Shouldn't this be called* mixed *doubles?*'

He wanted a quiet night in, that was all. Just him and Sue and a couple of glasses and maybe something mindless on DVD. He didn't want to think too much, to make smart conversation, to entertain. Sunday tomorrow, then Monday and a fresh week to kill. It was necessary, of course it was; but the deceit was starting to wear him out, the effort required far more tiring than the work itself ever was.

Leaning close to the mirror, he decided it was starting to show in the laughter lines and the darkening half-moons beneath his eyes. Jesus, even *this* was an effort he could do without. He was fairly certain that Sue's mate fancied him, he knew those looks well enough, and that meant he couldn't relax, he couldn't just slob about in a ratty old sweatshirt or whatever.

It was a pain in the arse.

He grinned at himself in the mirror. That was a good joke. Pain in the arse . . .

He snatched at the deodorant and squirted. Once under each arm, then he lifted his balls and squirted once more down there, for luck.

Right.

Khakis and a polo shirt and that would have to do. Then a quick 'hello' and Gay Graham could sling his hook.

When Ed came back down, Sue and Graham had opened another bottle, so he sat and joined them. They talked about school—about teachers they hated and kids who were borderline feral—and when Graham asked Ed how work was, Ed shrugged and told him he would much rather hear some more of Graham's hilarious staffroom stories.

After half an hour, Ed went and helped himself to the leftover pasta, ate standing up, leaning against the worktop on the other side of the kitchen.

Just as Graham appeared—finally—to be leaving, he said, 'Sue tells me you're having dinner with your new friends again next week.'

Graham had put 'friends' in inverted commas and Ed asked himself how much Sue had told him about their holiday.

'Hardly friends,' he said.

265

'So why are you going?'

'Because they came here,' Sue said. 'Everybody gets to be host, I suppose. Kind of a three-way thing.'

Graham raised his eyebrows. 'A three-way? Sounds interesting.'

Sue grimaced. 'No, thank you. Mind you, I think Ed might be up for it.' She nudged Ed, and he smiled politely.

'Course, you've got that business in Florida,' Graham said. 'Probably something to do with that.'

Ed said, 'Right.' It was obvious now that Sue had told him what had happened back in Sarasota.

'Horrible.' Graham shook his head, reaching for his coat. 'That poor girl. Mind you, things like that bond people, don't they?' Then, when he was almost at the door, 'There's that wonderful Roald Dahl story about the people that survive an air crash and all meet up for dinner every so often. You know the one?'

Ed said that he did, but the truth was he'd never heard of it. Didn't Roald Dahl write kids' books? Willy Wanker and giants or whatever?

'Of course, in that story there's that lovely twist, isn't there?' Graham said, leaning in, conspiratorial. 'They'd all eaten their fellow passengers after the crash and so they'd developed a taste for human flesh. That was why they kept having those *special* dinners.' He shuddered theatrically and grinned. 'I hope there's nothing like that going on with you and your new mates.'

Sue laughed. 'When they came here I just made spaghetti . . .'

When Graham had gone, Sue said, 'How was the gym?' It was where Ed was supposed to have been going.

'Fine,' he said.

'How come you didn't have a shower there?'

Ed walked back into the kitchen and Sue followed him. 'There wasn't much of that pasta left,' he said.

'Sorry.'

'I wouldn't mind a bit of toast.'

'Not sure there's any fresh bread—'

'So, defrost some.'

And opening the freezer like a good girl, Sue thought—as she did a hundred times or more every day—*that's* how easy it is to flick the switch marked 'normal'. They had not spoken about their terrible argument, that night everyone had been round for dinner, though Sue guessed that Ed had been thinking about it when Graham had raised the subject of the coming weekend's gathering at Marina and Dave's.

No mention of what had been said. The poison spat out and Ed's broad back to her on the edge of the bed.

The photograph.

That was how they handled things and Sue supposed it was what all husbands and wives did from time to time. There was always *something* a couple fell out about. Something that would simmer and spark and blow up in their faces every so often, that they would have to put behind them in order to keep inching forward. A little piece of them chipped away each time, the stings that little bit more painful, the damage lived with until it became irreparable.

All couples had their tender spots; the ulcers they bit down on.

With many it was money of course, or the lack of it. It was family or politics or previous sexual partners. The things they left alone until they became impossible to ignore.

With them it was a dead child, simple as that.

Carrying the frozen loaf across to the toaster, she saw Ed running fingers through his hair, his palm stroking to assess the amount of stubble on his cheeks, and Sue reconsidered that earlier thought. Was her husband really thinking about anything other than the lies he could invent to explain away his empty days and the smell of perfume in the car that most definitely wasn't hers? Was his mind occupied with anything more complex, more hidden than improving his cross-court forehand and the things he was going to ask her to do in bed later on?

She doubted it.

She slipped two slices of bread into the toaster thinking: there is almost certainly nothing about this man that I did not know within a day of meeting him. Ed looked up to check her progress and she smiled.

Thought: and that is probably a very good thing.

267

FORTY-FOUR

Walking from church, Dave took Marina's hand and squeezed and when they reached the car, he said, 'That was nice, wasn't it?'

'Yeah,' she said.

'Not a great turnout, but that's not how we measure these things, is it?' He opened the car doors. 'It's how you feel afterwards.'

Driving home, Dave felt pretty good, always a lot calmer at this time on a Sunday than he had been walking into the cool and the silence of the church. The stress and the tension built up during the week, every petty annoyance and painful memory lodged like a small, sharp stone in his chest, until by Saturday night the weight of them had become almost unbearable. With the worn wood of the pew solid at his back though and the words of the sermon echoing around, the weight was lifted, he could *feel* the rushing wind and once he began to sing—loud enough sometimes to make Marina wince next to him—it was as though he weighed nothing at all, and nothing mattered but God and forgiving, and nothing and nobody could ever wind him up again.

Only for an hour or two, the anaesthetic bliss of that, but still . . .

'You know the smell?' he asked. He was waiting patiently to pull out into traffic on the main road, no hint of irritation, not a single angry gesture as bastard after bastard refused to let him out. 'Mothballs, candles, whatever it is. The smell in the church.'

'What?' Marina said.

Dave smiled, waved a thank you and eased out. 'It's *faith*,' he said. 'I heard an old woman telling her friend. The "glorious stink of faith", she said.' He chuckled. 'That's great, don't you think?'

'Smells like old clothes to me,' Marina said. Her eyes were fixed on the blur of shops and houses moving past the passenger window. 'A charity shop or something.'

She didn't say a great deal else for the rest of the journey home, but Dave thought that was OK. They never talked much afterwards, each enjoying the moments of quiet reflection after a service in their own way. Dave believed it was important that they respected one another's headspace, especially at times like this, but all the same he wondered and could only imagine that, while it lasted, she was relishing the same feelings of peace and calm that he was.

Of course she was, he could see it on her face.

They certainly never discussed their beliefs with anyone else. Not with work colleagues or friends and definitely not with that Florida lot. Nobody's business but theirs, same as everything else. Yes, it was partly because they were private people, but Dave was not the sort to foist his opinions on anyone else. He couldn't stand those idiots who tried ramming their religion down your throat, and besides, if he was going to respect the beliefs of others, surely that included the freedom to believe in bugger all. Not that he would have minded half an hour with Richard bloody Dawkins, put him right about a few things . . .

He knew others might find it all a bit . . . strange, what with him being such a science geek and all that, but he'd never found the two things to be incompatible. Like he'd said to Marina once, 'Why can't I have God *and* an iPhone?' He'd been very pleased with that one, had passed it round the congregation the following Sunday.

'Quiet night in, yeah?'

Marina nodded.

He'd taken her to church for the first time a day or two after they'd met. That party when they'd found out how much they had in common. He'd told her just how much his faith had helped him with all the bad stuff, told her it would do the same for her.

Which it had, that was obvious.

'Stops the hate eating you up,' he'd told her. 'And the guilt.' They both agreed that was the worst thing.

They never really *dis*agreed, not about anything that mattered, which Dave reckoned was what made them such a perfect team. I'm the brains of it and you're the heart, he would say to her. Give me the best computer in the world and I couldn't design anything better. You and me versus the rest of them kind of thing.

God, the Florida lot . . .

Turning into the street where they lived, he felt a nice fresh stone heavy in his chest, the jagged edges of it.

'Nowhere to park,' Marina said, quietly.

He could just imagine how they would react. Barry sniggering like a kid and Ed making 'God Squad' remarks, the wives meek as mice. Well, Barry was thick as mince and the only divinity Ed believed in was between his legs, so screw *them*!

'When are we going to get Residents' Parking?' He felt for the inhaler in his pocket, the stone settling in. 'How many emails have I sent now . . .?'

Ten minutes trying to find a space, and walking back from the next road along, Marina's hand still hot in his and the sun on his back, Dave could see nothing but their faces. Smirks and knowing glances and Ed pretending he was a deep thinker; trotting out the usual tired shit.

'So, if God is *love* or whatever, how do you explain tsunamis and babies with AIDS? How do you explain murdered girls?'

Dave imagined it all very clearly. Barry nodding, impressed, and Ed waiting with his arms folded. *Go on then, smartarse, answer that.* He wouldn't of course, not because he couldn't but because they were

270

not worth it. He would say nothing. He would just smile and hope they understood how worthless he thought they both were.

He would say nothing.

Marina went straight to the fridge and began swigging water from the bottle. She'd nearly been sick in the church, but now, when Dave came across and rubbed the small of her back, mouth twisted in concern, she just put the bottle back and smiled and said she was fine. A bit hot, that was all.

He'd trotted off to check on the thermostat.

But not for long.

More than anything she wanted to be on her own, just for five bloody minutes, but he kept following her; upstairs, then from bedroom to bathroom and back again like a puppy. He spoke in that high, silly voice he reserved for times like this. He reached out to stroke her neck when she passed and, in all the ways she had come to recognise, made it blindingly obvious that he was hoping for his Sunday night special.

She could never understand it. Why did God make him so horny? The last thing praying made Marina feel like was fucking.

She wanted a hot shower.

Not that she *had* been praying, of course.

At first she'd gone along because she had nothing better to do, happy enough to make him happy; clinging to the hope that it might help, that maybe belief was something you could get better at, like table tennis or a foreign language. It couldn't hurt, could it? But she'd known almost straight away that it wasn't for her. She'd found it all a bit creepy to tell the truth, a bit desperate, and she could never quite bring herself to tell him, to destroy his image of them as ideally matched. Beautiful, he'd said, that's what we are, like the perfect bit of software.

MarinaDave Version 1.0. He'd actually written that once, in a Valentine card!

She didn't know how he managed to . . . disassociate himself the way he did. Like he was a character in one of the games he designed, like what had happened wasn't real. She envied it, if she was honest,

271

couldn't find anything that worked better than spliff or red wine. Maybe she didn't *want* to let go of the hate, not completely. Sometimes she felt it crackling through her and it was like she was empowered by it, staring at some of the idiots on the other side of the reception desk and feeling so much stronger than they could possibly imagine.

The guilt was something else though.

Today, Dave belting out some dirge about kings and shepherds next to her and she could feel it coming off her like sweat. She half expected that her fingers would leave it there for everyone to see, in tell-tale, guilt-greasy smudges on the hymn book.

What she'd done. What she wanted to carry on doing.

She wasn't stupid, I mean you didn't need to be Freud or whoever to work out that this was probably why she wanted to be an actress or a writer. Why she wanted to tell *other* people's stories.

'You look tense,' he said.

'Just tired,' she said.

'How about a massage later?' Behind her now, his small hands on her shoulders. 'I could run you a bath . . .'

She knew what people thought, how they looked at her sometimes when she told them she was an actress. An actress . . . who works as a dental receptionist. *Oh right . . . you get a lot of work?* She'd seen that look from Angie and from Ed, from Sue even and she was probably the only one with a creative bone in her body.

'That would be lovely,' she said. 'Thanks, babe . . .'

Nobody knew how good an actress she really was.

FORTY-FIVE

'It's me.'

'Hey, Jeff . . .'

Hey, like she was happy enough it was him, but also *hey*, like she was not that surprised, like who else would it be? Gardner could not help asking himself how many other people were calling Patti Lee Wilson these days to see how she was. When he'd been up there he hadn't seen too many signs that anybody else had been around to check up on her. There were no cards, no food in Tupperware from neighbours in the fridge. There had been a handful of distant relatives at the funeral, a few of Amber-Marie's friends, but nobody had seemed keen to stick around afterwards.

'What you doing?'

'Just watching TV,' she said.

'Anything good?'

'Some gameshow. It's OK.'

'Nothing wrong with gameshows.'

'Hey, I got a job.'

'You did?'

'Just the checkout at Best Buy, but that's fine, you know? Pays the bills, right? No point waiting around for IBM to come knocking at my door.' She laughed, and Gardner heard applause from the TV. 'How *you* doing?'

'Busy,' Gardner said.

'People never get tired of killing each other, huh?'

'Seems that way.'

'It's a sick world, Jeff.' She paused and the volume from the TV was turned down. 'It's kind of ironic, but sometimes I think my baby was too good for it, you know? Better off . . . somewhere else. Does that make sense?'

Gardner had no idea if Patti was religious or not. The ceremony had been pretty much standard, except for a short reading from *The Prophet* and the pop song Patti had said was her daughter's favourite. Something about fireflies.

'Yeah, I see that,' Gardner said.

'Wouldn't you rather *not* be busy?' she asked. 'Trying to catch murderers, I mean. Wouldn't you rather be giving out tickets or chasing the assholes who didn't pay their taxes or whatever? I bet you'd sleep a damn sight better.'

'It's my job, Patti. I just deal with what comes my way.'

She sighed a 'Yeah, I know,' then said nothing for a few seconds. 'So, this part of your job, Jeff?' Her voice was quieter now. She sounded sleepy. 'The aftercare?'

'Listen. I wanted to ask you,' Gardner said. 'When you were at the Pelican Palms, you remember the three British couples?'

She said, 'Sure,' but there was hesitancy and a question in it.

'The three guys, you remember them?'

'Yeah . . .'

'Ed Dunning, Dave Cullen—'

'I don't remember their names—'

'That's OK—'

'Which of them was which, anything like that.'

'Look, I'm just asking if maybe one of them was a bit friendlier with Amber-Marie than the others.' Gardner was struggling to find the right words. 'Did you notice . . . anything that might have been a little off?'

'Don't you think I would have mentioned that?'

'Maybe something that didn't seem strange at the time, I don't know. I know I'm asking you to think back, but—'

'They were nice,' she said. 'It wasn't like I got real friendly with any of them, it was just a few words once or twice, you know? But they were nice . . .'

'OK.'

'Why? You think one of those guys . . .?'

'No . . . look, it was just a shot, OK?' There was more noise from the television, bells and klaxons sounding. 'I'm just following up on a few things, loose ends, you know?' He did not want to say anything else. She did not sound tired any more.

'Shit . . .' He heard a noise, a hand slapped down on the cushion of the settee, maybe. 'Now I'm going to have to take some pills.'

'Excuse me?'

'I've just started to sleep a bit better, four or five hours the last few nights, but now . . . well, I think I may need a little help after this.'

'Really, there's no need.'

'Easy for you to say.'

'I'm sorry.' Gardner held the phone to his chest for a few seconds, cursed quietly. 'Like I said.'

'Your job, right.'

He told her that he needed to go, then said the same things he'd said countless times. He told her that he would let her know as soon as there was any real news, that the case was anything but closed. He tried to make it sound fresh, *meant*, half expecting to hear a sarcastic 'blah blah blah' coming back at him.

'You like Lucinda Williams, Jeff?' she asked when he was done.

'I don't know,' Gardner said. 'I mean . . . I've never really listened to any of her songs.'

'There's this one of hers, "Sweet Old World". It's a real sad one, where she's talking to some fool who's killed himself, telling him about all the great stuff he's left behind.' She began to softly hum a few ragged bars and, when she stopped, the breath catching in her throat, the muted applause from the TV sounded as though it might be for her.

'Patti . . .?'

'I love her stuff . . . always have. She's got this *voice*, you know? You can hear the hurt in it and the pack of Marlboros a day and all the great sex she's having. She can give you chills, I swear . . . but I'm telling you right now that's one stupid song I'm never going to listen to again. "See what you lost when you left this sweet old world". You see what I'm getting at, Jeff?'

He saw it, but let her say it anyway.

'Nothing sweet about it.'

FORTY-SIX

The house was in a long, leafy street in Tilgate, a quiet neighbourhood a mile or so south of Crawley town centre. Jenny grabbed a parking space a few doors down. She turned off the radio and took a last look at the notes she had prepared.

Wilson/Gold Interviews 2.

She had written most of it up at home the day before, her flatmate thankfully away with friends for the weekend, but an extra page had been added to the file first thing that morning, after a short session on the Police National Computer. Running the six interviewees through the PNC would normally have been standard procedure, but she had not been able to do it first time round. Any access to the database was strictly monitored—the log-ins timed and registered, the electronic fingerprint unmistakable—and that had not been something Jenny had wanted to risk while she was working rather more off her own bat than might have been tolerated. Now though, she had been given the all-clear. Trainee or not, she had been . . . endorsed.

No more coffee-runs or photocopying, for the time being at any rate.

Jenny looked at the printout and got excited all over again. Half an hour on the PNC—a request to pull a file sent straight through to the

General Registry—and she guessed that one of her interviews was going to be rather more lively than it might otherwise have been. Four of the six were, as expected, clean as a whistle. One had been cautioned four years before for possession of a Class C drug. Another—though all charges had eventually been dropped—had been arrested six years earlier for something altogether more interesting.

She had fired off an email to Jeff Gardner straight away . . .

The front door was open, so Jenny walked in. She showed her warrant card to the first workman who looked her way and asked where the boss was. The house was cold, the air thick with plaster dust and in the room where the kitchen used to be—where she guessed a new one would appear at some point—three more labourers were hard at work, while a fourth stood leaning against a wall taken back to the brick, fag in hand. Jenny raised her voice above the hammering and the sound of talkSPORT from a paint-spattered radio and was pointed towards the garden. She walked out through the shell of an extension and found Barry Finnegan talking to a short man wearing an anorak over a shirt and tie. The architect, she guessed. Planning officer, maybe.

'I just need a couple of minutes,' she said.

Finnegan nodded slowly and Jenny waited patiently while he finished up with the man in the suit, shook hands and told the man to 'bell me as soon as'. The conversation was semi-shouted, punctuated by the loud *snap* of the plastic sheeting in the window-frames, the bursts of noise from a jackhammer back in the house.

'Right,' Finnegan said, when the man had gone. He led her towards the end of the smallish garden, lighting a cigarette as he went. 'How did you know I was here?'

'I called your office,' Jenny said. She stepped carefully. There was as much mud as grass. 'Very helpful bloke gave me the address.'

Finnegan nodded. 'Adrian.' He took a deep drag. 'My brother.'

They reached a dilapidated shed, its windows thick with cobwebs and a child's plastic slide up against the door. They turned to look back at the house.

'Big job,' she said.

'Not for us. Pretty standard kitchen extension.'

'Looks like a bit more than that. I mean not as grand as what you've had done at your place, but . . .'

Finnegan nodded towards the scaffolding at the side of the house. 'Yeah, well, you start a job and other stuff comes up, doesn't it? Brickwork turns out to be buggered or like this place, you point out to the woman that her roof could do with sorting out while we're here. Tiles are blown. There's always something.'

'Something that means you can whack the price up.'

'We're not that sort of firm.'

'An honest builder,' Jenny said. 'You should be on *The X-Files* or something.'

Finnegan snorted a laugh, but there wasn't much to it.

'So, while you're being honest, I wanted to ask you about that trip to buy cigarettes. When you left your wife on the beach and drove back into Siesta Village.'

Finnegan's shoulders sagged and he let out a long breath. 'I told you.'

'It took you how long? That wasn't very clear first time round.'

'I don't know, half an hour, something like that.'

'Your wife said it was more like an hour.'

He said nothing for a few seconds. Lifted the cigarette to his mouth but didn't draw on it. 'I suppose.'

'Right, so you bought your fags and then decided to stay and have a beer. You went to what, the nearest bar?'

'Yeah. It was hot and I fancied a beer.'

'You can't remember the name of this bar?'

Finnegan shook his head.

'And you didn't see Dave Cullen and Marina Green at any time?'

Another head-shake, the cigarette in his mouth.

'Thing is, they told us they were having lunch at the same time you were having your beer and it's just that the whole stretch of the village is shorter than this street we're on right now.' She had spent a useful hour or two on Google Earth, mapped the place out. Half a dozen bars, a few souvenir shops, an upmarket strip mall. No more

279

than five minutes' walk end to end. 'Just worth checking that you didn't see them, maybe while you were driving past whichever bar they were in.'

'Well, unless they were sitting outside I *wouldn't* have seen them, would I? Like I said, it was hot, so they were probably inside.'

'And obviously you didn't see Amber-Marie Wilson.'

'Obviously.'

One of the labourers appeared on the patio, shouting something about the sparks and where the woman wanted her power points. Finnegan shouted back, said he'd be in to sort it in a minute. The labourer gave a thumbs-up and went back inside.

Jenny said, 'This bar.' She scraped mud from her shoe on the edge of a stone. 'It was probably the one nearest the place you bought your fags. I'm assuming you didn't get back in the car and drive to it, did you?'

'No. Yeah, it was close to the 7-Eleven,' Finnegan said. 'I got the fags from a 7-Eleven.'

Jenny nodded. She remembered the map. There was a 7-Eleven a few doors down from a bar called Gilligans. That was one of the places Dave Cullen had said he and his girlfriend might have eaten lunch in.

'Are we about done?' Finnegan asked. He tossed his fag end into the bushes. 'If I'm going to whack my prices up, I need to crack on.'

They walked back towards the house. The wind was up and a few leaves skittered about on the shitty lawn. A pace or two behind him, Jenny thrust her hands into the pockets of her jacket and said, 'Can you tell me where you were a week ago today? Last Monday. Late afternoon . . .'

Finnegan turned to look at her but kept walking. He stopped at the doors to the extension and waited for her to catch up. She saw the question on his face. 'I'm sorry, but I just need you to tell me where you were.'

'I'll check,' he said, finally. 'God knows what it's got to do with anything, but far as I can remember I was in the office. Me and my brother had a business meeting. Yeah, I reckon . . .'

'Thanks,' Jenny said. 'I'll talk to Adrian.'

He nodded, looked away for a few seconds. 'Listen, I should probably tell you me and my brother haven't exactly been seeing eye to eye lately. A few silly rows, that's all, nothing major. Anyway, that's why I was in such an arsey mood when you came round before. A bit of a ding-dong, you know? Just wanted to let you know that . . . say sorry for being out of order.' He reached for his cigarettes again. 'I got a right ear-bending from the missus when you'd gone.'

She told him it was fine, that she'd known worse. All the same, she wondered why he was telling her. Was it a genuine apology, or was he making it clear that he and his brother were not close; providing a reason in advance if his brother failed to back up his story? Then again, alibis from family were usually treated with a degree of scepticism anyway, so perhaps she was reading too much into it.

'You going to talk to Angie?'

'Yes, I'll be calling her,' Jenny said. She clocked his expression, guessed that the minute she was out of there, he would be calling her first.

They stepped inside. It was quieter and, looking through into the kitchen area, she could see that the workmen were taking a tea break.

'What have you got?' Finnegan asked. 'A flat or something?'

'Yeah, a flat.'

'Renting?'

'For now,' she said.

'Well, as soon as you get your own place, if you need any work doing, you know where to come. I was being straight with you before. We don't rip anybody off . . .'

Walking back to the car, Jenny asked herself if Barry Finnegan was just supremely confident or a bit thick. Or so completely innocent of anything that it hadn't seemed remotely inappropriate. It was certainly an odd moment to be touting for business. Then again, she had once had a sex offender try to advise her on where to buy clothes that would make her look a bit sexier.

She supposed she shouldn't be too surprised by anything any more.

FORTY-SEVEN

It wasn't easy doing the normal things and I wasn't sleeping too well either. You never know how good you're going to be at something like that, I mean, how can you? All that pretending and carrying on like none of it means anything, and even though I turned out to be a damn sight better at it than I would have guessed, it was definitely a strain. It got a lot worse, of course, after the police came sniffing around again, and I'd known that they would. I'd taken all that into account before I'd made that first drive out to Sevenoaks, but there was no backing out, not once I'd sat and watched that playground for a while.

Two decisions at once, one leading straight to the other. Once I'd decided I was going to take the girl, I'd started making plans.

I knew I needed to think ahead, because it was pretty obvious they'd be putting things together once I'd done it again. I know they talk to each other, police force to police force or whatever, and these days, with the internet and everything, the connection was likely to get made very bloody quickly.

I'm not denying I was lucky because I was *stupidly* lucky. The people I needed to behave in particular ways behaved in exactly the ways I thought they would, said the right thing. Said the wrong thing. Of course, luckiest of all, there'd been so many of us out there enjoying the Florida sunshine to begin with. Let's hear it for the crappy British weather. Plus, once the connection was made between the two girls, they widened the investigation out and started looking into all the British holidaymakers who had been in the area at the time. That silly cow, WPC Smartarse . . . Quinlan . . . thought she was being entrusted with chasing up on the, what do you call them, prime suspects or something. She probably never clicked that they were running about like chickens with their heads cut off on the other side of the pond, desperately trying to track down *all* the Brits who'd been anywhere near Sarasota when Amber-Marie was taken. A waste of time obviously, and you'd think they'd have worked that out for themselves, wouldn't you? I mean, it's not rocket science to figure out she would only have got into a car with someone she recognised.

So, as it turned out, that jumped-up trainee detective *cunt*stable was closer than she knew all the time. She'd been almost spot on from the word go. Big things predicted for that one, future commissioner I shouldn't wonder, blah blah.

Luck and lies then, that's about the size of it. The other thing, the 'why', well that's not really for me to say, is it? Anyway, I'm not sure I could put it into words that made sense and how could anybody? Whatever it is that makes your blood race and puts your hands where you know they really shouldn't be.

The thing that opens the cage.

FORTY-EIGHT

'There's something different,' Jenny said. The three of them were seated at the same table as before in the Dunnings' living room; mid-afternoon sun cutting in through the windows on to the polished pine. The weather was better than it had been first time round and the small garden had more colour in it, or seemed to.

Sue Dunning looked around, shrugged. 'I think it's just because I had the chance to tidy up a bit,' she said, laughing. 'School hadn't broken up when you were here before.'

Jenny nodded. 'Well, thanks for sparing me the time, anyway.'

'Tell you the truth it's nice to talk to anybody who's not making up some story about why they haven't done their homework.'

'Dog ate it, that always did the trick for me.'

'We're not quite as gullible these days.'

Jenny looked at Ed Dunning. 'And thanks for taking the time off work.'

Ed gave a small nod. Said, 'Why *do* people tidy up when the police are coming round?' He quickly answered his own question, which was clearly just the set-up for a punchline of some description. 'I mean obviously it's a good idea to get the body out of the way. The bottle of poison and the bag marked *swag*.'

Sue laughed a little and rolled her eyes, but Jenny just looked down at her notes. She did not feel inclined to humour either of them at this stage.

'So, how can we help you?'

Moving things along was fine with Jenny. 'You could start by telling me why you lied about going shopping that day.'

'Sorry?' Ed looked at his wife.

'We checked the CCTV at the shopping mall,' Jenny said, enjoying the *we* rather than the *they*. She looked at Ed. 'We know you weren't there.' They didn't know any such thing of course; the absence of Ed Dunning on four sets of CCTV pictures being far from conclusive and Gardner having said as much.

Jenny could see straight away, though, that they'd been right.

'So, I don't particularly like being dragged around shopping centres looking at candles and cushions,' Ed said. 'I don't *think* that's grounds for arrest, but maybe they've brought in some new law.'

'I'm not a big fan of shopping either,' Jenny said. 'It's not just a bloke thing. I'm just a bit confused as to why you felt the need to tell the police in Sarasota that's what you were doing.'

'We had a flight the next day.'

'I'm still not—'

'We didn't want to get held up, that's all. I know what they're like over there and I didn't fancy giving them any reason why they might want to keep us hanging around.'

'Ed dropped me off,' Sue said. Her hand moved reflexively across the table towards her husband's, stopped just short of it.

'Yeah, I dropped her off. I went off on my own for a bit then came back to pick her up.'

'A couple of hours later,' she said. 'Something like that.' She watched Jenny taking notes. 'For the record, I didn't buy any candles or cushions.'

'Where did you go?' Jenny caught movement out of the corner of her eye and turned to see a skinny ginger cat in the doorway, watching her. 'I didn't see him last time either,' she said.

'*Her*,' Sue said. 'She's not very sociable.' She pursed her lips, made kissing noises. 'She's old . . .'

The cat turned round and padded out. Jenny turned back to Ed. Perhaps the distraction had given him time to gather his thoughts, she could not be sure.

'I drove to the harbour,' he said. 'Wandered about looking at the boats for a while. Watched a couple of the charters come back, tourists thinking they're what's-his-name . . . Ernest Hemingway or something.'

'Did you talk to anybody?'

He shook his head. 'Just wandered around, keeping the tan topped up. It's one of our favourite places over there, isn't it?' His wife nodded. 'We've taken a little boat out ourselves occasionally, rented kayaks, all that.'

Jenny wrote down what Ed had said and thanked him. 'I also need to know where you were rather more . . . recently.' She turned back a page or two to check the date she had written. Like it was just a small thing. 'A week ago yesterday. Monday . . . the eleventh?'

'Why do you want to know?'

It was a reasonable enough question. While a detailed description of Samantha Gold had been circulated, together with photographs, no mention had been made of the girl's learning difficulties, which were not considered relevant to the hunt for her. There was no reason for anyone—if they were innocent—to have made any connection to the murder of Amber-Marie Wilson. Still, reasonable or not, innocent or not, Jenny wanted none of these people anywhere but on the back foot.

'Can you just answer the question, please?'

'How should I know?'

He looked to his wife and when Jenny did the same she saw Sue Dunning smile and nod; saw that she had got it. A look to her husband. Isn't it obvious? 'That girl who went missing last week. In Kent, wasn't it?'

'You're kidding,' Ed said.

'Can you tell me where you were that afternoon?'

He raised his hands, opened his mouth and closed it again. 'At work. *Obviously.* I was at work . . .'

'So . . .?'

286

'God, I had calls all over the place, same as always.' He shook his head, thinking. 'Size of the territories these days, you know? Maidenhead, Reading, High Wycombe, out that way. Might even have gone as far as Swindon. I'll have to check the diary.'

'I think I spoke to you on the phone at lunchtime,' Sue said. 'Yeah, I think you told me you'd just finished in Reading.' When she saw Jenny looking at her, Sue said, '*I* was almost certainly lying around on my fat arse watching *Loose Women*.' She blushed slightly. 'Making the most of the school holidays.'

'I can send you the names of the bookshops,' Ed said.

Jenny said, 'That would be helpful.' She checked that he still had her number then closed her notebook. This was going to be the good bit. 'What you said before, about knowing what the police were like . . .'

Ed blinked.

'That's presumably got something to do with the way they've treated you before. The police over here, I mean.'

Ed began shaking his head. 'Here we go.'

'Something to do with a woman called Annette Bailey.'

He turned to his wife with a look that was almost triumphant. 'You see?'

'Relax,' Sue said.

'Fucking *Annette Bailey*?'

'Anything you'd like to say about that?' Jenny asked.

'Not a damn thing.'

'You might be doing yourself a favour in the long run.'

'A *favour*? Is this some kind of a wind-up?'

'Look.' Jenny was pitching for 'trustworthy' but worried as she spoke that her tone was closer to downright patronising. 'I can understand why you might have thought it would be held against you in some way, if the police in Florida had done some digging and found out about it, but I'm giving you a chance to tell me—'

'I'm telling you bugger all.'

'Your prerogative,' Jenny said.

'What the hell d'you need me to tell you anyway? You obviously know all about it.'

Jenny knew no more than the basic details. The PNC gave the names, dates and little else. She would not know any more until the file she had requested arrived from the General Registry. She gathered her things together, dipped for her handbag.

'Maybe I should be calling a solicitor,' Ed said.

'Maybe you should,' Jenny said.

She stood up and stepped away from the table. Sue moved quickly to join her and at the doorway they both cast a look back to Ed, who had not moved and was not bothering to watch them leave. He rubbed the back of his neck, stared out towards the garden. There had been agitation certainly but he had not raised his voice and now he looked calm enough. Jenny felt sure there would be shouting after she had left.

At the front door, she turned to Sue Dunning. Over the woman's shoulder she could see the ginger cat perched halfway up the stairs, licking itself. Jenny said, 'You really shouldn't have bothered to tidy up.'

FORTY-NINE

Marina said that she needed a large glass of wine and Angie had no problem keeping her company. The good weather was holding, so they sat outside a Pizza Express in Crystal Palace. It was only ten minutes from the practice where Marina worked in South Norwood and Angie had been happy enough to drive up from Crawley.

'Diary's not exactly packed,' she'd said on the phone.

When she'd got there and they'd ordered, Angie explained that they were going to have company. Marina seemed a little shaken.

'Sorry, but there wasn't a lot I could do,' Angie said. 'I told her I was meeting you for lunch and she said how much easier that would be for her. Two birds with one stone sort of thing.'

'It's not fair,' Marina said. She turned her mobile phone over and over in her hand, then laid it on the table. 'Like it's being sprung on us.'

'She's already spoken to Barry. So, you know, I think they want to talk to us all again.'

'Talk to us about what?'

'No idea,' Angie said. She seemed perfectly at ease with it, happy even, and, as the waiter laid their pizzas down, Marina decided that being spoken to by a police officer was probably as exciting as Angie's life got. Being married to Barry was hardly going to be a rollercoaster ride, after all.

'This is lovely,' Angie said.

Marina grunted her agreement, mouth full.

'I mean the two of us having lunch like this. I know you and Sue have been getting together, so . . .'

'Just once.' Marina swallowed fast.

'It's fine.'

'We just met that one time. Just for an hour or something. Sue thought it would be a bit far for you to come.'

Angie smiled. '*We* haven't really had a chance for a proper girlie chat, have we?'

Marina shook her head.

'I love what you're wearing, by the way.'

Marina wore a thin white cardigan over a fifties-style, floral-print dress. The tips of her hair were still dyed red, though most of it had been gathered up beneath an oversized tweed cap.

'Sue's got one like that,' Angie said.

'Has she?'

'Don't you remember? We saw it when we were in her bedroom. I don't know, maybe it was Ed's. I'm sure it looks better on you.'

'Your bracelet's gorgeous,' Marina said, reaching towards it.

Angie stretched her arm across the table. 'Got it from Barry for Christmas.'

'So, how *is* your old man, anyway?'

For some reason, Marina had asked the question with more than a trace of a cockney accent. If Angie noticed, she didn't seem to mind and she told Marina all about the problems Barry had been having with his brother and his ex-wife. Marina made sympathetic noises and they both agreed that families could be a nightmare.

'Dave and I are lucky,' Marina said. 'Neither of us has anything at all to do with ours, for one reason or another.'

'Oh, that's a shame.'

She shook her head. 'Like Dave says, we're self-contained. Better off that way.'

Angie cocked her head, considering it. 'Different things work for different people, I suppose.' She was about to say something else, then saw the woman walking towards the table. She leaned towards Marina and whispered, 'Here we go.'

A few seconds later, Jenny Quinlan was pulling a chair across and joining them without a trace of awkwardness. As though she were simply a friend who had not been able to make it in time for the main course.

'God, wine would be nice,' she said, eyeing their glasses. 'But I'd better not. Those boys on traffic would love nothing more than to pull over a female detective with a couple of glasses of Chardonnay inside her. Make their bloody day, that would. *Major* stiffies all round, I promise you.' She smiled at Angie then turned to Marina. 'So, how was work this morning?'

'Same as usual,' Marina said.

'I bloody hate the dentist,' Jenny said. 'Well, I don't suppose *anybody* likes it very much, do they?'

'I'm a receptionist,' Marina said. 'Part-time.'

'Right.'

'Leaves the afternoons free for auditions. Or to get some writing done.'

'What are you writing?' Jenny asked. She appeared to be genuinely interested.

Marina looked embarrassed.

'Oh, go on,' Angie said. 'I was going to ask how all that was going.'

'Actually, I'm working on a short story about what happened when we were in Florida,' Marina said. She was more confident suddenly, cocky almost. 'That girl.'

'Ooh, a crime story.' Angie hunched up her shoulders, excited. 'I love those.'

'Me too,' Jenny said. 'But they always get things wrong.'

'Like what?' Angie asked.

'Well, they always manage to catch the killer for a start.' She rummaged in her bag, brought out her notebook. 'Talking of which . . .'

'So they still haven't caught him then?' Angie said.

Jenny looked at her. 'We're still working on it.'

She asked the two women what they had been doing nine days earlier, on the eleventh. Then she asked if they knew what their other halves had been doing, in Angie's case to confirm what Barry Finnegan had already told her. When she had been given the information, she asked them if they were going to have pudding, told them she could murder a piece of chocolate fudge cake. Angie said that she would join her, and when it arrived, Jenny said, 'So tell me what you make of Ed Dunning?'

Angie and Marina said nothing for the ten seconds or so it took for their expressions to change a number of times. Surprise, confusion, then contemplation, which Angie at least appeared to find enjoyable. Though clearly both were bursting to do so, each seemed a little afraid to ask Jenny the obvious question.

'He's . . . nice enough,' Angie said, finally.

Marina's pause suggested that she didn't wholeheartedly agree. 'I think he'd be thrilled that we were talking about him,' she said. 'He likes to be the centre of attention.'

'Oh, definitely. He's never short of an opinion.'

'A very *odd* opinion.'

'But he's funny.'

'Well, he *thinks* he is.'

'Yeah, I suppose he can be a bit . . . sick sometimes,' Angie said.

'Only because he likes shocking people.'

'I never really know when he's taking the mickey, if I'm honest.'

'He's just a wind-up merchant,' Marina said.

'Really? Sometimes I think it's a bit nastier than that.'

The dessert arrived. Jenny got stuck in, continued to listen.

'I suppose you'd have to say he's quite good-looking.'

'Oh God, no,' Angie said.

'I'm not saying he's *sexy* though.'

'Well, I can see what you mean, but not my type at all.'

292

'He's always *talking* about sex for a start. I find all that a bit sleazy, to be honest.'

'He certainly likes to flirt,' Angie said.

'Bit of a bully too, I reckon.'

'Well, yes, but between you and me, I think Sue quite . . . *likes* that.'

'Over-compensating, if you ask me.'

'Maybe he can't get it up,' Angie said.

Walking back to her car, already regretting the chocolate fudge cake, Jenny got a call from the man she had spent the previous half an hour talking about.

'About yesterday,' Ed said. 'I just wanted to clarify a couple of things.'

'You want to talk about Annette Bailey?'

'No, I told you.'

'And I told you, it might help you if you did.'

'I said everything that needed saying at the time, told the police everything and it didn't help when it came to getting an apology, did it? Not a single word, not a "sorry, we fucked up" after weeks of hell. No charges ever made, not a single one, but in the end it doesn't matter, does it, because the shit sticks. Sits there stinking on some computer somewhere until it gets dragged up years later by the likes of you.' He said nothing for a few seconds. 'And you wonder about my attitude towards the police.'

Jenny pressed the remote on her keyring to open her car. 'So, if you didn't call to talk about Annette Bailey, what exactly do you want to "clarify", Mr Dunning?'

'Those bookshops, on the eleventh. I was going to give you a list.'

'It's a bit tricky at the moment. Can you email it to me?'

'It's not worth it, because I didn't go to them,' Ed said. 'Not all of them anyway.'

'I see.'

'Sue doesn't know, that's why I didn't say anything yesterday.'

'So, what were you doing?'

'Look, things are a bit stretched at the moment and I don't make anything like as many calls as I used to. I'm not exactly . . . busy.' He let out a long breath. 'I sit in car parks and listen to the radio, I go to the pub. Cinema sometimes. All right?'

'So you lie to your wife.' Jenny opened the car door and got in.

'Yes, I lie. It makes things easier for both of us, and although this is none of your bloody business I'd really rather not have her finding out that I haven't been able to pay the mortgage for the last few months, so if there's any way we can avoid that . . . you know.'

'I'll see what I can do.'

'You'd be doing me a favour.'

Jenny closed the car door and slid the key into the ignition. She said, 'Thank you for being honest with me.'

FIFTY

The truth was, Gardner had been thinking about flying over there for a week or so, ever since he'd received that email about the girl going missing in Kent. It was only now though, three days since he'd spoken to Jenny Quinlan, that he brought the subject up at home. Nice and casual, over grilled salmon steaks and salad.

'Really?' Michelle asked.

'Well, there's nothing definite,' Gardner said. He knew how much his wife hated him going away unless it was absolutely necessary. That overnight in Atlanta had led to an atmosphere for a couple of days. 'I just had a conversation with the lieutenant about it. That's all.'

'It sounds a bit vague,' she said. 'This so-called connection.'

'Well, we'll see.'

'Can't the police over there handle their side of it?'

'Yeah, I'm sure they can.'

'So what's the point? Besides, wouldn't they be a little pissed, you showing up? Barging in, like they couldn't do their jobs properly?'

The point was that rotten tooth and him doing everything he could to get it out. But Gardner just said, 'It's only an idea, that's all.'

He was getting sick of wading through the paperwork on all the British tourists they had so far been able to track down. Ticking one off after the other, eliminating them from the investigation. Every UK passport holder who had been staying on Longboat, Siesta or Casey Key when Amber-Marie was taken. Anywhere as far as Anna Maria island to the north and Venice to the south. It felt as though his end was now all about the people who *didn't* do it. There was nothing to get excited about, nothing he would be able to tell Patti Lee Wilson.

A bit vague . . .

His wife was probably right.

He never usually talked to her in any great detail about the cases he was working. Michelle's choice as much as his. She was not exactly itching to hear about the latest drug deal gone bad in Newtown. Some sixteen-year-old shot dead for selling a few wraps on the wrong corner. In fact, she wasn't crazy about any of it and more than once she had tried to get into the subject of them moving out of Florida altogether. She was originally from the Midwest and once in a while she talked about a small town somewhere, some three or four-man police department Gardner might be able to head up. He would listen and pretend he was thinking about it, then remind her that even if Sarasota had its problems—and the homicide rate per head of population *was* way higher than it should have been—at least he wasn't working in Atlanta or Detroit.

He didn't tell her that he could not imagine anything worse than running some two-bit department in Bumfuck, Indiana. Spending his days sorting out disputes between noisy neighbours or whatever it was. What had Patti said? Overdue taxes and parking tickets. Yeah, maybe he'd sleep a little better, but he'd feel like he was in a coma the rest of the damn time.

'Make sure you pack sweaters,' Michelle said, a little snappy.

'It wouldn't be for long and it probably won't happen anyway.'

'Look, it's up to you,' she said.

They might normally have gone outside after they'd eaten, finished the wine off by the pool, but it was way too humid for that. The late summer months were brutal, you just moved from house to car and car to air-conditioned building as fast as you could. The temperature might come down once in a while, enough for him to take a beer out on to the deck maybe, but right now at seven-thirty in the evening it was still pushing 80 degrees. So they took their glasses across to the couch.

'Well, it's not my decision ultimately,' Gardner said.

'If you're pushing for it though.'

'Who says I'm pushing?'

'I know you,' Michelle said.

'You think?' Her face told him exactly what she thought. 'Like I say, it's only an idea.'

'Right . . .'

He leaned across to kiss her. He was thinking about the emails he'd received from London over the last few days, the phone calls from Jenny Quinlan. He said, 'I just want to be where the action is.'

On cue their daughter began calling out from upstairs.

'How about you start with that?'

Gardner sighed and quickly finished what was in his glass. 'Talking tiger time.'

FIFTY-ONE

Thursday morning, the file arrived from General Registry. Jenny opened up the green cardboard folder, sat at her desk with a coffee. Around her, the office was buzzing—a domestic murder in Catford, a stabbing at a club in New Cross, serious gunshot wounds following a drive-by in Lewisham—but Jenny had no trouble zoning out; the chatter and the laughter and the ringing of phones fading into the background as she concentrated on the report.

A white printed sticker, peeling at one corner from the front of the file. *Edward Charles Dunning. Charge of rape. January 17, 2005.*

There was not much of it. The case against Dunning had collapsed at a relatively early stage with all charges dropped well before pre-trial preparations.

Didn't help when it came to getting an apology, did it?

Despite the distinctly unfunny nature of the subject matter, Jenny found herself smiling as she read, picturing the outrage on Dunning's face, enjoying the memory of his self-righteous ranting the day before.

The shit sticks . . .

Dunning had been charged with the rape of Annette Bailey, a thirty-seven-year-old woman who worked as a bookseller at her own premises in Wokingham, a shop on Ed Dunning's patch. He had invited her for a drink, having called at her shop at the end of the day. After a couple of hours in the pub, they had gone back to the small flat above the shop. They had opened another bottle, ended up in Annette Bailey's bed.

It was at this point that their versions of events began to diverge.

Jenny read the initial statements made the following morning by Dunning and by the woman accusing him. She looked through the results of the rape kit that had been run earlier the same day. These confirmed that sexual intercourse had taken place and detailed the multiple injuries consistent with a serious sexual assault. She read the results of the subsequent DNA test, which left no doubt whatsoever that Ed Dunning had been responsible, then she read—and reread—Dunning's interview following his arrest, five days after the alleged offence.

Then, it was just admin.

Back and forth between the senior investigating officer and a lawyer from the Crown Prosecution Service. A second round of interviews requested along with 'background information' on Annette Bailey. The growing list of 'concerns' on the part of the CPS.

Miss Bailey had invited Mr Dunning to her flat.

She admitted that she had been drinking and smoking marijuana.

She admitted to finding Mr Dunning 'fanciable'.

She willingly climbed into bed with him.

The assault was not reported until the following morning.

Then, finally, the CPS's conclusion that having considered the evidence carefully, it was not in anyone's interest, including Miss Bailey's—Jenny had to read that line twice—to take this case to trial.

All wrapped up nicely in a dozen pages, plus a few unpleasant pictures.

The sounds of the office faded up again as Jenny noted down the salient points. Then, together with her own thoughts as to how she should proceed, she transferred them into an email, which she sent to Jeff Gardner. Well aware that any kudos coming her way was dependent on following the necessary chains of command, she took care to copy in the relevant SIOs from both Kent and the Met.

She took down the contact details she needed from the file. Checked again to make sure there was nothing else she should do, no procedure she had neglected to follow.

Job done.

Half an hour later she was perched on the edge of a desk, sharing a joke with Adam Simmons, when the call came through to say that a visitor was waiting downstairs.

She watched Dave Cullen stand up when he caught sight of her through the window. A nod of recognition. He reached into a pocket for his inhaler and took a swift puff as she opened the door into the reception area and walked across to join him.

'Mr Cullen?' She shook his outstretched hand. 'I was going to call you.'

'I thought I'd save you the trouble,' he said.

'You're obviously getting fond of this place.'

He laughed. 'Well, it's exciting to see where it all happens, isn't it?'

'Shall we talk here?' He hesitated, as though waiting for a better suggestion. 'Or I could try and find us a nice quiet room somewhere?'

'That would be great,' he said.

She swiped him through the security door and he followed her up the stairs. Walking along a corridor towards the suite of rooms occupied by CID, she was aware of him glancing into offices as they passed, scrutinising noticeboards.

'Can I see the Incident Room?' he asked.

'I'm afraid not,' Jenny said. She did not bother to point out that as far as the case he had presumably come here to talk about went, the Incident Room amounted to little more than a single drawer in her desk. She glanced over her shoulder at him as they walked. 'I didn't think you were here for a tour anyway.'

He managed a tight smile. 'They're just like ordinary offices,' he said, peering through another small window in another plain wooden door. 'I bet you've got stationery cupboards and everything . . .'

Jenny found an unoccupied interview room. Before that, she'd tried one of the briefing rooms, but the large whiteboard at one end was still

300

decorated with photos of the targets in a forthcoming drugs operation. She had quickly closed the door again. 'Not allowed to see those,' she said. 'Sorry.' His disappointment had been obvious.

As they sat down on opposite sides of the metal desk, Cullen said, 'I wasn't far wrong with sixty-five per cent, by the way.'

'Sorry?'

'Your chance of catching the killer. I've done a bit of checking and it's actually a bit less than that in the US. Closer to sixty per cent according to the most recent set of figures, but that's nationwide of course. Obviously it's way lower than that in some places.'

Jenny nodded. Obviously.

'We really need to factor in the UK figures though, don't we?'

'Do we?'

'Well, the investigation has obviously widened out to include the disappearance of Samantha Gold.' Cullen smiled. 'Bearing in mind the questions you've already asked the others.'

'So?'

'Oh, it's way higher over here,' he said. 'Closer to ninety per cent, but that's based on figures from Scotland Yard, so, you know, pinch of salt and all that. Also, that applies to what they call "detected" murders. Problem is, that can mean murders where someone is convicted, but it also applies to anyone who's been charged and cleared later. So, it's a bit . . . muddy.'

'All the same.' Jenny did her best to look pleased. 'Higher's good, isn't it?'

'Yeah, definitely. There are only a thousand or so unsolved murders in the whole country, going right back. That's pretty impressive, I reckon.'

'I'll pass that on,' Jenny said. 'It's nice to be appreciated.'

Cullen nodded and looked around. He sat back in his chair, his hands thrust into the pockets of his hoodie. 'So, how's it going, anyway?'

'Early days,' Jenny said.

'That's the important bit, isn't it? Those first few days, that's when they say you've got the best chance to find someone who's missing.'

'Most of the time, yes.'

'After that it's always a murder inquiry, isn't it? I mean I know you don't say that to the family or anything, but that's what you're thinking, right?' He shook his head. 'Way past that already for Samantha Gold, I would have thought . . .'

He stretched his legs and Jenny shifted hers back beneath her chair when Cullen's feet nudged her own. She glanced down and saw a pair of orange and white New Balance trainers. They looked familiar and she remembered that Ed Dunning had worn a pair exactly the same.

'I need to ask you some questions,' Jenny said.

'Course. That's why I'm here. Fire away.'

She'd always thought Dave Cullen was weird—had noted that down after the first interview—but now she was struck by just how arrogant he was. It was interesting, as it was not how others had described him. The day before in Crystal Palace, once they had finished discussing Ed Dunning, Jenny had taken advantage of Marina's visit to the ladies to ask Angie Finnegan what she thought of him.

'Dave's lovely,' Angie had said, her voice low even though Marina was no longer with them. 'He's quiet and I think he's a bit shy really . . . even though he's clearly a right brainbox. Lovely to Marina as well. *Attentive.* I wish Barry was a bit more like that, tell you the truth . . .'

'The eleventh,' Jenny said to Cullen. 'In the afternoon.'

'I know Marina already told you that we were both at home, but I'm guessing you need to hear it from me as well.'

'Please.'

'Like she told you, I was off work for a few days because my asthma was bad. Still is, actually. Smog levels have gone through the bloody roof in London. There's plenty of work I can do on the computer at home. So . . .'

'So Marina came back when?'

'Same time she always does when she's on mornings. Half one, something like that. We had lunch, a sandwich or whatever and we sat and watched a film.' He looked at her. '*The Romantic Englishwoman.* It's a Joe Losey movie . . . Michael Caine and Glenda Jackson. Not exactly one of Caine's best, but he *has* made a lot of rubbish.' He smiled. 'Now obviously I could have just found out what was on by looking at the *Radio Times* or something. But I didn't. I think it was Channel 5 if you're interested.'

Jenny scribbled it down. 'I won't bother looking out for that one.'

'Just out of interest, why *do* you think the Samantha Gold case has got anything to do with what happened to Amber-Marie Wilson?' As Jenny was about to trot out the usual line about being 'unable to divulge that information', Cullen held up his hand, knowing what was coming. He said, 'Fine,' and shrugged, like it didn't matter. Or like he knew the answer anyway.

'Right then . . .'

'Should be interesting on Saturday,' he said.

'What's happening on Saturday?'

'Dinner round at our place. Ed and Sue and the others.' He smiled. 'The Sarasota Six . . .'

'I'm sure you'll have plenty to talk about,' Jenny said.

FIFTY-TWO

Mid-morning on Friday, Sue Dunning received a call from Marina Green.

'I know it's late notice and it's probably a mad idea, but I was thinking we could make Saturday night into a Saturday night *and* Sunday morning thing. You could all stay over.'

'Oh,' Sue said.

'There's this fantastic greasy spoon round the corner which me and Dave go to all the time and they do the most amazing fry-up. Not first thing or anything, I mean I'm sure we'll have several bottles of wine to sleep off.' Before Sue could say anything else, Marina carried on. 'Which is another thing. I mean everyone can have a drink Saturday night then, can't they? What do you think? Go on, it'll be a laugh . . .'

'Well, I'll need to talk to Ed.'

'I mean our place isn't as big as yours, but we've got a spare room and a sofa-bed, so we can easily do it.'

'He sometimes plays tennis on Sunday morning, that's the only thing.'

'Come on,' Marina said. 'Which sounds better? Running about on a tennis court or a late night piss-up and a full English . . .'

As soon as she had hung up, Sue called Angie Finnegan. She told her what Marina was suggesting. Sue said it was a bit late in the day and even though Angie agreed, she still seemed quite excited by the idea.

'So, what do you think?' Angie asked. 'Sounds like fun.'

'Well, we won't do it unless you do.'

'I'll see what Barry says. I'm sure the kids will be delighted to get rid of us for a night.'

'I told her Ed might be playing tennis to give ourselves a get-out if he doesn't fancy it.'

'Just tell him you want to have a drink. I'm sure he won't fancy being the designated driver!'

'Well, maybe. I mean it's the last one, isn't it?'

'What do you mean?' Angie asked.

'Well, you know. We'll all have done it once, kind of thing.'

'So are we not going to carry on seeing each other?'

'No . . . sorry, that didn't come out very well.' Sue struggled for a few seconds. 'Just me being stupidly British about it all, I suppose. Somebody invites you for dinner, so you have to invite them. That's all I meant really.'

Angie laughed. 'Well, we're *Irish*, so you know . . . we don't *need* an excuse for eating and drinking.'

'Obviously we'll stay in touch,' Sue said.

'If we do stay over, we'll have lots more time to talk about you know what,' Angie said.

'That's true.'

'It was on the news again last night by the way. About halfway through, police still searching, you know. Did you see the press conference thing the other day? God, those poor parents.'

'I didn't see it,' Sue said.

'Barry reckons it was the dad.'

'Really?'

'Oh, you know. No smoke without fire, all that.'

Sue thought: now that really *is* British.

305

FIFTY-THREE

Jenny was standing on the pavement, looking at the front door, mobile pressed to her ear. Stupid, but she still got excited hearing that single, long ringtone. Those few seconds of . . . somewhere else. The thought that her call was flashing off a satellite somewhere, racing along wires or whatever from a dreary Berkshire market town all the way to the Florida sunshine.

She still hoped she might get the chance to go. If Samantha Gold was dead and the killer was caught and if it did turn out to be the *same* killer, would there be two trials? One here, one over there? She wasn't certain, but if all those things happened and it turned out that she had played even the smallest part in catching the person responsible, then surely she would be asked to give evidence.

She would stay on for a while afterwards, she had decided, try and see something of the place. Maybe someone would volunteer to show her around . . .

Gardner answered on the third ring.

'It's Jenny Quinlan . . .'

'I know,' he said. 'I've got your number programmed into my cell.'

306

It made her absurdly happy to hear him say that. 'Listen, just to let you know that none of these alibis are exactly gold-plated.' She wedged her phone between chin and shoulder, flipped the pages in her notebook. 'Barry Finnegan's doesn't hold up because his brother says their meeting was all over by two o'clock. Crawley to Sevenoaks is fifty minutes, an hour at the most, so he could easily have made it and his wife can't vouch for where he was the rest of the afternoon. Marina Green *is* vouching for Dave Cullen who claims he had the day off sick which is bloody convenient, but she would, wouldn't she . . . so that's not what you'd call watertight either, and Ed Dunning freely admits to not being where he originally claimed to be.'

'What about the other thing?' Gardner asked. He sounded a little distracted. 'The rape or whatever.'

'I'm on it.'

A few minutes later, standing in front of the narrow, off-white door, she was still chiding herself for the stupid Americanism. Would Gardner think she was taking the piss? Trying too hard . . .?

Annette Bailey was not what Jenny had expected.

Actually, she was unsure what she had expected, but the fact was that the woman at the door looked far older—Jenny quickly did the maths in her head—than her forty-three years. She looked fifty-something, not much younger than Jenny's mother. She was wearing baggy, department store jeans and Crocs, a long blue cardigan over a pink patterned blouse. Her face was pale and puffy and if she'd ever bothered she had long since stopped colouring the grey out of her hair.

Jenny introduced herself. Said, 'Thanks for seeing me.'

She was invited in and followed the woman up a narrow staircase—junk mail piled neatly on a tread about halfway up—into what appeared to be a one-bedroom flat. Annette Bailey walked straight into the living room and sat down, waited for Jenny to take a seat opposite her, the two of them at right angles around a low, glass-topped table.

'I had to sell the shop in the end,' Annette said. She unscrewed the top from the small bottle of water she'd been holding when she answered the door. 'It was just me, and I'd had to take so much time off after what happened and I couldn't afford to take anyone else on.' She took a swig. 'I managed to hold on to the flat though.'

Jenny looked around. There were three or four manuscripts of some sort piled up on the table. A copy of that day's *Guardian* and an empty ashtray. Aside from the single armchair and two-seater sofa, there was only a small dining table and two chairs against one wall; a smallish TV and DVD player in the corner, a couple of IKEA table lamps and rugs of various sizes scattered across white-painted floorboards. There were half a dozen pictures in clip-frames on the walls. Paintings, Jenny noticed, not prints, but either way, she did not think they were much good. Landscapes, sea and sunsets, that sort of stuff. Like the kind of things they had in her doctor's waiting room that she always suspected had been done by the doctor himself.

There was a distinct smell of marijuana.

'It's nice,' she said.

Annette nodded at the floor. 'They're OK, the new people, not that they sell many books in there these days. It's all handmade cards and pottery, that sort of thing. I think they make more money with the coffee than anything else.'

'Yeah, I was here a bit early,' Jenny said. 'I had one.'

'A latte, was it?' When Jenny nodded, the grimace of distaste was momentary, but clear enough. Perhaps Annette Bailey was simply not a fan of the stuff, but for a few seconds Jenny found herself imagining that this woman somehow believed the nation's love affair with fancy coffee had played its own small part in bringing her to where she was. Negligible of course in comparison to the event Jenny had come here to talk to her about. The man they had yet to mention.

'So what do you do these days?' Jenny asked.

Annette nodded towards the manuscripts. 'I get paid to read. Not a lot, but it's fine. New fiction for a few small publishers. That, and some other bits and pieces. I live on my own, so it's not like I need to be making a fortune.' She raised the bottle to her lips again. 'I *am* seeing someone though. Not for very long, but it's . . . nice.'

'That's good,' Jenny said. Once again, she found herself reading things into the woman's words; an expression that suddenly was almost defiant, forbidding even the smallest shred of pity before it dared to surface.

Yes, he fucked my life up, but he did not *destroy me.*

'I also volunteer at a refuge up the road,' Annette said. 'I man a helpline sometimes. It's one of the reasons I agreed to see you.'

'I'm grateful that you did.'

'So, what? Has he done it again?'

Jenny blinked. 'He's . . . someone we're looking at in connection with a serious offence,' she said.

Annette put the bottle on the table. 'Well, you can stop looking.'

Jenny said, 'Can you run me through what happened that night?'

'It's all in the file, isn't it?'

Jenny said that it was.

'Well, I stand by that statement. I'm not changing a single word of it, even though I was strongly advised by certain people to do so at the time. Could I *maybe* think about taking out the stuff about fancying him and the amount I'd drunk?'

'So why didn't you?'

'Because it would have been a lie. I mean I was probably a bit stupid not to, looking back. Mind you, how long would he have done, realistically? He'd probably be out by now anyway.' She sat back, spat out a laugh. 'He could have gone to prison back then and still have done whatever it is you're after him for now.'

'Tell me what happened,' Jenny said.

'You know.'

'I've read what you said then, but . . .' She let the words tail away.

Annette took a few seconds, then began tugging at a loose thread on the arm of her chair. 'We went out to a local pub. We drank a bottle of wine and I asked him back here.' She looked hard at Jenny. 'Because I was horny and he was clearly interested, fair enough? We opened another bottle when we got in, we smoked a joint and then at some point we started . . . you know. Ended up in the bedroom.' She nodded towards the hallway, a stripped wooden door on the far side of it. 'In *there* . . .

'We got into bed and started to . . . have sex. It was OK for a minute or two, maybe a bit longer, but then he got rough. It got very . . . rough and it was hurting and I told him to stop. I thought maybe he hadn't heard me because he was making a lot of noise, so I shouted. I told him to get off, that I wanted him to stop, but he wouldn't stop.

'He wouldn't stop.'

She tore away the thread and balled it up into her fist. 'That's rape, isn't it? Whatever I'd felt before, whatever I'd said to him before. That's *rape* . . .'

'Yes, it is,' Jenny said.

'I think it's because he was angry with me. I mean, I worked that much out afterwards, but I never said it in the statement. By the time I'd sat down and thought about it, about why he'd been *so* angry, they'd already dropped the charges.'

Jenny nodded. 'Rape's always about anger. It's never about sex.'

'I know all that,' Annette said, irritated suddenly. 'I mean, he was angry because I wouldn't go along with his stupid game.'

After a second or two, Jenny realised she was holding her breath. 'What game?'

'Some stupid fantasy . . . role-play thing. I told him straight off I didn't want to. I'm a grown woman, for God's sake, I mean I'm happy to have fun, but this was just stupid. No, it was . . . creepy.'

'What did he want?'

'I don't know if he actually wanted me to . . . dress up or anything and I mean, dress up in *what*? Like I've got a uniform hanging in the wardrobe or something. I think he just wanted me to play the part. Say the right things.'

'What things?' Jenny asked. 'What did he ask you to do?'

This time, the grimace of distaste stayed put. 'He wanted me to be a schoolgirl.'

Jenny knew there was a protocol she should follow. There were basic rules of politeness, thank yous to be said. But all she could think about was getting out of there as quickly as possible and calling Gardner again.

FIFTY-FOUR

Angie thought that Barry was in a good mood. This was because each time he came into the bedroom, he talked back to the radio, which was tuned in to some programme about the day's football fixtures. He stood at the end of the bed and listened for a minute or two, then muttered, 'Bollocks,' or 'He doesn't know what he's talking about,' before wandering out again.

It was only eleven o'clock, something like that, but Angie was already packing their overnight bag. She carefully pushed her toiletries to one end of the small case. She placed her make-up bag at the other, leaving plenty of room in the middle for clothes.

She shouted to Barry. 'I've put clean pants and socks in for the morning, all right? Tell me what shirt you want.'

'I don't know . . . the light blue?'

She collected the shirt from the wardrobe, folded it and put it into the case together with a choice of tops for herself. There was plenty of room and she didn't know what she'd fancy wearing the next day. Then she took out the new pyjamas she'd bought from M&S, a red pair with cartoon monkeys on them. She stood in front of the full-length mirror on the back of the wardrobe door and held the top up against herself. She'd liked them in the shop, thought they were fun. She'd imagined that she would look good drinking tea the next morning at Marina and Dave's, but now she wasn't sure.

'What are you going to sleep in?' she shouted.

She would look like a tomato on legs. A fat-arsed tomato.

Barry shouted back, 'Why do I need to sleep in *anything*?'

Angie was excited about the evening ahead. It would be good to have a night away, a laugh with mates. She also hoped that the change of scene might shake things up a bit in the bedroom. End the drought. Messing around under someone else's roof was a *bit* off, but it was . . . naughty and just the thought of it was causing her to flush a little.

Same colour as these stupid pyjamas, she thought, folding them.

Once or twice in the last few months, she'd suggested that they have a weekend away somewhere. A romantic break, though she was careful not to call it that and always talked about the great food and the scenery instead. She fancied a little hotel in Devon or Cornwall, somewhere like that, but Barry had never been keen. He always told her it was too far, there was too much on at work, but she suspected it was because he knew it wasn't really cream teas and sunsets she was looking forward to.

'Why can't I sleep bollock-naked, like I always sleep?' Barry had come in again, this time cradling a mug of tea.

'Well, we might be walking around in the morning and you've got to look decent.'

'So, I'll get dressed.' He held up his tea. 'Kettle's just boiled if you want one, by the way.'

'I'm fine, love.' She folded up a towel, watching him. She said, 'You're chirpy.'

'Am I?'

'You all right about going then, now?'

'Long as we're not the ones who end up with the sofa-bed. Bugger *that*.'

Angie laughed. 'That all you're concerned about?'

'No. I'm also worried that this breakfast might not be as great as she says it is. I'll be having words if there isn't decent black pudding . . .'

She could only put his good mood down to the fact that he wasn't working today. That things—as far as he was telling her, anyway—had eased off a little between him and his brother. Maybe he *was* looking forward to the evening ahead; a few drinks and something to eat and who knows, maybe he was even thinking about getting those stupid red pyjamas off her later on. Whatever the reason, she was happy not to feel those eggshells under her feet.

'That woman told me you said sorry to her.' She put the towel into the case. 'That copper.'

Barry looked down into his tea. 'Yeah, well.'

'Was that sorry because you were stroppy with her, or sorry because I had a go at you afterwards?'

'Doesn't matter, does it?'

'I told you I'd been on the internet, didn't I? Found out about that girl.'

He puffed out his cheeks. 'Tonight going to be another *Crimewatch* special then, is it?'

'Well, it's big news.'

'I don't know about *big*.'

'It's the link though, isn't it?'

'They might already know.'

Angie felt a little deflated, but tried not to show it. She didn't want his mood to change. She liked it when it was like this, she didn't mind him taking the piss. It was like when they first met and he would wind her up about the building work, the things she was asking for, tell her she didn't know her arse from her elbow.

She would tell the others what she'd found out anyway. She might even use Barry's line. Here's a Finnegan Crimewatch update, sort of thing.

Make a joke of it.

She suddenly imagined Samantha Gold; vividly pictured her grinning in a pair of silly red pyjamas. They were the sort of thing a girl like *that* would like, weren't they, even at her age?

Childish things. Bears and glitter and sweet surprises.

'Why don't I put one of your polo shirts in?' she said, as Barry walked out of the bedroom. 'Gives you the choice then, doesn't it?'

Barry had started to learn that not *showing* your mood was the most important thing. A bad mood, anyway. You had to learn to hold it in, live with it for however long and not show a thing until you got the chance to let it out safely.

Like disposing of dangerous chemicals.

He walked back downstairs, turned on the TV and settled down in front of *Football Focus*.

He sometimes thought that if he wasn't such a fat bastard, sport might be the answer. He never got the chance to go to the Emirates these days, but you could let off a lot of steam watching a match. At the ref, the players, the other team's fans obviously. Maybe he could even try and shift some weight and play a bit. Kick a few lumps out of somebody or other in the local park of a Sunday morning.

Yeah, that would make him feel a lot better.

As it happened, he wasn't dreading the evening ahead . . . the whole overnight business . . . quite as much as he had been when Angie had first suggested it. He knew things might get a bit awkward, mind you, that Angie would most likely fancy it later on. He'd just have to make sure he had a bit too much to drink, avoid a row. Even before the problems started, booze had always successfully scuppered any downstairs business.

It wasn't like he wasn't trying, for crying out loud. Angie hadn't been the only one on the internet lately. He'd been checking out a few of those dodgy sites that sold Viagra, but he hadn't quite been able to bring himself to click that *buy* button. It felt like admitting you were past it, besides which you could never guarantee what you were getting, could you? Not when one little blue pill looked much the same as another.

'We need to leave some cash for Laura and Luke,' Angie was shouting from upstairs. 'Enough to order pizza. I've told them they can have a couple of friends round as well, is that OK?'

315

'Yeah, fine,' he shouted back.

A night away from Angie's kids though, that was worth having. He loved them, course he did; not quite like they were his own, that would be stupid, but . . . enough. Lately though, the mouthing off and the liberties with money and lifts and all that, he'd felt like swinging for them.

He thought about his son. He wondered how Nick would be spending his Saturday night. Hiding the moods, the blackest of them at least, was bound to make relations a bit smoother with his ex-wife, wasn't it?

Anything at all to make it easier, that had to be the way forward.

What were they called, those stupid bastards who dressed up as Spiderman or Batman or whatever and protested on roofs?

On TV they started talking about Division One, so he flicked the set off.

I mean really, what did they think making tits of themselves like that was going to achieve? Who the hell was ever going to take that sort of carry-on seriously?

There were better ways to get your point across.

FIFTY-FIVE

'Have you really got nothing better to do on a Saturday morning?'

'Depends what you mean by better,' Quinlan said. 'More enjoyable, almost certainly. More important, no.'

'Well I have,' Ed said. 'So, are you asking me or telling me?'

'At this moment, I'm asking you.'

'Right then.'

'But I *can* tell you it would be a good move to come in and talk to me.'

'Like I thought, an invitation. It's not formal because you haven't got anything worth *making* it formal.'

'I spoke to Annette Bailey . . .'

Ed had been pacing up and down the living room with the phone. He stopped at the garden end and looked out. It was a good day for tennis. Maybe he could take a walk down to the club, see if there was anyone hanging about who fancied a game. Somebody he could beat.

'Mr Dunning?'

He could still remember every detail of that evening. Six years ago, nearly seven. A month or so after everything had fallen apart. He remembered her wanting it and then not wanting it, changing her mind in a heartbeat. How insanely unfair it had seemed to him that she still had the choice.

He remembered standing in the garden, taking that bloody swing down.

'Maybe I should think about getting that solicitor.'

'Like I said . . .'

'My prerogative, I know.' He began to pace again. 'Maybe I should start talking to one about suing you people for harassment. How does that sound?'

'Go ahead.'

'I might, because this is getting ridiculous now.'

'Quite pricey though, I would have thought.'

'What?'

'Legal fees. For someone who hasn't paid his mortgage in three months.'

Sue appeared in the doorway. She saw his face, mouthed, 'What?' He shook his head. She stood watching him until he waved her away and she backed out of the room.

'I'm only thinking of you, Mr Dunning.'

He walked to the doorway, pushed the door closed. 'So, come on then, what did she say? *Annette* . . .'

'It's not something I really want to discuss on the phone.'

Ed turned and leaned back against the door.

'I'm sure you can understand that, Mr Dunning.'

That woman . . .

Wanting it then not wanting it, blowing hot and cold. *Hurting* her? Jesus Christ . . . like she had any idea what it meant to be in pain, what it really *meant*?

It had poured with rain, that day he'd stood in the garden and taken the swing apart. His hands had slipped, bled as he tore at the wet, cold metal and he remembered turning and looking up to see Sue watching him from an upstairs window.

'I don't understand a fucking thing,' he said, quietly.

318

'Well I'll explain, if you come in.'

'No . . .'

'You can tell me all about the game you wanted Annette Bailey to play.'

'*What?*'

'The things you asked her to do.'

He pushed hard away from the door. 'I'm not telling you anything, because there's nothing to talk about, all right? This is just getting ludicrous now . . . it's stupid. Like thousands of other people I happened to be in Florida when a girl went missing, and I made the mistake of lying about what I was doing at the time. That's all. I lied because of exactly what you're doing now, dredging up shit that has nothing to do with anything. You want to push this any further, you'd better get some evidence and then I'll find the money to hire the best legal team I can and make you look stupid.'

He was feeling a lot better suddenly, stronger. 'Thinking about it, I don't think that's likely to cost me very much . . .'

Sue was in the kitchen, waiting for Ed to finish on the phone. He walked in and went to the fridge, spoke with his back to her.

'Quinlan.'

'What did she want?'

'She spoke to Annette Bailey.'

Sue said, 'Oh,' and waited again. When Ed closed the fridge door and turned to her, he had a carton of orange juice in his hand. He looked calm. There was even a hint of a smile.

'You ask me, she's pretty well qualified to be investigating the murder of that girl in Florida,' he said. 'Quinlan, I mean. She's got about as much going on upstairs as that girl did.' He raised the carton in a mock toast and drank from it.

'It's not just Florida though, is it?' Sue sat down at their small kitchen table. 'They're investigating two crimes now.'

'What's that supposed to mean?'

'It's not supposed to mean anything. They are though, aren't they?'

'I don't know *what* they're doing.' He reopened the fridge to put the carton back. 'I don't think *they* know what they're doing.'

'So what did she say?'

'She wants me to go in and talk to her.'

'I meant the Bailey woman.'

He stared at her for a few seconds, then shrugged. The half-smile was still there. 'Doesn't matter, does it? She was probably pissed anyway.'

'Or stoned.'

He nodded, pleased. 'I told her where to get off, in so many words. I don't think she was expecting that. They think you're going to be intimidated or scared of them. They *love* that.'

'Yes, but you don't want to antagonise her.'

'What's she going to do?' He walked behind her to the worktop, turned and walked back again. 'I'm going to really enjoy telling everyone later on. I'll bet none of *them* told her where she could go.'

Sue thought, why would they? but she said nothing. Ed was moving easily, on the balls of his feet, like he was stalking a baseline. He was making a good job of hiding the tension, the nerves, but Sue knew him better than anyone. Knew how much he hid.

'Listen, we don't have to go tonight.'

'Course we do,' he said. 'I'm very much looking forward to getting completely and utterly slaughtered.'

'There's no need to do that.'

'Oh yes there is.'

'One of us should stay sober though, yes? Then we can always chicken out and drive home if it gets too horrendous.'

'Fuck *that*,' he said. 'Horrendous is exactly the way I want it.' He stopped behind her and began to rub her shoulders. 'You really want to see any of these people ever again?'

Sue said that she didn't and told him not to stop.

FIFTY-SIX

Dave held out his bag and the man behind the stall emptied the onions, okra and sweet potatoes into it. He handed over the cash and the man gave him his change. The man said, 'Take care, yeah,' and turned towards his next customer. Dave said, 'You too,' and held out his fist. The man looked a little awkward, but eventually turned back and touched his fist, just for a second, to Dave's.

Dave said, 'Thanks, man,' and walked away to buy the meat.

He loved Brixton Market on a Saturday morning. The music, the crowds, the vibe of the place. It was pulsing with energy, thronged with shoppers, black, white and Asian faces. It fascinated him, these hundreds of people going about their business. The way that, for those few minutes or even seconds when their lives intersected with others—a look or a word exchanged here, a bump of the shoulders there—there was a connection made and that connection was passed on. Everyone had a link with someone else, like electricity moving between circuits, but once that power was cut and the connection was dead, each person went back to their own life. Drifted quietly back into the shadows of themselves and got on with it.

They ate, they slept, they did what bodies needed to do.

They fucked or got fucked over.

They beat their children.

Whatever, didn't matter.

Here though, buzzing under a clear blue sky, everyone was just part of a crowd. As happy or as miserable as the rest of the mass, each one moving in whatever direction the whole dictated. There were a few of course, like himself, who stood in isolation from it, though he had no idea how many like him there were. A handful, no more than that. Just a few, moving through the crowd easily but without ever quite becoming part of it. It wasn't just about being smarter; it was something he could never quite define, but it felt like being tuned to a different frequency.

He saw the wannabe guitarist from the coffee shop talking to someone in a small cluster of people outside the bakery. He raised his hand and the man nodded a cursory hello.

Dave grinned and pushed on.

He enjoyed this 'joining in' precisely because, however much it seemed that way, he never really was. Not quite.

The result of things that had happened to him in the past, maybe. Or perhaps it was hard-wired, this ability, and he truly believed it *was* an ability. Yes, it was standing above or . . . apart, but he could honestly say that he never thought of himself as special in any way, or any better than anyone else. He wasn't arrogant like the Ed Dunnings of this world. He never assumed he knew better.

He knew *different*, that was all.

He stopped at the stall in the indoor market that sold organic meat—always organic—but he still felt a little uneasy staring at the slabs of beef, the glistening bodies of chickens and rabbits, the unplucked game birds on hooks at eye level. More than once he had tried to convince Marina that the two of them should become vegetarians. He showed her a grisly documentary about the workings of an abattoir and cut out magazine articles that proved a meat-free diet was healthier. He told her it was the right thing to do, but she was having none of it and, watching her tucking into a bacon sandwich or feasting on pork crackling, he knew it was a lost cause. It wasn't a problem though.

However *he* felt, if that was what she wanted then he was never going to push it. That was not the way a unit like theirs worked. They would do it together or not at all.

Same as everything else.

He picked out the lamb and paid quickly, keen to make a getaway before the smell of the meat had him reaching for his inhaler. He checked the list he had written before coming out. Satisfied himself that he had not forgotten anything.

They would shine tonight.

Competition was ultimately pointless, but the others had clearly entered into one and even if their crockery was not quite as fancy and things were a little more crowded around the dinner table, this would be the evening that stood head and shoulders above the others.

He and Marina had been . . . underestimated, he knew that.

He very much looked forward to setting things straight.

He eased back into the crowd and moved slowly outside again, towards the coffee shop where he would sit and wait until it was time to collect Marina from rehearsals.

In the crowd, and out of it.

He subscribed to more than a dozen magazines which he down-loaded regularly on to one of his three tablets. Science and technology, philosophy, politics, true crime. In truth, he never got round to most of them or gave up after a few pages when he did, but in one he had read an amazing article about people who had died for a few minutes on the operating table. Died and come back. They all talked about feeling as if they were floating and looking down on their own bodies.

In the crowd and out of it.

It felt like that.

A man in a hurry bumped into him and kept walking. Without looking round, the man held up a hand and shouted, 'Sorry.' Dave smiled and said, 'Not a problem.' The connection, made. A few paces further on and Dave dropped his shoulder, stepped across and eased it into a woman coming in the other direction.

323

She turned and told him angrily to look where he was going.

Dave smiled again.

Passing it on.

Marina walked out of the toilet cubicle, adjusted her skirt and sat down in front of the dressing-room mirror. Her hair was a mess and her skin looked terrible. She leaned closer to the mirror. There was a small cluster of whiteheads at the corner of her mouth.

Fuck!

She did *not* want to look shit, tonight of all nights. Skinny Sue and Fat Angie dressed to the nines like Laurel and Hardy in expensive frocks. It wouldn't matter how great Dave told her she looked, how many times he tried to persuade her.

You're perfect. We're *perfect.*

She knew the truth.

She opened her bag, took out a smaller one and laid her make-up out in front of her.

The toilet flushed and a few seconds later Philip emerged, zipping up his jeans. He stood there with his hands on his hips, grinning like a schoolboy and watching her in the mirror. He said, 'You are *seriously* good at that.'

'Yeah, well, I'm a good actress.'

'I know that. I mean—'

'I was *acting*, all right?'

He laughed, just a little. 'Not what it looked like to me.'

'You had your eyes closed.'

'You telling me you didn't enjoy that just as much as I did?'

'Remember Kelly, the sex worker from Camberwell?'

He waited.

'I used it, just like you told me. I *focused*.'

'Bullshit . . .'

'Centred enough for you, was I?' She picked up a lipstick and met his eyes in the mirror.

324

He nodded slowly, smiling with his eyes half closed, like he was enjoying being had. Like he could not help but admire what she had done. He said, 'Right,' and 'Well.'

'So do I get the part then?'

He nodded towards the cubicle. 'What . . .?'

'In the show.' She finished applying her lipstick, leaned forward and pursed her lips. 'The part you told me I had when you were still trying to get in my pants. You know, the main one?'

He shifted from one foot to the other for a few seconds, then dragged out the chair next to Marina and sat down. He took his tobacco tin from a waistcoat pocket, took out the rolling papers. 'Listen, there isn't a *main* one, you know that. This is an ensemble piece . . . this is devised around everyone in the group. I can't play favourites just because . . . you know.'

Marina nodded and picked up an eyebrow pencil.

'You're an arsehole,' she said. A simple statement of fact, because she'd known this pussy-arsed little speech of his was coming; known it before she'd let him persuade her into that cubicle. It was the reason she'd got down on her knees. 'I was acting and you're an arsehole.'

'Well, I'm sorry that's the way you feel.' He licked a rolling paper. 'I genuinely am.'

'And you can stick your poxy devised piece of shit up your arse.'

'As you wish.' He popped the roll-up between his lips and lit it. 'You know I can't refund any of the tuition fees, don't you?'

'Whatever.'

'Course rules, I'm afraid.' He picked a strand of tobacco from his lip, watched her for a few seconds, then slapped his hands on his thighs and stood up. He turned at the door and said, 'Just so you know, you weren't *that* great in there.' He nodded towards the cubicle again. 'Maybe you weren't the only one who was acting, you know?'

She spun round fast. 'Just watch yourself walking home at night. All right, *Philip*?'

He snorted. 'What the hell's that supposed to mean?'

'You heard me.'

'This some "black" thing, is it? You got gang connections? Shagged a Yardie or two?'

She spat at him, but it didn't even reach halfway to the door.

'So what, you going to come at me with a hairbrush up some dark alley?'

'Not me, wanker. People who care about me.'

He laughed at her. 'Seriously? Your *boyfriend*? That ratty little toe-rag who looks like an am-dram Raskolnikov?'

Marina didn't know what he was talking about.

She pointed at him, hard.

She said, 'You have no fucking *idea* what we are capable of.'

FIFTY-SEVEN

So, all set for the last supper.

Or at least, the last three-course dinner for six, with nibbles before-hand, chocolates of some description with coffee and a cheeseboard, you know if you're really pushing the boat out.

Stupid isn't it, these games we play? The conventions that tie us together, come hell or high water. The rules that make us do things we don't really want to do: talking to people we despise; shacked up with people we don't love; sleeping with people we don't fancy any more or who we suspect don't fancy us.

Yes, these are only small things in their way, though believe me they can do plenty of damage. Small, though, compared to the important rules that govern us all, that are supposed to make us into a decent and caring society.

All kicked off with the big ten, I suppose.

You know, those ones that begin *Thou Shalt* or *Shalt Not*, though I'm guessing we're all way past coveting our neighbours' oxen these days, aren't we? So, why is one life supposed to be as important as any other, when it so obviously isn't? I can't honestly tell you my life is really worth more than the person who's going to cure cancer. That would be stupid, wouldn't it? If you had to get rid of one of us, which one are you going to pick?

Life isn't fair. Fair is somewhere you go to ride the dodgems and win a goldfish. A goldfish that will probably die within a week, by the way, because life tends to be shit and not all creatures are created equal.

Sorry about that.

So, am I saying that what I've done up to this point would be worse if those two girls had not been . . . the way they were? Yes, I am. I'm sorry if that sounds horrible. It's not meant to upset anyone, honestly, I'm just trying to explain. I don't expect anyone to like me, and before anyone starts jumping up and down and crying, 'Good job!' it's worth pointing out that none of this has been about getting anyone to like me.

There's no point screaming about Hitler or any of that, either. Not if you've ever killed a wasp or really been honest about how you'd react if you were carrying a child that was damaged.

Go on, ask yourself.

I'm not expecting anything but simple hatred. I'm not an idiot. And I'm also honest enough to admit I might not have been able to take those girls in the first place if they hadn't been quite so trusting.

If they'd known that the world *was not fair.*

I know it might seem strange that I go along with some ways of doing things and not others. With the trivial stuff. But we draw our own lines, and besides, going along with some of life's stupider conventions was all part of it.

We've got to talk to people after all, we've got to play the game.

And who doesn't like chocolates with coffee?

THE FINAL
DINNER

FIFTY-EIGHT

They stood around in the living room, it being fairly apparent that there were not enough comfortable chairs for six. It was similar in layout to the Dunnings' place, but the two connecting rooms on the ground floor were smaller and squarer. The one in which they were clearly going to be eating did not look as though it was a dedicated dining room, but rather one without any specific function into which Dave and Marina had simply moved the table from the kitchen.

'It's got those extra bits you put in at either end,' Marina said.

'Leaves,' Dave said.

Dave and the three women were drinking wine. Barry and Ed nursed cans of beer. Marina had set out bowls of olives, nuts and spicy trail mix on a side table.

'I like your cushions,' Sue said.

Marina smiled, but she was watching Barry stare at the plain rectangular hole in the chimney breast which housed the largest of the dozen or more candles that were burning around the room. 'I know,' she said. 'Probably used to be a gorgeous old fireplace there. Idiots who were here before us took all that stuff out. Got rid of the sash windows and put double glazing in, for God's sake. Be really nice to put everything back one day if we can afford it.'

'Maybe Barry can sort something for you,' Angie said.

Barry said he'd keep an eye out.

'Double glazing's a damn sight more efficient though,' Dave said.

Marina curled her lip. 'Ugly, though.'

'Our gas bill's ridiculous,' Sue said.

'Only because you keep the central heating turned up.' Ed rolled his eyes at Barry. 'It's like a bloody greenhouse.'

Sue shook her head. 'Who leaves the lights on in every room in the house? I spend my life turning lights off.'

'Barry's the same,' Angie said, laughing. 'Not to mention the dirty pants left lying around.'

Barry grunted and helped himself to a handful of trail mix.

Ed raised his beer can. 'As long as it's only the little things we argue about, eh?'

'Blimey, that's a bit poky,' Barry said, chewing and pointing at the bowl.

There was music coming from small speakers on a computer table in the corner. Guitar and piano, a smoky, swooping voice. Sue nodded. 'God, I listened to this album non-stop when I was a student.'

'Yeah, I *love* Joni Mitchell,' Marina said.

They all listened through another mouthful of wine and beer, for the time it took Sue to wander across and start looking at the books on shelves to one side of the chimney breast. Self-help, astrology, fringe theatre; pristine-looking paperbacks by Alice Walker and Margaret Atwood. Then Dave said, 'Right, I'd better see how dinner's going. Who's hungry?'

'You're cooking?' Ed shuddered theatrically. 'Is it too late to send out for pizza?'

'Hilarious,' Dave said. 'I'll try and remember to spit in yours.'

'It's one of my mum's recipes,' Marina said. 'Caribbean lamb, so I hope it's not too spicy for anyone. I did pudding though. Well, I *bought* pudding . . .'

When Dave and Marina had gone into the kitchen, Sue walked back across to the group. She nodded towards a framed map on the wall behind the sofa. 'See that?'

'I noticed,' Ed said.

'What?' Angie said. She looked at the map, and said, 'Oh, it's like that one you've got. We used to have those in school.'

'We've got a few actually,' Sue said. 'The school I used to teach at was cleaning out an old storeroom, so I pinched them and got them framed. Look . . . same cushions as ours as well.'

'Right,' Angie said.

The two women turned and stared around the room.

'I don't see what the problem is,' Ed said.

'Well, it's not just this, is it?'

'What, that dress?'

'I'm sure I had Joni Mitchell on as well, when they came round . . .'

'What's going on?' Barry asked.

'Sue thinks Marina's copying her.'

'Not just Marina,' Sue said, her voice hushed. 'Dave's wearing a pair of trainers the same as yours.'

'This is stupid,' Ed said. 'So they think we've got good taste.'

'Keep your voice down . . .'

'I can't see anything of ours,' Angie said, a little disappointed.

'Sorry, I think it's spooky,' Sue said.

Barry nodded. 'It is a *bit* strange.'

'Like they're trying to steal our lives or something.'

Ed said, 'That's just mental,' as Marina walked back in.

'What's mental?' she asked.

'Bloody football,' Sue said, with barely a second's hesitation. 'Barry reckons his team's going to do better than Man United this season.'

'Right,' Marina said.

Ed swung round and nodded towards the sofa. 'We were all just admiring that fantastic map.' He ignored the look from Sue. 'That's really nice.'

Marina walked across and stared at the map, spoke with her back to the group. 'Great, isn't it?'

'How long have you had it?' Ed asked.

'Oh, ages,' Marina said. 'I found it in a junk shop in Islington.'

Sue looked at Angie and shook her head. Barry looked at Ed and shrugged. Dave appeared in the doorway.

'Grub's about ready . . .'

Marina ushered Barry and Angie across to the table, while Ed and Sue lagged behind.

'Maybe she doesn't even know she's doing it,' Ed said, quietly.

'Course she does.'

'Like an unconscious thing.'

'Just sit anywhere,' Marina said, waving Ed and Sue across.

Sue hissed, 'She knows exactly what she's doing.'

'I hope you two aren't having a domestic!' Marina patted the back of a chair.

Ed led the way. 'Like I said . . . only the little things.'

Sue said, 'It's certainly spicy, but it's nice.'

Barry said, 'Yeah, very nice.'

Ed said, 'The spicier the better as far as I'm concerned. And I'm not just talking about food.'

Angie waited another minute or two, then said, 'So, come on then, who's ready for Angie's latest *Crimewatch* update?'

'That must be a record,' Ed said, looking at his watch. 'A whole forty-five minutes before we get into the Florida thing.'

'Not just Florida any more,' Dave said.

'Oh here we go, Inspector Morse has kicked off.'

'Well, do you want to hear it or not?' Angie looked annoyed. She laid down her fork. 'I mean, I'm really not bothered.'

'Go on,' Marina said.

'Well, it's like Dave said . . . it's not just about Florida any more.'

'I think we'd all worked that much out,' Ed said.

'Yes, but I know *why*,' Angie said. She smiled, pleased with herself and clearly delighted to finally have their attention. 'I did a bit of digging on the internet, OK? It took a while, but I finally came up with an article from a few years back in one of the local papers. *Sevenoaks Chronicle*, I think. Anyway, it was all about that poor girl Samantha Gold and there was a picture and everything . . . all because she'd won some art competition for children with special needs.' She waited. Looked from one face to another. 'She's got learning difficulties, you see . . . same as that girl in Florida. *That's* the link.'

'That's why they're talking to us then,' Marina said. 'Bloody hell.'

Ed pushed his food around for a few seconds. 'They're probably talking to lots of other Brits if that's the case though, don't you reckon?'

'That makes sense,' Angie said.

'Anyone who was there, right?'

'Hang on though,' Marina said. 'Why are they presuming it's someone British who was on holiday or whatever? Why can't it be an American who's come over here?'

Barry said that was a good point.

'Why does it have to be a Brit *or* an American?' Dave said. 'The killer could be from anywhere, when you think about it. He could be moving around deliberately to disguise where he's from.'

Angie nodded, impressed. 'God, I never even *thought* about that.'

'Why not? He could be from bloody Timbuktu for all we know, could be doing this all over the world. He could be in Italy or Sweden or Australia already. Eyeing up another girl.'

'Oh that's horrible.' Angie turned to Sue and pulled a face. 'Makes me feel a bit funny.'

'It's perfect when you think about it,' Dave said. 'Another stamp in his passport, another victim.' He banged his fist lightly on the table. Once, twice, acting it out. 'Easy as that.'

'The EasyJet Killer,' Barry said, his mouth full.

Angie looked at him.

'What? They always have a nickname, don't they?'

'What do you know?' Angie said. 'You thought it was that girl's father.'

'Still do,' Barry said. 'A tenner says it was the dad. He abused her then killed her. What d'you reckon, Ed?'

Ed poured himself another glass of wine.

Marina asked if anyone wanted second helpings, despite the fact that only Dave had so far cleared his plate. He was the only one to take her up on the offer. As the food was being spooned on to his plate, Sue leaned across the table towards him.

'So you really think the girl's dead then? The second girl.'

'Definitely,' Dave said.

'Why?'

'Well, it certainly looks like the same person took both girls and he killed Amber-Marie Wilson, so . . .'

'And you definitely don't think it's a . . . *sexual* thing?' Angie asked.

'Why are you asking *him*?' Ed said. 'He's like the . . . oracle now, is he?'

Dave ignored Ed and considered Angie's question, a forkful of food halfway to his mouth. 'Still impossible to say. There was nothing to indicate there was anything sexual with the first girl, but if you remember the DNA evidence had already been destroyed because of the time she spent in the water. So we'll have to wait and see.'

'Never really about sex though, is it,' Sue said.

Dave nodded. 'Right, it's actually about power. Same as rape.'

'There's no end to your expertise, is there, Dave?' Ed said. 'It's Italian food one day, serial killers the next. Now you're an authority on rape all of a sudden.'

'I'm not claiming to be—'

Ed reached for the wine bottle again and winked at Marina. 'I should watch him if I were you.'

Seeing that the second bottle they had opened was already empty, Marina stood up and said she was going to fetch another couple. Ed told her to be sure and open the one he and Sue had brought with them. It was a decent red, he said, though *obviously* he'd need to confirm that with Dave, who'd probably been on some course or other. Or watched a *fascinating* documentary . . .

'It's actually about being a nutter, isn't it?' Barry said. 'Doing this stuff, you've got to be sick in the head, surely.'

336

'That's the big question, isn't it?' Dave said.

'Is it?' Ed said.

Marina returned with the wine. Ed opened a bottle and poured himself a large glass. He leaned towards Sue, but she shook her head and covered her glass with her hand. He topped up Marina's when she sat down and held it towards him.

'What have I missed?' she asked.

'If a killer's not in control of themselves because of some mental problem, how should we treat them?' Dave looked around the table for a reaction. 'If they can't help themselves.'

'We should bang them up,' Barry said. 'Simple as that.'

'I'm not saying we shouldn't, but—'

'Or worse. Anyone who hurts kids is an animal, end of story.'

Angie nodded. 'Doesn't matter how mental they are,' she said. 'I still think it's evil.'

'Loads of people are evil,' Marina said. She swirled her wine around in the glass. '*Loads* of them and you wouldn't even know it.'

Dave said, 'Yeah, but what does "evil" mean?'

'Hang on though, Dave's got a point.' Ed cleared his throat and held up his hands, a wine glass in one of them. 'Let's say I had some physical problem, like a twitch or whatever, and I wasn't in control of my limbs, right? If I was to suddenly lash out and smash Dave here in the face . . .' He moved his hand quickly towards Dave's face, spilling a small amount of wine on to the table.

'All right,' Sue said. She leaned across with a napkin to dab at the spilled wine.

'No, hang on . . . if I was to smash Dave in the face and he fell over and cracked his head open and died, does that make me a murderer? I mean, obviously I couldn't help myself, could I?'

'It's not quite that simple though,' Dave said, quietly. 'Some people pretend they can't help themselves.'

'Right,' Ed said, taking a drink. 'Tricky . . .'

'I don't care,' Angie said. 'It's evil and it's always worse when it's kids.'

'"Beasts", that's what they call them in prison,' Barry said. 'Anyone who hurts a kid . . . and that's what they are.'

'I don't see why it's worse,' Dave said.

'Course it is,' Angie said. 'Kids have got their whole lives ahead of them, haven't they?'

'Yeah, but that's not always a good thing though, is it?'

'What are you on about?' Barry said.

'Some people's lives are shit.'

'Bollocks.'

'It's a fact.'

'Listen, mate, things haven't exactly been a barrel of laughs for *me* lately, but I'm still better off than a lot of people. Better off than those two girls for a start.'

'Really? What kind of life would those two girls have had anyway?'

'That's not your . . . decision though, is it?' Angie said.

'No, it's not and whatever God you believe in, we all get tested in different ways.' He glanced at Ed, who stared at the table. 'I'm just saying that we over-romanticise this whole thing about kids. Like they're the be-all and end-all.' Dave reached across and took Marina's hand. 'Me and Maz don't want them anyway, so it's not an issue . . . but even if we did, I'm really not convinced this world is a particularly nice place to bring kids into.'

Dave removed his hand from Marina's and went back to finishing up his dinner. Nobody spoke for fifteen seconds and then Angie said, 'Well, if you don't want to bring children into the world, that's up to you, but what about the ones who are already here and need good homes?'

'You mean adopt?' Marina asked.

'I know it's not easy, but a lot of people go to China now, don't they?'

'We're not all cut out to be parents,' Dave said.

Marina said nothing.

'You don't know until you try though, do you?' Angie said.

'Look, it's not *compulsory*.'

'No, but think of all those babies whose parents don't want them . . .'

Marina stood up and began gathering plates. 'Do people fancy pudding straight away?' she said. 'Or shall we leave a gap?'

Angie turned to Sue. 'I mean, now I come to mention it, you and Ed could always—'

Sue pushed back her chair quickly and picked up her plate. She smiled at Marina. 'I'll give you a hand.'

Sue piled plates on the draining board then began rinsing them under the tap, while Marina sliced up a cheesecake in its foil container and poured cream from a carton into a small jug. When she could see that Sue was about to speak, Marina smiled and said, 'Dave's not interested in having kids, simple as that.'

'What about you though?' Sue asked. 'I mean it's not just up to him.'

'It doesn't matter anyway, because I probably couldn't have them even if I wanted to.' Marina put the knife down, licked her fingers. 'So, you know . . . no need to argue about it.'

They could hear voices from the next room. Just Angie's and Barry's, but it was not possible to make out what was being said.

'How do you know?'

'I had an abortion a long time ago and there were complications . . . and they told me it might be difficult.'

'Still a chance though.'

Marina took a bowl of mixed berries from the fridge and removed the clingfilm. 'It's a horrible world to grow up in. That's what Dave says. He didn't have a particularly great childhood himself, so . . .'

Sue turned off the tap, bent and began to load the dishwasher, reaching up for dirty plates and cutlery from the worktop. 'That business about "whatever God you believe in". Is Dave a bit . . . religious? I mean sorry, maybe you both are. I didn't mean . . .'

'I don't really know if he is or not,' Marina said.

'I wasn't trying to pry.'

'It's just something we do. When he gets into something he really goes for it, you know? Like cycling or whatever. You know he shaves his legs, right?'

'God, *really?*'

Marina leaned towards Sue and whispered, 'Do you know why I wanted everyone to stay over?' Sue shook her head. 'Just to get out of going to sodding church tomorrow morning.'

'Seriously?'

'It's so bloody *depressing.*'

'I *was* wondering about that . . .'

Marina told Sue to leave the dishes and asked her if she could get some ice cream from the freezer. They listened to Angie laughing at something in the next room.

'What Angie said in there about you and Ed . . . adopting or whatever.' Marina gathered up a stack of small dishes. 'That was out of order.'

'She means well.'

'Didn't look like Ed was very happy. He went very quiet.'

'We should be grateful for small mercies.'

'Did you see his face though?'

'Ed's had too much to drink,' Sue said.

'He's not the only one. I should probably stick to water from now on.'

'So should he,' Sue said. 'But there's no point me telling him. I never know how he's going to react when he gets like that.'

'Who needs an old man that's predictable?'

'I suppose.'

'Don't worry,' Marina said. 'Nothing like a fry-up for sorting all the hangovers out. Help me carry this lot in . . .'

'Does he know?' Sue lowered her voice. 'About the abortion?'

Marina shook her head. 'He knows *way* too much about me already,' she said. 'Everyone needs a secret, don't they?' She took half a step towards the door, but Sue did not step aside.

'This business with the handbag and the dress,' Sue said. 'What's all that about?'

'Sorry?'

'That map as well and the same cushions on the sofa as us. Why are you doing all that?'

340

Marina's shoulders rose and fell slowly. She pushed her tongue against her lips, as though her mouth were dry. 'Are you angry?'

'I'm just . . . why are you pretending you don't know we've got those things?'

Marina pulled the dishes tight against her chest. 'I like your . . . taste in things, that's all.'

'So why didn't you just ask me?'

'I don't know.'

'Anyway, *you're* the one who always looks amazing,' Sue said. 'You've got fantastic taste.'

'None of it's mine.'

'Don't be silly—'

'No, really . . . *nothing's* mine,' Marina said, her eyes on the floor. She looked up and nodded in the direction of the living room. 'Nothing except Dave, anyway. I know he'd do anything for me . . .'

After a few seconds, Sue stepped forward and gently eased the shield of plates away from Marina's chest. Then she moved around her and picked up the platter with the cheesecake on it. 'Come on,' she said.

Back at the table, the appearance of dessert was greeted with applause from Angie and Barry. While Sue dished it up, Marina walked across to swap Joni Mitchell for Marvin Gaye and Ed opened another bottle of wine.

Dave said, 'Looks gorgeous, Maz . . .'

The noises of contentment as everyone got stuck in suggested that the cheesecake tasted every bit as good as it looked. Marina watched Angie happily tucking a large slice away and said, 'I don't think that's too spicy for you, is it?' She was smiling as she spoke, but the look on Barry's face was enough to wipe it quickly away.

When Ed had finished, he helped himself to another glass of wine then turned slowly and deliberately towards Dave.

'So . . . have you been sharing all this with your friend Detective Quinlan then?'

'Sharing what?' Dave asked.

'Your new theories. Killers not being able to control themselves. Rape. All that.'

'Come on, don't be daft,' Sue said.

'She *asked* him,' Angie said. 'And he was only trying to help.'

Ed ignored them. 'Well, you might be interested to know that I told your friend where to get off.'

'She's not my friend,' Dave said, quietly.

'What did you say to her?' Marina asked.

Ed shrugged. 'I told her I wouldn't bloody well talk to her any more. Simple as that. I told her she was taking the piss, which she was.'

'How?' Angie asked.

'She was . . . overstepping the mark,' Ed said. He stumbled over the big word, repeated it. 'Let's leave it at that.'

Angie looked at Barry and, when she turned back to Ed, she could barely conceal a smile. 'I knew there was some reason why she was so interested in you.'

'How do you mean, interested?'

'Asking so many questions.'

'What questions?'

'What we thought about you, what you were like.' Angie looked at Marina. 'It wasn't just *you*, by the way. She asked me what I thought about Dave as well.'

Marina looked at Dave. 'When?'

'You were in the toilet.'

'Right, for about five minutes,' Marina said. She pointed at Ed. 'She spent twenty minutes quizzing us about *him*.'

Sue was staring at Angie. 'What did you tell her?'

'Nothing,' Angie said.

'Nothing? For twenty minutes? She must have been asking some very long questions.'

'Oh, you know.' Suddenly, Angie looked a little less comfortable. 'I said he was funny, that he liked a laugh.'

'What did you say about me?' Dave asked.

'I really can't remember,' Angie said. 'Nothing . . .'

342

'Incriminating?' Dave shook his head. 'Well, that's good. Jesus . . .'

Ed had not taken his eyes off Angie. 'Tell me what she wanted to know, *particularly*. Was it more stuff about the girl in Florida or did she ask if I'd said anything about the second girl?'

'Not specifically.'

'Did she or didn't she? Come on, it's not hard.'

'It was just general stuff.'

'What kind of stuff?'

'Background . . . you know.'

'What the hell for?'

'Leave it, Ed,' Sue said.

Ed shot her a look and she shrank back in her chair. He held his arms out wide. 'Come on . . . we're all *friends*, aren't we?'

'Maybe you should take five minutes,' Barry said. 'Go and have a coffee or something.'

'I just want people to be honest,' Ed said. The words were starting to thicken and slur and his face was red. 'Fair enough? To tell me what they said to that nosy fucking bitch policewoman.' He blinked, waited, pointed at Angie. 'Come on, fucking *tell* me.'

'You need to watch your mouth now,' Barry said.

Angie laughed it off. 'You think I'm frightened of *him*?'

'I'm just trying . . . trying to find out why she's so interested in me,' Ed said. 'That's all.'

Sue leaned across, spoke quietly. 'Why do you think they're so interested in you, darling?'

'Shush . . .'

'Go on, take a wild guess.'

'I said, shut up.'

'Why should I?'

'Because I told you to.'

'I don't care.' Sue leaned forward. 'You've had plenty to say all evening . . . though you *were* suspiciously quiet on the subject of dead children. Funny that, don't you think?' She smiled and looked around the table. 'Strangely quiet about that.'

Ed stared at her. His face was as pale as the wash of melted ice cream in the bottom of his dish.

'It's like some kind of blind spot with you,' Sue said. 'I mean, you're happy enough to shout your mouth off most of the time. Crack your stupid jokes, take the piss out of Dave, try and shag anything that moves.' She looked from one face to another. 'But one little mention of a dead girl and all of a sudden he's quiet as a mouse.' She drew an imaginary zip across her mouth. 'We all get the silent treatment then, don't we? It's like Kryptonite to him, a dead girl. Now, I'm sure you've all had a good old chat about everything by now, so you've probably worked out that I'm not just talking about *any* old dead girl—'

Ed pushed his chair back hard enough for Sue to move a hand instinctively up to her face and for Angie to gasp. He looked hard at Sue for a few seconds, then stood up and walked unsteadily out of the room. Sue let out a long breath. She picked up her napkin and pressed it across her eyes. She croaked out a 'sorry', then followed her husband, closing the door behind her.

Without a word, people began passing dirty dishes around the table to Marina. Angie raised her eyebrows at Barry. Dave was about to say something, but they could hear voices in the kitchen and Angie quickly told him to be quiet. The four of them sat and listened. The words were indistinct at first, so Marina quietly got up, walked across to the computer table and turned the volume of the music down a little.

They heard Ed say, 'What the fuck did you start on about that for?'

They heard Sue say, 'Why can't we talk about it? Why is it always off limits?'

They heard Ed say, 'You'll be fucking sorry . . .'

A few moments after the sound of heavy footsteps on the stairs, the door opened and Sue came back into the room.

'God, I'm so sorry,' she said.

'Don't be silly,' Marina said. 'It's fine.'

'He's pissed,' Barry said.

'I'm not though,' Sue said. She walked calmly back to the table and sat down. 'He's gone to the toilet. Looked like he was going to be sick.'

Barry caught Angie's eye.

'I think we should probably head off,' Angie said.

'No, please stay,' Sue said quickly.

Marina looked at Dave. Said, 'Oh, but I presumed you'd be . . .'

'He's in no condition to drive,' Sue said. 'And I *really* don't want to take him home.' Her face crumpled, leaving nobody at the table in any doubt that the last thing she wanted at that moment was to be alone at home with her husband.

'Right then.' Dave stood up and rubbed his hands together, absurdly cheery. 'I suppose we should think about who's having the spare room.'

'They can have it,' Angie said. It took a second or two, but Barry nodded.

'No, that's not fair,' Sue said.

'It's fine, really.'

'Hang on a minute,' Dave said. He walked across to the computer table, rummaged on a shelf above it and came back with a deck of playing cards. 'Here you go.' He shuffled the cards. 'Highest card gets the spare room. The sofa-bed's pretty comfortable, mind you. I've been on it a few times myself.'

'When he's had a cold,' Marina said. 'Not wanted me to catch it.'

Sue nodded, whispered, 'Fine.'

'Yeah, why not?' Barry nudged Angie. 'Go on, you do it, love.'

Dave fanned out the pack and proffered it, and while Marvin Gaye sang 'If I Should Die Tonight' and the toilet flushed somewhere above them, Sue and Angie each took a card.

An hour and a half later, one of the couples is just asleep—the man snoring gently—while in the next room another talks in hushed voices about the evening's events. He tries to make a joke about dinner parties from hell, but she doesn't think it's particularly funny. He says, to be serious, it makes you realise how strong your own relationship is, but she just says they should probably try and get some sleep and leans across to kiss him; dry and quick.

The third couple is arguing.

Within a minute or two of the shouting starting, all the people upstairs are wide awake. One couple throws off the duvet at the sound of something smashing below them. Things clattering to the floor. Encouraged by his wife, one man creeps to the bedroom door and opens it. Both couples meet on the landing just before the screaming begins and without a word they hurry downstairs.

They stop in the doorway, stare horrified into the kitchen.

At the body, and the blood; its fine, bright spatter on blue cotton and yellow silk. Thick and livid where it spreads slowly across the black and white floor tiles. Trickles along the grout lines.

The kneeling figure and the knife.

The wide eyes and the scarlet fingers, wet against the sucking wound, and the mouth twisted in confusion as it repeats and repeats.

'Both those girls. Both those girls . . .'

FIFTY-NINE

The 999 call was received at the national emergency call centre in Hendon and was immediately patched through to Lewisham station. Within a few minutes of the response car and the ambulance service being dispatched, Jenny Quinlan was woken up.

'Jenny . . . it's Sandra from the control room. Listen, we've caught a nasty-looking one and there's a flag come up on the address.'

Shivering in the hallway in nothing but a T-shirt, Jenny immediately began walking back towards her bedroom. Suddenly she had goose-bumps on goosebumps. She ignored her flatmate who was peering angrily around her own door, having only recently returned from a late shift.

'I flagged up three addresses,' Jenny said. 'Which one is it . . .?'

Fifteen minutes later, she was pulling up behind a paramedic motor-bike on the small street in Forest Hill. There were already two other marked police vehicles parked up parallel to residents' cars; the blue lights still flashing on one of them, a uniformed officer digging a roll of crime scene tape from the boot of another.

She showed him her warrant card then stood back and looked at the house while he made a show of studying it. The only one she hadn't visited.

As the PC tied tape to a fence post behind her, Jenny walked the few steps from pavement to front door and pushed through it. She took a deep breath and, in that moment before she released it, she could feel her heart racing.

I was right. I knew there was something. Right from the kick-off . . .

There was another uniform standing at the foot of the stairs and she could see movement on the landing one floor up. Training shoes were lined up neatly just inside the door. A pushbike was leaning against a radiator.

Jenny could smell something like curry, and blood.

Has anyone called Gardner yet? It should be me, of course it should.

The door to her right was closed, but the one directly ahead opened and a man she recognised as the on-call uniformed inspector stepped out and walked towards her. She could see straight away that he had come from the kitchen. Over his shoulder she caught a glimpse of the body; a red smear on a low cupboard and a paramedic getting to his feet and snapping off protective gloves.

'Who are you?'

Jenny introduced herself, though once the man knew she was Job, he did not seem overly interested in exactly what her connection to the people in the house might be. He had more important things to think about. She had seen him stalking around the station and knew that he had only recently been transferred south from the other side of the river. There were rumours he had been bumped down from CID to uniform; a major slap on the wrist for something or other, though nobody was very sure what. On the few occasions Jenny had run into him, it had been clear enough that he was not thrilled about the situation, though now—watching him taking in his surroundings, seeing the way he carried himself—he seemed a little more energised than usual.

One of those who came to life at a crime scene, she guessed.

Easy enough to recognise, because she was one of those too.

She heard a siren growing suddenly louder and guessed that the HAT car had arrived. A minute or so later she was proved right when the two plain-clothes detectives from the Homicide Assessment Team stepped into the house. She saw the uniformed inspector's expression harden.

The banter was not long in coming, the habitual Suits v Lids wind-ups, though it *did* seem a little less good-natured than Jenny was used to.

'All right, Thorne, we'll take it from here.'

The inspector glared at them.

'Why don't you make yourself useful? Actually, the car needs parking . . .'

Grinning, the detectives pushed past the inspector towards the kitchen, just as the paramedic was on his way out.

'Straight through the heart by the looks of it,' the paramedic said. 'More or less instant, I reckon.'

'What about the weapon?' one of the detectives asked.

The paramedic pointed back down towards the officer who was standing at the bottom of the stairs. He turned and for the first time Jenny noticed the plastic bag he was cradling as if it were a newborn. The blade pressed against the plastic, a tablespoon of blood pooled at the bottom of the bag.

What had Dave Cullen said to her?

'Should be interesting on Saturday.'

Christ . . .

The detectives stood in the doorway staring at the body, still sharing a laugh at the things they'd said to the inspector. The paramedic smiled as he walked past Jenny. Now it would just be a question of the formal pronouncement of 'life extinct', but the doctor would not need to hurry. The on-call scene of crime officer would be on their way together with a forensic photographer, but the body would be staying where it was for a few hours yet.

Jenny took a step closer to the inspector. Said, 'Where's the suspect?'

'Upstairs,' he said.

'The witnesses?'

He nodded towards the room with the closed door. 'You know them then?'

349

Jenny said that she did and that she'd interviewed all of them.

'There's a new lad in there with them,' he said. He took a few steps back towards the kitchen. 'Why don't you go in and give him a hand?'

As soon as Jenny stepped through the door into the living room, two of the four people who had been sitting on the edge of the sofa-bed got to their feet. The uniformed officer standing on the other side of the room stepped forward, a little concerned, but Jenny showed him her warrant card, assured him that there was nothing to worry about.

'What's happening?' one of the witnesses asked.

'How long do we have to stay here?'

'I think they're just trying to organise some vehicles,' Jenny said. She looked around, saw a duvet lying in a heap next to the fireplace. 'We'll need to get you down to the station in separate cars if possible.'

'Why?'

'So we don't talk to each other. They need to make sure our statements aren't tainted.'

'That's right,' Jenny said.

'Any chance we could get a drink?'

Jenny looked at the uniform. 'They've had some tea,' he said.

'I was thinking about something a bit stronger. I mean, it's been a bit . . .'

'I'm afraid that won't be possible,' Jenny said.

'Because they've got to make sure our statements stand up in court or whatever. If some lawyer finds out we were drinking after it happened . . .'

'I don't think one drink's going to make any difference, the amount we've put away in the last few hours.'

'I'm sorry,' Jenny said. 'Just try and get comfortable and we'll get this sorted as quickly as we can.'

'Is he dead?' Angie asked. 'Nobody's told us anything.'

'Yes, he's dead. I'm sorry.'

The woman shook her head, though it was not possible to tell if it was disbelief or a simple indication that the apology was unnecessary.

Barry put his arm around his wife and Jenny was about to settle down on the arm of the sofa when she heard footsteps on the stairs.

'Is that her?' Angie asked. 'Are they taking her out?'

Jenny opened the door just the few inches necessary to see out and watched as a uniformed officer led a handcuffed Sue Dunning down the stairs. She stared at her feet and her lips were moving just a little. Her cheek was marked high up, as though she'd been slapped hard. There was dried blood on her face and hands and a patch that still looked wet on the front of her blouse. She and the uniform were joined at the foot of the stairs by the inspector and when he glanced across at Jenny, Sue followed it and caught her eye.

She stopped.

The uniformed officer laid a hand on her arm to urge her towards the front door, but the inspector told him to wait.

Sue licked at a flake of dried blood at the corner of her mouth. Swallowed and shuddered. She looked as though she had just woken from a nightmare and had yet to discover if she was still dreaming.

When she spoke, her voice was cracked and colourless.

'I know where she is.'

PART FOUR

SUE

From: Detective Jeff Gardner [mailto: j.gardner@sarasotapd.org]
Sent: July 30 09.48
To: Jennifer Quinlan
Subject: My Visit

Jenny,

First off, thanks for sending the transcript of the witness interviews. Were you in there for those? Sounds like quite a night!

All being well I should be arriving in London sometime tomorrow evening and coming to your station first thing the following morning. Hoping there's a cab as I have no idea where the hell "Lewisham" is or how to get there from the center of town. On the SPD budget, I seriously doubt my hotel's the kind of place that will have a concierge! Apologies for not making contact sooner, but have spent the last few days talking to the top guy in your Homicide Command and it looks like he's finally agreed to let me do the interview.

I'm looking forward to it, if that doesn't sound too weird.

Be good to finally meet you too. Put a face to the name.

See you in a couple,
Jeff

SIXTY

*DI STEVEN BARSTOW (Homicide Command): How soon after
the noise started did you go downstairs?*
*ANGELA FINNEGAN: Straight away, near as damn it. I
mean . . . a few minutes? Barry got up to see what on earth was
going on and when he opened the door, Dave was already standing
at the top of the stairs. I came out the same time as Marina did and
then we all went down. God, I couldn't believe it . . .*
SB: What did you see?
AF: She'd killed him, hadn't she?
*SB: If you could stick to what you actually saw, that would be
helpful.*
*AF: Sorry . . . he was lying on the kitchen floor and she was sitting
back against one of the cupboards and she sort of had his head in
her lap and she was . . . Her hand was on his chest and there was
just loads of blood. And the knife was in her hand. In her right
hand, I think. Yes, must have been. There was a red mark on her
face where he'd hit her. Sorry . . . where it looked like he'd hit her.
We just stood there, you know? Listening to her . . .*

★

357

DAVID CULLEN: She was gabbling a bit, hysterical sort of thing. She was saying sorry all the time and talking about how he'd told her what he'd done. Just come out with it. All the details. She said he was expecting her to be on his side, to stick up for him, I suppose, and then when she wouldn't he'd just lost it and gone for her.
SB: This was after you'd called the police?
DC: Right, yeah. Marina wanted to go into the kitchen, try and help Sue or whatever, but I knew that she shouldn't really be touching anything because it would contaminate the crime scene. Somebody said, 'What if he isn't dead, shouldn't we try to help or something?' But he definitely wasn't moving and something on Sue's face sort of made it obvious he was already dead. So I went to get a phone and made the call and the others stayed where they were. She was talking all the time though, telling them everything. The girl in the boot of his car in Florida and what he'd done with that girl in Kent. Like I say, it was a bit hysterical. I don't know what the others thought and maybe they're saying how shocked they were and all that. I mean seeing what had happened was definitely a shock . . . the blood and everything else . . . but about him and the business with those girls . . . I can't honestly say I'm really surprised.
SB: Any particular reason you say that?
DC: I just think he had it in him.

MARINA GREEN: It was funny because all I could think about, standing there and seeing what had happened, was that we'd heard him threatening her before. When we were eating, I mean. They went out into the kitchen after this big argument. He said, 'You'll be sorry,' or something like that. He was really drunk and getting aggressive and he seemed OK when everyone went to bed, like he was just going to crash out, but I suppose it must have all kicked off again. There was this thing about kids, you know? They had a daughter who died.

★

BARRY FINNEGAN: Is that true? The stuff she said about him killing those girls? Jesus . . .

SB: Obviously we've passed that information on, but right now we're just interested in the incident this evening.

BF: Well, it was pretty bloody obvious what had gone on, her sitting there with this dirty big carving knife in her hand and him covered in blood and that. She was looking at us all standing there in the doorway, but it was like she couldn't really see us properly. I suppose that's shock or whatever. Then she starts saying that it was him who'd done it . . . the girl who was killed when we were in Florida and that one who went missing a couple of weeks ago. She said he'd told her where she was, that girl . . . what he'd done with her. I mean I don't know if she knifed him because of that or because he attacked her or what. Not sure I care very much, if I'm honest. I was probably the only one he hadn't had a pop at over dinner and that's only because he knew I'd smack him if he tried it on. I never really liked him, no point me sitting here and pretending I did, but still . . . I can't say I had him pegged for that. Just goes to show, doesn't it?

DC: He was always pushing her around a bit, but some of us thought she liked that. You know, like she wanted to be . . . dominated or something. He was definitely the boss though. He didn't like not getting his own way.

SB: Had you heard him threaten her earlier on that evening?

DC: Yeah, we all heard it. 'You'll pay for that,' or 'You'll be fucking sorry.' Something like that. She was really upset when she came back in . . . it was almost like she was trying to defend him because he'd had too much to drink, but you could see she was shitting herself.

SB: You said that after things started breaking downstairs, you heard screaming.

DC: Yeah, Sue was screaming.

SB: Like she was angry? Like she was scared?

DC: I don't know . . . just this scream that went on and on. Because
of things getting smashed up, I presumed she was screaming because
he was trying to hurt her, but I suppose it could have been after
he'd told her what he'd done. One sort of scream probably sounds
much the same as another, doesn't it? She was definitely terrified,
I can promise you that, but if the person you were married to
just came out and told you they'd killed two people that's pretty
understandable. She still looked terrified, just sitting there on the
kitchen floor. I don't know . . . terrified because of what she'd done,
I suppose.

SB: Can you remember any of the things she said? Specifically?
AF: I don't know about word for word.
SB: Do your best.
AF: She definitely said, 'It was him.' And she said, 'He told me
what he did to them.' Then she was sort of ranting and raving,
talking about water and kayaks and keeping a body in the boot
of his car. Something about chocolate and a place in the woods. I
remember there was one point, not long before the police came, when
she suddenly looked even more scared than she was already. She
looked at us and said, 'I didn't know. I swear I didn't know.'

MG: Yeah, she kept on saying that, right up until the police and the
paramedics arrived. She was saying it to them too, I think. We got
taken into the living room as soon as they arrived, so I don't know
what happened after that. I heard someone asking her to put the
knife down . . .
SB: How much had Mrs Dunning had to drink?
MG: I don't know . . . not much. Probably less than anybody
else. That's the stupid thing, because she could easily have driven
home. She was just too scared to, I think. She probably thought
she was safer here with everyone else, that he wouldn't do anything
with other people in the house. I reckon they started fighting in the
living room, because there were a few things knocked over in there.

He probably tried to tell her what he'd done when they were still in bed and she freaked out . . . I mean quite understandably, and then when he attacked her she ran into the kitchen and . . . I don't know . . . just grabbed the knife. Is that about right, you reckon?

SB: We'll know more when we've finished in the house.

MG: If it was me . . . if I found out that Dave had done something like that . . . I'd want to kill him.

BF: I'm not even sure she really knew what she'd done, you know. She looked . . . dazed or something sitting there like that. Like a kid with ketchup round her mouth. She had her hand on his chest, where the knife had gone in I suppose, sort of patting it, and she was stroking his head with her other hand . . . the same hand she still had the knife in. All the while she was telling us this stuff, the things he'd done to these girls, it was like part of her just thought he was asleep or something. Like she didn't know there was blood everywhere.

SB: OK, thank you. I think we're about done. Interview terminated at—

BF: Listen, I know she stabbed him, nobody's arguing with that . . . but if he did kill those two girls and, you know, she only did it because he was trying to kill her or whatever . . . will she still get done?

SIXTY-ONE

'You look tired,' she said.

'Yeah, overnight flight. Jet lag's a killer, right?'

The woman did not react to the unfortunate choice of words, though the man next to him shifted slightly in his chair. Gardner looked down, a little embarrassed, doodled something in the corner of his notebook.

'Police don't fly business class then?'

'You kidding?'

Four days after her arrest for the murder of her husband, Gardner was finally sitting down opposite Sue Dunning. Next to him sat Detective Inspector Steven Barstow of the Met Homicide Command, a bluff Scotsman who was leading the investigation into Edward Dunning's murder. As Sue Dunning was being interviewed primarily as a witness and not in direct connection to the murder for which she was now on remand in Holloway prison, she had dispensed with legal representation. As far as her own offence went, she had thus far seemed content with the solicitor appointed on the night of her arrest. Happy enough to do whatever she was told, or advised.

'Thanks for agreeing to talk to me,' Gardner said.

'Nothing to thank me for. But I do want to help . . .'

'Shall we get this started?' Barstow said.

They were gathered in an interview room at Holloway station. A remand prisoner was only allowed out between the hours of 9.00 a.m. and 5.00 p.m., so as a matter of course interviews were conducted at the nearest available station. Not that it made a great deal of difference.

One interview room was very much the same as another.

In jeans and a plain T-shirt, with her hair scraped back, Sue Dunning was not what Gardner had expected. She was smaller than he had imagined, slighter. She did not look like the sort who would do well in prison. She looked like a victim. Despite what she had done, Gardner supposed that, given everything they had discovered about Edward Dunning since his death, that's exactly what she was.

'We're now as certain as we can be that your husband was responsible for the murders of Samantha Gold here in the UK and Amber-Marie Wilson in Florida,' Gardner said.

Sue Dunning nodded slowly, swallowed hard.

'Obviously you'd got no reason to think otherwise, bearing in mind everything he told you. You're aware that they found the location of Samantha Gold's school programmed into the GPS in his car and I know you've already been informed that the remains of a young girl were discovered in woods just outside Sevenoaks.'

'It was her.' Not a question.

'Yeah, it was her. She was still . . . identifiable.' Gardner had spoken to the officer leading the hunt for Samantha Gold. There had been a lot more left of her than there had been of Amber-Marie Wilson. 'What you don't know is that they got a provisional DNA result back late yesterday and samples taken from the burial site are a match for your husband.'

'Late husband,' Sue said.

It was a simple statement of fact. If there was any malice there, it was well disguised and it struck Gardner more as a reminder to herself than anything else. An explanation as to why she was sitting where she was and not at home watching daytime TV or marking homework assignments.

'So . . . we're trying to piece together what happened in Sarasota when you were there and I was kind of hoping you might be able to fill in some of the gaps.'

'I'll try.'

'Well, we think he took Amber-Marie during the hour or so you were at the Westfield mall and kept her in the trunk of the car for the rest of the day.'

'But that would mean the body was there when he came to pick me up.'

'That's right.'

'Wouldn't there have been a . . . smell?'

'Not straight away, no.'

'What if I'd seen it?'

'I'm betting he put your shopping bags in the trunk.'

Sue thought about it. 'I suppose he *must* have. I mean otherwise . . .'

'I'm not sure he thought it through real carefully, you know? Sometimes these are spur-of-the-moment things.'

Sue looked doubtful. 'I don't know. I've been thinking back and trying to remember the way he looked at that girl . . . if it was any *different*. All the lies he'd been telling me about his work, the covering up. He wasn't particularly . . . impulsive.'

Gardner nodded, like he was considering it. 'I'm not trying to be funny, but you know, bearing everything in mind, maybe you didn't know him as well as you thought you did.'

'We were together twenty-five years,' she said, simply.

'Well, whether putting her in the trunk was part of the plan or not, he got away with it and then it was just a question of getting rid of the body.'

'It had to be during the night,' she said. 'We put our suitcases in the car the next morning.'

'We can't be sure of the time, but we think he drove down to the fishing dock at Turtle Beach, took one of the kayaks that's moored up there.'

Sue opened her mouth and closed it again, looked down at the table.

'What?'

'We went kayaking there last year.' She managed a half-smile. 'I saw a manatee.'

'Right,' Gardner said, pleased. 'So he knew the place . . . knew where to find a kayak. Maybe he put the body *in* the kayak or laid her across it or something, we'll probably never know. It's no more than a fifteen-minute paddle from there to where we found her in the mangroves. Then he wedged her in under the roots there, paddled back and left the kayak where he'd found it. Whole thing could have taken him less than an hour. Maybe he had a change of clothes—'

Sue had been shaking her head and rubbing her hands together for the last few seconds before she cut him off. 'How though? How on earth was he gone for an hour in the middle of the night? Why didn't I wake up when he left? Or when he came back?'

Gardner raised his arms. It was just another thing he would probably never know. 'Are you a heavy sleeper?'

'Well, I'm not a *light* sleeper.'

'Had you been drinking?'

'A little,' she said. 'It was the last night, so . . .'

'Fact is, he got away with it,' Gardner said. 'Same as the trunk thing. And you know what, there's no point beating yourself up about it, because even if you had woken up, he could just have said he was going for a walk or he'd been for a walk. He couldn't sleep or whatever.'

Sue looked at him. 'I don't think that's going to be particularly easy.'

'What?'

'Not . . . "beating myself up".'

'Yeah, it's easy to say, right?'

'He told the police he was with me at the shopping mall and I went along with it. That first day when she went missing.' She was still rubbing at her hands, one laid flat on the table and the other pressing down as though trying to wear it away. 'If I hadn't, Samantha Gold might still be alive, that's right, isn't it?'

Gardner was aware of Barstow looking at him. 'There's no way of knowing that.'

'I *lied* for him.'

'I know,' Gardner said. 'I wanted to ask about that . . .'

'He said it was because of the rape. He said he couldn't tell them he was on his own driving around, because if they thought he was any sort of a suspect they'd dig around and find out about what had happened with that woman six years ago and then . . . you know.'

'He'd be even more of a suspect.'

'He said I had to back him up.'

'Did he threaten you?'

She shook her head, sadly. 'I wish I could tell you that he did, but it wasn't really like that. Not like . . . the other night. It was more like he was begging me.' She looked at him again, licked dry lips. 'That's something else I've been thinking about. One of many things. The rape . . .'

Gardner glanced at Barstow. 'I spoke with Jenny Quinlan, who I believe you know?' He waited. A small nod. 'She interviewed Annette Bailey and she's fairly convinced that your husband did rape her.'

She did not look surprised. A little extra tonnage to a weight that was already unbearable. 'Right. Of course he did.'

'Something . . . interesting, though.' Gardner hesitated, embarrassed once again by his choice of word. Clumsy, considering what he had to tell her, though he could not imagine it would make this woman feel any worse than she already did. 'Miss Bailey told her that Ed asked her to dress up as a schoolgirl.'

Sue Dunning looked genuinely shocked for the first time, shaken out of a dark torpor. She lowered her head. She said, 'Oh God.'

'Sorry,' Gardner said. He asked himself what the hell he was apologising for. Why this in particular?

Sorry that your late husband, the rapist and double child-killer, had a bit of a thing for gymslips and training bras.

'It's all about children, isn't it?'

'Excuse me?'

'What he did,' Sue said. 'It's all about our child. About Emma.'

Gardner felt a little uncomfortable. 'I'm not a shrink, Mrs Dunning.'

'I should have known. He was always so weird about Emma, refusing to discuss it, like he was trying to pretend we'd never had a daughter. Now, of course, I'm asking myself if Ed ever . . . when Emma was alive, you know?' She shook her head, firm with herself. 'No, not that. Whatever else has happened, I can't go *there* . . .'

Nobody spoke for a while, until eventually Barstow said, 'We should probably wrap it up, unless there's anything else?'

Gardner said he was about done, but when he looked back at Sue she was staring at him, as if she'd suddenly seen something in his face. 'Do you think I *knew*?' When Gardner did not respond immediately she carried on, producing a smile that looked almost painful. 'Don't worry, I've already had a few comments from women in prison. It's obvious what they think from what they've said they plan to do to me when they get a chance. I know that's what most people will think. It's what I'd probably think. *The wife always knows.*'

'I think you're in hell,' Gardner said, quietly. 'And it's not your fault.'

For the first time, Sue Dunning looked as though she might weep. 'Thank you,' she said.

Gardner started to gather his papers.

'Do you talk to her mother? Amber-Marie's, I mean.'

'Sometimes.'

'Please say I'm sorry, if you remember. I'd really like her to know that.'

Gardner assured her that he would pass the message on.

Twenty minutes later, Gardner and Barstow stood at the rear entrance to the station, watching the blue metal gates slide back and the van carrying Sue Dunning back to prison disappearing through them.

'So how do you think it's going to go?' Gardner asked.

Barstow sniffed, reaching into his jacket for cigarettes. 'Noises the CPS are making . . . the provocation, the self-defence angle, I think they might decide to go for manslaughter as best chance of a conviction.'

Gardner was still having a little difficulty with the Scottish accent. He had lost the odd word, but got the gist of it. 'That's good news,' he said.

The DI nodded as he lit his cigarette. 'Bloody right it is, pal, and between you and me I don't think there's too many round here are going to be trying awfully hard, if you know what I mean.'

Gardner looked at him.

'Like you said in there, she's in hell. Can't see what good prison's going to do on top of that, can you? Ten years dodging bull-dykes with home-made blades.'

'I guess not,' Gardner said.

'Especially not when she's done the world a favour.'

SIXTY-TWO

Patti Lee Wilson topped up her glass, sat down and, for the third time in the last thirty minutes, picked up the phone. This time, after emptying half the glass in one, she dialled. She waited for the connection to be made; a few more seconds during which she had to fight the urge to hang up.

The woman who answered sounded sleepy, a little worried.

'Is this Sonia Gold?'

'Who's this?'

Patti heard a man's voice, muffled. 'Who the hell's that?'

'I'm Amber-Marie's mother,' Patti said. 'Amber-Marie Wilson?'

There was a pause, then the woman said, 'I know who you are.'

'God, did I wake you? I wanted to call earlier, but I was a little nervous, you know?'

'It's fine,' the woman said. 'We're in bed a bit earlier than normal, that's all. The trial starts tomorrow, so . . .'

'Yeah, that's why I called. To wish you luck, kind of thing. Does that sound strange?'

'Not really. Well, perhaps a bit.'

'Maybe I should be wishing *her* luck,' Patti said. 'You want her to get off, right?'

Another pause. 'I don't know what I want.'

Patti swung her feet up on to the couch. 'I know, it's messed up.'

'I mean, yes . . . I think so. There's still a little part of me though that wonders if she . . . you understand.'

'No way,' Patti said. 'I talked with the detective who questioned her over there. He's a pretty good friend of mine, actually. He looked into her eyes, you know?'

'There's a part of me that hates her, if that makes sense.'

'Sure.'

'I want it to be *him*.' The woman's voice was still quiet, but the passion was clear enough. 'I wanted to see his face when he got put away. When he got to really understand what he'd done . . . what he'd taken from us. From you, too.'

'I near enough jumped for joy when I got the call saying the fucker was dead, excuse my language.'

The woman laughed a little. She told Patti that she'd said a lot worse.

Patti said, 'If we'd caught up with him over here, he'd be getting the needle and I'd be sitting right there in the front row, laughing my ass off.'

'Would you?' the woman asked. 'Honestly?'

It took Patti a while, the rest of the glass, before she said, 'No, I guess not.'

'It won't bring our girls back, will it?'

Patti heard the man's voice again, could not make out what was being said. 'Listen, I should probably let you get some sleep.'

'It was kind of you to ring.'

'I wasn't sure if I should.'

'Did you not think about coming over yourself?'

'Money's kind of a problem right now,' Patti said. 'Maybe I should've saved up though. Be worth it just to shake her hand.'

'Well, anyway . . .'

'Listen . . . I guess I really called just to say hang in there, OK? I know it's been a while already since your little girl passed, but I've got a bit of a head start on you and I wanted you to know that it gets easier. Not *easy*, nothing like that, but it's more like an ache, you know, instead of just something . . . raw. It'll get easier, honey. I promise.'

She heard the woman suck in a breath.

'God, I hope so . . .'

'And you know what else? That bastard didn't take her from you, not really. Not all of her, he didn't. Not the very best part.'

Then Patti sat, cradling an empty glass and listening to a woman three thousand miles away, whom she had never met, starting to cry.

SIXTY-THREE

'So, can you tell the court what happened when the argument moved from the living room into the kitchen?'

Sue stood three-quarters on to the jury in the way she had been told would be most effective. For the last six months she had done everything she had been instructed or advised to do. By prison officers, solicitors and by her defence counsel, who now stood looking up at her. What to wear and how to present herself. She had chosen a dark skirt with a simple white blouse and, even though she'd put on weight in prison, she thought she looked as respectable as could be expected, given the circumstances.

'Mrs Dunning?'

She looked at the barrister's face; jowly with a drinker's nose, but creased into a suitably compassionate expression. She knew what was coming and how painful it would be, but understood that it was necessary if she was to avoid spending years in prison. Certain facts had come to light since her arrest that it would be stupid to deny.

She knew what she would need to confess.

'Ed was . . . storming around,' she said. 'He'd thrown the duvet off the sofa-bed and a few things had got knocked over, candles and things.

I was telling him to be calm and to stop shouting, because at that stage I was only concerned about waking the others up. I was . . . *embarrassed* more than anything.'

'Then what happened?'

'Then he hit me.'

'Had your husband ever struck you before?'

'No, never. If he had then I don't think I would have been so shocked. He had this look on his face though that I'd never seen before. It was as if he was suddenly stone-cold sober and while I just stood there holding my face he started telling me . . . what he'd done.'

'What did he say to you, Mrs Dunning?'

She took a deep breath, but it was not quite enough, so she took another. She leaned forward and grabbed hold of the rail that ran around the witness box. 'He said that for all these years he'd stood by me. He'd supported me no matter how stupid I'd been, no matter what I'd said and what I'd done because he loved me so much . . . and now it was my turn to do the same for him.'

'To stand by him?'

Sue nodded. 'I asked him what he meant.'

'And this was when he told you what had happened in Florida.'

'It was so strange, because as soon as he started to tell me it was like I . . . wasn't surprised. I mean, I didn't shout out or fall on the floor or anything. I just stood there and listened to this . . . what he'd done to that girl and how he did the same thing all over again when we came home. I was just so cold, that's what I remember most. I was suddenly shivering.'

'So, what happened after he told you about these murders?'

'I was just standing there, like I said . . . frozen, almost literally . . . and he said, "Aren't you going to ask me *why*? Don't you want to know *why*?" He looked . . . desperate and his face was getting redder and redder and when I said no, I didn't want to know why because there couldn't be any reason that would explain something like that . . . he got angry again and started coming towards me.'

'And how did this make you feel?'

'I was frightened,' she said. 'That was when I was suddenly very scared and I bolted out of the door and ran into the kitchen.' She lowered her head for a few seconds. 'I should probably just have gone upstairs and knocked on one of the doors. I should have woken up Angie or Dave or someone and told them what was happening, but I didn't think. I panicked.'

'Did your husband follow you?'

She nodded. 'Yes, he was right behind me. He was ranting about how I never supported him and how it wasn't fair. He kept saying that he *needed* me and that if I wasn't going to stand by him there wasn't any point to it.'

'What did you think he meant by that?'

'I don't know,' Sue said. 'Thinking back now, I wonder if he meant that he was going to kill himself, but right then I was just thinking . . . just . . .'

'What were you thinking, Mrs Dunning?'

She blinked, breathed heavily. 'I was thinking that he was going to kill me. He kept coming towards me and I didn't have anywhere to go and I couldn't take my eyes off his hands. I couldn't stop thinking that he'd strangled those girls with them and the edge of the worktop was digging into my back . . . I just kept looking at his hands.'

'Was your state of mind affected by the threats your husband had made earlier in the evening? The threats to which other witnesses have already referred?'

Sue said that it was and the QC asked her to repeat them so that the jury could hear.

'So, what did you do then?'

'I just put my hand out without thinking and there were all these dirty plates and knives and forks. The dishwasher was already on, you see, but there was lots of stuff that wouldn't fit in . . . I knocked a lot of things on to the floor . . . scrabbling around. I was still looking at his hands and he was shouting and I just put my hand around this knife. This knife . . .'

'Do you need to take a minute, Mrs Dunning?'

She shook her head, swallowed. 'He put his arms out in front of him and he lunged and I sort of . . . pushed forward.'

'With the knife?'

She nodded. 'I remember screaming when I did it. I thought his face . . . the *look* on his face was just because I'd let out this God-awful scream, you know? I wasn't even sure what had happened until he stepped back and he was looking down and his mouth just sort of fell open.'

'Take your time. There's no rush . . .'

'Then I saw the blood on the knife, and he sat down . . . dropped down and he was up against the cupboard.'

'What did you do then?'

'I got down on the floor with him. It was just a natural reaction, I suppose. I got down there and I lifted his head up. I put my hand on the . . . on the hole in his chest and the blood was bubbling up through my fingers and the next thing I remember was seeing everyone in the doorway and wondering what they were doing there. They were staring and I was saying things, but I don't know what. It's stupid . . . but I can remember feeling bad because I'd woken everybody up. Because of all the mess . . .'

The QC nodded and said, 'Thank you, Mrs Dunning. I know this can't be easy for you. However, if you'll bear with me, I do need to take you back to what happened between you and your husband just *before* the alleged offence. To the argument itself. Do you feel up to that?'

Sue knew what he wanted. What was coming. She told him she felt fine.

'Earlier on you told the court that your husband had said'—he read from his notes—'he'd supported you no matter how stupid you'd been, no matter what you'd said and what you'd done because he loved you so much. Do you know what he meant by that?'

Sue looked at him, her breathing growing heavier by the second.

'Mrs Dunning, what was your husband referring to?'

She said, 'Our daughter.' She cleared her throat and said it again.

'Your daughter, Emma?'

Sue nodded.

'Did your husband want you to talk about Emma?'

'No, he hated it,' she said.

'Why was that?'

She shook her head.

'Mrs Dunning, you are giving evidence under oath and this is your opportunity to explain things to members of the jury. Now, you made a statement shortly after your arrest during which you talked about your husband's attitude towards your deceased daughter, Emma. How much it upset him when you talked about her. We have also heard from two different witnesses who have testified that privately you told them all about Emma's illness and her tragic death from leukaemia. Is this true?'

Sue nodded.

'Mrs Dunning, you do understand that while you're telling the truth about what happened that night, about your husband threatening you . . . the truth about fearing for your life after he had confessed to a double murder, that you must tell the truth about everything? You do see how important that is, don't you?'

Sue nodded again, barely perceptibly.

'Good. Thank you.' Standing behind the table that Crown and defence shared, the QC glanced down at his notes and cleared his throat. His voice dropped a little. 'Now this will inevitably be extremely painful for you, but can you please tell this court the *truth* about your daughter Emma?' He waited, knowing that there would be a reaction in the courtroom. There was an outbreak of low chatter in the public gallery and several of the jurors leaned forward in their seats. 'Can you tell us about Emma? Mrs Dunning . . .?'

Sue closed her eyes. Seconds passed. 'There was no Emma . . .'

'Could you speak up, Mrs Dunning?'

'I never had a daughter.'

The chatter in the gallery grew louder and more than one juror looked stunned. The barrister waited for the noise to die down.

'Did you purchase clothes for her?'

'Yes.'

376

'Did you put up a swing in the back garden for her?'

'Yes.'

'Did you frame pictures of a girl you cut out of a magazine and hide those pictures away in drawers?'

'Yes.'

'Can you tell us why you did those things?'

Sue shook her head again, then opened her eyes. 'We wanted children, both of us did, but it just . . . never happened.' Her eyes were fixed on a point just above her counsel's head; eyes that brimmed and spilled tears down her face as she spoke. 'We had tests . . . all the tests, and nobody could find anything wrong, but just . . . nothing. Ed bottled up all the pain . . . all the *grief*, and I thought I'd done the same. Then one day I just woke up and Emma was there.' She put a hand to her chest. 'In *here*. An Emma that *had* been. I don't expect anyone to think it makes any sense, but I never even questioned it. Suddenly I was able to get up in the mornings and get through the days, because I had a reason for the grief. It filled me up. I had memories of this girl and they were real, do you understand? Every . . . detail of her. Things we'd done and places we'd been together. I could hear her laugh and I knew what vegetables she hated and I remembered the pain of watching her slip away in that hospital. I remembered *all* of it.

'The smell of the place. The clothes I picked out to dress her in afterwards . . .

'Of course, Ed wanted me to see somebody, to get some help. He thought it was unhealthy . . . no, worse than that, he said it was "sick". In the end he just left me to it, because he could see I wasn't going to stop, because I wasn't going to say goodbye to her again. I couldn't do that. He was concerned about me, in the beginning at least, I know that . . . but sometimes I'd need to talk about her, to share it with him and we'd always end up screaming at one another. So sometimes I'd tell somebody else. I'd talk about Emma to complete strangers when I was shopping or having a coffee or something. They'd say how sorry they were and they'd ask me what she was like, and I felt *alive*. Like I was worth something.

377

'I know it's . . . I know what it sounds like and I know it's time to move on, but those years I had with Emma, with Emma's *memory*, were . . . well, I wouldn't swap them for anything. I'm probably not . . . explaining it very well, but I felt as though I was a whole person again because of this special girl I'd lost.' She lowered her head for a few seconds, nodded. 'This girl I hadn't *really* lost.'

The QC leaned even closer, asked if she would perhaps like a drink of water. Sue raised her head, but managed only a few more words before the sobs took hold completely.

'I felt like a mother . . .'

After a nod from the opposing counsel, the judge announced that the court would rise and that questions from the Crown were to commence after an early lunch. He told Sue that she could step down. When he saw that her fingers were still wrapped tightly around the metal rail, he asked an officer of the court to come forward and help her from the witness box.

SIXTY-FOUR

There was a good-sized crowd at the bottom of the steps when they emerged. Members of the public jostled for space with newspaper reporters and TV crews, holding up mobile phones to take blurry pictures or shoot video. Some had gathered well in advance of the verdict and were there to show support, while a good many others— passers-by who had spotted the cameras and decided that something important must be happening—simply took the opportunity to stand around or record proceedings.

You never knew what you might get outside the Old Bailey.

Several uniformed police officers gathered themselves into an impromptu cordon as Sue Dunning's solicitor stepped forward to make a statement.

'We are obviously relieved and delighted at today's verdict,' he said. 'At seeing justice done in *every* sense. Mrs Dunning will not be speaking or taking any questions this afternoon, but she has asked me to say a few words on her behalf . . .'

Angie, Barry, Marina and Dave stood close together a few feet behind and to one side. Next to them, Sue's colleague Graham Foot stood with his arm around Annette Bailey. They had all appeared as witnesses for the defence. They stared at the back of Sue's head, at the ranks of microphones thrust in her direction and the line of camera vans beyond. They struggled to hear the solicitor's words above the noise of passing traffic and the constant clicking of camera shutters.

'I am so relieved that this nightmare has finally come to an end. Or at least this part of it, because I don't expect that living with what has happened, with what my late husband did, is going to be easy . . .'

Dave leaned across to Barry. 'Do you fancy going to get some lunch?'

'What about Sue?' Angie asked. She saw Sue angle her head slightly, and thinking that she might turn round, she raised a hand to wave. Sue didn't see her.

'I think she's probably going to be a bit busy for a while,' Barry said. 'I'm up for it though.'

'I'm starving,' Marina said.

Angie nodded. 'Be good to celebrate.'

'Be even better if that murdering prick had been banged up for the rest of his life.' Dave took Marina's hand. 'He got off lightly if you ask me.'

'Yeah, but how much does it cost to keep someone like that in prison though?' Angie said. 'PlayStations in their cells, some of them.'

'Right result, I reckon,' Barry said.

'I wonder what *they* think.' Dave nodded across to where Sonia Gold was standing with her husband and son. Their faces were grim as the solicitor continued to read out Sue Dunning's statement.

'Above all, I want to take this opportunity to pass on my sympathies to the families of the two girls that my late husband murdered. However hard this has been for me, I cannot begin to imagine what they are going through.'

'God, that stuff about the daughter though,' Angie said. 'I still can't get my head around it.' Then Sue did turn round and Angie caught her eye, then raised her little finger and thumb to her ear and mouthed, 'Call you later on.'

Sue gave a small nod and turned back towards the reporters again.

Jenny Quinlan had mixed feelings. She was as pleased as anyone else that Sue Dunning had been acquitted, but this was not her case.

Connected, but not hers. Jeff Gardner had made a point of thanking her, as had the SIO on the Samantha Gold investigation, but she still felt as though Ed Dunning's death had robbed her of the kudos that should rightfully have been hers. She'd been moaning about it the night before while she and Steph had put away two large pizzas and a bottle and a half of wine. Steph had told her she was being stupid, that she was the one who had drawn all the attention to Ed Dunning in the first place and hadn't *she* been the one who had found out what had really happened to Annette Bailey? That was important stuff, wasn't it? I mean, surely all the work she had done would be noticed.

Jenny could only hope her friend was right.

She looked across to where Jeff Gardner was drinking takeaway coffee and talking quietly to Steve Barstow from the Homicide Command. Barstow didn't look too disappointed with the outcome, despite the failure to secure a conviction. It was hard to read Gardner though. He seemed a bit . . . bemused by the whole thing.

She smiled when he glanced in her direction, wondered how long he was planning on staying in London.

Steph was right, of *course* she was. Whichever way you looked at it, it had to be a feather in her cap, didn't it? There had certainly been talk in the pub about fast-tracking her up to DC, plenty of banter and backslapping from Adam Simmons and the rest.

She'd gone back to making them coffee anyway, just in case.

'. . . *and I hope that you'll understand my need for some privacy at this time. To come to terms with everything that's happened and to try and rebuild my life.*'

Jeff Gardner stepped away from the English detective and reached into his jacket for his phone. God, it was every bit as cold as his wife had said it would be. He couldn't wait to get back to the sunshine and the ocean. Back to courtrooms where they didn't wear those stupid wigs . . .

He thought about calling Patti Lee Wilson to give her the news, then decided it could wait until later. When he got home would be fine. She would probably pick it up on CNN or something anyway, if she was tuned in.

There was movement on the steps below him, as the solicitor tried to move Sue Dunning towards a waiting car, as police tried to keep the scrum of reporters at bay, despite the solicitor's insistence that no questions were going to get answered.

Sue Dunning was pale and still looked as if she wasn't quite sure where she was. He was grateful for all her help in putting the final pieces together for him on the Amber-Marie killing, but having heard what had been said in court, he was still shocked at the way she had spoken about her daughter in that interview room in Holloway.

What had he said to her? Something about not being a psychiatrist. He hoped to God she was able to find a good one.

He watched her now as she suddenly stopped a few feet from her car and stared across its roof at a BMW parked on the opposite side of the road. Gardner craned his neck to see who was sitting at the wheel, but couldn't make him out. Her solicitor laid a hand on the small of her back and, after a few more seconds, they both climbed into the car, which quickly pulled away from the kerb and out into the traffic.

'It's all about children, isn't it?' Sue Dunning had asked him.

She'd been in hell a lot longer than he'd thought.

As the crowd dispersed and a few reporters lingered to talk to senior detectives, Gardner saw that Jenny Quinlan was on her way over. He smiled as she approached and when she was next to him, he said, 'You did well in there.'

'Thanks.'

'No, really. Nice job.'

Quinlan shrugged like it was no big deal, but Gardner knew it was the first time she had given evidence in court. She'd seemed confident and calm as she'd read excerpts from her interviews with Edward Dunning and with others. When she was questioned by the defence, some of the comments made about Dunning by Angie Finnegan and Marina Green had clearly resonated with the jury.

'Not that it did any good,' she said. 'I mean we didn't win.'

'One of those cases,' Gardner said. 'Not sure anyone won. We all get those occasionally, right?'

'Right,' she said. Once again trying to sound like the seasoned pro she so clearly wanted to be. 'So, when are you heading home?'

'Tomorrow.'

'All set for a last night on the razzle then?'

'I've got an early flight.'

'You sure?' She rocked from foot to foot, her hands stuffed into the pockets of her jacket. 'I know some good pubs. Happy to show you the town.'

'It's an early flight,' he said.

'You could always sleep through it.'

'Probably not a good idea.'

She looked away for a second, then turned back and nodded towards the phone in Gardner's hand. 'I'll let you make your call then,' she said.

Gardner watched her move away, then looked down at his phone and began to dial. Thinking about it, a last night out in the city might not be such a terrible idea. It wouldn't take him long to pack, after all. Maybe he could find an old-fashioned English pub whose name he would not be able to remember on the flight home and it *was* always better to drink with somebody else. He looked across at Jenny Quinlan standing alone, then remembered who he was calling and decided that he should probably do the sensible thing and ask Barstow.

Yeah, he seemed like a good guy.

When Michelle answered the phone, Gardner told her about the 'Not Guilty' verdict. She said she was pleased and that their daughter was missing him. She asked him when he was coming home.

'First flight out tomorrow,' he told her. 'You can tell her I'll be back for talking tiger time . . .'

SIXTY-FIVE

And Marina Green was supposed to be the actress.

I was amazed, I still am, at how well it went. There'd been tears when they were needed and each sob, every catch of the breath and agonised pause had done its job brilliantly. To be honest, it wasn't actually very hard because I *was* sad that Ed had died. It might sound strange, but I missed him and I knew that adjusting to life on my own was not going to be easy. And I *did* think all those things they'd said he'd done were appalling. I mean, looked at objectively, how could you think anything else? Of course they were terrible.

Except it wasn't him who had done those things, was it?

I was staggered by the size of the crowd afterwards. Well-wishers, gawpers, whatever. Standing there listening to my solicitor making his speech, delivering my words with just the right amount of compassion and sincerity, I couldn't help thinking how many more people there were on those courtroom steps than had bothered to show up at poor old Ed's funeral. Just a few members of his family—none of whom had ever liked me much, as it happens—and a couple of morons from the tennis club. Not a bumper turnout, but what can you expect?

I half expected a queue to spit on his coffin.

It all started with that first, stupid lie of his and the ironic thing is that I was actually angry about it at the time. He'd panicked, worried that the cops over there would find out about his record at home, that he might get held up. As it was, that paved the way for everything. One stupid little lie, saying he was with me when the poor sod had actually slept the afternoon away in our cabin. I gave him the second lie of course, when I told Quinlan he'd dropped me off at the mall. He was *grateful* at the time, like I was backing him up somehow, like I was getting him out of a hole or something when all I was really doing was putting him right in the frame. Ed, the man with a previous arrest for rape, alone in the car and driving around just when Amber-Marie Wilson was snatched off the street in Siesta Village.

And the police here were happy enough to believe I'd gone along with that first lie because he'd made me do it.

Did he *threaten* you?

Were you *scared*?

It's *OK*, Mrs Dunning . . . we understand.

Which all fitted in perfectly with the witness statements, thank you very much. Ed wearing the trousers and being a 'bit of a bully' . . . God bless you for that, Marina and Angie. The fact is, I've never done *anything* he or anyone else told me unless I wanted to. Yes, in the bedroom perhaps, but I happen to have . . . preferences in that department that have got nothing to do with this, so no need to dwell on that, is there?

Lies and luck then, like I've said before, and plenty of the latter.

The seven of spades, that was another bit of luck! Being downstairs that night meant I was nice and close to the kitchen, handy for the knives. Don't get me wrong, I would have found a way to do it if we'd been upstairs in the spare room. A lamp or a shoe or something. The knife was way better though, and it *did* make the whole self-defence thing a damn sight more credible. I'm not sure I could have convinced the thickest copper in the world that I was just trying to defend myself if I'd had to batter him to death with one of my high heels.

Winding Ed up and getting that row started had been the easiest bit of the lot. He was pissed anyway, which helped, and a few words about what had happened with him and Annette Bailey had been more than enough. He started trying to tell me that it was me and the whole 'Emma thing' that was to blame. *That* was why he'd gone with other women, he said, *that* was when it had all started to come apart. I told him I was starting to think that maybe he *had* raped that woman—which, let's face it, is neither here nor there—and that was when he slapped me. Bingo! A cut lip or something would have been even better, a nice black eye . . . but it did the job.

He tries to apologise but I bolt for the kitchen and he comes after me. I grab the knife and he puts out his arms.

He says, 'Please, darling,' or something and I bang the knife in . . .

Not too much else to say, though of course there are always the Angie Finnegans of this world who can't bear a loose end. The ones who like everything nice and neat. The location of the school on Ed's sat-nav . . . well, that's pretty self-explanatory I would have thought, and a clump of his hair teased out of the shower drain, dried and folded into Samantha Gold's fist, did the job nicely as far as DNA evidence was concerned. As for what happened in Florida, well, there were clearly things that needed to be done after that initial . . . rush of blood. Gardner was more or less right about the disposal of Amber-Marie's body, except that I *pushed* the kayak, because the water's no deeper than three feet most of the way. I remembered that from when Ed and I had been there before, as well as where the kayaks were tied up. I got to the tunnels and back in about forty minutes, was out of my swimsuit and back at the resort in another fifteen while Ed was still dead to the world. Because he *was* a heavy sleeper.

Talking of 'heavy', Amber-Marie could certainly have done with losing a few pounds. I'm stronger than I look, so it wasn't *too* much trouble getting her bagged up and in the boot of the hire car, but still I was sweating like a pig on the way to that mall. Mind you, even tying your shoelaces gets you hot and bothered in that kind of climate and the air-con soon cools you off.

Oh, and that line I put into Ed's mouth?

'Don't you want to know why?'

Come on . . . *really*? Girls like Amber-Marie Wilson and Samantha Gold walking around. *Creatures* like that, breathing through their mouths, flapping and grinning, when I know my own girl would have been perfect.

So, in a word: balance.

I was aware of Angie and the others behind me, desperate to get my attention as things were finishing up and turning to look at them I realised I would have a few phone calls and invitations to ignore. They'd all played their part in what had happened, albeit without a clue they were doing any such thing, but I can't say I was mad keen to stay in touch.

Life's too short and I've got better things to do.

As I was bundled down towards the car, I noticed the BMW on the other side of the road and I recognised the man at the wheel. He slid the window down, as if he wanted me to see him. That inspector I'd met at the house on the night of Ed's death and at the police station later on. It was a little disconcerting, I'll admit that, but only for a few seconds.

Him staring across at me like that, like he *knew* something.

I managed a smile before my solicitor urged me forward and we got into the car. As it drove away, he was asking if I was all right and I probably said that I was, but I was already miles away.

All I really wanted was to get home, to make some tea and get busy.

I was so looking forward to taking Emma's pictures out of the drawer. To polishing them up until they shone and putting my daughter on display where she belonged.

Acknowledgements

Though *Rush of Blood* is a very different book to any I have written before, my need for help and support was as great as always and I am hugely grateful to all those who gave generously of their time and expertise and made the novel far better than it otherwise would have been.

Thank you to my new friends in Sarasota, Bob and Marie Black, and to Michael Connelly for the warm welcome, the generosity and, of course, the fishing.

Not for the first time I am grateful to Caroline Haughey for her legal expertise and Wendy Lee for her eagle eye. NH was indispensible and Tony Fuller was, as always, a mine of useful advice and procedural brilliance. At Little, Brown it continues to be an enormous pleasure to work with Tamsin Kitson, Hannah Hargrave, Thalia Proctor, Sean Garrehy and Emma Williams. Rob Manser and the Sales team are workers of wonders when it comes to getting the books out there to as many readers as possible. So, thanks to them.

When a writer steps outside their comfort zone—as they certainly should from time to time—the support and enthusiasm of publisher and agent is more important than ever. In David Shelley at Little, Brown and Sarah Lutyens at Lutyens & Rubinstein, I have the finest editor and agent that any writer could wish for. Simple as that.

And thanks most of all to Claire, of course.

One day we'll have that view of the water . . .